BACK WITH VENGEANCE

BACK WITH VENGEANCE

C. J. Carver

This first world edition published 2009
in Great Britain and 2010 in the USA by
SEVERN HOUSE PUBLISHERS LTD of
9–15 High Street, Sutton, Surrey, England, SM1 1DF.
Trade paperback edition published
in Great Britain and the USA 2010 by
SEVERN HOUSE PUBLISHERS LTD

British Library Cataloguing in Publication Data

Carver, Caroline, 1959-
  Back With Vengeance.
  1. Missing persons–Investigation–Fiction.
  2. Amnesiacs–Fiction. 3. Russians–Great Britain–
  Fiction. 4. Suspense fiction.
  I. Title
  823.9'2-dc22

ISBN-13: 978-0-7278-6847-3   (cased)
ISBN-13: 978-1-84751-192-8   (trade paper)

All Severn House titles are printed on acid-free paper.

Severn House Publishers support The Forest Stewardship Council [FSC],
the leading international forest certification organisation. All our titles that
are printed on Greenpeace-approved FSC-certified paper carry the FSC logo.

Mixed Sources
Product group from well-managed
forests and other controlled sources
www.fsc.org Cert no. SA-COC-1565
© 1996 Forest Stewardship Council

Typeset by Palimpsest Book Production Ltd.,
Grangemouth, Stirlingshire, Scotland.
Printed and bound in Great Britain by
MPG Books Ltd., Bodmin, Cornwall.

Acknowledgements

Thanks to Broo Doherty, my agent, for her unfailing support and enthusiasm.

Also thanks to a number of people who helped me as technical advisers: Randall Smith for helping me with all things Russian; Deborah Siggery for her always generous and immediate input; Anthony Weale for his inimitable proof reading; Dr Michael Seed for his extensive knowledge on weaponry.

Thanks to Steve Ayres for loaning me his Brussels home while I completed the final edit. Sorry I drank all your wine. *Za vasheh zdarohvyeh!*

One

Jay McCaulay's consciousness crawled awake. Her head was thick and her mouth tasted sour. Nausea rolled through her belly. She cracked open an eye to see she was lying on a hotel bed, fully dressed. The curtains were drawn. Where was she? She couldn't remember this room. She couldn't remember booking into a hotel, but her tote bag was on the suitcase rack at the bottom of her bed.

She rolled her head to check the bedside table. She could see her passport, along with a hotel room key, a paperback, a tube of lip balm and her old army-issue watch. Everything appeared normal, aside from the fact she hadn't got undressed before she'd fallen asleep. Daylight seeped through a crack in the curtains making her wonder what time it was.

She took in the fact she was incredibly thirsty. Her mouth felt as though it had been packed with sand and her head had started to ache.

Why couldn't she remember what hotel she was in?

There had to be a logical explanation, like she'd had a reunion with her old regiment and drunk too much, or maybe someone had spiked her drink. It wouldn't be the first time. Not only had she appeared to have lost half her brain cells but she also didn't think she'd ever felt so dreadful.

She struggled to get up, and the nausea rushed over her like a tidal wave. She only just made it to the bathroom in time, but barely brought up anything. Just a thin, mean trickle of saliva, but she couldn't stop retching.

After a while the sensation passed, and she sank on to the bathroom floor and wiped her mouth. Sweat prickled her forehead. Her hands were trembling, her skin cold. She hadn't felt so bone-marrow ill since she was eight and had contracted chicken pox. Her parents had taken one look at her weeping outside their bedroom and had taken her into their bed to comfort her. The memory gave her a little strength and she got to her feet. She poured a glass of water, drank it, then poured another and drank that as well. She glanced at the toiletries in the little basket by the vanity mirror. She looked again, her skin crawling. She picked up the miniature bottle of shampoo and stared at the letters. They were Cyrillic.

In a rush she crossed the hotel room and flung the curtains wide. For a moment, her mind went blank; it couldn't process what it was seeing.

Faceless, grey blocks stretched as far as her eye could see. There were wide grey roads with six lanes of rushing traffic and, just below, a quiet acre of park. She could see the Kafe Biskvit and the Smolenskaya Metro, and beyond that was a broad, grey river flowing in front of the Kremlin.

She was in Moscow.

And she had no idea how she'd got there.

Two

Jay turned back to the bedroom. Her breathing was tight. *Keep calm*, she told herself. *You'll remember, just give it time. You've had too much vodka or maybe something bad to eat, like a dumpling filled with rotten meat.* At the thought of food, her stomach rebelled, and she bolted for the bathroom and threw up the water she'd just drunk.

Shivering, she flushed the loo and dashed her face with cold water, rinsing out her mouth before returning to the room. She checked the hotel directory to see she was staying at the Hotel Oktyabrskaya II, which appeared to be one of the better hotels in Moscow – having five stars and prices to match. She had to be here on business. She couldn't afford such an upmarket hotel and would normally have stayed in a two or three star Intourist hotel further from the centre. Closing her eyes, she pictured the office back in London – cramped, overflowing with paper and smelling of coffee and pastries – and tried to think why Nick might have sent her to Moscow. Nothing. Not even a whisper of a meeting or a mission in her memory.

Panic rose.

Why couldn't she remember?

Feeling dizzy, she returned to the bathroom and drank two glasses of water. She couldn't seem to rehydrate and her head was now pounding. She wondered if she should call for a hotel doctor but decided against it for the moment. She needed time to fill in the blanks.

First, Jay studied the hotel room. Aside from the crinkles of the bedcover where she'd lain, the hotel room appeared unused. The sanitary strip across the toilet bowl had been intact, the towels perfectly hung and the minibar's security tab unbroken.

She turned to look for her mobile phone – which she'd normally put on the bedside table – but it wasn't there, nor was her recharger. Carefully, she checked her tote bag. Spare jeans, socks, washbag, she picked through everything. Eventually, she sank back on her heels. Everything was there, including her phone, but what troubled her was that they were in her tote bag. She always kept her phone and iPod in her handbag; she never packed them in her general luggage. It was a small thing – tiny compared to not remembering what she was doing in Moscow – but it felt important.

She wanted to check her phone messages but the battery was flat so she put it on to charge. Massaging her forehead, she tried to think. She needed help. Backup. Someone or something to kick start her memory and jog everything into place. A single word might do it. She picked up the hotel phone, wondering who to call. She didn't dare call her mother. What about Nick? Not a good idea either. Her boss always saw straight through her if she tried to fib, and if he thought anything was wrong he'd be on the next plane out, which was nice – at least she knew she didn't have to be alone – but she decided to wait before she pressed that particular panic button. She frowned. Why could she remember Nick and her mother but not anything about her trip to Moscow?

Her mind turned to her housemates, Angela and Denise, whom Nick had nicknamed the girl squad. Both women were tough ex-special-reconnaissance soldiers supporting 1 PARA, both of whom Jay had met on her tour in Kosovo. Like many soldiers, they'd bonded hard and fast after doing a dangerous op together, south of Pristina, and when Jay was invalided out of the army two months later she was delighted that the girls kept in touch. When the women had left the army the following year and had set up house in Fulham, they'd invited Jay to move in with them. Both Angela and Denise were no nonsense, practical and trustworthy, and neither likely to overreact when she called.

Her head was now pounding relentlessly so she swallowed two Panadol with another glass of water. While she waited for the painkillers to kick in she turned on the TV – tuned into Channel 1, the main national channel – and laid everything from her tote bag on to the bed, hoping something might jar her memory. She did the same with her handbag before checking her passport and air ticket to see she was here on nothing more than a flying visit; she'd flown in Friday the sixteenth of June and was due to fly out of Moscow Sunday late evening. A trickle of relief gave her a boost of energy, and she picked up the hotel directory and dialled British Airways.

BA was an automated service, and Jay had to dial another number and wait for five minutes before she managed to get hold of one of their operatives, called Dmitry. Her Russian wasn't bad, but unfortunately Dmitry had a thick accent, maybe from the east, which forced her to concentrate, making her headache worse.

'I just want to check my flight departure.' As Jay gave Dmitry her flight details, her stomach gave a swoop. She didn't even know what day it was. As she reached for her mobile to check the date, she heard him tapping on his keyboard. He said, 'Your flight was on Sunday. Do you need to book another?'

'I'm sorry?'

'Your flight left at twenty-one fifteen on Sunday the eighteenth of June. Three days ago.'

'Three days?' Her voice was pitched several notes higher than usual. 'Are you saying it's Wednesday today?'

'Yes. Wednesday, twenty-first of June.'

Jay's legs almost went from beneath her when she checked her mobile phone display to see he was right. She'd lost more than her memory. She'd lost five days of her life.

'Hello?' Dmitry said. 'Are you still there?'

'Yes.' She cleared her throat. 'I'm here.'

'You'd like to rebook your flight?'

'Yes.' She started trembling again. She was overcome with an urge to see her mother, and allow her to fuss over her until everything was all right. 'I'd like the next flight out of Moscow, please.'

'The first seat I have available in business class is tomorrow evening.'

Business class? Her mind reeled. She never flew business class. 'Economy is fine.'

'If you're sure.' He sounded disapproving.

'Yes, I'm sure.'

'I have one tonight, at the same time as shown on your ticket. Nine fifteen in the evening.'

'Perfect.'

After she'd hung up, Jay switched on her mobile to see she had a text from Nick, asking her when she was coming home, and two from her mother, asking the same. Both had left messages this morning. Jay dialled the hotel concierge. 'I'd like to confirm when I checked in.'

There was a brief pause, then he said, 'Yesterday, at six p.m.'

'Have I ordered any room service since I arrived?' She knew it was an odd question, but she was sure the concierge had answered far more peculiar ones.

A small pause while he checked his screen. 'No, madam. You have not used room service. You also requested not to be disturbed by housekeeping for the duration of your visit.'

'How long am I booked in for?'

'Until tomorrow.'

'Did I give you my card details?'

A small pause. 'According to my records, the room was paid for in cash.'

She mulled this over. 'And you say none of your staff have entered my room since I arrived?'

'That is correct.'

'Thank you.'

Jay hung up. If she'd flown in on Friday, she must have stayed elsewhere for the past few days. Where?

She checked her watch – just after twelve o'clock – which made it around nine in the morning in London. Ten hours until she got home. It was too long to wait. She needed answers now. Picking up the phone again, she dialled. Listened as the phone connected and began to ring. Outside it was cloudy and looked bleak and windy, but since people were wearing cotton trousers and sleeveless dresses, she assumed it was warmer than it appeared.

Her heart sank when there was no reply.

She was about to redial, in case Denise and Angela were having coffee in the garden, when she remembered they'd been on holiday in Cyprus. They'd asked her along, and although she had been tempted – she hadn't had a holiday all year – she'd decided to save her time to go hill walking in Scotland later in the year. Were they still in Cyprus? Jay dialled Denise's mobile.

Denise picked up on the third ring. 'Hello?'

'Hi, it's me.'

'Hey, you! What's happening? The house burned down yet?'

'I wouldn't know. I'm in Moscow.'

'Holy cow. What the hell are you doing there?'

Jay took a gulp of water. 'That's what I want to know. Look, don't freak out, but I seem to be missing part of my memory. I can remember pretty much everything – Nick and work, you and Angela, my family – but not what I'm doing here. I woke up in a hotel room I'd never been in before about half an hour ago and don't know what's going on.'

'Wow, some party.' Denise sounded impressed.

'But I *can't remember*.' Despite making an effort to remain calm, panic edged her voice. 'I can't remember flying in – apparently I flew business class, something I'm not likely to forget – nor checking into the hotel. I've been here for five days and can't remember a *single thing*.'

'You're serious?'

'One hundred per cent.'

There was a brief silence. Denise's tone turned brisk. 'OK. What's the last thing you remember?'

There was a flash of blonde hair, a brief glimpse of a woman laughing, but when she chased the vision a grey wall descended.

'I don't know.'

'OK, when did you last see Nick?'

'At the airport.' She was surprised at how easily the memory returned. 'He drove me there. He was on his way to Reading and said he'd drop me off.'

Her boss, Nick Morgan, an ex-marine in his late fifties, was as hard and rugged as an old tree stump, but his heart was as soft as sap. The image of him made something loosen inside, and, for the first time since she'd woken, she took a full breath. She hadn't realized she'd been breathing fast and shallow for so long.

'He dropped me outside the terminal. We weren't in his car, but Gill's. His was being serviced.'

She could almost smell the jet fuel as she climbed out of Nick's car, the memory was so vivid. He came round to open the boot – as was his custom before she left on a mission – before pecking her on the cheek and telling her to keep safe. As she pictured Nick, his pale eyes scanning the crowds – the marine in him always aware, on duty – the greyness in her mind abruptly dissolved and a name sliced hard and bright across her consciousness.

'I know who I was supposed to be meeting here.' Her voice came out excited. 'They're a reporter for a weekly paper, *Mokovskie Novosti*, Moscow News. Her name's Anna Vorontsove.'

'Hey, that's great.' Denise sounded relieved. 'Maybe you can ring her, get her to fill in the blanks.'

'I'll do that.'

'What else can we do? You want us to fly out? You know it's not a problem. We love Russian women.'

The thought of having the girls with her was immensely tempting, but she hadn't reached that stage yet. 'I'll ring Anna first, OK? When I've done that, I'll let you know what's happening.'

'Good plan. Where are you staying?'

Jay gave Denise the hotel's name and phone number.

'When are you back home?'

'I get in tonight. My flight lands at ten fifteen.'

'Look, you need to know we're leaving Cyprus in a couple of hours. If our flight's on time, we'll pick you up, OK?'

'Please don't.' No matter what was happening in her life, Jay hated putting people out. 'Just having you back at the house will be great.'

'OK. I reckon we'll be there around six. I'll leave the mobile on when I can, OK? And if you need us, we won't hesitate. You know that.'

'I do. And thanks.'

'Look after yourself, babe, and keep safe.'

Jay took a breath and crossed her fingers. 'See you tonight.'

Hanging up, she fetched some more water, downing two more glasses. She couldn't believe how thirsty she was. Her headache had receded a little but was still there, softly pulsing against her skull.

She tried to remember if she'd seen Anna Vorontsove over the past five days, but the grey wall was impenetrable and there were no clues in her luggage or handbag. No diary showing an appointment or an address. She tried to picture Anna and for a second she got a flash of a gold earring, a wide mouth and an infectious laugh, but then the memory was gone, swallowed in grey. Carefully, she moved her thoughts sideways, keeping Anna at a distance, and suddenly her cousin Cora's voice rang clear as a bell in her mind.

I'd love a holiday in Moscow.

For a second Jay was taken aback by the vision of Cora crowding her mind and almost pushed it away, but it was so bright and intense – a bundle of auburn curly hair, amber necklaces and flowing yellow and orange scarves – that she relented and opened herself to the memory. Cora was in the living room at Norridge Farm along with the family, all eleven of them, including the grandchildren. Even Fitz and Amelia were there, having driven down from Fife. They were standing in a semicircle, looking at her solemnly.

'It's not a holiday, Cora.' Jay's mother sounded cross as she walked into view, as short and round and homely as a cottage loaf. Jay's aunt Elizabeth, almost a foot taller, followed. Elizabeth's normally pretty face was thin and drawn, her eyes circled with bruises from lack of sleep. She gave Jay a hug and kissed her on both cheeks. She said, 'Thank you so much for doing this. Be careful, won't you?'

Jay couldn't see her uncle Duncan – Elizabeth's husband – and, for some reason, this brought a sensation of anxiety into her chest. Opening her eyes, she searched the memory for Duncan several times, but he remained absent. After she'd allowed the memory to fade, she picked up the hotel phone, dialled, and asked for the *Mokovskie Novosti*.

When she was put through, she asked for Anna Vorontsove. The Russian felt like fuzzy pebbles in her mouth. Each language she spoke reminded her of a different sensation and taste. French was like smooth butter, German reminiscent of gravel, and Italian warm treacle.

She was asked to hold a moment and there was a click, followed by a man saying, 'Who wants Anna?'

'I'm a friend. I was supposed to meet with her at the weekend.'

'Is that Jay?' The man spoke in English. He sounded incredulous.

Instinct told her not to confirm her name although she couldn't think why. She said, also in English, 'No. It's Frances.' She used her middle name. 'Can I speak with Anna, please?'

'She isn't here.'

'Oh.' Jay thought fast. 'Can I catch her at home?'

'No. She isn't there either.' The man cleared his throat. 'Anna hasn't been seen since Saturday morning. She's missing.'

Three

'Missing?' Jay repeated blankly.

'It's vital that we meet.' His tone turned urgent. 'I will be at the bar of the Hotel Intourist in half an hour . . . You are in Moscow, I take it?'

'Yes.'

'In that case you must come. Anna's life may depend on it.'

He gave her an address near the Kremlin and Red Square. It wasn't far away, just across the river.

'How will I know you?' she asked. She was aware he hadn't given her his name.

There followed such a long silence that for a moment she thought they'd been disconnected.

'I'm Vladimir. You don't remember me?'

Her brain made a wild search only to come up against the grey wall. 'I'm sorry. No.'

'OK,' he said. 'I'm not so tall. And I need to lose weight. I'll be carrying a guide book to Paris.'

'OK.'

When Jay hung up her fingers started trembling again. She forced herself to the bathroom again and drank another glass of water. In the mirror her face was bloodless, her normally glossy conker-coloured hair lank. She fetched her washbag and put on some blusher and lipstick, but it made her resemble a corpse so she scrubbed it off and decided to have a shower instead. As she stripped, she paused when she saw the bruises. Grey and green, they were on her thighs, her ankles, her upper arms . . . and then she became aware her body was tired and achy, as though she'd done some intense physical exercise. If she was still in the army she'd guess she'd been on a weekend operation, the physical effects felt so familiar. The bruises weren't serious, no deep tissue damage. It was as though she'd pelted over an assault course.

Climbing into the shower, she gently soaped herself. She felt better after blow-drying her hair and putting on clean clothes, spraying herself with scent. A gift from her mother, she remembered. She'd ring her when she got back, once she knew what was going on. Passport inside her handbag, hotel map of the inner city in her pocket, she picked up the hotel key and headed for the door, but, when she went to open it, a rush of fear flooded her. She didn't want to go outside. She didn't know who might be there.

Going to the minibar she unlocked it and pulled out a litre bottle of vodka by its neck. Now she had a weapon she felt more confident, but as soon as she stepped into the corridor, clutching the vodka, she felt foolish and put it back inside the room.

Two people were in the lift when it arrived, and although it was a large lift – it could have taken twenty people, no problem – she waited for one that was empty. She didn't want to be shut inside with people she didn't know.

The reception was busy with businessmen, tourists checking in, and the odd prostitute hanging around in hopeful expectation. Jay steered a path through the melee, trying to avoid coming too close to anyone, not wanting anyone to touch her. When an American woman in a too-tight dress bumped into her, Jay leaped aside.

'Jeez,' said the woman, as Jay hurried away. 'You sure need something for your nerves.'

Wasn't that the truth? Seconds later she made it on to the street. She paused in the cool air, and concentrated on controlling her breathing. She didn't think she'd ever felt so jumpy. She'd seen combat in Kosovo and Iraq, but she couldn't remember being so skittish, so frightened of coming into physical contact with people. In theatre – the military term for being on operations, in combat or at war – she'd been scared, even terrified, but she had controlled her fear either by channelling it into action or shoving it into a box deep inside her and locking the lid. What she was feeling now was completely different. It was as though her body knew there was an imminent threat and was screaming at her to *watch out*, but her mind wasn't able to listen to the warning due to the shrouding grey curtain.

She hoped she hadn't gone over the edge. She knew several soldiers who'd cracked up after they'd left the service, needing hospitalization and round-the-clock suicide surveillance. Please God she wasn't going to join them.

A taxi drew to a halt beside her. The driver gestured, asking if she wanted to hire his vehicle, but she shook her head. She wanted to walk. She hoped it might help clear her head and let another memory through. As she strode out, she purposely didn't think of Anna but let her mind drift. She kept seeing the Goodwins – her mother's side of the family – looking anxious and upset. She felt as though they were urging her to do something, but she didn't know what.

In the middle of the bridge, she paused to look at the line of severe, grey blocks curving round the bend of the slate-coloured Moscow River.

The same thought she'd had when she'd first seen this stretch of water ten years ago rose: why hadn't anybody thought to name the river something more majestic or romantic?

When she was nineteen the army had sent her here on a language course, and she had fond memories of the place – the different neighbourhoods, and the alleys and courtyards that contained the flats of millions of Muscovites. There was more neon in the city than she remembered, more music and fashionable clothing on the streets, but the atmosphere still felt severe.

She only needed to use the map once, which made her wonder if she'd walked this route before, but when she arrived nothing was familiar. Inside the hotel lobby was an expanse of white space and tiled floors, and she'd barely taken five paces when a man detached himself from a chair nearby and hastened towards her. He was short and running to fat, with red veins spreading from his nose to his cheeks, and as he approached he put out a hand.

She backed away. 'Don't touch me.' She spoke in Russian.

Immediately, he held up both hands. One was clutching a *Time Out* guide to Paris. 'Sorry. I didn't mean to scare you.' He was sweating heavily and wiped his forehead with a large, blue handkerchief that had threads hanging from one corner. 'Shall we go outside? We need to talk.'

Jay looked around the lobby, which was busy with tourists returning to have lunch. 'No. I'd rather stay here.'

He looked at her curiously, but relented by offering her the chair he'd just vacated. He took the next one along and sat perched on the edge, his belly straining over his waistband.

'What are you doing here?' His voice was low. 'I thought you had gone home.'

Jay stared at him.

'You went for drinks with Anna on Friday, and that was the last time I saw either of you. Where have you been?'

She studied him, wondering if she could trust him or not. He didn't look like anyone to be frightened of, with his shaggy mop of brown hair and myopic gaze, and he certainly didn't resemble a Mafia thug, let alone anybody from GRU, Russia's military intelligence, or the KGB, now known as the FSB.

'Vladimir,' she said. 'Tell me about yourself. About Anna. When you saw us. Where we were going.'

'You don't remember?'

She shrugged. 'I'd like to hear it from you.'

'I see.' He ran a hand over his eyes. 'Let us start with myself. I am Anna's colleague at Moscow News. We have worked together for five years. We're reporters; we cover everything from traffic accidents to drug busts to murders. We are good friends. The best of friends.' He paused and bit his lip. 'You see, Anna's father was murdered recently, last month. He was shot in the head, twice, at close range. Executed. She was trying to find out why. She was up all night, every night, trawling the Internet, but she wouldn't tell me what she was doing. She became paranoid and secretive. She lost weight.

'Finally, she got a lead in England. She was excited. I was worried she was getting in over her head and persuaded her to tell me who she was interested in over there, in case things went wrong or she needed help. She told me she was going to see a man called Duncan Bailey . . .'

Two things happened when he said her uncle's name. Firstly, she flinched as though she'd been electrified, but second, she felt a rush of nausea so violent that she had to bend double to hide the fact she was almost retching.

'Are you all right?'

Jay swallowed, but she had no saliva. She took several breaths and stared at the floor, at the handful of cigarette butts squashed flat on the marble. What on earth had her uncle got to do with this? Was it because, like herself, he could speak Russian? His mother – who was from Belorussia – had insisted he learn the language when he was a child. Jay tried to think if Duncan had ever been to Russia, or Belorussia, but came up with zilch. She'd have to ask Aunt Elizabeth when she got back.

'Jay? You don't look well.'

Vladimir was watching her anxiously.

'I'm fine. Just a bit dizzy. Sorry.' She straightened, making an attempt to swallow again but it was just a reflex. 'I think I ate something bad earlier.'

'Wait here. I'll get you some water.' He got up and walked out of the lobby briefly, returning with a small bottle of Stolichnaya vodka and a litre of locally produced mineral water and two glasses. She refused the vodka but took the mineral water gratefully. It was slightly fizzy and tasted metallic, oddly salty, but at least it took the sour taste out of her mouth and helped settle her stomach.

'Thank you.'

Vladimir poured vodka into his glass and took a slug. 'Anna flew to England ten days ago to see this Duncan Bailey. When she came back she said she was close to finding her father's murderer. Again, she was like a woman obsessed. She wouldn't tell me anything; she seemed convinced it might put me in danger.'

He paused for another gulp of vodka.

'And then you turned up. Out of the blue as far as I was concerned.

You arrived in the office, Anna embraced you – she only ever did that with someone she liked – and she picked up her bag and you left together. Anna mentioned you'd both be going away for the weekend, and I think she mentioned Aeroflot, an internal flight perhaps, but she never said where to . . .' He trailed off, looking despondent. 'You don't remember this?'

Jay didn't respond but sipped her water, thinking. There would be little chance of finding out where she and Anna had flown. Airlines were notoriously strict about what passenger information they gave out and would only relent if you were an official, along the lines of a cop or paramedic. Jay went for another angle. She said, 'Could you tell me about Anna's father's murder?'

'Ah, poor Eduard.' Vladimir sighed. 'He was a tough man, sometimes ruthless, but his job made him so. I know he believed in doing the right thing . . . Anna told me.' He studied her anxiously. 'We have to be careful. Anna is gone, and you are here, and you are not well . . .'

'No,' she admitted.

'But you want to know what is happening?'

'Yes.'

'I also.' He poured himself another shot of vodka and knocked it back. The bottle was now only a quarter full but he showed no signs of being drunk. 'OK. So Eduard was with the FSB. I have no idea what he was investigating, but I'm pretty sure Anna had.'

'You think what he was investigating might have got him killed?'

He nodded. 'This is what Anna believed.'

Jay took another mouthful of water. 'Where was Eduard when he was murdered?'

'Sinsk, Siberia.'

A high pitched ringing started in Jay's head. She was staring at Vladimir, but she wasn't seeing him. The word *Sinsk* had triggered something in her brain and she could see Anna as clear as day. About the same age as Jay, the journalist was small-boned and pretty, with dyed-blonde hair that was black at the roots. Jay had liked Anna enormously, she remembered now, not only because they shared many traits and skills – Anna was a black belt in Karate and spoke several languages – but also because they both shared the same sense of humour. She could picture them in a bar, and they were laughing and drinking vodka, and then the scene abruptly switched.

Anna was no longer laughing. She was cowering naked on a tiled floor. She had bruises all over her body, and she was bleeding from her mouth. She was sobbing.

Jay stood over her, a Sig Sauer 9mm pistol in both hands. It was pointing at Anna.

And then it fired.

Anna fell backwards, her legs kicking. Blood smeared her torso and dribbled over the tiles. She groaned for a long time before she finally lay still. Her arms were spread wide, her left leg twisted beneath her. Tears streaked her face. Her eyes were open. She was looking straight at Jay. Her expression seemed to forgive her.

'Jay? Are you all right?'

Vladimir was crouched at her side, offering her his tatty blue handkerchief. Tears were pouring down her cheeks. Her soul, the marrow of her bones, knew that the memory was real and not a dream. She'd killed before, shooting a Serbian soldier who was brutally raping a young girl, and another two men who would have killed her if she hadn't killed them first, but she'd never killed a woman. A naked and defenceless, terrified woman. A woman she liked.

What had Anna done to provoke Jay into killing her? Where was her body? Where had it happened? She scrambled to her feet. She didn't want to talk to Vladimir now, face his questions. 'I've got to go,' she said. Her words were choked.

'What is it? What's wrong?'

I killed your friend.

'Nothing's wrong.'

'Let me drive you. I have a car outside . . .'

'No. I'll take a taxi.' She headed for the lobby door. She felt as though her legs were far away, as if she were walking on stilts. The high-pitched ringing in her head increased.

'Can we meet again?' Vladimir was following anxiously. 'Maybe tomorrow?'

'Maybe.' She wasn't going to tell him she was flying out tonight in case he tried to find her at the airport.

'Where are you staying?'

'The Hotel Belgrad,' she lied.

'I'll come and see you for lunch at your hotel tomorrow,' he said. 'You were the last person to see Anna. You have to help me find her.'

To her relief, there was an empty taxi outside the hotel. As she climbed inside, Vladimir was almost treading on her heels. 'Lunch is OK?'

'Lunch is fine.'

As the taxi drove away, she twisted in her seat to see Vladimir staring after her. His face had crumpled. He looked as though he was crying.

Four

Jay spent the flight home drinking wine and trying to stop the memory of Anna's death endlessly repeating itself in her mind. Fortunately, a business-class passenger had failed to turn up so she was allowed a window seat near the front of the airplane. This meant the wine was on tap. Since Nick had driven her to Heathrow, she didn't have to worry about drink-driving. She would take the Heathrow Express train back to Paddington and then the tube.

At least now she had an idea why her brain was having trouble accessing her memory; it was trying to protect her from facing the same traumatic event all over again. She glanced down at her hands, strong and square and criss-crossed with the tiny, white scars she'd received when a roadside bomb had exploded in Basra. Five people had died and countless others had been injured. A fellow soldier, Steve Duffy, had tried to save an eighteen-month-old baby boy who'd had one of his legs blown off, but the boy died in his arms. When they'd met again months later, on manoeuvres back in England, Jay had said how sorry she was about the boy, and Steve had looked at her blankly. 'What boy?' Steve's memory had buried the event so deeply that it took weeks of psychotherapy to unblock it to a stage he could reprocess it, deal with it, and grieve.

Tote bag over her shoulder, she walked into the arrivals hall. Despite the fact it was nearly eleven at night, there was a surprising amount of people waiting for passengers to disembark. Jay walked past a handful of uniformed drivers holding up client names and almost jumped out of her skin when someone wrapped an arm around her waist and scooped her to one side.

To her disbelief she saw it was Tom, looking amused at having given her a fright. DI Sutton, six foot two of lean, hard-muscled undercover cop, wearing combat trousers tucked into a pair of big brown boots and a black T-shirt. If his hair hadn't needed a cut, he could have been taken for a marine.

'Did you get me some duty-free?' he asked.

She stared at him, astonished. 'What on earth are you doing here?'

'Maybe some vodka?' He made as if to peek in her tote bag. 'I fancy some on ice, since we're mid summer.'

She couldn't stop staring. He'd tanned since she'd last seen him, and she couldn't help wondering if he'd been on holiday abroad – and if so, with whom. Jealousy rose, making her feel as though she had a fragment of glass lodged in her heart. 'No vodka,' she managed.

He widened his eyes. 'Not even a miniature from the hotel minibar?'

She shook her head and began walking for the street. She was aware her heartbeat was up, her breathing shallow: symptoms of being within touching distance of him. Did he feel the same? She checked to see Tom walking alongside, seemingly impervious.

'The girl squad rang me,' he said. 'They said you were in trouble.'

'You came to rescue me?'

His eyes cut across to her. 'Why, do you need rescuing?'

She didn't answer, and when she made it outside she paused, unsure if she wanted to share a car with Tom right now. Her defences were down and she didn't want to make a fool of herself.

'My car's over there,' he said.

'Parked legally, as usual,' she muttered. It was angled on a double yellow line with a police notice shoved on the dashboard.

'I heard that,' he called. He was already halfway across the street and beeping the Vauxhall open.

Trailing after him, she made to throw her tote in the boot but her battered muscles – frozen after the long flight – were so stiff that she nearly dropped it.

Tom grabbed the bag and chucked it effortlessly inside. 'Don't tell me, you got into a fight with a Russian hood and you're covered in bruises.'

'Something like that,' she prevaricated.

He rolled his eyes. 'You can't stay out of trouble, can you?'

'I think the words "kettle" and "black" might be appropriate here,' she responded. She was aware she was being prickly, but it was better than the alternative – falling into his arms and begging him to take her back.

'Just because I don't always do things by the book . . .'

In the car she leaned back and closed her eyes, hardly able to believe Tom was driving her home. Last year he'd proposed marriage, but when he'd found Blake – an MI5 officer she'd worked with during a mission to the Balkans – on her doorstep, expecting to sweep her away to Italy for the weekend, he'd changed his mind and suggested they 'take a break'. By the time she'd managed to persuade him there was nothing going on between her and Blake it had been too late. Tom and his secretary, Sharon, had become lovers.

Whether he'd done it to sooth his bruised ego, or simply because he wanted to hurt her, Jay didn't know, but instinct told her that, Sharon aside, she'd probably made one of the biggest mistakes of her life. She'd been commitment shy about the whole marriage idea, stringing Tom along, not wanting to lose him but not wanting to pledge herself absolutely, but when he'd dumped her the shock had been immense. She'd been forced to take a long, hard look at herself and had belatedly realized she'd behaved appallingly, taking him for granted the way she had, and it was only at that point that she'd realized she felt more for him than she'd ever admitted.

What an idiot she was.

Snapping on his headlights, Tom pulled into the traffic, heading north for the M4. Although he drove fast, he also drove smoothly enough that if a passenger were to balance a cup of coffee on the back seat it would not spill, a skill he'd learned in a previous life when he'd gone through a chauffeur-bodyguard training academy to learn how to prevent VIPs from getting kidnapped. Now he was a cop and had been Jay's main police adviser in the UK since she'd started working for TRACE – the Tracing Reunion and Crisis Executive. When they'd split up, she'd put her job first, not wanting to lose such a valuable contact just because he'd once been her boyfriend. They'd held an uneasy truce over the past year or so, working together on half a dozen missing people cases, but when either of them tried to move things to a personal level they fought: Tom sniping at Jay over Blake, while Jay sniped over Sharon. They hadn't seen each other socially, outside work. Until today.

'What brings you to London?' she asked. Tom worked from the Trinity Road cop shop in Bristol, and she assumed he was up in town on business, either seeing Scotland Yard or meeting Goose, another plain-clothes cop, who Tom had known since he'd joined the force.

'Visiting a friend.'

'Goose?' she said, yawning.

'Another friend.'

Something in his voice made Jay look across. 'Anyone I know?'

'Nope.'

She had to force herself to ask the next question. 'Is she nice?'

'Actually,' he said, 'she is.'

Jay fixed her gaze dead ahead through the windscreen as a wave of heat washed over her, making her skin tingle. *He's not your boyfriend*, she reminded herself. *Sure, he proposed last year, but that was last year, and things are different, so get a grip and don't let your jealousy show.*

'You OK?' Tom asked.

'I'm tired. It was a tough trip.'

'So the girls said. Their flight was delayed, hence trying to find someone to meet you. Apparently, Nick's out of town tonight.'

'They're fussing. I'm fine.'

'They went through their entire address book until they got to T for Tom. Lucky for you, I was free.'

Jay didn't respond but leaned back and closed her eyes. The alcohol she'd drunk on the plane had rubbed the vision of Anna's body away and replaced it with blurred scenes of the grey buildings of Moscow. She felt disconnected and peculiar, as though she had jet lag, and she couldn't get rid of the sensation of wanting her mother. She wished Norfolk wasn't so far away or she'd ask Tom to drive her there.

All the lights were on when Tom drew up outside her house. 'You hop out,' he said. 'I'll park up the road and bring your tote with me, OK?'

She'd barely turned her key in the lock when she heard footsteps thundering along the corridor. The door was flung open to reveal her housemates.

'You OK?' asked Denise. She was looking her over as though checking for broken bones and bandages.

'Of course she isn't OK,' interjected Angela, pulling Jay inside. 'She looks like hell.'

'Nothing a good night's sleep won't fix,' Jay said, but her voice was faint. She didn't want to be here, but there was no way her housemates would let her drive to Blakeney tonight. She'd have to wait until everyone had gone to bed, to avoid an argument.

'Sleep's a great healer.' Angela had taken her arm and was leading her up the stairs for her bedroom.

Behind them, Denise said, 'Where's Tom?'

'Parking the car,' Jay managed.

'I'll wait for him.'

Jay's bedroom window was open, letting in scents of honeysuckle and jasmine. There was a vase of fresh flowers on her bedside table and a duty-free bottle of gin.

'Homecoming presents,' said Angela. She took Jay's face gently between her hands and looked into her eyes. 'You're safe now, OK? Nobody's going to mess with you while we're here. I swear it.'

It was exactly what the soldier in Jay needed to hear. Any energy she'd had left from Moscow faded the second she began to get undressed. She heard Tom and Denise's voices downstairs but not what they were saying. Everything fell quiet.

She'd just taken off her T-shirt and bra when there was a tap at the door. 'Come in,' she called, thinking it was one of her housemates, but it wasn't. It was Tom.

Snatching a robe she hurriedly wrapped it around herself as he closed the door behind him. His eyes were soft. 'Are you sure you're OK?'

'Sort of.' Which was a lie. She wasn't at all OK but she might be once she'd had some sleep. She added, 'Thanks for bringing me home. It was really kind. Saved me loads of time.' She suddenly felt self-conscious and awkward with him in her room.

'No problem.' He stepped close and gently brushed a lock of hair behind her ear. 'I haven't seen you like this before. It's not just exhaustion, either; there's something more. What happened out there?'

'Too much,' she said, rubbing her eyes. 'It's complicated.'

'They say a problem shared . . .'

She managed a smile. It was what they used to say to each other. 'I appreciate the thought, Tom, but honestly I'm too knackered. Sorry. All I want to do is go to bed. I could sleep for a week.'

'Fancy some company tonight? Keep the demons away?' His eyes held hers. Slowly, his gaze moved to fasten on her mouth. His eyes darkened from blue to midnight. It was a look she was familiar with, and when his hand moved to stroke the nape of her neck she felt heat pouring through her veins like liquid fire. A slow smile spread across his face. 'You missed me,' he said.

'Maybe,' she hedged, battling with her pride. She didn't want him to see how much he got to her, but she didn't want him to think she was a pushover either.

'What if I said I'd missed you?'

She said, 'What about your friend?'

For a moment he looked blank, and then he grinned. 'Don't tell me you're jealous?'

'Of course not,' she lied. She'd die rather than admit she'd like to scratch out Sharon's eyes, along with whoever it was he was now seeing. She lifted her chin. 'You're allowed to see whoever you like, whenever you like . . .'

He slipped an arm around her waist and lowered his head and kissed the skin behind her ear, nuzzling her neck. 'What about you?' he whispered.

'Me?' It came out as a gasp. He'd moved his hands to stroke the base of her spine. Then, out of nowhere, she had an urge to flee, to put some space between them, but she couldn't work out why.

He said, 'Seen Blake lately?'

She narrowed her eyes. 'What if I have?'

He shrugged. 'You can see whoever you like . . .'

This was not how she'd envisaged their reunion. She'd decided that if they got back together it would be for keeps, not a casual fling. If he was seeing someone else he'd better finish with them first. Jay wasn't prepared to share him.

She abruptly gave in to her need for space and stepped away from the heat of his hands, his gaze. She was shivering inside.

'What's wrong?' he said.

She wasn't sure, so she answered his question straight. 'I don't want to be second best,' she told him.

He looked confused.

'Your friend?' she reminded him. 'What would she say if she knew you were here?'

'Ah.' His frown cleared briefly, and then returned. 'Yes. I see your point.'

'Who is she?'

He looked away for a heartbeat. 'Another time,' he said.

'Is it Sharon?'

He gave her an exasperated look. 'Sharon and I had one night together. *One night.*'

'No reason why you might not have decided to make it two. Or more.'

'It's not Sharon, OK? It's not anybody, really.' He studied her at length as though thinking something through. 'But you're right. It needs sorting. Goodnight, Jay.' With that, he padded out of her room and downstairs.

When she heard the front door open and click shut behind him, she felt her body relax. Slowly, she eased into bed and pulled up the sheet, closing her eyes. The last thing she heard was the sound of a car starting up at the end of the street.

Jay woke in the middle of the night drenched in sweat and with a scream lodged in the back of her throat. She'd been running in her dream, fleeing for her life from a man with a face like a hatchet. He'd been wearing a lab coat and holding a syringe that contained the euthanasia drug that vets use to put dogs down.

Her heartbeat slowed as she recognized her room. The window was still open, letting in enough light for her to see the shape of her dressing table, the dark squares on the walls that were her pictures and photographs. Outside, she could hear the familiar hum of London. She felt wide awake and alert. Oddly, she was reminded once again of jet lag. Creeping downstairs, she turned on the kitchen light. Propped against the kettle, where she wouldn't miss them, were half a dozen letters and several phone messages. She made some coffee and opened the letters to find two invitations – one to an artist's exhibition in Soho, the other to a friend's party in Clapham – and a credit card bill for a pair of horribly expensive but gorgeously soft skinny jeans she'd bought last month. The rest was junk mail, the phone calls from a couple of friends and her family.

As she drank her coffee she thought over the past sixteen hours, but when she tried to push into the seemingly forbidden three days the grey wall repelled her.

Anna cowering naked on a tiled floor. Anna bleeding . . . dying.

The urge to see her mother returned. She swayed briefly. Her hands began to tremble with the strength of her longing. She'd never felt anything like it before. She had heard of brave, courageous soldiers crying for their mothers when they'd been wounded on the battlefield, and an SAS friend of hers admitting to calling for his mother during a mountaineering accident that left him dangling two thousand feet with only a thin, nylon rope between him and oblivion, but she wasn't injured. She wasn't dying. Why did she feel like this?

Jay crept upstairs and got dressed. Jeans, T-shirt and a pair of Moroccan twisted-leather sandals she'd worn all last summer. Back in the kitchen, she scribbled a hasty note to the girls before picking up her handbag and her car keys. She hoped she wasn't over the limit. She felt sober, but that didn't mean she didn't still have some wine from the flight in her system. Her tote bag was by the front door and, slinging it over her shoulder, she left the house. Logic told her she was safest with two ex-soldiers but something inside her, something primal, was screaming for her mother and it wasn't going to stop until satisfied.

The drive north was fast with little traffic, and she made it in record time. Parking next to her mother's Toyota, she climbed outside. A cool breeze, damp with coming rain, was blowing off the North Sea. She raised her face and tasted salt and brine on her tongue, the taste of her childhood, and felt a sense of calm descend.

Using her key, she let herself inside. She had planned to creep up to her old room and try and get some sleep before morning, but she hadn't bargained on her mother's miniature schnauzer, which rocketed down the stairs, barking fit to burst a blood vessel.

'Hey, Tigger, shhh.'

As soon as she spoke, the dog stopped barking and leaped up at her knees, making soft squeaky noises of greeting.

'Jessica? Is that you?'

Her mother was the only person in the world who used her full name and could get away with it. Normally, it drove Jay mad, but today it sounded as sweet as the dawn chorus.

'Yes, Mum,' she said quietly. 'It's me.'

The hall light snapped on to reveal her mother in a full-length nightie the colour of cornflowers. Her curly hair was awry, her eyes full of sleep, but the look of loving concern on her face was unmistakable.

'Darling, what's going on?'

'Mum . . .'

The child in her took over. She ran across the hall and fell to her knees and wrapped her arms around her mother's waist. She took a breath, inhaling the familiar scents of childhood night-time hugs – fresh linen and face cream – and then she lost all control. She opened her mouth and all the grief and horror and fear she'd felt during the past seventeen hours poured out like a stream of black filth, choking her, making her sob so hard that her voice cracked.

Her mother knelt and took her in her arms. She heard her say, 'No, Tigger, not now,' and then she was rocking Jay and stroking her hair, soothing her with gentle words, baby gibberish, but Jay didn't hear them. She couldn't stop seeing Anna, the way her legs kicked out as she was shot, the way she'd screamed, the blood that blossomed on her blouse.

Jay cried until her eyes were puffy and her sinuses so swollen that she could barely breathe. 'I'm sorry,' she sobbed. 'I'm so sorry.'

'Darling, what is it? What's wrong?'

I killed a friend.

She leaned back and wiped her eyes, looked into her mother's face. 'I didn't mean to wake you.'

'I know. Now, let's put on some hot chocolate. And then you can tell me what's been going on.'

Despite wanting to unburden herself to her mother, Jay couldn't do it. She couldn't bear to see her mother's confusion, or witness her fear over her daughter killing a woman. She admitted to having a hazy memory of her stay in Moscow, but didn't admit how bad it was.

'I'm exhausted,' Jay told her. 'That's all.'

'But what happened in Russia?' Her mother looked nonplussed. 'Didn't you meet with this woman, Anna?'

Alarm speared Jay. 'You know Anna?'

'You told us all about her last weekend. Anna Voro-something. I can't remember her name . . .'

'Vorontsove.'

'Yes, that's the one. You were supposed to see her over the weekend and find out where Duncan's vanished to. He still hasn't turned up. Elizabeth is going crazy with worry, along with the rest of us.'

A flutter of nausea rose at Duncan's name. 'You're saying he's missing?' She couldn't bring herself to say the word *Duncan* in case it brought on the nausea full throttle.

Her mother frowned. 'Darling, you really are in a state if you can't remember your favourite uncle vanishing like a puff of smoke last Monday.'

'Of course I can remember,' she lied. 'Humour me, will you? Pretend I know nothing about it and tell me the story from the beginning. It might throw up something new that we haven't considered before.'

Her mother seemed to think this a reasonable request and, between cups of tea and toasted crumpets in the kitchen – her mother seemed to think bread too ordinary for Jay this morning – she told Jay what had happened.

Apparently, Duncan had come home as usual after work on Monday the twelfth of June, around six thirty. He'd had a glass of wine before supper with Elizabeth, and after working in his study for an hour or so – just before bed – he'd taken out the rubbish. That was the last time Elizabeth saw her husband: as he wheeled the black bins down the drive. He'd changed out of his suit earlier, into chinos, checked shirt and fleece, and where he'd gone was anyone's guess. His Range Rover was still in the drive, his mobile phone and personal organizer in his study. He had, however, her mother added, taken a toothbrush and razor, his wallet and his passport, which Jay read as a sign that he hadn't been kidnapped. Had he planned to vanish? And what was the Russian connection? Was it because Duncan spoke the language? At least she now knew why her family had popped so vividly into her mind in the hotel room. They were depending on her to find Duncan. It showed her memory wasn't entirely ruined and was functioning reasonably well at a particular level. She just had to learn how to access it.

'I can't believe I flew business class,' Jay said.

'God bless Elizabeth.' Her mother smiled. 'She said she wanted you to arrive fresh and rested, but in all honesty she wanted to spoil you as a way of saying thank you. She knows how busy you are.'

Another question answered. Before long, hopefully all the blanks would be filled. 'It was kind of her.'

'Did this Anna help you?' her mother asked. 'She said she was sure she knew where Duncan was. Why he'd vanished. She even had lunch with him that Saturday.'

'I'm sorry, Mum. She never made the meeting. I'm no further to finding –' Jay took a breath to combat the drift of nausea – 'Duncan than when I left.'

Her mother glanced outside. Dawn was breaking over Blakeney Harbour, but there was no sun. The tide was in and the water was choppy and coloured brown.

'I wish she'd told you what she knew over the phone,' her mother grumbled. 'Talk about paranoid, forcing you to go to Moscow. Couldn't she have written a letter? Emailed you or something?'

'She was probably worried about security.' Jay yawned. Tears collected in the corners of her eyes. 'Mum, I'm going to get some sleep. I'm knackered.'

'You need more than sleep, darling. Whatever happened to make you so upset?'

'Nothing really. I just need some rest.'

'It's more than just being tired,' her mother insisted. She was frowning. 'I've never seen you like this before. It's not right, Jessica, so don't you try and tell me it is.'

Knowing she wouldn't be left alone until she'd provided a decent explanation, Jay went for the work angle. 'In all honesty I think I've hit an emotional wall. I've been doing nothing but work on human trafficking cases since I got back from my mission in Afghanistan. I think it's getting to me. I've eight Albanian women reported missing, assumed trafficked into the UK, another fifteen from Lithuania. It's not the most sanguine of professions, trying to fight the sex slavery business. I spent a whole day last week in Kentish Town trying to persuade two girls from Lithuania to go to the police. They'd been beaten and raped almost continuously since they arrived in England.'

'Oh, darling.' Her mother's face crumpled. 'You poor thing. No wonder you're at your wits' end. Trying to save all those girls . . . Why don't you stay here for a bit? Until you feel better?'

'I'd love to. I'll ring Nick in a couple of hours.'

Five

Jay didn't feel better the next day, nor the one following. She spent most of the time in her bedroom, lying on her bed and staring at her old school photographs on the walls where she looked young and happy, carefree. She felt no inclination to go outside, not even to walk Tigger along the coast path, which she normally loved. She didn't want to see or speak to anyone. She wanted to be left alone. Her mother had to tempt her appetite and was also worried about the quantity of wine she drank.

'It helps me sleep,' Jay told her. It was Friday lunch time and she was on her third glass. She never usually drank in the middle of the day, but she couldn't seem to help it. It was the only thing that kept the vision of Anna's death at bay.

'All afternoon?' her mother said, shocked. 'Darling, you must see someone.'

'Like who?'

'A doctor. Someone who can help you.'

'Mum, I'm fine. I don't need a doctor.' Jay took the bottle up to her bedroom, unable to work out why she kept telling her mother she was OK when she obviously wasn't. She didn't know what was wrong with her. Why didn't she want to go back to work? Nick had been understanding, as she knew he would be, giving her time and space to recover from her trip, but Tom was another matter. He'd rung the morning she'd arrived in Blakeney.

'The girls told me where you'd gone,' he said. 'I can't believe you drove. You weren't only over the limit, but you were also exhausted. I'm amazed you didn't fall asleep at the wheel and kill yourself.'

'I was fine, I swear. Refreshed and alert. I wouldn't have done it other-wise.' Which was a lie, and one which Tom saw straight through.

'Jay . . .' He sounded as if he could happily strangle her but was trying to restrain himself. 'Sometimes you have to ask for help. You don't have to shoulder all the world's problems on your own. You just have to open your mouth and *ask*.'

'I'm sorry. I'll do it next time, OK?'

'I'll hold you to that.' There was a pause, then he said, 'Seriously, Jay, what's wrong? What happened in Moscow?'

She watched a skein of geese fly across the sky, heading for their feeding grounds further west. A stout-looking birdwatcher followed them with his binoculars. He wore an orange shirt and so stood out from the rest of the group on the harbour. Everyone else wore country-coloured clothes in muted browns, greens and olives.

'I'll tell you when I've rested up, OK?' she told him.

'That's exactly what the girls said you'd say.' He sighed. 'When you're ready then. You know where I am.'

Jay hung up, grateful for her housemates' perception. Right now, talking was a real effort, and the thought of answering a barrage of questions from anyone but her mother made her feel faintly sick.

She continued to stare outside as she considered her housemates. Fit, bright and strong, neither of them – like Jay – had thought themselves exceptional until they'd left the army. It was only then that they'd understood how their training, their discipline and their physical stamina set them apart from the rest of the population. Most men ran a mile when Jay admitted she used to be in the army; they couldn't cope with dating a woman who was probably tougher than they were. Your average bloke on the street wouldn't know how to talk an armed insurgent into dropping his weapon, let alone put an enemy soldier in a headlock. They didn't understand she'd joined the army because it offered so much more than civilian life. At university she had majored in languages – French, Russian, Italian – but she also loved sport, and finding a job that didn't have her sitting behind a desk translating for hour upon hour had seemed almost impossible until her uncle Duncan had suggested she join the services.

Her memory of first meeting Duncan flashed across her mind, quickly followed by a rush of nausea. Clenching her fists she closed her eyes, refusing to allow her ruined memory to dictate the past. She wanted to remember the scene. Instinct told her she needed to remember Duncan.

She had, she recalled, just turned eighteen and was having an argument with her mother over her perceived career – translator for the diplomatic service – when Duncan and Elizabeth arrived. Elizabeth had arranged for them all to go to lunch to get to know her new boyfriend, and both Jay and her mother were so absorbed in each other and their argument that they were oblivious to anything else.

'I don't see why you're so against university.' Her mother's mouth was set tight.

'I want to live in France, Mum. I want to get a job in St. Petersburg or Berlin. I don't want to learn French and Russian stuck in some dusty old lecture hall, don't you get it? I want to *live!*'

'Don't be ridiculous,' her mother snapped. 'You are going to university and that's the end of it.'

'God, who made you Nazi dictator of the year?'

At that point Duncan had leaned between them and said hi. They'd immediately shut up and introduced themselves, and it wasn't until they were leaving the restaurant that Duncan had turned to Jay and said casually, 'If you joined the Services, you could do both. Travel and go to university. They would pay.'

Jay had signed up with the army two months later, and her mother had found it hard to forgive him.

Saturday morning, she was gazing through her bedroom window, frowning. The man she'd spotted birding yesterday, dressed in an orange shirt, was now sitting in his car down the street, reading a newspaper. Which wasn't unusual, but she didn't like the fact that he'd been there since yesterday evening, nor that he'd glanced at her mother's house on several occasions. Or was it her imagination? Perhaps he was looking at birds in the garden. Besides, had he really been there overnight? She remembered seeing him in his ancient Maestro before supper last night, but she hadn't looked later. Perhaps he'd gone home and come back and parked in the same spot?

She jumped when her mother knocked on the door. 'I've brought someone to see you,' she said.

Jay checked her watch. Ten o'clock. Two hours until she could pour herself a glass of wine. 'No thanks.'

'We're coming in anyway, so make sure you're decent.'

Jay wished there were locks on the doors, but her father had removed them years ago and nobody had thought to replace them. 'Two seconds,' she called and scrambled to pull on jeans and an old fishing sweater. Warily, she opened the door.

'You remember Dr Philpotts?' her mother said brightly.

Dr Philpotts was the family GP and had been for as long as Jay could remember. He'd stitched her knee after she'd torn it open falling from the tree house, and nursed her and her brother Angus through measles, stomach upsets and flu, prescribing painkillers and bed rest when needed. Dr Philpotts had been pretty ancient when she was a kid, and things hadn't changed. Today he looked about a hundred.

'Hi,' she said.

'Hello, Jessica. May I come in?' He raised an old-fashioned black doctor's bag that was worn to thready grey on the corners. 'Your mother's worried about you. I suggested a health check. Blood pressure, that sort of thing. All right?'

Actually, she thought, it wasn't such a bad idea. He might be able to prescribe a pill that would make her feel better.

'Sure.'

Sitting her on the side of the bed, Dr Philpotts brought out a little light and checked her eyes. Fine, apparently. Then there was the soft hammer to knock against her knees and check her reflexes. Again, fine. Her blood pressure was perfect, seventy-five over a hundred and fifty, and her nails and teeth were in good shape.

He asked questions about her stools and urine, her appetite, what she'd been up to recently, and Jay answered as best as she could while trying to hide the fact she'd lost five days from her memory. Finally, Dr Philpotts packed up his bag and made to leave. 'You're doing the right thing,' he told her. 'Rest as long as you think you need to, but if you haven't improved by the end of next week, call me.'

'But something's wrong with her,' Jay's mother insisted. 'She drinks too much, barely eats anything and spends all her time sleeping—'

'Sometimes we need time to ourselves,' Dr Philpotts said. He was looking at Jay as he spoke. 'Time to rest and to heal. Jessica's nearly thirty years old, she knows her own mind. I suggest we let her be.'

Jay could have hugged him, but settled for a peck on his cheek. 'Thanks,' she said.

Her mother saw Dr Philpotts out. Ten minutes later she came back upstairs. There was a determined lift to her chin that warned Jay she wasn't to be messed with.

'Sitting in your room all day isn't going to help, Jessica. So I've asked Sandra to come up and see you.'

Jay blinked. Sandra was her sister-in-law. She'd known her almost all her life – she'd been Angus's childhood sweetheart – and she bet her bottom dollar her mother had asked Sandra to check up on her.

'She's a fully qualified psychologist,' her mother said. 'She'll help you.'

'For goodness sake, Mum,' Jay protested. 'I don't need a shrink. I just need time to rest. You heard Dr Philpotts—'

'Sandra's on her way.'

'Well, tell her I'm sorry I couldn't be around.' Jay began throwing things into her tote bag.

'Darling, I'm only trying to help.'

Jay paused and looked at her mother. 'I know. And I love you for it, OK? But I've already seen a shrink, remember? When I came back from Kosovo . . .' Both of them looked away at the memory. 'I don't need another, I promise.'

Her mother looked doubtful. 'Are you sure?'

Travelling light had its advantages, and Jay had finished packing and was walking for her car in under five minutes. She was very fond of Sandra, but she had no intention of lying on her sister-in-law's proverbial couch. If she needed a shrink, she'd find one in the Yellow Pages.

The sea air felt good against her cheeks and in her lungs – refreshing. Perhaps this was the right thing for her, being forced to move from the safety of her childhood den. She couldn't believe she'd been indoors for half the week. It was so unlike her, so alien, that she couldn't blame her mother for worrying.

'Bye, Mum.' She hugged her mother and bent to pet Tigger goodbye. 'Thanks for looking after me.'

'You're going home now?'

Jay thought it over. 'I was thinking of dropping in to see Elizabeth en route. Talk to her about Duncan.' A flicker of nausea rose and fell just as fast at the mention of her uncle's name. She was, she realized with relief, getting better.

Her mother looked surprised, then pleased. 'Oh, darling. She will be glad to see you.'

As Jay drove down the street, she checked her rear-view mirrors but there was no sign of the birder and his orange shirt or of his Maestro.

Elizabeth was seven years younger than Jay's mother, and although the two sisters had never got on as children – the age gap was too wide – as adults they were firm friends, and Jay had happy memories of her aunt and her cousins coming to stay during the summer holidays.

When Jay arrived, she found her aunt in the garden, weeding her herbaceous border beneath a blazing sun. Where some families might flap or fall apart during a major catastrophe, the Goodwins did the opposite. They got busy. Fitz and Amelia were with the grandchildren, pickling eggs in the kitchen; David was washing everyone's cars; and Cora was spring-cleaning the cellar. It was a hive of activity designed to disguise their anxiety, and Elizabeth was no exception. She was weeding as if her life depended on it. She had dirt on one cheekbone, a leaf in her hair and her dungarees were smeared with earth.

The only two members of the family that weren't fully occupied were Duncan's two Labradors, Toast and Marmite – one yellow, one black – who were stretched in the sun, dozing. Both, however, leaped up to greet Jay with their usual doggy enthusiasm when she approached.

'Dearest Jay.' When Elizabeth got up to greet her, Jay fussed with the dogs, trying to avoid her aunt coming too close. Normally, she loved being hugged by her family, but since Moscow she didn't like being touched. As her aunt pulled off her gardening gloves, Jay studied her and saw that although her face was drawn, her eyes rimmed with red and circled with bruises from lack of sleep, she appeared remarkably calm considering her husband had disappeared less than two weeks ago.

'We were so worried when you didn't come home when you said you would,' Elizabeth said. 'I would have visited you in Blakeney, but Alice said you were exhausted.'

'I was a bit.'

'Always the master of understatement.' She wiped some sweat from her forehead with the back of her hand.

Jay bent to stroke Toast's sun-warmed head. 'How are you bearing up?'

Elizabeth looked away. 'Awful, since you ask. We don't talk about it because, if we do, we end up crying and that's no good for Charlotte and Katie. They think he's gone away on business. We can't bear to tell them the truth.'

'They're too young to hear it,' Jay agreed. Her cousins were only seven and five years old and wouldn't be able to understand their father disappearing. It was their mother who felt every second of his absence. Duncan was Elizabeth's second husband, and Elizabeth always smiled when she said, 'Second time lucky.' She had met Duncan when she'd just turned thirty-eight and had married him within the year. Charlotte and Katie arrived soon afterwards, and although it sometimes felt strange having such a young uncle – Duncan had just turned fifty, making him barely twenty years older than Jay – it meant she had more in common with him than she might with someone older.

Duncan had swept into their family like a benign whirlwind, and it hadn't taken long before they began to talk about BD and AD – Before Duncan and After Duncan – because their lives changed so dramatically. Almost overnight Norridge Farm became the hub of the Goodwin family, with huge family Christmas, Easter and bank holidays. It was as though Duncan had always existed, and now Jay kept looking around, waiting for him to pounce on her and lift her into one of his bear hugs. The energy seemed to have gone out of the place. Even the ants looked listless.

'Alice rang after you left.' Elizabeth led the way into the farmhouse, the dogs padding ahead of them. 'She said you found nothing in Moscow. After all that, flying over there, you never even got to see that Anna Vorontsove woman. What a waste of your time; I'm so sorry.'

'How did we get to know about Anna?' Jay asked. 'Who put us in touch?'

Elizabeth gave her an odd look. 'You found her.'

'Talk me through it. In case it jogs something free that we haven't thought of before.'

Like Jay's mother, Elizabeth seemed to think this made sense. 'You saw her name in Duncan's diary. Next you checked The Angel Hotel, where

they'd met for tea. You thought Duncan might be having an affair . . .'
Elizabeth kicked off her shoes in the boot room. Jay followed suit. The air
smelled of dogs, leather, and saddle soap.

'But then you spoke to the police and got Duncan's phone records.
Anna had gone back to Moscow by then. Flew out the day Duncan vanished.
You spoke to her and she convinced you that she knew where he was, and
why, but she wouldn't tell you over the phone. Which is why you went
to see her.'

Jay shook her head as if she had water in her ears. She wished she could
shake some kind of recollection into her brain. 'Do you have Anna's number?
I mislaid it.'

'Of course.' Elizabeth went to a dresser in the kitchen piled high with
paper and had a search. 'Here.' She copied the number on to a Post-it note
and passed it over. 'Can you stay for supper?'

'I'd love to.'

Using the phone in the hallway, Jay tried Anna Vorontsove's number in
Moscow but it had been disconnected. She wasn't surprised. There seemed
to be more dead ends than live ones.

Supper was a low-key affair. Usually, the family were noisy and rambus-
tious but everyone – even the children – was subdued. Their eyes darted
from Fitz, who was sitting in Duncan's place at the top of the table, to the
doorway, as though waiting for Duncan to suddenly appear and roar jovially
at Fitz for usurping his position as head of the family.

Afterwards, Jay helped Elizabeth wash up. There was a dishwasher, but
the messier cooking trays, good glasses and fine cutlery were always hand
washed. As she rinsed a silver butter knife free of suds, Jay gazed outside,
contemplating Duncan's success. He'd done well for himself, establishing
a solid, dependable and trusted accountancy firm in town since he arrived
eleven years ago, but the real money hadn't been made with accountancy
fees.

Duncan, it appeared, had a bit of a flair for the stock market. Not only
did he dabble with his own money successfully, but he also gave tips and
advice to his friends. When Jay had muttered about the lack of pension
should she leave the army in her twenties, he'd advised her to sink as much
as she could afford into a media company she'd never heard of, and Jay –
wary and unsure – had invested three hundred pounds. A year later, that
three hundred pounds was worth five hundred and forty, an eighty per
cent increase. When she'd asked Duncan how he'd known about the takeover,
Duncan had shrugged. 'I have a knack for it, that's all. Always have.' His
eyes had gleamed. 'Did you invest much?'

'Not enough.' Jay had been rueful.

'Never invest more than you can lose,' Duncan had said, nodding sagely. 'That way madness lies.'

The relief of being able to think of Duncan without feeling sick was intense. It was as though by coming to his home she'd managed to eject some poison from her mind. Her mother had been right. Sitting in her room all day hadn't helped, but being active and facing the world had.

Jay picked up a glass and started washing it. Where was Duncan now? Was he all right?

After a couple of minutes, she glanced across at her aunt. She'd stopped drying up and was staring through the window. Jay turned to see what had caught her eye. Briefly, she saw a light flash in the woods. Something was reflecting the setting sun.

Elizabeth said, 'It looks as though someone's on Barrett's Hill. How odd.'

Jay studied the slope with its occasionally flashing light. 'Maybe it's a gamekeeper or something.'

'Duncan doesn't have anyone like that. Nobody should be up there. It's private land.'

'Kids then. Drinking, partying. Whatever.'

'Jay, it's miles from anywhere. You have to walk half an hour from the road to get to that point.'

Jay took off her rubber gloves and put them by the sink.

Elizabeth was still staring at the darkening slope. She said, 'Do you think it's Duncan?'

'I'll go and find out.'

The sky was clear, beginning to darken into a deep blue edged with stars. The ground was dry underfoot, the dirt as pale and crumbly as crushed shortbread. As she walked, Jay felt the temperature drop slightly. The warm smell of flowers intensified.

Elizabeth had wanted Fitz to join her, but Jay insisted on going alone. 'Less noise,' she said, but when Elizabeth looked worried, Jay added, 'I'll take the dogs. They'll look out for me.' Which was rubbish. The second she'd let them off their leads they'd vanished. They would, no doubt, turn up in time for their bedtime biscuits, but in the meantime they'd gone hunting rabbits.

When she reached the gate leading into the woods, she switched on her torch and started up the slope. She'd taken an educated guess where the light had flashed from, and was headed for a rough open piece of ground that gave views of the farmhouse and surrounding area. As she approached, Jay slowed, wanting to creep up on whoever it was and see what they were up to. She just had to pray it wasn't a farmer friend of Duncan's, or even a poacher, out hunting. She didn't want to startle them so their gun went off. She didn't want to get shot.

Carefully, she pushed her way through the bushes, the only sounds she made being her soft footfall and tiny snicking sounds as branches tugged at her shirt. She was nearing the top when there was a rustling and crackling of branches from further up the hill. Her torch had been spotted. Immediately, she broke into a jog. It didn't take long before she reached the lookout point. Sweeping her torch around she saw two empty drink cartons, a sandwich and Mars bar wrapper, and a pile of cigarette stubs. One was still alight, still smoking, and Jay ground it out with her boot. Then she ducked down and shone her torch on it. Her breath hissed between her teeth. The stub had a Cyrillic stamp.

She pocketed the stub along with the others, the Russian connections making her skin crawl. Moscow, Anna Vorontsove and now someone on Barrett's Hill smoking Russian cigarettes . . . She studied the position of the rubbish and the cigarette stubs, the scuff marks and the crushed grass where the person had sat. Jay settled in their place, putting her boots where his feet had been.

Dead ahead, the farmhouse was lit from every window. You could even see people moving from room to room with the naked eye, the view was so clear.

There was no doubt about it – the Goodwins were being watched.

Six

All eleven of the Goodwin family, predictably, erupted in a cacophony of shock and confusion at the thought of being watched. Fitz immediately closed all the curtains while Jay faced her family with every ounce of aplomb she could muster, answering their questions patiently, until one by one they finally quietened, allowing her to pour herself a well-earned glass of whisky.

She'd only taken a sip when her cousin Cora came over, a bundle of blonde, curly hair and brightly coloured scarves. An amber necklace that David had given her at Christmas bounced between her breasts. 'I got that number you wanted.' She delved in her maroon velvet handbag and passed over a piece of paper with a mobile number on it.

Jay tried to look as though she knew what Cora was talking about. 'Great.'

'Nikolai rang this morning, wanting to chat to Dad. Mum told him Dad had disappeared. He left his number. You know, saying he'd do anything he could to help, blah blah blah.'

'Nikolai?' An alarm bell began ringing. 'He's Russian?'

'He could be, I suppose, but I wouldn't know, sorry. One accent sounds much like another to me. The family language gene passed me by.'

'Does he have a surname?'

'Sorry.' Cora ran a hand through the curls. Like her mother, her eyes were red and she obviously hadn't been sleeping much, if at all. 'I wasn't thinking straight.'

'Tell me about him, would you?'

Cora gave her a strange look, prompting Jay into giving a revised version of what she'd said earlier to her mother and Elizabeth, in order to hide her shattered memory. 'You might have forgotten something small, that might be important. Repeating things sometimes does that. Shakes something new free.'

Cora gave a shrug. According to her, Nikolai was an old friend of Duncan's and had popped in for drinks on Sunday evening, the day before Duncan vanished. Apparently, Jay had spoken to everyone Duncan had seen over the past week except Nikolai.

'You wanted to check him out as well as get his viewpoint on Duncan's state of mind,' Cora finished.

Jay turned Cora's note over in her hands, wondering if Nikolai had anything to do with her extended stay in Moscow. 'I'll ring him now.' Her curiosity was too piqued to wait until morning.

The number was for central London and answered on the second ring by a man saying, 'Koslov residence.' His voice was heavily accented Russian.

Having ascertained that Nikolai was in fact Nikolai Koslov, Jay introduced herself, saying she was a cousin of Duncan's, and the man told her to wait. Listening to emptiness echoing down the receiver she drank her whisky, studying the photographs on the wall. There was one of her at her passing out parade at Sandhurst, another of her in her desert combats in Iraq. Duncan, she remembered, had sent her a letter unfailingly every week during her Basra tour, along with a gift of some sort: a book; a packet of treacle dabs – her favourite sweet; a miniature game of Scrabble; a jar of Fortnum and Mason's goose pâté. Little treats that had lifted her spirits each week and meant far more than she could ever tell him. There were depths to Duncan that few knew about. On the surface he was bluff and jovial, but beneath he could be introspective and melancholy. Whatever mood he was in, however, he was always kind.

'I am sorry, Mr Koslov is not here at the moment. He is overseas at present. You would like an appointment?'

Before she could reply he went on, saying, 'He tells me Wednesday is good for him, at ten o'clock.' He rattled off an address in Hampstead, which she scribbled down, thankful that Elizabeth kept a pad and pen by the phone, because she'd barely copied the postcode when he hung up.

'He said he was an old friend of Duncan's,' Elizabeth said when Jay asked her about Koslov, 'although I'd never heard Duncan mention him before. They talked mostly about racing. You know what Duncan's like about the horses.'

'Could he be a business colleague? Maybe a client?'

'Most of Duncan's clients are friends and vice versa.'

'Would you mind if I checked Duncan's office tomorrow?'

Elizabeth looked surprised. 'You already did that last week.'

'I just want to double-check something, that's all.'

'The keys are hanging up in the kitchen. Help yourself.'

Nine a.m. the next morning Jay arrived at the eighteenth-century trading house and let herself inside. Nobody was at work since it was a Sunday, and the air was still and silent, as well as incredibly hot. She'd barely walked into reception when her skin started to spring with sweat. Like many old buildings in England, Duncan's offices had no air-conditioning. Although it was cosy in the winter, the building sweltered in the summer.

She started in Duncan's office, which was where most of the business was done. There were tax forms, files and surprisingly neat heaps of paper-work in progress. Highlighter pens, pencils and erasers. A calculator, some business envelopes bound with a rubber band. She checked the drawers and found more office supplies: compliment slips and business cards, notepads, more pens. She went to open the filing cabinet, but it was locked.

Unsure whether to force it or not, she paused, raising her hair from the nape of her neck in a vain attempt to cool down. It was no good; she had to open a window or she'd pass out. Unlatching both lead-lined windows she swung them wide. Below, people in shorts and T-shirts were heading to prepare themselves for the Sunday market. She saw a woman pushing a trolley loaded with basil plants, her companion carrying a tray of French cheeses. Duncan loved shopping in his home town. He'd take Toast and Marmite, and despite Elizabeth giving him a detailed shopping list he'd buy barely half of it because he'd be chatting too much.

Out of nowhere, the grey curtain in her mind parted and a sliver of light shone through. The memory of Elizabeth calling her to tell her that Duncan had gone missing arrived, clear as day.

'We've searched everywhere but we can't find him. Please, Jay, say you'll come and help?'

Jay's fingers clenched as she pictured Duncan the last time she'd seen him, on the May bank holiday weekend, thundering around the sitting room on all fours giving 'horsey' rides to Katie and shouting, 'Giddy-up!' at the top of his voice. He would have done the same for Jay if she'd been younger when he'd married into the family, but even though she'd insisted that, at nineteen, she was too old, he'd taught her how to ride a horse: a gentle giant of an Irish draught called Polo because, like Duncan, he loved mints.

Looking around at the pictures of racehorses on the walls, the family photographs prompted another memory to ease from the grey wall: her asking Duncan's secretary if anyone had a grudge against him.

'Nope,' said Chrissie. 'Everyone *loves* Duncan. Oh, that's aside from Mr Stamper, an organic pig farmer, of course. He refused to pay Duncan's last invoice because he considered it an outrageous rip-off. But he wouldn't do Duncan any harm. He's all bluster and bluff, that bloke.'

Jay shuffled through files labelled with stickers: Marsh Chickens, Stony Grove Cereals, Parsonage Pork. It appeared that Bailey & Co. did the accounts for every farmer in Suffolk and Norfolk combined. No wonder Duncan had such a beautiful home, Jay thought. He must be raking it in.

She flicked through the in tray, pausing when she came to what looked like a birthday card, unopened, and marked Personal. Sending an apology to Duncan for the intrusion, Jay extracted the birthday card. It was a watercolour painting of a yacht sailing on a calm, flat sea. Inside, the handwriting was tremulous.

Darling,

Wishing you plain sailing always.

From your loving mother.

On the opposite flap was a note telling Duncan that she was fine, that she'd taken a walk to the shops earlier and that, although she was as slow as a snail, she wasn't as slow as Boots. The vet had apparently diagnosed Boots with kidney trouble and prescribed him some pills that cost more than her annual pension. Boots sounded as elderly as his owner.

It was a normal, everyday birthday card from a loving mother to her son.

Which Jay wouldn't have found unusual, except the postmark was dated the ninth of June, fourteen days ago, and Duncan's mother, Kristina, had supposedly died in 1995.

She was still studying the card when she heard footsteps in the corridor. Light footsteps, soft footsteps. Footsteps that were muffled, almost as though their owner didn't want them to be heard . . .

A wave of white cold washed over her, leaving a prickling sensation along her hairline.

She stepped to the doorway. She didn't duck her head into the corridor and back – she didn't want an abrupt movement to alert whoever it was – but inched it around the door jamb until she got a clear view.

A short, chunky man in jeans, sneakers and a blue T-shirt was prowling around reception, opening and closing drawers, pulling things out and letting them fall to the floor. She waited for him to turn to show his face, and, when he did, another wave of cold hit her.

It was the man she'd seen in Blakeney, she was sure of it. The man in the orange shirt. Or was it? She hadn't seen him up close at her mother's house, so how could she be so sure? Quickly, she studied his features: pale skin, a narrow mouth, short, mouse-coloured hair. No distinguishing marks that she could see. No visible moles or tattoos. Imprinting his face in her mind as best she could, Jay inched back into Duncan's office and crept behind his desk. Ducked down out of sight, she switched her mobile to vibrate and started to dial the police.

She stopped when she heard him moving down the corridor. He was coming towards her. Then she realized the windows were still open – a dead giveaway that someone else was there. Nerves jumping, she scrambled up and pulled them to. She didn't dare shut them properly, in case she made a noise. His footsteps were getting closer. Ducking beneath the desk once more, she made herself as small as possible, praying he wouldn't want to open Duncan's desk drawers as he'd spot her in an instant. Should she make a noise and hope it frightened him off? Or would it make him aggressive? Tom had told her never to surprise a burglar. Apparently ninety-five per cent of them fled when they were disturbed, but the remaining five per cent, fuelled by fear and adrenalin, went berserk, sometimes killing the person confronting them.

What should she do?

Sweat streamed down her face, her flanks. His footsteps came closer. He was at the doorway, and then he paused.

Silence.

Had he seen the windows weren't latched? Muscles tense, heart racing, she waited.

The seconds ticked away.

He stepped inside. She heard him move to the left and try and open the filing cabinet, and then rattle it in frustration. He grunted, and next came the jingle of what sounded like a bunch of keys. There was a scraping sound, and then he started banging the filing cabinet. He was trying to break the lock. He was absorbed. He didn't know anyone was here. Could she tiptoe out of the office without him noticing? No chance.

She felt her mobile vibrate but didn't answer it. She considered sending a text to the police, but didn't dare in case the man heard the tiny metal clicking of the keys.

A drop of sweat worked its way down her cheek but she didn't brush it away. She squatted, as still as stone.

She heard a final bang, and then the metal rush as he pulled open a drawer. She had to move, she realized. She couldn't sit and wait for him to find her. She had to take the initiative.

Slowly, she inched to the edge of the desk and peered around the corner to see he was taking files out and throwing them on the floor. She glanced at the door. Only five paces and she'd be in the corridor. She could out run him once she was there.

As she tensed her legs, readying herself to spring up and race outside, the man must have caught her movement out of the corner of his eye because he turned his head and looked straight at her.

Jay didn't hesitate. She uncoiled, leaping for him with her fingers hooked, going for his eyes. She was screaming as loud as she could.

He stumbled backwards with his arms raised, protecting his face.

Jay kicked his knee but as he fell he grabbed her arm. She fell with him, still going for his eyes. He tried to punch her face but she deflected the blow with her elbow. He cursed. It was a messy scuffle until he feinted with his right arm and let loose with a punch from the left. It hit her on the side of the head like a mallet.

'Hope it hurts,' he said in Russian. His words were strangled from where she'd hit his windpipe. 'Bitch.'

He turned and ran into the corridor. Dizzy, ears ringing, Jay let him go. She scrambled to her feet. She was about to ring the police when her phone vibrated again. It was Tom.

'Are you psychic?' she said and started to laugh, a reaction from the adrenalin release. 'I was just about to call the cops.'

Seven

'He spoke Russian?'

'Yes.' Her head was still aching from the burglar's punch, so she opened the cupboard above the bread bin and helped herself to two extra-strong Panadol.

'And you think he was the same man you saw outside your mother's house?'

'Yes.'

Tom stared past her shoulder. He'd driven from London to Suffolk in less than an hour, which was fairly impressive considering he wasn't using his own car but an undercover vehicle he'd swiped off Goose: a five-year-old Skoda with dents in every panel. After she'd rung Elizabeth – her aunt had joined her along with Tom as she'd made a report to the local police – they had returned to the farm. Tom and Jay were ensconced in the kitchen, while Elizabeth had called the family into the drawing room to fill them in on the burglary.

He said, 'Tell me about Moscow.'

'I went to meet a journalist . . .' She couldn't say Anna's name. She felt as though once she did the whole festering story would pour out and Anna would appear between them, bleeding, groaning, dying.

'Jay,' he murmured. 'What's scaring you?'

The answer came straight from her heart. 'I'm not the same person I was before. And I don't know if I can get her back.'

He nodded, as if what she'd said made sense. 'What happened?'

'Moscow,' she blurted. 'I lost my memory there.'

He didn't turn a hair, just nodded. 'Tell me.'

She began to shudder as she recounted everything – waking up in the hotel room, clutching the bottle of vodka outside her hotel room, talking to Vladimir, the sense of jet lag, the Cyrillic cigarette butts left on Barrett's Hill – but she couldn't bring herself to tell him about Anna. As she spoke, a part of her wondered why she could tell all this to Tom but not anyone else.

When she finished, Tom came and stood in front of her. His movements were slow and steady, as though he was wary of disturbing a wild creature. When he raised both hands to her face, she didn't move away but let him wipe away the tears she hadn't realized she'd shed.

Tom dropped his hands but didn't move away. 'I want to check something,' he said. 'OK if I do that?'

'OK.'

Gently, he took her left wrist and turned over her arm, exposing the pale underside. Goosebumps rose all over her body at the feel of his touch and for a second she forgot about Duncan and Moscow as she gazed at his hair, thick and richly coloured and as shiny as tortoiseshell. She had to resist the urge to stroke it.

He said, 'How did you get this?'

He was pointing at the inside of her elbow, the faint blue vein lying proud on her skin.

'What?' She couldn't see what he was referring to.

'There's a bruise. See?'

She peered closer. 'It's tiny.'

'You gave blood recently?'

She stared at him. 'Not for ages.'

'Hmm. Can I check your other arm?'

Jay let him inspect her skin. Now she knew what he was looking for, the bruises – there were five of them – seemed to stand out like fluorescent beacons.

'What the . . .' She touched them carefully but they weren't sore, which was probably why she hadn't noticed them.

Tom lowered her arm. He said, 'You've been quite a pin cushion, haven't you?' There was something in his voice that she hadn't heard before, something tight and hard. With a start, she realized what it was. Anger.

She opened her mouth, but nothing came out. She was too appalled to speak, too horrified, and too scared.

'Whoever did this wanted something from you, and they wanted it badly.'

She found her voice. 'They drugged me?'

He didn't say anything, just looked at her. Of course she'd been drugged. How stupid not to have thought of it before. By whom? Had Anna been involved? Was that why she'd killed her, because she'd been betrayed?

'You say you lost five days?'

'Yes.'

'That figures. Takes at least that long to knock your defences flat and get to where they want to go.'

Fear crawled over her skin. 'What were they after?'

'I'd say the initial nausea you felt whenever your uncle's name was mentioned might be a clue.'

'Right.' She swallowed. So they wanted information on Duncan. She thought further before recalling what Vladimir had told her about Anna trawling the Internet until she found Duncan in England. 'Anna was trying to find her father's murderer. Eduard Vorontsove. He was with the FSB. He was killed in Siberia, apparently.'

Tom thought this over. 'Anna believed Duncan had something to do with her father's death?'

'Vladimir certainly thought there was a link.'

'But what's the connection with your uncle?'

There was a pause as they looked at one another.

Jay sighed. 'Only Duncan knows the answer to that.'

'Agreed.' Tom gave a nod. 'The sooner we find him, the better.'

She moved to put the kettle on the Aga. Her mouth was dry from a combination of anxiety and too much talking. 'I don't think I should tell the family I was drugged, do you? Not until I have more information. It'll only give them sleepless nights.'

He nodded. 'What's next?'

'I'm going to try and track down Duncan's mother.'

Tom looked startled. 'His mother's alive?'

'Yes,' said Jay. 'I found this in his office.'

She fetched the card from her handbag and handed it over. He said, 'She's Russian, right?'

'Belorussian. Duncan's half-Russian, remember?'

Tom glanced at the card. 'Her English is perfect. I'd never guess it was her second language.'

'She's lived here for over fifty years.' Jay picked up the envelope and studied the postmark for the umpteenth time. 'Minton? Ington? I can't work it out.'

Tom plucked it from her fingers and gave it a cursory glance. 'Lymington.'

She raised her eyebrows.

'I used to go on holiday there as a kid,' he said. 'From there we'd catch a ferry to the Isle of Wight.' After he put down the envelope he checked his watch. 'I'd better be getting back.'

'To London?'

'Yup.'

Jay said lightly, 'Visiting your friend?'

There was a long silence and then he said, 'Yup.'

She fiddled with a thread that was hanging from her sleeve. 'Thanks for coming. You didn't have to.'

'I know.' Before she could move he ducked his head and kissed her mouth. He murmured, 'Please try and stay out of trouble.'

* * *

After staying overnight with the family, trying to settle their nerves without much success, Jay headed to her office. She was jumpy, her nerves still tight after her brawl with the burglar, but at least the Panadol had kicked in and her headache had eased. Despite being unable to stop checking the tiny bruises on her inner arms – shuddering in horror each time – she felt more in control now she had some idea of what had happened to her. Tom had told her she wasn't responsible for what happened in Moscow. 'You were drugged,' he said. 'It wasn't your fault.' But he was wrong. She *was* responsible. She hadn't told him she'd killed Anna, but come hell or high water she was going to find out why. First, however, she had to find Duncan. She was convinced her uncle held all the answers.

While she waited for her computer to boot, she let her eyes roam the office, familiarizing herself with the photos of happy families displayed on the walls. They could be seen as corny, but TRACE was a close-knit team and when they reunited a family – especially a child with its parents – the news flashed around their organization like wildfire. And no matter how tough a day they'd had, how difficult and emotionally brutal, at that moment everyone walked on air.

It was no accident that she'd chosen to work for a non-governmental organization. The transition from military to civilian life, from conflict to peace, had been one of the hardest things she'd done, mainly because she'd discovered she had nothing in common with her old friends. They were into shopping in their spare time, watching TV from the sofa and eating out, and although she also enjoyed these pursuits she didn't want to do them all the time. When she'd fallen on TRACE, a private aid agency with twenty-seven people employed worldwide – all but three were ex-Services – she had just about fainted in relief.

Online, she saw she had over a dozen emails from Lithuania and four from a Nigerian cop about two brothers, whose parents insisted they had gone missing in Manchester; but none were about Duncan. She checked through her files and saw she'd arranged a lot of publicity about Duncan's disappearance before she'd flown to Moscow. She recalled Duncan's birthday card from his mother, Kristina, and its message: *Wishing you plain sailing always.*

What did that mean? Was it a hidden message of some sort? Was he on a boat somewhere? Checking further, she saw she'd begun collating information about her uncle and his friends and acquaintances, but not as much as she'd expected. Considering she'd had four working days between Duncan disappearing and her trip to Moscow, the file should have been bulging. Wondering if the file had been dropped and some papers lost beneath her desk, she bent to check and found another file. This one was marked *Parnell's,* but oddly it held nothing but a legal document. Looking further, she saw it detailed a trust fund of a million pounds, set up by Duncan for someone called Justin Parnell in 1996. Jay rang the solicitors who'd drawn up the document, who were based in London, and introduced herself to the receptionist. 'Oh, you'll need John Ciszek. John looks after trusts.'

John apparently remembered Jay calling him two weeks ago, even if she couldn't remember him. 'I'm sorry,' she said, 'but I need reminding about Justin Parnell's trust. What were the details, exactly? I'm sorry, but I've mislaid them.'

'Ah, yes. We had to do a fair digging around to get the information you wanted. Let me check and get back to you with the notes I made. It shouldn't take long.'

While she waited, Jay logged into the Internet and Googled the Parnells. They popped up immediately at the top of the page as some of the best racehorse trainers – not just in Britain, but around the world. Apparently, Magnus Parnell had died in 1995, leaving the stables to his son Crispin, who'd continued the business with barely a hitch, building on his father's fame. The cream of the world's bloodstock was sent to Crispin's stable, and Crispin could, from the sound of it, pick and choose which horses he wanted and – more importantly – which owners.

Her pulse jumped when she saw that Nikolai Koslov was one of Crispin Parnell's owners, with eight horses under his care. Koslov had seen Duncan the day before he vanished. When was her appointment? She checked and saw it was two days away, on Wednesday. She nibbled the inside of her lip. Why was her file on Duncan so empty? Had she taken the papers home? Or had the burglar turned TRACE's office over as well as Duncan's? Hastily, she double-checked the front door was locked, along with the windows, but she still jumped when the phone rang: John Ciszek.

'I have my notes . . . The trust, for one point two million pounds, was set up for one Justin Parnell, in perpetuity, in 1996. The trustees are Grace Holger and her parents, Mr and Mrs Patrick Holger. The money is held by a private investment bank . . .' He rattled off the details of a well-known city firm. 'If you need information about the money, you'll have to approach the bank directly. You'll need police authority.'

Jay thanked him and hung up. Flipping through some more pages on the Internet she saw that Justin was Crispin's younger brother. Why had Duncan settled such a large sum on this man? Had there been some sort of blackmail threat?

Her heart leaped to her throat when she heard the front door bang but immediately relaxed when she recognized the footsteps striding across the hall and into the office.

'No news on your uncle, I take it?'

She turned to see her boss, Nick Morgan. Nick was as scarred as an old fighting dog, with a torn ear and broken knuckles, but not all the scars were visible. He'd been deployed in the Falklands and the first Gulf War, but it was only after a lengthy tour in Bosnia that he'd found his vocation and set up TRACE in the belief he could help more people as himself than as a marine. He was a practical man, not a visionary, and he'd employed mainly ex-service personnel like Jay because he felt comfortable with others whose lives had been structured and strictly disciplined.

'Not a squeak.' She indicated the files on Duncan. 'Has anyone been using these?'

He paused. 'Not that I know of. He's all yours.'

'They're incomplete.' She pushed back a lock of hair and told him about the burglary, the watcher on Barrett's Hill. 'I think they're looking for Duncan too. I don't suppose we got burgled?'

Nick looked at her in surprise. 'Put it this way, if we've been burgled, I'm the last person to know about it. Look, I've got a meeting with the Albanian Embassy in twenty minutes; you want to bring me up to date when I get back?' He vanished into his office before she could speak and returned in a rush with a bulging folder in one hand and a tattered briefcase in the other. He said, 'Don't forget to check Duncan's old school friends. Sometimes they can trigger abnormal behaviour, especially if they've rocked up out of the blue.' His gaze turned distant. 'An old flame could have contacted him.'

'But he adores Elizabeth.'

Nick looked at her steadily.

'OK, OK.' She held up her hands. 'I'll check out his old school buddies.'

'Did he go to university?'

'No, but he did an accountancy course. I'll check for old flames there too.' She told him about Duncan's mother, Kristina, and what was written on the card. 'And what about her cat? If I could find a vet that had recently diagnosed an elderly cat called Boots with kidney disease . . .'

Nick snorted. 'Now you're clutching at straws. You want to call every vet in the south of England? Besides, I doubt they'll release personal information about their precious patient's owner.'

'It's worth a try. You know as well as I do that sometimes it's when we're working on the periphery of an investigation that we get a real break-through.'

'OK, call the vets then.' He glanced at his watch. 'I really must go . . . You want me to take over the Lithuanians for a bit?'

'You wouldn't mind?'

'Since you're not going to be functioning at your best until you find

Duncan, no.' He gave her a stern look. 'Besides which, you look terrible. Gill and I will take up the slack for say, the next fortnight or so, OK? Gill owes you anyway; she won't mind.'

As he swept into the hall she called after him, 'Thanks!'

'You owe us!'

Jay went to the wall chart and re-colour-coded her clients so that anyone wanting a quick reference to who was looking after whom could do so easily. Gill was currently at the Sudanese Embassy and working on the mess in Darfur, which normally would send anyone suicidal, but, having reunited six families split by the conflict in the past ten days, Gill was on a roll and brimming with enthusiasm. Jay hoped Gill wouldn't resent the extra work, but, as Nick had said, Gill owed Jay from last year, when Gill's mother had fallen ill. Gill had been away for a month, and Jay had shouldered the majority of her work. It had just about killed her but she hadn't complained. It was one of the bonuses about having a small team. Everyone helped everyone else when times got tough.

Jay rang Elizabeth and asked her which school friends Duncan was still in touch with. 'None that I know of,' her aunt responded. 'I've never met another Marlborough boy.'

'Do you know when he left?'

'Golly, now you're asking. Nineteen eighty or eighty-one, at a guess. He started when he was eight years old. I always thought it was criminal sending a child so young to board away from home. Should I have met his mother – God rest her soul – I'd have given her a jolly good talking to for doing that to him.'

Little did Elizabeth know she might just get to do that, Jay thought, but didn't say anything. Instead, she asked, 'What about old friends from his accountancy course? Any of them still around?'

'I haven't a clue.'

'Can you remember the name of the course? Where it was held? What year he started?'

'It was in London. At the City College for International Business Studies. I only remember because Fitz's best friend got a job teaching there recently. Duncan would have been twenty or so. I never met anyone from that period of his life. I'm sorry. Is it important?'

'I'm just making sure we don't leave any stone unturned.'

They talked a little further, and then Jay rang the City College in London and gave her credentials, explaining what she wanted. If she could speak to an old tutor of Duncan's, or a mentor of some kind, it would cut through a lot of tedious legwork, but when the records manager came back on the line, he was apologetic.

'We don't have any Duncan Bailey listed. We put all our records on computer recently but nothing is coming up.'

'Could you try the next year? His wife must have got it wrong.'

'No, I'm sorry. I mean we have never had a Duncan Bailey attend our course. We have four Duncans listed, and two Baileys, but no Duncan Bailey.'

Puzzled, assuming there was some mistake, Jay rang Marlborough College and asked the same questions.

'Please hold.'

Jay held. Finally, the woman returned to the line. As soon as she spoke, Jay had the inkling that things were going to get very complicated.

'There's nobody in either year called Duncan Bailey.'

Jay cleared her throat. 'Could you do me a favour and check ninety-nine and eighty-two for me?'

'Give me five minutes and I'll call you back.'

True to her word, the woman did ring back, not in five minutes but in twenty. She said, 'I'm sorry. I've checked the records several times. There's no Duncan Bailey listed. You must have the wrong school.'

Jay thought fast. 'Do you keep photographs of school-leavers?'

'Of course.'

'Perhaps I could come down and have a look. If I got to you, say, in an hour, would that be OK?'

'I'll leave the books with the bursar.'

Jay drove like the wind to arrive just after lunch. Boys in uniform looked at her curiously as she passed, one giving a wolf whistle, which she ignored. The school smelled of polish, old wood and toasted cheese. The books lay on the bursar's desk, along with a pot of freshly picked herbs. As directed by the bursar, Jay settled to flick through the photographs, starting with Elizabeth's first hunch: 1980.

To her relief, Duncan appeared on page fifteen, saving her hours of searching. He was smiling, his eyes creased and happy, and his skin was tanned, flushed with youth and good health, but the boy shown wasn't called Duncan. He was someone called Trent Newton.

Eight

Telling her aunt that her much loved husband had lied about his past wasn't something Jay enjoyed.

'There must be a good reason for it,' Elizabeth kept saying, over and over again, her face pale and drawn. 'If he was here, he wouldn't hesitate to tell us. There must be a good reason . . .'

Jay's mother had driven down from Blakeney – and, although she'd been sympathetic towards her sister, she reacted as Jay had expected, triumphant to be proven right. She said, 'I always knew there was something not quite right about Duncan. Things rarely added up to how he presented them . . .'

Jay didn't have the mental strength to stay for long. Luckily, the farm was only an hour and twenty minutes from home, and she was in bed by eleven o'clock.

She slept badly, haunted by images of Anna. Occasionally, she'd find herself dreaming that she was floating above a broad wilderness, an iron land of silence under a strange half-lit sky, dotted with remote villages. There were no roads, just handfuls of dusty looking trails and mud tracks, and when her alarm went off she awoke feeling tired and in need of another night's sleep.

Lying on her back, she studied the ceiling. She felt tense and anxious, and she was reluctant to get out of bed. It wasn't like her to be like this. She hated herself and was filled with shame, an all-pervasive sense of guilt about who she was and what she'd done. For no reason she could think of, tears began to seep from her eyes.

'Hey, Jay.' It was Angela, outside her bedroom. 'You want some coffee?'

She coughed and cleared her throat of tears. 'Later, thanks.'

'You're running late,' Angela warned. She knew Jay liked to beat the traffic by leaving before seven thirty.

'Doesn't matter.'

'If you say so.'

Jay lay in bed listening to her housemates bathe, dress and breakfast, and eventually leave the house. She had to force herself into the shower, and each time she heard a sound she couldn't identify, she jumped, her heart flipping. Back in her bedroom, she struggled to get dressed, fighting against the urge to climb back into bed. Her skinny jeans weren't where she remembered leaving them, hung over the back of the chair, but slung in the bottom of her wardrobe. Puzzled, she picked them out, along with a crumpled piece of tissue paper and a cashmere sweater that her father had bought her two birthdays ago. The sweater should have been wrapped in the tissue paper and stacked with her other woollens on the wardrobe shelf . . .

Had Denise or Angela been in here, looking to borrow things? It wasn't unlikely, but it was highly unusual. The girls were highly protective of personal space – their own as well as others – and only entered her room when necessary, like they smelt burning and suspected a fire, or wanted to check for a burst water pipe.

Slowly, she turned and surveyed her room.

She studied the positioning of the pictures on the walls, her jewellery scattered across her chest of drawers, her alarm clock, her childhood stuffed toys on top of the wardrobe – Eeyore, Tigger, and a worn looking lion she'd called Howard – and, although everything looked fine, there was something off about the room. Her silver necklace wasn't to the left of the mirror as she remembered leaving it, but in the centre, and the pile of paperbacks by her bedside had been reshuffled.

Uneasy, Jay rewrapped her sweater and put her jeans back on the chair. She hoped this wasn't a memory problem tied into her Moscow experience, and that it wasn't going to get worse. Still uncertain, she checked the front door, always double locked, but the back door was on the latch. Any intruder worth his salt would barely pause at such a pathetic attempt at security. They'd grown slack over the summer, pottering in and out of the garden, and now Jay bolted the door from the inside.

In the kitchen she poured herself some Special K but, after two mouthfuls, pushed the bowl away. It tasted of sawdust.

She gazed outside – yet another peerless, sunny day – thinking about Duncan. She was unsure how she felt about her beloved uncle being someone else all this time. Oddly, she didn't feel as shocked as she thought she should be and couldn't work it out. Perhaps she'd suspected something from the start? However, she couldn't remember being suspicious about him at any point in the past. She'd liked him straight away, as most people did. What on earth had made him change his identity? It was a drastic step, not one easily undertaken considering the type of person Duncan – she couldn't think of him as Trent – was: steadfast, reliable, family-orientated.

Jay turned on her laptop and, coffee to hand, settled herself for a lengthy session on the Internet. She noted someone had logged on since she'd last used her computer and, after her disquiet over her room, she checked her files. A band of tension increased in her shoulders when she saw some files had been opened during the week she'd spent in Blakeney with her mother.

Had the girls used her computer? She'd ask them later. Meantime, she'd Google Trent Newton. She had to search for a while, but she finally hooked into a series of old newspaper reports, mostly in the financial sections. Apparently, Duncan used to be an extremely successful broker and investment adviser. As she read further, it appeared he'd made millions for his clients, and millions in bonuses; he was a revered financial master, a veritable god in the City of London . . .

And then, in June 1995, he'd apparently suffered a mental breakdown and gone to live in the Shetland Isles, far away from the stress of city life. That was pretty much the last anyone heard of him. One day he was in the thick of the City, the next burnt out and living on a remote island. Nobody had turned a hair.

Jay sank back in her chair, emotions all over the place as she tried to take in the fact that behind the bluff, ruddy expanse of Duncan the country accountant had been a revered City guru. She'd known he had a knack for working the stock market, but not how *much* of a knack. She then considered his so-called move to the Shetland Isles and guessed it was a smokescreen. He'd last two seconds up there – the winters were truly tough – but pretending to have a breakdown was a neat way of removing himself from London without causing any waves.

Tom's phone was engaged, so she dashed off an email asking him to ring her when he was free; she wanted to see if the police had any files on Duncan in his past life. Then she started ringing as many of Duncan's friends as she could. Nobody could remember meeting or knowing Duncan before 1995, not even his bank manager or the tax man. Which she assumed meant he'd changed his identity from Trent Newton in the same year. The identity change was so complete – including national insurance as well as his passport – that Jay reckoned there had to have been a real Duncan Bailey at some point. Either the man had died, or he'd sold his identity. She was fetching another coffee when Tom rang. 'How's the headache?' he asked.

'Gone, thanks.'

'Do you fancy meeting this weekend? I'm in town. Maybe we could catch an exhibition or something?'

Jay's heart gave a hop. 'That would be nice.' She decided not to mention his 'friend'.

'I'll ring you, OK?'

Very OK, she thought, but she didn't say so, just, 'Great.' Then she said, 'Are you sitting down?'

'Do I need to be?'

'It might be wise.'

Pause. 'OK. What's happened?'

'It transpires that Duncan isn't Duncan at all, but someone called Trent Newton.' She brought him up to date with her findings.

'He's had another identity all this time?' Tom sounded amazed. 'He didn't seem the type. Bloody hell.'

'That's rather how I feel. Could you do me a favour and check that he wasn't in witness protection or something? It's the only thing I can think of that might fit the bill.'

'Sorry, no can do. Only two – maximum three – officers are allowed to know the true identity of someone who's gone down that route. It's the only way we can keep their identity and whereabouts absolutely secret.'

'Oh.'

'Good idea though. Worth looking into.'

When the doorbell rang, she peered cautiously out of the window to see who it was. Standing on her doorstep and looking straight back was a handsome woman with shoulder-length auburn hair and skin the colour of cream. She wore a pretty summer dress patterned with lavender flowers, and carried a voluminous canvas bag over her shoulder. She waved, smiling, and despite Jay's feeling of annoyance – she bet her mother had put Sandra up to this – Jay waved back. She liked Sandra a lot, and she was glad Angus had married someone she got on so well with, but if her sister-in-law brought out her psychobabble she'd have to give her short shrift.

Jay opened the door.

'Hi, you,' Sandra greeted her, advancing to give Jay a hug.

Jay stepped back and Sandra immediately halted and stood aside, giving Jay lots of space.

'Did Mum put you up to this?' Jay asked. She was fiddling with her hair, unsure whether to ask Sandra in or not.

'She's worried about you.'

'I'm *fine*. I wish she'd stop worrying.'

'It's only because she loves you. Look, let's get some coffee and sit in your gorgeous garden. Give me a break from the twins. They're driving me insane today.'

'We won't have to talk about my mental health?' Jay was suspicious.

'Only if you want to. I admit Alice asked me to drop by and see you, and now I've dropped by I can at least report I've completed the mission.' Sandra reached into her bag and withdrew a box of croissants, bought from a very expensive, very delicious deli in Putney. 'Come on, we haven't seen each other for ages.'

'I'm meant to be finding Duncan.' Jay knew she sounded stiff and unfriendly but couldn't seem to help herself.

Sandra rolled her eyes. 'I'm sure Duncan won't mind you pausing for two seconds to have coffee with your sister-in-law. Even superwomen need time off.'

Reluctantly, Jay let Sandra inside and brewed coffee, reheated the croissants, and put everything on a tray. Outside Jay brushed down the deck chairs before they sat. Already it was warm, the air thick with the scent of jasmine. It felt more like the South of France than London.

'Hmm.' Sandra bit into a pastry. 'This is good. Heaven. So peaceful without the little horrors. Mark got a trumpet for his birthday and won't be parted from it for a minute. He even sleeps with the thing.'

Jay sympathized, and as Sandra chatted about Angus and the kids, and their Eastern European nannies, Zamira and Hana, she gradually stopped sending surreptitious glances towards her watch and settled back and let the sun warm her face and throat. Sandra began telling her a story about Mark trying to feed his twin sister some soap when – without realizing it – Jay fell asleep.

She awoke bleary eyed and feeling as though she'd been knocked out by an industrial-sized tranquillizer. Sandra was still talking, but softly, and for an instant Jay thought she'd only been asleep for a minute or two until she saw the sun had climbed into the sky. Her watch told her she'd been out for over an hour.

'Sandra.' She struggled to sit upright. 'I'm so sorry . . .'

'You needed the rest. You're obviously exhausted. As well as stressed.' Sandra surveyed her steadily. 'How do you feel now?'

'As if I've been slugged with a sandbag.' She eyed her sister-in-law suspiciously. 'Did you put something in my coffee?'

Sandra looked shocked. 'No way! All I did was prattle on about my boring old family life and before I knew it you were snoring!'

'Well, you did something,' Jay grumbled. 'I never kip during the day.'

A swallow swooped low through the garden, grabbing insects on the wing. In the distance she could hear an airplane approaching, crossing the city to land at Heathrow.

'All I did was respect your personal space and talk about safe subjects. If I'd started with, "Good grief, Jay, you look awful," you'd have bolted for the horizon, correct?'

Ruefully, Jay nodded.

'Am I right that when anyone presses you about what's happened to you recently, you feel threatened?'

Immediately she thought of Tom, the way he'd kept his distance, understanding and aware.

'Jay? What are you thinking?'

'Why can't I remember things?'

'Like what?'

Jay told Sandra about the missing five days in Moscow, her dreams of shabby villages set in a wilderness of scrub, but she couldn't make herself share the vision of Anna dying, nor the fact she'd been drugged.

Sandra let a short silence develop before she said, 'I don't want to alarm you, Jay, but – talking professionally – you appear to be showing indications of post-traumatic stress disorder. I'm sure you've heard of the symptoms from your army days, but they include difficulty sleeping, sometimes not wanting to get out of bed and face the world, having a poor appetite, feeling restless, tense and anxious . . . avoiding other people, feeling guilty, plus being unable to recall the precise trauma.' She took a breath. 'I think something catastrophic happened to you and you're suffering the consequences.'

Jay hunkered down in her deck chair as she remembered the roadside bomb in Basra, and her fellow soldier, Steve, who later couldn't recall the baby dying in his arms. But she wasn't like Steve. She could remember shooting Anna. She could even remember the spots of blood on her face, the splashback missing the mole on the journalist's jawbone.

'Would you trust me to help you?' Sandra's expression was gentle and composed. 'Or would you rather go to a colleague of mine, who specializes in PTSD?'

'I don't know.' It was a child's response, but Jay couldn't think of any other.

Sandra let a silence drift, turning her head briefly to watch another airplane pass overhead before she said, 'If you want to remember everything fully, there's a technique we can use that might help. It's called EMDR – Eye Movement Desensitization and Reprocessing. It's a method used to uncover traumatic memories. Eye movements help to access the channels of the brain that hold the traumatic memory. It could help us bring the memories of those five days into the open and replace the imprints of terror or fear, or feelings of disempowerment, with the truth of the incident so you can process it properly, and move on.'

Jay crossed her arms. She didn't say anything.

'For what it's worth, I think it would help enormously.' Sandra paused. 'You're very strong, Jay, especially mentally, but you're not strong enough to face this alone. If you don't deal with it, it could alter your behaviour with your friends and your family irrevocably, and not necessarily for the better. Do you want that?'

A shiver ran through her. It was already happening. She just had to look at how she reacted to Elizabeth and Nick. No touching, no hugging, leaping aside if they got too close.

'I'll let you think about it.' Sandra stacked the tray and got to her feet. 'Let's ring each other tomorrow and see how you feel.'

Jay followed her inside, anxiety nipping her heels. Did she really have to do this EMDR thing? Why couldn't she just *remember*?

At the front door, Sandra turned to Jay and looked at her straight. 'Normally, I wouldn't say this to a client, but, while you're thinking this over, don't forget to consider the fact you might remember a vital clue that might help you find where Duncan has gone.'

Nine

Jay decided on doing some legwork to settle her mind and, after picking up a couple of photographs of Duncan and checking the map, drove out of London on the M4. After she'd taken the Newbury exit, she opened the sunroof and switched off the air conditioning to let in the smells of the countryside: cut grass, pollen and the occasional waft of cow muck. Normally, she would have revelled in the drive. To her, England in June was incomparable, with the countryside cloaked in every shade of green imaginable, from the trees and fields to bursting hedgerows, lawns and roadside banks. However, today she barely saw it because her mind was taken up with questions.

Why had Duncan changed his name all those years ago? What had Nikolai Koslov to do with his disappearance? As she headed west, towards Marlborough, she thought over Anna visiting Duncan. Anna had been a journalist. What if Anna had shared something vital with Duncan that had put him in danger? That had prompted him into protecting his family by vanishing? Quite liking this theory, she toyed with it further. What if Duncan had originally changed his name to keep himself safe from something? What if he'd had to do the same thing all over again? Was he now living somewhere else with another name? Maybe the million pound trust to Justin Parnell was an insurance policy of some kind.

She slowed as the road narrowed. Two horses were trotting fast towards her, slender legs stretching out, ears pricked and tails high. Both riders raised their whips as she pulled over. She watched them go in her rear vision mirror, beautifully balanced and as elegant as anything she'd seen in years.

Holbrook Park Stud Farm was a hundred yards further along the road. It had a lodge at the end of the drive and an avenue of beech trees leading to the main house and stables. On either side mares and foals grazed, tails and ears flicking. The railings were painted white, the drive immaculately maintained with perfectly mown verges.

When she drove up and parked, half a dozen dogs came trotting over, barking. There were four Labradors and two Jack Russell terriers, and since all the tails were wagging Jay reckoned she was safe enough. She climbed out and said hello, the dogs' tongues drooping in the summer heat but their tails wagging harder.

On the left was an Elizabethan manor house, two stories, with wisteria surrounding large windows letting in lots of light. On the right was a smaller version of the manor house, which Jay reckoned had been built in the last ten years or so. Everything was spotless: shrubs and grass trimmed, the gravel raked, the tubs of flowers bursting with colour.

Jay walked ahead for the stables, counting the cars. Five grubby, cheap and cheerful Japanese makes – which she took to belong to jockeys and stable lads – along with a BMW estate, a Maserati and a battered looking Range Rover. If his cars were anything to go by, Crispin Parnell looked to be doing pretty well for himself.

As she approached the yard a man in a wheelchair arrived very fast. Wiry, thick blond hair, probably in his late thirties, he had the golden boy athletic good looks that some women went crazy for, aside from his legs. They were wasted, barely threads in his trousers, and were as twisted as a pair of tortured willow branches. Jay knew from experience with disabled soldiers not to avoid the issue, and said, 'Yikes, what happened to you?'

'Got mugged in Bristol.'

'Good grief.' She could feel the horror form on her face. 'They certainly didn't mess about.'

'One of them had a baseball bat. I hit him – I was scared he was going to attack my girlfriend – and he took it personally.'

Jay almost didn't dare ask but curiosity got the better of her. 'And your girlfriend?'

'She ran to the local pub to get help.' He looked past Jay's shoulder briefly, then back. 'If she hadn't returned with half the pub's customers as fast as she did, I might have died.'

'What a terrible thing to have happened,' she said. 'I'm sorry.'

'Kind of you.' He gave her a cheerful grin. 'Now, what can I do for you on this beautiful, sunny day?'

'I'm here to see Crispin. I rang earlier. I'm a friend of Nikolai Koslov's.'

At the mention of Koslov's name he blinked. 'Oh. You're Jay? Forgive me, I was expecting a . . . er, because of your name . . . sorry.'

'You're not the first person to think it's a man's name,' she told him.

'Sorry,' he said again. He stuck out a hand. 'I'm Justin. Crispin's brother. Do you want to see Flashman Flyer?'

Justin Parnell was the beneficiary of Duncan's one-point-two million pound trust, and although she wanted to ask him about it she decided to hold off for a while. She didn't want to spook him too early.

'Sure.'

Flashman Flyer was an enormous chestnut with a broad chest, a white blaze and a pair of ears that reminded Jay of swords. Jay dredged up a favourable horse comment that Duncan always used. 'He looks well.'

Justin beamed. 'He's the favourite for the Derby next month.'

'I'll make sure to back him.'

En route to the next horse, Justin brought out a mobile phone and dialled. 'Hi, bro,' he said. 'Jay's here and she's a girl. Just warning you . . . Sure. Will do.' He pocketed his phone. 'He says to come to the house.'

As he escorted her back across the yard, smoothly dodging the odd wheelbarrow of horse muck, Jay took in the quantity of CCTV cameras. Just about every inch of the yard was covered. If someone tried to nobble one of Crispin's horses, they'd have to nobble the cameras first.

Crispin Parnell greeted her at the front door. He was dressed in a pair of tatty corduroys and a checked shirt with threadbare elbows. Dirty blond hair framed a round, ruddy face. He looked like a farmer instead of the immensely successful trainer he was.

'Miss McCaulay?' He shook her hand. 'What can I get you? Something soft, or a glass of wine? I'm sorry it's just me today. Jane's gone to London.' He ran a hand over his head, looking harassed but trying not to. 'The drawing room's a bit of a mess . . .'

'The kitchen's fine.' Jay knew from Duncan and Elizabeth's house how things were on working farms. 'All I need is a cup of tea. I won't take much of your time, I promise. And please, call me Jay.'

Relief flooded his face. 'If that's OK . . . It's not often we get friends of Nikolai's here, and, when we do, they rather expect the stops to be pulled out. The last lot drank a case of champagne and ate pretty much the entire contents of our larder.' He glanced at his brother. 'Thanks, Justin. I'll catch you later.'

Jay thanked Justin for the stable tour, which was returned with a genial salute.

'See you, Jay,' he said and wheeled away.

Crispin led the way into the kitchen, which, although huge, was crowded with dog beds and bowls, a variety of ancient armchairs, and a big, pine table covered in cereal boxes and packets of biscuits. Photographs of horses covered the walls. A television in one corner was tuned to horse racing at Bath racecourse.

Crispin put a kettle on the Aga and turned to face her, resting his hips against the towel rail. 'So, what brings you here?'

'I fancied seeing the Derby favourite.'

His eyes lit up. 'Beautiful, isn't he?'

They talked horses a bit and drank their tea, and then Jay said, 'I gather you took over the training when your father died.'

'Mum and I, actually. People forget Mum. Funny that, really, considering it was her who kept the place together when Dad died.'

'You've done well.' She reached into her handbag and withdrew a photograph of Duncan, taken six years ago on holiday in Cornwall when he was tanned and smiling. She passed it to Crispin. 'You don't recognize this man, do you?'

He took it warily. 'Why?'

'He's gone missing. He's a great fan of horse racing. I just wondered if you knew him.'

When he looked at the picture the colour left his face so fast that Jay thought he might faint. She put a hand out but he waved her away.

'Christ,' he whispered. 'I don't fucking believe it. It's him. It really is.'

'You know him.' It was a statement, not a question.

He strode to the far end of the kitchen and pointed at a photograph of two men standing with a sweat-streaked horse in a winner's enclosure. They had their arms around one another's shoulders and were grinning.

Jay felt a small shock beneath her breastbone when she recognized her uncle. Pointing at the man standing with Duncan – straw hair, pale eyes – she said 'Who is he?'

'Nikolai Koslov.'

Jay pointed at Duncan. 'And that's Trent Newton.'

'Yes. He's also Justin's godfather.' He swung to face her. 'You say he's missing? From where? Where the *fuck* has he been?'

Not wanting to get into Duncan's life with Elizabeth just yet, she said, 'When did you last see him?'

'The day Dad died. Thirteenth of June, 1995. My father –' he ran a hand over his face – 'committed suicide. Trent was his best friend, part of the family, and when Dad blew his brains out with a shotgun, Trent vanished like a puff of smoke.' Old anger rose, making his voice tremble. 'The *bastard*.'

'Crispin . . . would you mind . . .' She wasn't sure how to put it. 'Why did your father . . .?'

He moved across the room and pointed at another photograph. This one was of Justin in his mid twenties. He was astride a big, grey hunter jumping a hedge the size of a sedan car. 'Did Justin tell you what happened to him?'

'Yes.'

He nodded. 'Dad took it badly. He blamed himself . . . They'd had a row the previous day over Justin's girlfriend, Grace. Dad couldn't stand Grace, thought she was a religious nut, and refused to let her stay here for the weekend. So Justin went to Bristol . . . where it happened. Dad never forgave himself. Every time he saw Justin's legs . . .' His mouth twisted and he turned away sharply, pain etched on his face.

'I'm sorry.'

He thrust Duncan's picture at her without looking round. 'When you find him, tell him not to bother coming round here.'

'Would you mind telling me Duncan's . . . I mean, Trent's relationship to Nikolai?'

'Best buddy and drinking companion.'

'Do you know if Nikolai's seen Trent since ninety-five?'

He shook his head. 'Nikolai actually offered a reward for any information on Trent, can you believe it? Ten thousand quid. He was as furious as we were that he'd disappeared. Worthless piece of shit. Would you mind going now? I've a lot to do before the end of the day.'

His tone warned her not to ask any more questions. The man was hurting and she had to respect that.

'Sure.' Jay put the photo back in her bag and let him walk her to her car before turning to face him. 'I'm sorry,' she said again.

His eyes were shiny. He scrubbed them hard. 'Tell me, where has he been all this time?'

'He married my aunt. He's got a family in Suffolk. A successful accountancy practice.'

'And he's missing?'

'Yes.'

'Good riddance to him.'

For the first time in days she felt as though she was getting somewhere. Knowing that Duncan used to be Koslov's best buddy and drinking companion was a huge breakthrough and shone a new light on everything. She wondered why Koslov hadn't told Crispin that he'd had drinks with his old pal Trent cum Duncan two weeks ago, and then she turned her mind to Crispin's father. A tragedy, and, in the middle of it all, Duncan had vanished and changed his identity. The trail was heating up.

Walking towards the stables, she saw Justin talking to a small-boned man perched atop a tall black horse. When Justin spotted her, he waved her over. 'This is Gerry Townsend.' He introduced the jockey. 'He'll be riding Flash in the Derby.'

Jay promised to back him, and the jockey grinned, sending her a wink before he walked the black horse away and into the next yard.

'I hope you don't mind,' said Jay. 'But I've a question for you.'

'Fire away.'

'I was wondering why your godfather set up a trust worth one-point-two million pounds for you.'

'Who are you?' Justin was obviously taken aback. 'The Inland Revenue?'

'No. I'm Trent's niece.' She told Justin what she'd told his brother and watched his expression turn from confusion to astonishment.

'He's *alive?*'

'Nobody knows. He's being treated as a missing person.'

'And he's got a whole other family. Another name. Another *life?*'

'Yes.' She talked it through with him for a while, letting him settle through the shock until he was calmer.

Eventually, he said, 'You didn't tell Crispin about the trust, did you?'

She shook her head.

He raised his eyes skywards. 'Thank God. He loathes Trent.'

'So I gather.'

Justin rubbed a hand over his golden curls, making them dance. 'Nobody knows the truth about the trust, except me and Grace and her parents. Grace wanted to put a stop to it, she was sure the money had something to do with Dad's death, but I said I couldn't be so cavalier. I survive on the dividends I get from that money. Trent was clever, you know. Even after the credit crunch, I still live really well . . . Crispin would go nuts if he knew I was living off Trent's money. He thinks it's Grace's family who look after me, out of guilt because I was walking her home when we were attacked, and I let him.'

He looked at her expectantly. 'Where's my godfather? I'd like to thank him. I wanted to before, but the solicitors wouldn't let me know where he was. I wrote a letter, several letters actually, for them to forward to him, but I never heard back.'

'I'm afraid I don't know.'

Justin looked aside as a stable lad walked past, lugging a couple of hay nets. 'I don't know what to make of it. Vanishing a second time? It's bizarre.'

Jay thought over what she'd learned so far. 'Why did Grace think your godfather's disappearance had anything to do with your father's death?'

'No reason, really. It just seemed odd that both things happened on the same day.'

'Very odd,' she agreed, and went on to ask him a variety of questions about Nikolai, but he couldn't shed any more light than his brother. She ended up saying, 'Should you hear from Duncan . . . I mean, Trent . . .'

'I'll let you know.'

Swinging on to the M11, Jay planned what to do next. Firstly, garner what information she could on Justin's mugging and his father's suicide and see if Duncan was involved in any way. Secondly, find Duncan's mother. From the affectionate tone of the birthday card, Duncan could well be staying with her. Kristina might shed some light on events in 1995, especially since that was when she had supposedly died. Thirdly, talk to Nikolai Koslov, best buddy and drinking companion of Duncan's. Which she was due to do tomorrow, at his house in Hampstead at ten o'clock.

The traffic thickened as Jay drove through London – early rush hour – and when the temperature rose to a scorching thirty-three degrees she decided a cool shower was a priority and went straight home. The girls were just back from work and they cracked open some beers and took them into the garden. Denise lit the barbecue and tossed on some sausages and chicken.

When the girls had kicked back and were relaxed, Jay asked them if they'd been into her room lately or borrowed her computer. 'I don't mind,' she added hastily. 'You're welcome, you know you are . . .'

'No way,' said Angela. 'I haven't touched your computer, nor have I been in your room.' She glanced at Denise. 'You?'

Denise shook her head. 'Nope.'

'Have you noticed anything odd about your rooms?' Jay said. 'Things moved around?'

Angela looked amused. 'You think we've a poltergeist?'

'Nothing,' said Denise. 'Why?'

'I must be imagining things,' Jay murmured, but she couldn't get rid of the feeling someone might have been in there, having a look. What if it had been the Russian burglar? What felt like a dozen ants scurried over her skin. Why her? What had she to do with anything? What had happened during her five lost days? She slugged back the rest of her beer and fetched a bottle of red wine while Denise served the meal. Jay normally loved barbecues, but her appetite was dull and she barely ate anything, just drank wine.

Denise eyed her still-full plate at the end of the meal, the empty bottle of Rioja. 'I'll only say this once, babe, but you've got to talk to someone about this. It's not like you.'

'I know,' Jay replied.

'You got anyone you can go to?'

She shrugged. She wouldn't meet her housemate's eye.

'Then go. Because if you don't, I'll drag you there myself. And that's a promise.'

Jay thought she'd sleep well, having drunk so much, but once again she had a restless night haunted by images of an asphalt courtyard leading to what appeared to be a block of offices. Men filed back and forth a long corridor lit with bare bulbs, coughing, and when she woke in the middle of the night she was coughing too.

Ten

'I have an appointment with Mr Koslov.' She spoke into the microphone by the massive wrought iron gate. 'Ten o'clock.'

'Your name again?'

'Jay McCaulay.'

'Please wait.'

She surveyed the brick wall topped with vicious curls of razor wire. Two security cameras were pointed directly at her. Since nothing was going to happen until she'd been checked out, Jay tried to settle her nerves by listening to some music. It didn't work. Her pulse was up, her heart thumping. She'd taken her usual precautions before she'd come here, but she still felt as though she was preparing to put her hand inside a sack of snakes. Her boss, Nick, knew where she was, along with Tom, her house-mates, her mother and everyone in-between. If anything happened to her, the entire Goodwin family, along with the girls and Nick's marine buddies, would parachute in and rescue her, all guns blazing.

She closed her eyes briefly. Why did she feel as though she might need rescuing? It was her body trying to get her attention again, as it had in Moscow, warning her, screaming at her to *watch out*.

To distract herself, she switched radio stations and listened to the news. More talk about the Treasury squeezing the armed forces into dropping yet more army jobs – how were they supposed to succeed in Afghanistan without any troops? – and then a piece about a man's body that had been found in Epping Forest, naked, his skin ripped and torn, apparently savaged by dogs.

A buzzing sound alerted her that the gate was opening. Letting off the handbrake, she eased her Golf down the gravelled driveway, trying to keep her breathing steady, her nerves under control. She absorbed the stretches of perfectly mown lawns, the beautifully manicured box hedges. There were three gardeners working near a Romanesque swimming pool and another two beside a lily pond. She parked next to a life-sized stone statue of a lion and climbed out of her car. Above the rhythmic hiss of a sprinkler she could hear the rumble of London's traffic and, in a nearby shrub, the fierce chatter of a blackbird. Jay crunched across the drive. Koslov's house was a huge, red-bricked, modern square with a marble porch flanked by a pair of massive stone urns. The front door was already open. A man with a buzz cut, dressed in an oversized, pale-grey suit, stepped out.

'Please, if you follow me.' His accent was thickly accented Russian. 'Mr Koslov wait for you inside.'

Sweat pricked her inner arms as she followed the man through a marble hallway and along a corridor that sported a fresco of blue sky and soaring eagles on its ceiling. When they came to a pair of double doors, he opened them and led her into a massive oak-panelled room. He asked if he could get her a drink. She said, 'A glass of water would be great.'

Jay walked around the room, trying to ignore her jangling nerves, but it was difficult against the backdrop of stuffed animal heads on the walls leering down at her. There were African antelopes – sable, waterbuck and a magnificent kudu – along with buffalo, warthog and wild boar. Lion and tiger skins were scattered across the floor. A polar bear stood on all fours at the far end of the room. Jay had a closer look and saw its claws were intact, and its skin ruined above its nearside front paw, indicating that it had been trapped and killed in the wild. A bronze plaque said it was from Wrangel Island, Siberia.

In the centre of the room stood a glass case, inside which was a bust of Stalin carved out of shiny black ore. There was a massive fireplace with a crest above it. Lots of crossed swords and leather armchairs. She picked up an ashtray, which looked remarkably like a horse's hoof, and hurriedly put it back. It wasn't ceramic as she'd thought. It was real.

A movement caught her peripheral vision and she glanced through the window. Two male Dobermans, ears and tails cropped, trotted past. They wore no collars, and looked as lean and muscular as a pair of sharks. Despite the fact the room was warm, she shivered as she recalled the man's savaged corpse in Epping Forest.

The double doors clicked and the man with the buzz cut returned to put a glass of water on a table inlaid with onyx. She was about to thank him when a man with a mop of shaggy fair hair padded inside. In Crispin's photograph he'd been clean-shaven and wearing a jacket and tie, but at home Nikolai Koslov obviously liked to dress down. He wore an oversized linen shirt, shorts and flip flops, had three days' worth of stubble and needed a haircut. He looked as though he was about to head to the coast to go surfing, except for the fat cigar he was smoking.

'Fuck sake, Gusev. I told you to bring her to the kitchen. You gone deaf or something?'

Gusev cringed. 'Sorry, boss. I thought you said—'

'You're not paid to think. Get out.'

Gusev scuttled for the door like a big beetle scared of getting crushed.

'Jay McCaulay.' Nikolai walked towards her. His hand was outstretched, his eyes smiling.

The smell of his cigar – cold leather and almond with a hint of honey

– swept through her senses. The nausea returned in a rush. She didn't know this man, didn't recognize him, but her body did. Every nerve was shouting at her to run, to flee, before it was too late.

At the last second, he paused. His eyes held hers. They were pale blue and as shiny as newly minted coins. 'I'm sorry,' he said, with his head on one side, 'but have we met before?'

Jay felt the familiar adrenalin surge as her automatic fear response kicked in at full throttle. For a second, she was so petrified she couldn't move, couldn't think at all. She was paralysed.

'There's something about you that's very familiar,' he added.

Instinct told her that her survival rested on the fact he mustn't know she recognized him. 'I don't think so.' She picked up an ashtray and pretended to study it, desperately trying not to show her fear. 'Is this real?'

'Absolutely.' Clamping his cigar between his teeth he stepped forward to take it from her. 'Look.' He pointed at a slim, silver strip around the base of the hoof, made to look like a horse's shoe. 'It's engraved. See?'

Pobyeda, Cheltenham 1992.

'I like to remember my winners,' he added. 'Victory did me well.'

Jay looked around the room, seeing half a dozen more horse hoof ashtrays. 'Are they all, er . . . from different horses?' She was amazed she sounded so normal. She felt dizzy and as though she might faint at any moment. *Breathe*, she heard her father's voice command.

'Yup.' He gave a laugh as he tapped a length of cigar ash into Victory's scoured-out hoof.

She took a gulp of oxygen and put out her hand. She didn't want to touch him, but knew she had to. *Dear God*, she prayed, *give me the strength to get through this . . .*

'Thank you for seeing me, Mr Koslov.'

'Please, call me Nikolai.'

His grip was cool and firm and thankfully brief.

'Nikolai,' she repeated. 'Please call me Jay.'

'Follow me.' He turned and began to walk outside, speaking to her over his shoulder. 'I'd rather chat somewhere less formal if that's OK.'

Unlike his manservant, Koslov's English was fluent and barely accented, indicating he was either more educated or he'd spent a lot of time in the west. He led her down two more corridors, passing an ice-blue dining room with gold-edged chairs and a table that could easily seat two dozen people, then another sitting room – with a full sized snooker table – before they came to the kitchen. The room was cavernous, with a central console and a conservatory filled with greenery, which overlooked the swimming pool.

'Coffee?' he asked.

'Gusev got me a glass of water but I left it behind. Shall I fetch it?'

'No. I'll get you another.'

She watched him move around the kitchen — cigar smoke drifting — grabbing a bottle of fizzy water from the fridge, putting on the kettle, spooning Italian coffee into a pot. 'I rang Elizabeth,' he told Jay. 'Told her to call me if she thought I could do anything to help . . .'

He trailed off as a girl entered the room. Eighteen, maybe nineteen years old, she had a reed-slim body and wore nothing but a man's shirt. Her hair was uncombed, her eyes thick with sleep.

Nikolai's squeeze, she thought.

But then she noticed a mark on the girl's skin.

A mark that froze the blood in her heart.

A cigar burn. A cigar burn on the inside of her thigh, freshly made and still weeping blood. Jay recognized it from her days in the Balkans, when the Serbs tortured women.

Jay clenched her fingers as she looked further. At the rope burns on the girl's ankles and wrists. The marks around her neck where she'd obviously worn a collar. She'd seen it before but she still had trouble choking back the shout in her throat, the groan. Her legs were stiff, her breathing unsteady, but she controlled herself.

'Nicky,' the girl said. 'Can I get some coffee?'

'Get dressed first.'

'But you said you wanted me . . .'

'I changed my mind.' He jerked his chin. 'Go.'

'Please. Just one cup.'

'What did I tell you yesterday?'

The sleep abruptly cleared from the girl's gaze. Fear stood in her eyes. Her mouth began to tremble. 'I'm sorry. I'll leave . . . I didn't mean . . . Sorry.' In a flurry of long legs, she vanished.

Jay opened her mouth.

And closed it.

She watched Nikolai set the water and coffee in the conservatory, and let him usher her to a wicker sofa with overstuffed cushions before taking the chair beside it. He said, 'I saw Duncan only last week. I can't believe he's disappeared.'

She was unprepared for the violence of her response when he said Duncan's name. The nausea rose in a tidal wave, jamming her windpipe. Eyes watering, shaking inside, she bent over, pretending to fiddle with the strap of her sandal. She felt worse when she saw his eyes slide to her ankle, and she wished she'd worn her usual uniform of jeans instead of a skirt and bare legs. She'd much rather be overheated beneath her denim armour than feeling cool but exposed.

Nikolai Koslov took his coffee black, and he downed his first cup in three quick swallows. Jay didn't dare touch her water. She knew her hands would tremble and she'd give herself away.

'You said you wanted to ask some questions.' He put his cup back on the glass table. His movements were surprisingly quick and delicate, like a cat's, and at odds with his otherwise mellow demeanour.

'If you don't mind.'

He spread his hands, expression open and helpful. 'Not at all.'

Jay tried not to swallow but couldn't help it. Her throat felt as though it had been filled with the ashes of his cigar. 'You had drinks with Duncan and Elizabeth a couple of weeks ago. Sunday the eleventh of June.'

'Yes. I hadn't seen Duncan for a while, and since I was in the area I dropped by.'

'Did he know you were coming?'

'Of course. I rang him in the office to check it was OK.'

'How did he seem?'

'I thought he was fine, the same as always, but when I heard he'd disappeared there was something that made me wonder . . .'

Jay could feel sweat trickling down her flanks and spine and prayed he wouldn't see. 'Wonder, what?' she prompted when he didn't continue.

'If he wasn't slightly discontented.'

'What made you think that?'

Koslov shrugged and looked at the windows. 'Call it male instinct.'

'He didn't say anything?'

'Of course not, with Elizabeth there.'

She could hear her pulse thudding in her ears. 'Why would Duncan be discontented?'

'I think he was missing some excitement in his life. Everything had become so easy for him. He didn't have to worry about paying the bills or the mortgage, school fees, whatever. I think he wanted a change. Something to challenge him.'

'He could have gone mountaineering for that. He didn't have to leave his family.'

Koslov turned his head to study her, his gaze bright. Too late, she realized what he was doing. He wanted to give her a red herring to follow – that Duncan was unhappy at home – but she wasn't playing ball.

He gave a self-deprecating smile. 'I spoke out of turn. I shouldn't have said anything.'

'No, no.' Jay clamped her fear. 'Please. Anything that might help me understand his state of mind.'

He shrugged. 'That's it.'

She ran her tongue nervously across her lips. She desperately wanted some water but couldn't risk it. 'How do you know Duncan?' she asked.

'Through horse racing. We met years ago at Cheltenham.'

'How many racehorses do you own?'

'Come now, Jay. I think you know the answer to that since you've already visited my trainer.'

There was a long silence during which she screamed at herself to *say something*.

'It's an expensive hobby,' she managed. She couldn't think of anything else to say. Her brain appeared to be seizing up.

Something cold slithered into his eyes. 'You're not a tax inspector in disguise, are you? They're always on my back about how much I earn. I tell them if I put fifty thousand down to win, and I win at five to one . . . Well, do the sums.'

A quarter of a million. She wanted to affect a look of admiration but her facial muscles refused to respond. 'Even so, you must lose a lot.'

'Now you're scaring me.' He gave a chuckle but the cold gleam remained. 'That's exactly what they say.'

'Sorry.' She gave a light shrug. 'I don't suppose Duncan owes you any money, does he?'

'Good heavens, no.' His surprise appeared genuine. 'If anything, I owe him.'

'How come?'

'Oh, for introducing me to one of the best racehorse trainers in the country.' His answer was smooth, but she detected a lie and filed it away for future reference. What had Duncan done for Koslov? Maybe he'd given him some hot stock market tips when he'd been a city guru? She couldn't think of anything else her uncle, the rural bean counter, farming accountant, family man and friend, might have to offer. To Jay, Duncan and Koslov went together as well as vindaloo and ice cream.

'Parnell's ranked in the top ten international racehorse trainers,' Koslov went on. 'We've won at Newmarket, Hong Kong and Kentucky. He's just bought me a stunning new filly. We're going to wipe the floor with her at Ascot next year.'

Jay wanted to cut short the interview, get herself as far away from Koslov as possible, but she didn't want to give him any suspicions. She had to wait until he was ready. She counted the minutes, sweating another litre as she learned that he was a property developer and that, although he'd been married in his twenties, he was now divorced. He had no children. He told her he'd lived in England since the early nineties, that he thought football was for idiots and that the British public lived with their heads in the sand with no idea of what went on in the real world. Jay discovered nothing new about Duncan, except that he'd won three thousand pounds at the Cheltenham races in 1987, and that his friendship with Koslov had suffered a hiatus when Koslov moved to live in Hong Kong for two years.

Finally, Koslov put his hands on his knees and made as if to rise. 'I'm sorry, Jay, but I have to be somewhere in half an hour.'

She had to compel herself not to slump with relief and to contrive a convincing display of dismay. 'Please, isn't there anything else you can think of?'

'I'm sorry, but I can't help you any further.' He looked genuinely regretful.

'No idea where he might have gone? Where he might be staying?' She pushed harder, knowing that the more she did, the more she'd convince Koslov she couldn't remember him.

More regretful gestures. 'Sorry, no.' He led her outside to her car. She was aware the temperature was hot, the sun beating down, but she couldn't feel it against the chill sliding through her veins.

He shook her hand again and wished her luck. 'I might drop by and see Elizabeth next week,' he said. 'Make sure she's OK. Do you think that would be all right? I'll ring ahead, of course, and make sure it's conven-ient.'

Over my dead body, she thought, but she said, 'I'm sure she'd appreciate it.'

She took rapid, shallow breaths as she drove through the electric gates, concentrating on driving smoothly. As she glanced in her rear vision mirror, she saw the two Dobermans were standing in the middle of the drive, watching her go.

Eleven

Jay was still trembling as she left Hampstead and began threading her way home south along Fitzjohn's Avenue, but not so badly that she couldn't drive. She couldn't remember whether the girls were working today or not – they did shift work as security guards at Heathrow – and decided it didn't matter. She could trust them not to have hysterics if they saw her like this.

The sun was beating relentlessly down from the sky and her clothes were sticking to her skin with sweat. Opening her sun roof, she buzzed down her windows. Her core still felt cold. It was almost as though she was suffering from shock. What she needed was a shot of whisky to warm her from the inside. Turning on the radio, she half-listened to a programme talking about the importance of godparents for young children, which helped ground her slightly, giving her a feeling of normality as she thought of her own godchildren – aged two, five and eleven – Monte, Maddie and Kate.

After negotiating Swiss Cottage, she picked up the Finchley Road. She wasn't driving at her usual crisp pace but her senses were heedful after her meeting with Koslov, and it didn't take long before she pinged the grey Ford, two cars behind her. Thanks to her experiences in Iraq, where there was always the possibility you might be rammed by a suicide bomber, she was unusually aware of the vehicles around her, and the Ford Mondeo was no exception. She could no more ignore a car tailing her on the same journey than she could a meteorite landing in the road.

Eventually, she crossed from Kensington into Chelsea, the Ford still on her tail. There were two men inside but she couldn't make out their features. Was one of them the burglar? Her nerves were tight as she considered what to do next. The Ford was still behind her as she turned into Fulham Road. She was three streets from home, and, although she was certain she was being followed, she decided to double-check before she took evasive action.

She'd already memorized the Ford's number plate, so all she did next was turn right at the next corner, and then right at the next, until she had completed a square and was back on Fulham Road. The Ford dropped back, trying to hide behind a taxi, but there was no doubt about it. The Ford was tailing her.

Heading east, Jay chose to turn right again, but on this occasion she timed it so that she dived through a fast-flowing stream of traffic, making it almost impossible to follow. While the Ford tried to force its way after her, Jay ducked left and then right, weaving her way through Chelsea until she was certain she'd shaken the Ford free.

Her heart was thumping as she parked at the end of her street. She tried to remember when she'd first noticed the Ford. Had it followed her from Koslov's? Or had it been tracking her from Duncan and Elizabeth's? She doubted she would have pegged it on the M11; it was only when she was in town and in heavy traffic that her awareness became heightened. Why were they following her? Or were each of the family members being watched?

Mind buzzing, Jay let herself inside the house. The air felt cool after the heat outside. No music, no sound of the TV. The girls had to be at work, and a note in the kitchen confirmed that they were on nights for the next few days. Moving through the house, she wished her housemates were there. She could do with someone normal to decompress with, who wouldn't bug her with questions but let her be, maybe talk about what was on the news, or try and complete today's *Evening Standard* crossword.

Upstairs, Jay flung open the windows. Even though she felt wired, on edge, she couldn't help thinking the garden was looking gorgeous. All of Angela's hard work had paid off. She had edged the long, rectangular lawn with shrubs and flowers – roses, delphiniums, irises and lilies – and Denise had laid some reclaimed flagstones to create a patio area with a brick-built barbecue. Not for the first time she mentally thanked Angela's ex-husband because without his generosity none of them could have afforded to live in one of the most expensive areas of London.

She angled the shutters to give her some privacy before pulling off her clothes and taking a shower. Afterwards, she wrapped her hair in a towel and sprawled naked on her bed. She couldn't believe the heat. Who needed to go abroad with weather like this?

Using the phone on her bedside table, she rang Tom.

'Sutton,' he barked.

'Can I ask a favour?'

'It depends.'

'Can you run a number plate for me?'

There was a long silence, then he said, 'Why?'

'I'll take you for a curry at Mr Singh's.'

'That's not the right answer,' he told her. 'Although a curry would be nice.'

'A Ford Mondeo followed me.'

Another silence.

'I won't ask why right now,' he said. 'It can wait until we're eating our curry. How about if I pick you up in half an hour? We could have a beer first.'

She sat upright. She hadn't been ready for that. 'You're in London?'

'Yup. Something came up. I mean, with Scotland Yard. I know it's Sunday, but it was urgent, something that couldn't wait, that sort of thing.'

Jay swung her legs off the bed. 'Tom, if you've been seeing your friend –' she emphasized the word 'friend' – 'just say so. We don't own each other.'

Pause.

'You're right,' he said. 'I saw her today. But it's not what you think. I'll tell you about it over our curry.'

She hung up and stared at the phone. Perhaps his friend wasn't another woman after all. Perhaps it was a pet dog or something. A long-lost cousin?

In a flurry of hopeful expectation she blow-dried her hair, moisturized, sprayed scent behind her ears and slid into her favourite peach-satin under-wear. Expensive undies always made her feel good. What had Nicola – her father's second wife – said?

Whatever you wear under your clothes dictates the person you are.

Which meant that this evening she would – hopefully – feel confident and beautiful, if not downright sexy. Whether this was a good idea or not, she wasn't sure, but she needed the confidence. Koslov had shaken her foundations to the core today.

She jumped when the doorbell rang. Tom must have driven like the wind to get here so soon. She wasn't even dressed. Flinging on her robe she trotted downstairs and opened the door. 'Sorry,' she said, 'but you caught me—'

'Nice outfit.'

Max Blake stood on her doorstep, an appreciative grin on his face.

Jay gave a yelp and slammed the door in his face. What in the hell was Blake doing here? The last she'd heard he was in Iran undertaking a clan-destine mission that she wasn't supposed to know about. Glancing down at herself she groaned to see her robe was gaping. Hurriedly she belted it together.

'Jay?' He was knocking on the door. 'We need to talk.'

'We do?'

'It's about Nikolai Koslov.'

She opened the door a crack. 'What about Nikolai?'

'You're on first name terms?' He didn't look as though he approved.

'He's an old friend of Duncan's. My uncle. Who's gone missing.'

Blake's eyebrows rose. 'We definitely need to talk.'

She was clutching her satin robe at her throat, feeling vulnerable and off balance. Blake on the other hand looked cool and calm in black jeans and a grey T-shirt that had had its sleeves stripped off. He looked more like a fitness instructor than an MI5 officer.

'Can I come in?' he asked.

'Tom's coming over,' she blurted.

'In that case,' Blake said without turning a hair, 'I'll brief him at the same time.'

Oh, that's just great, she thought as she flung open the door and pelted upstairs. Tom and Blake under the same roof and me in my sexiest under-wear? Dragging on jeans she then yanked an old sweatshirt of Tom's over her head. She was pushing her feet into a pair of old deck shoes, faded almost grey by salt and the Mediterranean sun from last year's holiday, when the doorbell rang. 'I'll get it!' she yelled, rushing for the stairs, but it was too late.

Blake was standing in her doorway while Tom stared back.

'What the . . .' Tom's gaze went to Jay who was standing at the top of the stairs.

'I came to talk to Jay about Nikolai Koslov,' Blake said.

Jay hurried downstairs. 'I didn't know he was coming. He just turned up. He said he'd brief you at the same time he briefed me. About Koslov.'

Tom gave Blake a hard look. 'Really.'

There was a small pause.

'Perhaps you'd rather I email you a report?' Blake suggested in a neutral tone.

'I'll expect it on my desk first thing tomorrow.' With that, Tom turned and walked down the street.

Jay hared after him. She couldn't believe Blake's timing. He couldn't have made more of an impact if he'd planned the entire event. No matter what Jay said, Tom refused to believe that her professional relationship with Blake was above board. Last year, Blake and Jay had been forced to team up – both of them on the run from the Albanian Mafia – and when Tom learned they'd slept together, he'd assumed the worst. It didn't seem to matter that the wooden pallets she'd shared with Blake had been in byres, sheep pens and the stinking bowels of a fishing boat – not exactly conducive for a passionate love affair – because once Tom got a bee in his bonnet about something that was that.

'Tom.' Breathless, she caught up with him. 'It's not—'

'Drop it, Jay.' His voice was hard and, from the way his shoulders were set, she knew she had as much chance of communicating with him as she would an angry armadillo.

'You said we'd talk over a curry.' She tried once more.

'Another time.' He didn't look at her. As he increased his pace, she dropped back, finally letting him go.

Blake was propped in the front doorway when she returned. She rolled her eyes at him. 'I need a drink,' she said.

'Good idea.'

Blake followed her into the kitchen and watched while she uncorked a bottle of white wine and poured. Her hands were unsteady as she passed him his glass, and she was glad that he didn't mention it, just took a sip.

'*Falederi. Passe a vilnus,*' he said. *Thank you. It's nice wine.*

'*Mire mundage,*' she replied. *My pleasure.* The Albanian response came from her easily. She had learned Albanian as a kid when the family had gone to live in Albania with their father, who was on a NATO diplomatic attachment in Tirana with the RAF. Yet another reason why Tom hated her relationship with Blake; they shared a language few people could speak.

Leaning his hips against the worktop, Blake took another sip of wine. 'So, what's with your uncle? How does he know Koslov?'

With an effort, Jay turned her mind from Tom. 'Apparently, they share a love of horse racing. How come you know him?'

'Horse racing?' Blake blinked. 'Talk me through it.'

She knew better than to try and get him to reveal any information before he was ready. Clams had nothing on Blake. Unsure where to start, she decided to begin by giving him a transcript of her meeting with Koslov. 'They met at the Cheltenham races,' she told him. 'In the early eighties. They remained friends, even though Koslov lived abroad for a while. In Hong Kong if I recall.'

'When did Koslov say he was in Hong Kong?'

Jay frowned. 'He didn't. Just mentioned that their friendship was put on hold for the time he was away.'

Blake took another sip of wine, expression shuttered. Eventually, he put down his glass and folded his arms. 'Koslov's well known to us, as well as the Russian authorities. He's one of their oligarchs. He looted the Russian economy during the good old days of Boris Yeltsin and stashed his stolen wealth overseas. He was a friend of the murdered Alexander Litvinenko.'

Jay felt her eyes widen. 'You're kidding.'

'Nope. Which is why we're keeping an eye on him. He has powerful economic and political interests both here and in Russia. Plus the fact that Litvinenko's radioactive trail led to one of Koslov's foot soldiers. . . .' Blake picked up his glass and raised it to the light as though studying the colour of the wine. 'We know there's been a demand for nuclear materials in terrorist circles for several years.'

'Koslov's involved?'

'Up to his neck.' He remained silent for a minute or so, then said, 'We're investigating a British company – Davenport Industries – which has been supplying Iran with material for use in a nuclear weapons programme. We tracked a group of Britons as they obtained weapons-grade uranium from Russia and followed them as they exported it to Sudan, and on to Iran. It was only thanks to one man that we discovered that Nikolai was behind this company. This man squealed and died two days later. His throat was cut.'

Jay swallowed. 'Nikolai had him killed?'

'That's our theory. Nikolai doesn't want anyone to know he's behind the UK's illegal nuclear trade with Iran. But more serious is the fact that the uranium is British.'

Jay felt her eyes widen.

'Yeah, I know.' He gazed outside as he spoke. 'The first batches of enriched uranium for warheads appeared in the nineteen fifties, early sixties, for the RAF Blue Steel and Thor programmes – cruise missiles and rockets – but when the MOD realized the rocket fuel was unstable on both projects, and that satellites could spot the weapons anyway, they decided to use the warheads on the Polaris submarine deterrent. However, when moving the uranium from one place to the other, some went missing.'

'How much?'

'Enough to build half a dozen atomic bombs. A little of that stuff goes a long way.'

'Was it stolen?'

'We're not sure. But somehow it got shipped to Russia, maybe as part of an industrial products order, and eventually Koslov got his hands on it. We don't know exactly how, or how much he's still got. But we want to find out.'

She followed his glance outside. Two teenage girls, slim as pencils and wearing skirts that barely hid their knickers, were walking arm in arm down the street, laughing. Blake turned his gaze to Jay. His eyes were flat. 'Iran going nuclear will only fuel US and Israeli aggression. This could destabilize the whole area. Who knows where that'll lead, especially if Iran starts lobbing nukes around.'

'You're talking world war three,' Jay said. 'Do you think he knows what he's doing?'

'I don't care if he does or not.' His face was like granite. 'Britain will take the fall because it's our uranium, and I will do anything to get Koslov, close him down. If I could get him thrown into jail for not paying a parking ticket, I would.'

He went to the fridge and withdrew the wine and topped up their glasses. 'I've been working with SOCA and the FSB, keeping a close eye on Koslov to try and see if we can find a new avenue of intelligence. My team picked you up at his house, followed you here. I gather you lost them on the Fulham Road.' The corner of his mouth turned up fractionally. 'Good to know your surveillance skills are up to scratch.'

'The grey Ford was SOCA?'

'Yup.' He gave a nod. 'Now, tell me about your trip to Moscow.'

Talking about her memory loss was easier the second time around, but she still couldn't bring herself to talk about shooting Anna. When she mentioned the bruises on her inner arms, from which Tom had suggested she might have been injected with drugs, the muscles in Blake's jaw tightened.

'My body was bruised all over from being manhandled . . .' She was rubbing her arms, almost unconsciously. 'I have to find Duncan, Max. Not just for the family, but because I want to know what happened.'

There was a silence.

'Promise me something?' he said. His tone was hard and low, scraping like gravel, and there was a light in his eyes she hadn't seen before.

'Yes,' she said cautiously.

'You find out who did this to you, you let me know.'

'OK.'

'And if you see anyone you don't like the look of, I expect you to let me know. Immediately. OK?'

'OK.'

Immediately, the muscles in his cheeks relaxed. He gave himself a shake, like a hunting dog might after a close encounter with a snake. 'What about your uncle? Where does he fit in with Koslov?'

'He's not involved with your missing uranium.' Her tone was sharp. 'He's a good man. One of the best.'

'Hey, take it easy.' Blake held up both hands.

'Sorry.' She rubbed her forehead. 'I'm very fond of Duncan. I owe him so much . . . He's the reason why I joined the army. Without him I'd probably be in some grotty office in Slough getting paid nothing for taking shorthand from some fat middle manager with halitosis.'

'You know, yesterday I couldn't see you as a secretary,' Blake mused, 'but today I'm not so sure. I bet really good secretaries wear satin lingerie. Like some kind of uniform.'

She willed herself not to flush.

He said, 'You free for dinner tonight?'

'I don't think so, Max.'

'Not even if I tell you I've booked a table at La Flamma?'

Since the Alsacien restaurant around the corner was renowned for its candlelit, romantic atmosphere, she said, 'Definitely not.' If there was the remotest chance of her getting back together with Tom, it would be shot down in flames the second Tom heard she'd been there with Blake. She didn't want to risk Tom for a smoochy evening with Blake, no matter how smoochy it might be.

Seemingly unconcerned, Blake finished his wine and set the glass on the draining board next to the sink. He paused, staring out over the street, and then he turned and looked at her. 'You're holding something back, Jay. I need to know what it is.'

There was a silence while she stared at him. Blake was probably the one person in the world who could help her. She ought to tell him everything, but she wasn't sure if she could. Then she remembered he'd helped her before, when she'd had nightmares. Could she tell him about Anna?

He came and stood in front of her. 'I've had operatives come back unable to talk about what they've been through. There's usually a delay before they can tell me what happened.'

She bet they hadn't killed their friends. Or had they? Maybe she wasn't alone in this. Maybe there were others who woke up in the middle of the night sweating, reliving every agonizing moment.

He plucked a thread of stray cotton free from her blouse. 'Whatever it is,' he said, 'you know you can tell me. Maybe not today, but when you're ready.'

'Yes.'

'So what's next?'

'Track down Duncan's mother. See what she knows.'

'Watch your back.'

Twelve

Before she got stuck into the search for Kristina, Jay rang Elizabeth and warned her against Nikolai Koslov.

'But he seemed so nice.' Elizabeth sounded confused. 'Really charming. Toast and Marmite liked him.'

'Even Stalin loved his pet snake,' Jay said drily.

'Stalin had a snake?'

'No idea. But you know what I mean . . . Look, MI5 are involved, OK? So if Nikolai turns up, either lock all the doors against him or make an excuse to turn him away.'

'MI5?' Elizabeth's voice wavered and for a moment Jay regretted mentioning the security service, but then she firmed her resolve. She wanted her family to be aware that Koslov wasn't all that he seemed.

'Yes. Warn everyone, would you?'

'Of course. I'll do it straight away. Thank you, Jay.' Her voice steadied as she spoke.

After she'd hung up, Jay decided to have a quick look at the Internet to see what she could find on Nikolai Koslov and hopefully find out what he had to do with Duncan. The first page she read told her that Nikolai Koslov was, according to the *Moscow Times*, the patron saint of a town called Sinsk.

As soon as her brain computed the word *Sinsk*, her body shuddered. What was it about that word? She'd had a similar reaction when Vladimir had mentioned it in Moscow. Sinsk was the place where Anna's father, Eduard, had been shot twice in the head: executed. Jay stared at the word Sinsk for a long time, but the grey fog, the blanket that clouded her memory of her lost five days, wouldn't lift.

She stretched, gave herself a shake. Made a cup of tea, more to distract herself than because she needed one. She sipped it slowly, staring out of the window, only half registering the cars driving past, the middle-aged woman walking her miniature dachshund – the dog wearing a diamanté collar, the woman a similar pair of earrings.

Finally, she returned to her computer. Apparently, before Koslov bought his first mine, just outside Sinsk, the eastern Siberian region had been impoverished. Then Koslov arrived and started developing mines, employing hundreds of people. Then came schools, a hospital and a food-processing plant, even a church. Every resident of Sinsk considered him their saviour.

Jay started digging into his background. *Know your enemy.*

The son of a miner, Koslov completed his military service before working as a minerals and metals trader, but it wasn't until the early 1990s, when Yeltsin announced that Russia was to become a stakeholding society that Koslov joined the scramble for state assets. Every citizen was issued with a voucher worth 10,000 roubles – then worth about thirty pounds, the equivalent of an average monthly wage – that they could exchange for shares in any state company. Unfortunately, the majority of Russians didn't understand the concept of owning shares, but Koslov did. He apparently bought up blocks of vouchers from oil workers, miners, soldiers, and converted them into shares. Perfectly legal.

As the rouble fell, from 230 per dollar to 3,500, it wiped out most people's savings. Stalls appeared in Siberian towns, offering cash in exchange for vouchers that were worth only a handful of kopeks. Koslov created front companies to run these market stalls. Again, he converted hundreds upon hundreds of vouchers into shares. Opportunistic, but not illegal. Jay sighed. No wonder the people hated these New Russians. Talk about taking advantage. If the people had known what to do, and had held on to their vouchers, they could have made a lot of money. Jay continued to trawl through the information – old newspaper articles, academic studies – but she didn't find anything remotely criminal beyond rapacious greed and opportunism. Koslov, it appeared, had been too clever.

She leaned back, rubbing her eyes. Had Anna's father, Eduard, uncovered something Koslov wanted to keep quiet? Eduard had been murdered in Sinsk . . . However, even if Koslov appeared to be a ruthless son-of-a-bitch, she doubted he would be stupid enough to murder an FSB officer. Shutting down her computer, she tried to think of another route to link Duncan to Koslov. After thinking for a couple of minutes, she rang Tom.

'Hi,' she said.

Small pause during which Jay prayed he wouldn't hang up.

'Hi,' he replied.

'Tom, please don't be mad at me—'

'Who you see is your business.' His voice was tight.

'I'm not seeing Blake!' she protested. 'He turned up out of the blue, wanting to know why I'd seen Koslov . . . Did he brief you?'

'Yup.'

'And?'

After another pause, he said, 'I got a full report this morning, emailed at four a.m. If the man ever sleeps, I bet it's in a coffin . . . Look, I'm not sure I like the fact you and Koslov have met. You're on his radar now.'

'I think it's been longer than that.' She told him about the man in the orange shirt and that she suspected her room had been searched.

There was a brief silence.

He said, 'Why do you attract trouble?'

'I don't! It's Duncan's fault, not mine.'

She heard him sigh.

'Tom . . .' She hesitated, unsure how approachable he was.

'Don't tell me,' he said. 'You want a favour.'

'Only a little one.'

Another pause, then, 'Does this mean you'll take me out for two curries, not just the one?'

Her heart lifted. 'Absolutely.'

'Two it is,' he said. 'Fire away.'

'Look, I want to dig deeper into some contacts of Koslov's.' She told him about the Parnells. 'And since it's your patch . . . Do you think you still have files on them?'

'Remind me, what's the connection to Duncan?'

'Duncan was Justin's godfather. Six months after Justin was mugged, his father killed himself, and Duncan – or rather Trent – vanished, and changed his ID.'

Tom made a humming sound that she knew meant he was thinking. Eventually, he said, 'Sounds like the past is repeating itself.'

'My thoughts exactly.'

'I'll see what I can find,' Tom told her. 'Can I stay the night after the curry?'

'Don't push your luck.' She was smiling.

Hanging up, Jay turned her attention to Duncan's mother. She rang five veterinary surgeons before she hit the jackpot. She lied through her teeth to get the information she wanted, pretending that she was looking after Kristina Newton's cat while Kristina was away, and that she'd mislaid Boots's medication and needed to collect some more. The vet's receptionist happily gave her their address and said the pills would be waiting after midday.

Before she headed south, she decided to duck into the office. Unable to find a space close by, she parked around the corner and walked the rest of the way. She'd just passed the Moroccan supermarket when her phone beeped, reminding her that its battery was low and that she'd left her charger in the car. Spinning on her heel she stalked back, narrowly missing colliding with a slim young man in jeans and brown shirt who had stopped to peer in a hardware store window.

Putting her phone on to charge, she checked the office but it was empty.

A note on the main board informed her that Nick and Gill would be back at lunchtime. They were, apparently, across the river today, talking to the Home Office. Their agenda was pinned on the wall. It appeared Darfur was still at the top of the list. She scrolled through her messages. More from Lithuania and Somalia, and a couple from Darfur, which she forwarded to Gill. What a nightmare civil war was. It made her problems seem trivial in comparison to having friends and family, people you knew from school, turn on you and kill you.

She didn't spend long in the office, no more than fifteen minutes, and when she left she was still thinking about the appalling conflict in Darfur and what the world ought to be doing about it. She was halfway to her car when she remembered her mobile phone was still recharging in the office. Cursing, wondering if her memory would ever be normal again, she swung round and began to march back. The same young man in jeans and brown shirt had stopped twenty yards or so behind her, this time to tie the lace of his trainer.

Instinct had every hair on her body standing upright. The man was following her.

Nerves quivering, Jay returned to the office wishing Nick was there, but at least she had backup working close by. She picked up the phone, and dialled, praying he was in the office and not on a mission elsewhere.

'It's me,' was all she said, but immediately he came alert.

'What's happening?'

'I think I'm being followed.'

'How many?'

'Just the one that I saw, but I guess there could be more.'

'Where are you?'

'At the office.'

'Sit tight. I'm on my way. Ten minutes max.'

'Wait. I need you to do something. Remember the spider you dealt with last time? I'd love you to dispose of it. I hate spiders.'

'Make it fifteen.'

She returned the phone to its cradle. She'd used a coded reference to spiders before with Blake, when her house had been bugged and she'd wanted him to disable them. She was glad he remembered.

She was pacing the hall some time later when she thought she heard a sound come from Nick's office, as though someone had knocked against his filing cabinet. Her heart started tripping. She remembered Duncan's office being turned over and wondered if she should go and lock herself in her car.

'Didn't mean to startle you.' Blake stepped into view.

'Can't you come through the front door like a normal person?' Nerves made her sharp-tongued.

'Wanted to check your security. It's not bad, but it's not great either.' He held up a leather bag and extracted a piece of wire and a small screwdriver. 'These opened your boss's office window. Tell him he needs deadlocks.'

'I'm sure he'll be delighted.'

Bag in hand, he moved to the window. 'So, where's the guy?'

'I haven't checked. I was worried he might see me looking and then he'd be forced to put someone else in his stead, who I might not spot.'

'Good thinking.'

'He's young, wearing sneakers, jeans and—'

'Brown shirt.'

She blinked. 'You've seen him?'

'Yup. And one other. As far as I know it's just the two, but we'll find out in a minute. First things first.'

He rested the bag on the floor and opened it. Neither spoke as he withdrew some tools and a machine that could have been a Geiger counter, but was in fact a piece of equipment designed to detect listening devices, both VHF and UHF – legal and illegal.

'I'd love a coffee,' he told her, and then vanished into Nick's office.

She went to the kitchenette and made it fresh – Fairtrade from the high Andes – it was the least the man deserved. She was glad he was here. Not only did she need the company, but having an experienced MI5 officer on her case also made her feel much safer. She still didn't know much about Blake's history, and since he rarely talked about it she had to survive on the odd tantalizing glimpse. For instance, when she'd mentioned his mission south of Tripoli years ago, where he'd briefly met Nick, she'd asked him what the place had been like, hoping to prompt him into telling a story, but all he'd said was, 'Hot.'

He drank three cups of coffee while he moved from room to room, and it was past midday when he finished. Returning his tools to his bag, he locked it before turning to her, both palms spread.

'Nothing,' he said.

'Really?' She was taken aback.

He rested his hips against her desk and folded his arms. 'Tell me who you think is eavesdropping.'

'Nikolai Koslov.'

'Why?'

'I think he's been keeping tabs on me since I came back from Moscow.' She told him about the items in her room being moved, along with the fact she thought someone had checked her computer. 'It's my guess he wants to see what I remember, how much I know . . .' Another thought occurred to her. 'He might be hoping I'll lead him to Duncan.'

Blake mulled this over. 'You could be right. But why bug your office?'

'I don't know.' She felt embarrassed. 'I wasn't thinking straight after I'd seen the man on my tail. It was an instinct thing.'

He frowned. 'I'm all for instinct. It's got me out of trouble more times than I can say. Let's do some dry-cleaning.'

Dry-cleaning, he told her, was a counter-surveillance technique, which provided several opportunities to observe a tail. He talked her through what he wanted her to do, where to go, and finished by saying that he'd be following at a distance to see what happened.

As Blake instructed, Jay left the office and turned right. She walked to the end of the street, turned left, and went into a grocery store, bought a bag of mixed nuts, and walked out. Next, she crossed the road and paused at the window of a bookshop before going in and walking straight through and out the rear exit. She continued her seemingly aimless shopping exped-ition for another ten minutes, then hopped in her car and drove towards Clapham until she found the service station Blake had mentioned, where she refuelled. Blake joined her at the till.

'Only two of them,' he said. 'And only one car. I've called to get them picked up. You should be free in a few minutes.' He looked at a café oppos-ite. 'You fancy a coffee while we wait?'

Jay moved her Golf to join his ancient, sludge-green Land Rover Discovery across the road. 'I thought you would have sold it by now,' she remarked. The last she'd heard was that all its electrics had blown and it needed a new alternator.

'I like its anonymity.'

They sat outside and drank their coffee: double espresso for Blake, cappuccino for Jay. She told him everything she could think of that might be relevant to Duncan's case, and he did the same.

He said, 'Whatever happened back then between Koslov and Duncan was obviously pretty serious. Along with Magnus Parnell's suicide.'

Blake checked his beeper before leaning back and stretching out his legs. She looked down at his shoes, city smart and shiny, and suddenly took in the fact he was wearing a suit. Beautifully cut, it showed off his swimmer's build to perfection: broad shoulders tapering to a narrow, muscular waist. Her lower belly gave a swoop and instantly a wave of confusion crashed over her. How could she be so attracted to two men? One was enough, but two was plain greedy. Besides which, she ought to steer clear of Blake, who wasn't known for being ultra-reliable. Blake was notorious for vanishing without warning, and she had the feeling if they got involved it would only end in tears. Her tears.

'Something wrong?' he asked. He was watching her carefully.

'Not cat-burgling today?' She tried to make light of the fact she'd noticed what he was wearing.

He angled his head to look down the street. She couldn't see his face. 'No. I had an interview.'

'Oh. How did it go?'

'Good, I think.'

'What's it for?'

'A posting in South America.'

Jay studied the set of his jaw. It held a tension that hadn't been there before. 'How long for?'

'Three years.'

She blinked. She'd been expecting him to say three weeks, or perhaps a couple of months, but three *years*? A crazy mix of emotions rattled through her at high speed as she stood staring at the side of his face. Shock, dismay, confusion and, finally, a sharp sense of loss.

'Why?'

'It'll be good for my career. I speak Portuguese and Spanish.' He turned to face her. His eyes were shuttered. 'They're paying me enough to make it worth while.'

'You'll sell your house?'

He shook his head. Then he looked at her. His expression cleared. 'Hey, I'm looking for a tenant. Someone reliable, who'll look after the place. You interested?'

For a moment she was seriously tempted. His house was luxurious and beautifully appointed and snuggled in the countryside near Reading. It sported everything from a home gym to a sauna, Jacuzzi and state-of-the-art office, and had a cupboard full of honey collected from around the world.

'It's a lovely offer, Max,' she said, 'but when you consider the state of your kitchen the last time I stayed . . .'

'Ah, yes. I'd forgotten that.' He gave a small smile. 'It's amazing the damage a four-wheel drive can do to your granite worktop.'

She was going to ask when the job in South America started, but he wasn't looking at her any more. He was studying the beeper on his belt.

'They've picked them up. You're free to go.' He rose to stand, looking down at her. 'You want me to put in a panic alarm tomorrow? Hooked to the cops as well as myself? In case they try to snatch you?'

'Max, that would be fantastic . . .'

'I'll do the same at your home too. You got spare keys?'

After she'd rung Nick, Denise and Angela – all happy to have a panic alarm installed at no cost – she told him where the keys could be found, almost overcome that he'd seen her fear and was addressing it professionally. She said, 'You're wonderful.'

He quirked an eyebrow at her. 'So I've heard.'

The nurse at the Beeches Veterinary Centre had been true to her word and Boots's pills were ready for collection. Jay paid up – shocked at the cost – then pretended to remember something. 'Can I check that Kristina remembered to tell you she's changed her telephone number?'

The nurse tapped on her keyboard and then turned the screen so Jay could see. 'Is that right?'

Jay quickly memorized the address – 10 Sea View Road – as well as the phone number.

'It is.' She made herself sound surprised. 'Well done her. I thought she'd forgotten.'

She checked again that she wasn't being followed before she drove to the coast. Blake might be good at his job, but she'd still rather take extra precautions.

Sea View Road was a misnomer. The houses all faced the same way – towards the sea – but the view was obscured by trees and boat-building sheds. Number ten was a chocolate-box cottage with roses climbing its porch and a Nissan Micra in the driveway. Shoes crunching on gravel, Jay walked across to see the Nissan had a lipstick in the well between the seats, along with a floral-printed silk scarf and hairbrush. Did this mean there was no Mr Newton? Duncan had said his father died when he was seven, but, since she no longer believed anything he'd told her about his past, she was ready for anything. Or so she thought.

Kristina Newton was small and neat and looked as tough as old boots. Her hair was a steely grey, her eyes wary, and the second Jay mentioned Duncan's name – she'd said Duncan, not Trent – Kristina slammed the door shut and shot home the bolts.

'Go away!' she shouted. 'Before I call the police!'

'Mrs Newton, please listen to me. Duncan was officially reported missing by his wife and family on Monday twelve June, over two weeks ago. Did you know?'

'Why should I? I don't know any Duncan.'

Jay wished she could see the woman's face. She couldn't tell if she was lying through two inches of wood door.

'OK. You also need to know that I know that your son is Trent, but he changed his name to Duncan in 1995. I'm going to call him Duncan as that's how I've known him for the past twelve years. He's my uncle. I'm trying to find him. His wife, Elizabeth, is going crazy with worry, along with the rest of us. Fitz, Cora, and his daughters Charlotte and Katie . . .' Jay filled in the family tree as best she could. She hadn't heard any movement on the other side of the door and hoped Kristina Newton was still listening to every word.

'Even Toast and Marmite miss him. His dogs.'

'I'm sorry, I can't help you. I don't know what you're talking about. Go away.'

'I need to know what happened in ninety-five. Why Duncan – Trent – changed his identity. He told us you died the same year—'

'I'm calling the police. Did you hear me?'

'Yes, I heard you.' Jay suddenly felt intensely weary.

'I'm dialling now. Nine-nine-nine.'

'It's OK, I'm going.'

Unsure what to do next, Jay walked back to her car, hopped in and started it, and drove a little way along the lane before pulling over. She opened the sunroof and looked up at the sunlight slanting through the leaves of an oak tree. If Kristina Newton wouldn't speak to her, then perhaps it was time to beg Tom for another favour. Her only concern was that it was the third favour she'd asked within a week, and there was only a certain amount of curry a plain-clothes cop could eat. She nibbled her lip, undecided, and then decided to hell with it. She dialled his mobile number.

'Don't tell me,' he said. 'It's another favour.'

'How'd you guess?'

'What do I get in return?'

'Your pick of a movie followed by a Thai meal,' she replied.

'Not bad. But I was thinking more in line of a full-body massage.'

'I'm not sure if sports therapists are available that late,' she hedged. 'Don't they shut up shop around six-ish?'

'I was thinking something more personal.' His voice dropped slightly and she felt a flush rise over her body. 'Remember the Grange?'

The flush deepened into a burn. They'd spent a weekend in a country house hotel not long after they'd first got together and used up nearly a whole bottle of organic juniper massage oil.

'I need you in uniform,' she blurted.

'Hey, that's a first.' She heard the smile in his voice. 'I didn't realize you were into dressing up.'

'Not like that,' she told him, mentally rolling her eyes. 'I need you to persuade Duncan's mother to talk to me. She shut the door in my face and threatened to call the cops.'

'I don't need a uniform for that,' he said. 'I'll show her my warrant card. That usually does the trick.'

'So you'll come?'

Silence.

'I rather walked into that one,' he said with a sigh. 'Where are you?'

'Lymington.'

'Make it two full-body massages and you're on.'

Before she could respond, he'd hung up.

Thirteen

Duncan's mother opened the door a crack to inspect Tom's warrant card, but it still took another five minutes to persuade Kristina they weren't there to stab her to death.

Finally, they were inside the tiniest cottage Jay had ever seen; its exterior was deceptive. Tom was almost bent double as he squeezed beneath the beams in the hallway – the width of a single person – and into a living room that felt only slightly larger than Tom's king-sized bed. There were two armchairs and a two-seater sofa; as Kristina urged them to sit-sit while she made tea, Jay realized the furniture was smaller than normal. She'd heard of show houses using custom-built, bite-sized furniture to make the rooms appear larger to prospective buyers, but she hadn't realized people used them in real life.

She paused before she took a hobbit-sized seat. Everywhere she looked were photographs of Duncan. Duncan ten years ago, twenty, Duncan as a kid, Duncan with Elizabeth, his children, his ponies and horses. There was even one of her and Tom drinking Pimms in Elizabeth's garden. It was a shrine to Duncan's life. Jay went over and studied one of Duncan and Koslov, taken at least twenty years ago. The men were, again, at the races, in another winner's enclosure. They had their arms around each other's shoulders and their heads were flung back, laughing. From their body language they could have been brothers.

Kristina returned with a tray, which she popped on the mahogany table in the centre of the room. Tea and biscuits at seven fifteen in the evening. The quintessential English cure-all, except Kristina wasn't English but Belorussian.

'Who's the man with Duncan?' Jay gestured at the photograph. 'You don't mind me calling him Duncan do you? It's just that that's how I know him.'

'I like the name Duncan,' said Kristina. 'We chose it together.' She missed the startled look on Jay's face because she was pouring tea. She said, 'The man is a racing friend of my son's. Nikolai. I can't remember his surname.'

'Did you meet him?'

'Never.'

'Did Duncan talk about him much?'

'No more than any of his other friends.' Kristina passed over a mug of tea before settling on the sofa. Her fingers plucked at her skirt.

Jay had decided with Tom that she would lead the questions, and it didn't take long for her to realize that Kristina knew little about her son's activities before or during the mid nineties. She hadn't even heard of the Parnells.

'Did Duncan ever mention working for Nikolai Koslov? In the eighties and nineties?'

'He didn't talk about his work. He was a broker. Very successful . . .'

Jay listened to things she already knew as she glanced out of the window. Two men were walking past, talking, and her heart jumped until she took in that one was wearing a sailing cap. The other had mousey hair peeking out from a baseball cap. She couldn't see his face but, with his stout frame, for a brief second she'd thought it was the burglar.

'This is Boots,' said Kristina.

Jay glanced around to see a skinny black cat with white paws totter across the carpet. Despite the fact its fur had worn away along its spine and its steps were unsteady, its tail was high and it was purring. Kristina picked it up and let it settle on her lap. Purrs reverberated through the room, reminding Jay of a tractor engine.

'He's lovely,' Jay said.

'He's very old.' Kristina looked proud.

Jay let the silence drift before saying, 'Why did Duncan change his identity?'

'Because he was frightened for his life. And for mine. He told me that if his enemies knew where I was, they would use me to get to him. I had to become invisible. Not just to protect myself, of course, but to protect my son.'

'When was this?'

'June the fourteenth, 1995.'

The day after Magnus Parnell had committed suicide, Jay thought, which confirmed Crispin's statement. 'Did he give you a reason?'

'No. And I never asked.'

'Really?' Jay was sceptical.

Kristen's expression turned fierce. 'Do you have children?'

'No.'

'Then don't judge me.'

Jay held up her hands. 'I'm sorry. I didn't mean to upset you—'

'Upset? You don't know anything. Imagine being unable to get to know your grandchildren. Imagine if your son's family think you are dead . . .' Her voice caught.

Jay felt a wave of sympathy. 'I'm sorry,' she said again.

The woman flapped a hand at her. 'It's our life.'

'But his disappearance affects everyone. His family are going crazy with worry. Where is he? Do you know?'

'No.' Suddenly the strength went out of the woman's shoulders. 'He dropped in to see me on Tuesday, two weeks ago.'

The day after he'd vanished, thought Jay.

'He told me he had to go away and not to worry. I haven't heard anything since . . .' Her skin pinched, making her look as old as her cat.

'I'm sorry,' said Jay, and meant it.

'When he was here,' said Tom. 'Did he make any phone calls? Give you a clue to where he might have gone?'

Kristina thought this over. 'He made several. He used my phone. He said it was safer. I didn't listen.'

'What's your number?' Jay asked her. She was looking meaningfully at Tom as she spoke. He brought out his notebook, and when Kristina recited her number he jotted it down.

After a brief silence, Kristina looked between them. 'Is that it?'

'I think so,' said Jay. 'Thank you.'

'Now, you go. Leave me in peace.' She levered herself to her feet. 'The next time I see you will be when my son is here, correct?'

'I certainly hope so.'

On her way out, on the pretext of using the loo, Jay managed to surreptitiously pop Boots's pills in the kitchen. No way did she want to throw them away; they'd cost a fortune.

Outside, Tom leaned against his car bonnet and folded his arms. Two herring gulls cruised sideways on the breeze overhead, past trees and the distant clank of halyards.

'I guess you want me to pull her telephone records,' Tom said. 'See who Duncan called.'

'Yes, please.'

He put his head on one side, looking at her expectantly.

'OK,' she said, 'how about two curries, a movie, a Thai meal and two tickets to Twickenham to see England versus Scotland in the autumn.'

His eyebrows shot to his hairline. 'How on earth did you manage that? They're like gold dust.'

'Friends in low places.'

'It's a deal,' he said. 'I'll even throw in the Parnell file if you'll come to the match with me.'

'Done.' She turned her head to watch a car towing a sailing dinghy drive past. 'Can I come and get it now?'

He checked his watch. 'No reason why not, except it's not meant to leave the station.'

'You can trust me, Tom.'

'I know I can, Jay. It's the rest of the general population that concerns me. What if you have a car accident and the file gets nicked?'

'What if I read it in your office?'

He looked taken aback. 'Tonight?'

'Why not?'

'Because, unlike you, I have a life. I'm supposed to be in London this evening.'

Pause. Beat.

Jay said lightly, 'Visiting your friend?'

There was a long silence and then, holding her eyes, he withdrew his mobile phone and dialled. He said, 'Hi, it's me . . . Yeah, everything's fine. Look, I'm sorry but I won't be able to make it tonight, something's come up . . . You know I told you about Jay? Yes, well, I'm seeing her tonight . . . Yup, I'll try and make it at the weekend. OK, bye.' He hung up. 'OK?'

She stared, trying to make sense of the call. 'Who is she?'

'It's not what you think.'

'Tom . . .'

'I'll tell you later, OK?'

He'd used his cop voice, the one that meant he didn't want to talk about it any further, and she hastily backed off. She wanted to see the Parnell file before she pushed him any further.

'OK.' She took in a breath of air, let it out. 'I'll see you at the office.'

'Make it my place. It's more comfortable and there's beer in the fridge.'

She opened her mouth and closed it as he climbed into his car and turned on the engine. As he drove off, he stuck an arm out of the window and waved. Feeling off balance and muddled, she nearly didn't respond, but, just before he vanished around the corner, she waved back.

The last time she'd been to Tom's flat it had been winter, and the steps to the basement had been covered in ice, making them treacherous. This evening the ice was replaced by clumps of dandelions poking cheerfully through the cracks in the paving.

Previously, she'd walk down the side of the building to the back yard where she knew he'd be sitting in one of his battered deck chairs, but today she pressed the front door bell.

He opened the door talking into his mobile. He was holding a bottle of beer in the crook of his elbow and clutching two files. 'Sorry, work,' he mouthed. She took the beer and files into the kitchen. Behind her, she heard him talking, something about a Somali youth getting stabbed.

The French windows were open and evening sunlight poured into the room. She could barely see the table through clutter and she had to push aside a stack of weekend papers and piles of junk mail to make space for the files. As she looked around, nothing in the kitchen appeared to have changed aside from a sorry looking cheese plant that was drooping, begging for water. Curious, she had a peek in the fridge to see the remains of a takeaway pizza, some Cheddar and olives, eggs, bread and beer. She pinched a couple of olives and settled herself at the table and opened Justin Parnell's file.

After a while, she paused to study the identikit picture of Justin's attackers. Both men were Caucasian and appeared to be in their thirties, with short necks and crew cuts. They looked like your everyday, common garden thug, who you'd find lurking at the bottom of the muddy pond of the criminal world, making her wonder whether the mugging had been opportunistic or planned. If it had been planned, why? Was it a case of mistaken identity? Justin didn't gamble or take drugs, hadn't owed anybody any money and appeared to have no enemies.

Jay turned to Magnus Parnell's suicide, which appeared pretty straight forward, but she didn't like the fact Duncan had vanished pretty much on the same day.

She sat back, thinking. Could Duncan have had anything to do with Magnus's death? And what about Justin's mugging? Where they connected? Jay remembered Koslov offering a ten thousand pound reward for information on Duncan when Duncan had originally disappeared. Had Duncan run from Koslov back then? If so, it was her guess that Duncan had run again from Koslov two weeks ago. She prayed Duncan hadn't taken on another identity or they might never find him, and she wouldn't wish that on her family. It would tear them apart.

Jay reread the pathology report on Magnus's suicide – which, again, was pretty straightforward, aside from one thing. The body had traces of cobalt, an isotope of which can be made radioactive, on the cuffs of its shirt and fingertips. How the pathologist had discovered this wasn't detailed, but she guessed it had to have been a fluke. Cobalt was odourless, colourless and, unless you had specialist equipment, impossible to detect. Nobody had known what to make of this potential clue, and right now neither did Jay.

At that moment, Tom walked in. 'That was Peter,' he said. He chucked his mobile on the counter. 'He's a pathologist. He's been working on a body that was found beneath the floorboards of a disused warehouse last week. You heard about that man's body found in Epping Forest?'

She glanced up. 'The one attacked by dogs?'

'Yup. Well, it looks as though Warehouse Man, as we're calling him, died the same way. Teeth marks all over his bones . . .' He ran a hand over his face. 'It's been there a while, maybe two, three years.'

'It's connected to the Epping Forest one?'

'We don't know. Not yet. But maybe.' He leaned against a worktop and gestured at the files. 'How are you getting on?'

'Did you read them?'

'Yup.'

'What did you make of the radioactive dust?'

He came and stood behind her, peering over her shoulder at the pathology report.

'Not sure,' he said. 'I've got an appointment with the pathologist first thing tomorrow. You want to come? You can stay here tonight.'

'Does this mean I have to buy you another curry?'

'I thought we were negotiating body massages.'

He brushed her hair aside and pressed a kiss against the nape of her neck. 'Hmm,' he murmured. 'You smell nice.'

A surge of lightning seared through her veins at his touch, and then her skin tightened warningly all over her body. She tried not to flinch but couldn't help it. Pushing back her chair she got to her feet and stepped out of reach.

'Jay . . .'

'I'm sorry,' she said. She ran her hands through her hair. 'Since Moscow I've been all over the place. Jumpy, unable to sleep properly. I can't bear to be touched . . .' When he widened his eyes she said hurriedly, 'Not by anyone. Not even Elizabeth.'

'Ah,' he said. 'Shame. Because I have to admit I'm finding it difficult not to push you against the wall and kiss you until you're panting.'

Indignation overcame her nerves. 'I don't pant.'

He raised his eyebrows. 'Oh, yes, you do.'

'Dogs pant.'

'This conversation is null and void considering I can't even touch you to prove the point.'

She covered her eyes briefly, rubbing the space between her eyes. Out of nowhere, she felt the urge to cry. 'I want . . .' she began to say and amended it to, 'I'm a mess.'

She looked up to see Tom was smiling. He said, 'I guess there's only one thing for it.'

She tensed.

'I'll ring for pizza. You still like anchovies?'

'Love them.'

It was like old times, spending a companionable evening on the sofa watching TV and drinking beer, and when her mobile rang, just after ten, she nearly didn't answer it when she saw the number was withheld. Then her conscience pricked her in case it might be Duncan.

'Hello?'

'Jay? Is that you?' It was Kristina. She sounded close to tears.

'Yes.' Jay sat up. 'What's wrong?'

'There's a man here. He wants to speak to you.' She heard Kristina take a trembling breath. 'I wasn't going to give him your number . . . but he killed my cat.' She began to cry. 'He killed Boots.'

'Put him on.' Jay's voice was tight. She could feel Tom watching her, but she didn't look at him. She didn't want to be distracted.

'Jay McCaulay?' The voice was heavily accented Russian. She didn't recognize it.

'Yes.'

'Stop poking your nose where it isn't wanted, or I'll come back and do to the old lady what I did to her mangy old cat.'

'Who are you?'

Click.

He'd hung up.

Fourteen

Kristina was burying Boots when they arrived, or trying to. She had a spade, but the ground was hard, baked dry by the summer. She was crying. Beside her lay Boots, wrapped in a silk scarf. Jay could see the tip of his skinny black tail peeking out.

'Here,' said Tom, taking the spade. 'Let me.'

Jay touched Kristina's shoulder. The old woman was trembling, and tears were pouring down her face. Jay could feel a lump rise in her throat at the woman's distress. 'I'm sorry,' she said, feeling inadequate. She'd spent the drive down with Tom berating herself for not being more vigilant. She'd assumed that since Blake had removed the watchers in London, she was clean, but it appeared she wasn't. She had led the Russians to Duncan's mother, and she sent thanks to God that the man she'd spoken to on the phone hadn't harmed the old woman.

Ducking into Kristina's house, she unearthed a bottle of cooking brandy from one of the kitchen cupboards, poured a glassful and took it out to Kristina. The woman took a big gulp, choked slightly, then took another.

'What happened?' Jay asked.

'He said he was collecting for the Lifeboats.' Kristina scrubbed her eyes with a fist. 'He had a card and everything. My husband was a lifeboat captain . . . I'm such a fool. I opened the door and he forced his way inside. He wanted to know what you and I talked about. Who the man with you was. I told him to get lost, but then he grabbed Boots. He said he'd kill him if I didn't talk . . .' She began to cry again. 'I told him everything, but he still killed my beautiful cat.'

Jay put her arms around Kristina. 'I'm sorry,' she said again.

'He snapped his neck with his bare hands,' she said, her words muffled by Jay's chest. 'I couldn't believe it.' She gulped. 'At least it was quick . . .'

Small mercies, thought Jay.

It didn't take Tom long to dig the hole. Kristina lowered Boots's body gently, carefully into the ground. Tom scooped the earth back on top, and they stood silently, the three of them, under a starlit sky, until Kristina said, 'Bless you for coming.'

Inside, Jay asked Kristina what the man looked like, but the description she gave didn't sound anything like the man Jay had seen in Blakeney. When she suggested Kristina go and stay with a friend, the woman agreed.

'Just until we find Duncan,' Jay said. *Along with whoever killed Boots*, she added silently.

While Tom drove Kristina in his car, Jay followed in Kristina's Nissan Micra. She couldn't stop checking her rear-view mirror and nearly rear-ended Tom when he braked at a stop sign in the centre of town. Luckily, Kristina's friend wasn't far away, and lived in a cottage on the edge of the New Forest, near Brockenhurst. As far as Jay could tell, nobody had followed them, and once Kristina was settled – her friend was a retired merchant seaman who appeared only too pleased to be involved in a rescue mission – Jay walked the periphery of the property with Tom.

'Do you think she'll be OK?' Jay was anxious.

'Nobody followed us, so nobody knows where she is,' he assured her. 'She'll be fine.'

When an owl hooted in a nearby tree, she jumped.

Tom said, 'They wanted to scare you.'

'They've succeeded.'

'You've touched a nerve. Any idea which one?'

'I bet it's Koslov,' she said. 'He's warning me off. Initially, I thought he might be following me in the hope I'd lead him to Duncan, but now I think he doesn't *want* me to find Duncan.'

The owl hooted again. This time it was answered by a sharp 'kew-wit'.

Although the rational, cautious half of her brain told her she should stop searching for Duncan, return to London and her job, the other half, the bloody-minded bolshy part, told her not to be bullied, not to give up. She took a deep breath and swallowed. 'I can't stop looking for my uncle. The family are depending on me . . . I want to find Duncan and I want to know what happened to me in Russia. *I have to know.*'

'What if a member of your family is threatened next? Elizabeth, for instance?'

She pictured her aunt digging holes for Toast and Marmite's dead bodies and hesitated. 'I don't know what else to do,' she said. She felt a combination of frustration and misgiving start to itch in her stomach.

'You're playing with fire,' he warned.

She looked up at his face, but in the dark she couldn't read his expression. 'Does that mean you'll still take me to meet the pathologist tomorrow?'

'Only if you promise to make me breakfast.'

Since Tom's fridge was pretty much bare, breakfast consisted of orange juice, coffee and toast, letting Jay nicely off the hook. Unlike her mother, she hadn't turned out to be particularly domestic and had trouble boiling an egg, let alone producing scrambled eggs that weren't stuck to the pan, burned.

She spent the journey to the mortuary twisted in the passenger seat of Tom's car, watching the cars behind.

'What if they've got a team?' he asked.

'Then I won't know they're there.'

As far as she could tell they weren't followed, but when they were walking inside the building Jay added the extra precaution of doubling back a couple of times to try and surprise anyone behind them. She saw nobody suspicious, but it didn't stop the coils of anxiety wrapping through her gut.

Peter Greenslade had fifteen years on Tom and his dark hair was beginning to thread with silver and his laughter lines to deepen, but he was still popular with the ladies if what Tom said was anything to go by. As well as his steady girlfriend, Rosie, he had another three women he saw regularly. Apparently, none of them knew about the others, and how he managed it, Jay couldn't imagine. She found balancing Blake and Tom difficult enough, and she wasn't even going out with either of them.

She went and stood by the window. Outside, a crow was hopping across a patch of sun-scorched, brown grass. The sun beat down from an ash-white sky, bouncing off windows and car windscreens, making her squint. She saw no man in an orange shirt, no man sitting in a car ostensibly reading a newspaper while keeping an eye on them.

'You want to talk radioactive material,' said Pete.

'Yes,' said Jay, turning back to the room. 'And how you discovered it on Magnus Parnell.'

'It wasn't me,' Pete said. 'It was Arthur Wilson.'

'Who retired ten years ago,' Tom said. 'How handy.'

'I managed to speak to him though,' Pete said. 'Just before he flew out to China this morning. Gone for two months, lucky sod. Wish I was retired, but I'd rather head for Tahiti. Chinese women don't do much for me.'

Jay ignored this aside. 'What did Arthur say?' she prompted.

'Apparently we were having our X-ray machines checked, and the engineer thought one of them was leaking. But it wasn't. The radioactive dust his equipment picked up was on the corpse.'

'How could it have got there?'

Pete shrugged. 'Difficult to say. Cobalt is used in all sorts of things, from jet turbine engines and steel alloys to paint, glass, enamels and ink. Arthur got the sergeant at the time to check if Parnell had visited any manufacturing plants, but apparently not.'

'Could he get the dust from any of those products?'

Pete shook his head. 'No. They've been processed to the max – usually overseas – by the time we buy them. Aside from mobile phones, which, as you know, emit radiation. They contain cobalt in an alloy form. Use yours much, Jay?'

'All the time,' she said brightly. 'So when I die in a year's time, with my brain full of tumours, you can pat yourself on the back. So what about Parnell and cobalt?'

'Arthur reckoned he came into contact with whatever it was very briefly. His fingertips were literally dusted, along with his shirt cuffs. A couple of tiny patches on his upper arms, but otherwise he was clean. It hadn't got through his skin and into his blood stream or his urine. Arthur checked.'

Jay saw the crow was now pecking at a sandwich wrapper. An elderly woman was watching the bird as well, while she was being helped across the car park by a man who looked almost as elderly, perhaps her husband. Definitely not a pair of Russian thugs.

'If he'd breathed in any quantity,' Pete said, 'it would have been lethal. But as it was –' another shrug – 'he just got dusted.'

'But *how*?' Tom wondered aloud. 'From what I learned on the Internet yesterday, cobalt is incredibly rare. About the only place that produces it is the Congo.'

'And Russia,' Pete said. 'Siberia, to be accurate.'

The hairs at the back of Jay's neck rose. 'You're kidding.'

'I triggered something?'

Jay told Pete about Nikolai Koslov owning eight horses at Magnus Parnell's stables, and that Koslov also owned several mines in Siberia.

'He mines nickel and copper, though,' Jay added. 'Not cobalt.'

'But cobalt isn't mined alone.' Pete's face was alight. 'It's produced as a by-product of those exact mining activities.'

There was a silence as the three of them stared at one another.

Tom said, 'Could Koslov have collected the dust from one of his mines accidentally and—'

'Unlikely,' Pete interrupted. He was scratching his head. 'Cobalt isn't naturally radioactive, but it can be made radioactive by bombarding it with Neutrons. The link is mostly with nuclear plants and hospitals, not mining directly.'

Jay frowned. Koslov had built a hospital, she recalled. Did he have any links with nuclear plants?

'Can I borrow your computer?' she asked. 'I just want to check something.'

It didn't take long until she found what she was looking for. Koslov hadn't just developed mines in Siberia, but also, more recently, a nuclear power plant. She swivelled the screen so both men could see.

'What if Koslov accidentally picked up some dust from his nuclear plant,'

Tom continued, thinking out loud, 'and brought it to England, where he shook hands with Parnell . . .'

'Entirely possible, but impossible to prove,' Pete said.

'Would the dust have rinsed off when Parnell washed his hands?' Tom asked.

'Yes.'

'What about his clothes?'

'Same.'

'So I'd be right in thinking that Koslov could have touched or brushed against Parnell before Parnell changed his clothes or washed his hands . . .'

'Which means that, unless Parnell was particularly unhygienic, Koslov probably saw Parnell on the day of his suicide.' Pete narrowed his eyes. 'Or are you thinking it wasn't suicide after all? Because if you have some doubts . . .'

Both Jay and Tom stared. Tom said, 'Go on.'

'Well, reading the report . . . I don't like the fact he was so bruised. His ribs had taken a good blow, along with one against his head, and there were several on his legs and arms, almost like he'd been in a fight.' Pete studied the file in front of him. 'Arthur put it down to a fall from a horse the day before. Apparently, he was dragged across the cobbles a fair way before the animal stopped.'

'Witnesses?'

'Nikolai Koslov.'

All Jay's instincts were now quivering, and Tom's evidently were too, as he was standing slightly forward, on the balls of his feet, alert as a hawk. 'And?' Jay realized Tom didn't want to lead Pete in any way. He wanted to let the pathologist voice his doubts without influencing him.

Pete sighed. 'I just don't like the look of it, that's all. And there's the champagne glass. It was found perched on a stable door. The fingerprints didn't match Magnus Parnell's, or anybody that worked in the yard . . . I know I wouldn't normally be talking like this – it wasn't even my case – but we've known each other for long enough. I know I can trust you not to freak Arthur out if you start querying things.'

Tom said, 'I doubt we'll cross any swords considering he's in China.'

There was a long silence. Pete eventually said, 'What are you going to do?'

Tom glanced at Jay. 'I'm thinking that something stinks here, and we're going to find out what it is.'

While Tom stayed behind to talk to Pete about teeth marks on Warehouse Man, Jay drove to Clifton. After she'd parked, she implemented Blake's dry-cleaning techniques, slipping in and out of delis, boutiques, cafés and bars until she was certain she was on her own. Only then did she head for Lansdown Road and Grace Holger, Justin Parnell's ex-girlfriend. Jay wanted to talk to Grace about Justin's mugging as well as Magnus's suicide.

Grace Holger, now Grace Wilson, opened the door with a toddler in one arm and a wooden spoon in the other. Grace had bright, blue eyes and the fine, fair hair of a Scandinavian. The toddler looked identical. 'Jay McCaulay?' she said.

'Sorry I'm late,' said Jay.

'Come in.' She opened the door wide. 'You'll have to excuse the mess.'

It didn't look messy to her. Sure, there were plastic toys scattered across the floor and stacks of papers and magazines on just about every surface, but to Jay it looked homely. She'd been brought up in a house like this, slightly chaotic, with her, Mum, Dad and Angus, two dogs, a guinea pig and two cats, and obsessively neat homes always made her slightly uncomfortable.

'Coffee?' Grace asked. 'I've just brewed a pot.'

'I'd love one.'

Grace popped the toddler on the floor, who immediately scooted for a wooden train in the corner of the kitchen. The house was Victorian, with high ceilings and big bay windows letting in lots of light. She'd like a house like this one day, with space to breathe. It had a good-sized garden too. If she lived here, she'd build a tree house for the kids and grow roses up the fence. She wondered what Tom would think, and if it was his style or not, and immediately berated herself for thinking like that. They weren't engaged any more. They weren't even dating!

The toddler started banging the train against the floor with gusto.

'Sorry . . .' Grace made to pick him up but Jay stopped her.

'It's OK. He's only playing. What's his name?'

Grace gave her a smile. 'Ollie.'

'Play all you like, Ollie.'

Grace settled them at the kitchen table. Classic FM was playing softly in the background. Jay looked outside at the garden. Still no Russian thugs.

'You wanted to talk to me about Justin's mugging,' Grace said. 'DI Sutton spoke to me this morning and said it would be OK. I'd do anything to get the men who did it.' She cupped her hands around her mug. 'Crippling him like that. Destroying his life. Destroying us.' She looked up. 'Did you know we were going to get married?'

'No.'

'Well, we were. But then Justin got mugged and our lives changed forever. Nothing was the same. One day we were happy and in love, the next he was in hospital, his legs a mess . . .' She got up and crossed the kitchen for Ollie, pushed a train carriage towards him. 'He was awful in hospital. Really horrible. I couldn't handle it. I didn't know it was part of the process. I was only twenty-two.'

'I'm sorry.'

'Me too.' Grace returned to her seat, picked up her mug again. 'We don't see each other much any more. We tried for a bit, but it was too painful, and when I met Ash, my husband, it seemed the sensible thing to do was to move on. We meet at Christmas once a year. Share some mulled wine.'

Jay half watched Ollie trying to balance a stuffed monkey on his train.

'It may be thirteen years ago, but sometimes it feels like yesterday. I loved Justin –' she swallowed – 'very much.'

Jay allowed a beat of silence to pass before saying, 'And Justin's trust?'

'Trent set that up. Justin's godfather. He didn't want anyone to know, so we let everyone think it was Mum and Dad's idea. What Justin would do without it . . . He lives off the income it provides. At the time I was convinced it was a guilt gift over Justin's father's suicide . . . I mean, a million pounds is one hell of a lot of money, but now I'm not so sure. It was a typical Trent thing to do, to look after Justin even though he wasn't around.'

'Did you know Trent well?'

'Not really. We only met a few times, but I liked him.'

'Any idea why he vanished?'

'None.' She shook her head. 'That's what made it so hard. We couldn't imagine him being embroiled in anything criminal, or getting into a messy situation with a married woman or something . . . He wasn't like that. He was a nice, ordinary guy . . .'

Long pause.

Jay said, 'Would you mind telling me about the evening Justin got mugged? Anything you can remember.'

Grace spoke eloquently, giving the sort of details a lot of witnesses forget over time, like the fact there was a cool breeze and that she could smell frying bacon and garlic from one of the nearby restaurants. As she talked, Jay felt as though she was walking with her and Justin, and when the attack came she flinched inside at its brutality. It was just as Justin had described it in his statement. The two men hadn't asked for any money, they had walked up to Justin and simply laid into him. Hard, fast, and silent. They had ignored Grace, which is why she'd been able to run and get help.

'He'd have been killed if those men from the Albion hadn't come so fast,' Grace told her.

Apparently, half a dozen men drinking at the Albion – which back then had been a rough pub with a German shepherd chained outside – had taken one look at a hysterical Grace and galloped to the rescue.

'Can you describe the two attackers?' Jay asked. 'I know you've probably done it countless times before, but I'd like to hear it from you.'

Grace described two thugs with swarthy complexions, thick necks and stocky bodies, both with short-cropped hair and large boots. 'One was tattooed, the other wore a gold chain.'

Jay tried not to blink or look surprised at the mention of tattoos and the chain. 'Can you describe the tattoos?'

She frowned. 'Only one stood out. The police made a drawing of it. It was of a mythical creature. At least, I thought it was mythical. A funny looking sort of reindeer, kind of curled up.'

'Where was it?'

'On the back of his neck. I saw it as he attacked Justin. Sometimes I dream about it.'

'And the other tattoos?'

'All over him. All colours. Intricate designs. Green and red, blue . . .'

Behind her there was a soft thud, and then Ollie began to wail. Jay watched Grace scoop him up, shushing him and stroking his head where he'd bumped it against a kitchen counter. Something inside her softened, and she wondered if she'd be as motherly. She'd been wary about the whole children issue for as long as she could remember, cautious about losing her independence and identity she supposed, but she hoped she'd embrace motherhood when it eventually came.

She asked some more questions, but learned nothing new. Eventually, she thanked Grace and headed for the front door. On the doorstep, she asked Grace if she'd be prepared to identify the tattooed man and his buddy should they be found, perhaps even testifying in court.

'It would be my pleasure,' she said.

Jay walked back to her car, thankful she hadn't received a ticket. After climbing inside she sat quietly and closed her eyes. In her mind's eye, she brought into focus the identikit pictures she'd seen in Tom's file of the two thugs that had attacked Justin. Both were tall and Caucasian and had crew-cuts. Neither could be considered swarthy, or wore a gold chain, or sported a single tattoo. She rang Tom.

'We've got a problem,' she told him.

'Which is?'

'The identikit pictures in Justin Parnell's file don't match Grace's description. They're completely different men.'

'Not what I like to hear.'

'Who was the investigating officer?' she asked.

'Hang on a tick . . .'

She heard some shuffling sounds, then he said, 'Sergeant Philip Norton. He eventually got promoted to Superintendent. He's now retired.'

'I'd like to see him.'

'I'd like to join you, but the Warehouse Man case has just gone berserk. The press have got hold of it, and we're going to have to pull the stops out to find who he is and whether it's linked to the Epping Forest case.'

'I'm OK to do this alone . . .'

'He's an ex-superintendent, Jay. Be careful.'

Fifteen

An hour later, Jay drew up outside an immaculate, modern, villa-style house in Somerset. On the edge of a village, it was one of four identical houses. If they had stood alone they might have been perceived as grand, but seeing them together took away any individuality and, in Jay's eyes, made them nothing more than your average – albeit large – common suburban home.

Before she climbed out of her car, she studied each house, trying not to yawn, trying to concentrate. She'd slept badly last night, alone in Tom's bed, breathing his scent, longing for him, but unable to call him to her in case she freaked out. She wanted him, but the sensation she'd had since Moscow – of being unable to bear anyone coming too close – was holding her back. She rubbed her eyes, trying to awaken her brain from the fug of sleeplessness. She had to stop thinking about Tom and concentrate on the job in hand, keep in mind the bigger picture. Not just that Duncan was Justin's godfather, but that Nikolai Koslov – racehorse owner – was in the thick of it.

Instead of creeping around the houses like she wanted, spying, checking them out, Jay took Tom's advice to play things by the book and walked up the front drive and rang the doorbell of the house called 'Tuscany'. Whereas next door 'Provence' was pale yellow, Tuscany was painted faded peach. A young apple tree stood beside the gravel driveway, the same height as her. Three small apples hung from its branches, two glossy and green, but the third was blackened on one side, blighted by bugs.

Turning her attention back to the door, she saw the fisheye darken as someone peered at her. Then it went light. Nothing happened.

Jay rang the doorbell again.

Once more the fisheye darkened. A woman opened the door: slim, in her mid forties, with dark-brown, bobbed hair. She was frowning, suspicious. 'Can I help you?'

'Hi. I'm a colleague of DI Tom Sutton's,' she said, and put out a hand. The woman ignored it.

Jay let her hand drop and ploughed on. 'I was after Philip Norton. It's about an old case of his. We need his help.'

'Do you have a badge?'

As Jay began to bring out her wallet to show her the card Nick had printed for everyone at TRACE, the woman said, 'Don't bother.' She glanced over her shoulder then back. 'He's not in anyway.'

'Gone anywhere handy where I can catch him? It's fairly urgent.'

'Er . . .' She looked past Jay as she spoke. 'He didn't say. Perhaps he's gone to the gardening centre.'

'Don't worry,' Jay said. 'I'll try someone else.'

The look of relief on the woman's face confirmed Jay's suspicions.

'If you're sure,' the woman said.

'I'm sure.' Jay trotted down the stairs and climbed into her car. She drove a little way down the road, and when she was out of sight she parked and jogged back. This time she didn't walk up the front path but round the side of the house, to the back, where there was a long lawn, just mown, with a handful of young trees planted – mostly maples – and, to the right, a large garden shed. Cautiously, she peered around. All was quiet. She stood for a few seconds, listening to birdsong and the occasional bleat of a sheep. Faintly, she heard music. She turned her head to the garden shed, and saw its door was ajar. A radio was playing inside.

Jay walked over and stuck her head through the doorway to see a balding man sitting on what looked like a milking stool. He was staring through the Plexiglas window. It looked as though he was studying next door's sheep.

'Hi, Norton,' Jay said. 'Trying to avoid me?'

As soon as the man glanced round, Jay knew she was right. Norton had told his wife to get rid of her. Norton was an ex-cop and could spot any type of Service personnel at fifty paces.

'You do realize you're trespassing.' Norton smiled to take the sting out of his words.

'Your wife invited me in,' Jay lied. 'Told me where to find you. So legally, I'm not trespassing, am I?' She felt a kick of satisfaction at the man's look of dismay. 'Mind if I take a seat? Have a chat?' Jay picked out an old deckchair and levered it open, set it on the floor. There was just enough room for both of them between the lawnmower and a ceiling-high stack of seasoned wood. Jay knew the close physical proximity would bother Norton, but the ex-cop was too seasoned to show it. He barely moved a muscle.

'Who are you?' Norton asked. His tone was perfectly cordial, polite, but there was an edge Jay recognized. Norton wasn't a pushover and she reminded herself that the man wasn't just an ex-cop, but an ex-superintendent.

'Jay McCaulay. I'm a colleague of DI Tom Sutton's. I'm investigating Justin Parnell's mugging and his father's suicide in ninety-five.'

Although Norton's facial expression didn't change – he was too experienced, too wily for that – some colour faded from his cheeks.

'Who?' Norton asked, the amount of puzzlement in his voice perfectly pitched.

Jay ignored the question. 'I want to know why the file descriptions of the thugs that beat Justin's legs to a pulp aren't the same as the witness's. Justin's girlfriend, Grace, got a good look at one of them – the man was covered in tattoos – but her description isn't in the files.'

Still, Norton's expression didn't change. 'I don't know what you're talking about.'

'The pathologist's report says Magnus Parnell was heavily bruised from a riding accident, but a separate opinion says they're consistent with being in a fight. There was radioactive dust on Parnell's fingertips that hasn't been explained, nor was there an explanation for an errant champagne glass found on a stable window sill. Lots of anomalies for an open-and-shut case of suicide.'

Long silence.

'How did they get to you?' Jay folded her hands in her lap and put her head on one side, waiting. When Norton didn't respond, she gestured towards the Italianate-style house. 'Nice place.' Her tone was purposely soft and suggestive.

Norton leaned forward. He wasn't a big man, but he had presence as well as an aggressive light in his eye. His jaw was set, the muscles bulging high in his cheeks. 'Are you intimating something?'

'Me?' Jay affected innocence. 'No way. I know how it is. A couple of thugs get a baseball bat and smash the legs of a young guy so he'll never walk again, and you look the other way. I wonder why they did that. For fun? It's not as though they wanted his money because they never touched his wallet. They never went for his girlfriend either. It was a lesson, or perhaps a warning of some kind, wasn't it?'

Norton didn't move, didn't say a word, but his eyes hardened.

'And what about Magnus Parnell, the father?' Jay continued pushing. 'What happened there? The poor bloke shot himself four months later, guilt-ridden over banning Justin from having his girlfriend Grace to stay that weekend. Guilt, my arse.'

'Are you going to stay long,' said Norton, 'or do I have to call the police?'

Jay got to her feet, pushed back the deckchair. She could feel the blood rising and evidently so could Norton because he stood too. There was barely a foot between them.

'You were the investigating officer at the time of Justin Parnell's mugging,' Jay stated. 'What happened to the identikit pictures of the muggers?'

The ex-superintendent held Jay's eyes. The seconds ticked past. *Tick-tick-tick.* Neither of them moved.

'One of the muggers had a tattoo on the back of his neck,' Jay said. 'It's a tribal tattoo from Siberia. Ring any bells?'

Norton was still staring at her. 'You think I'm stupid?'

'No,' Jay admitted. 'I don't. But I'm struggling here. I have a missing person who changed his identity in ninety-five, a young guy who ended up in a wheelchair, his father dying of shotgun wounds four months later, and it's all regurgitating into today . . .'

'Best leave it alone, then.'

A picture of Duncan blazed into her mind: the way he limped slightly – an old injury apparently sustained in a car accident in his thirties – the way his eyes lit up when she walked into the room, his smile, his hugs, his bonhomie flowing like a fine red wine through the family.

She said, 'I can't. It's personal.'

Norton's eyes narrowed almost to slits. 'Not my problem.'

'Oh, yes, it is,' Jay said. 'Because I won't leave any stone unturned in the search for the truth, including the one you're currently hiding beneath.'

There was a long silence, and then Norton turned his head and gazed outside once more. 'If I give you something, you promise you'll leave me and Jeanie alone?'

'Promise,' Jay lied. She didn't care how hostile Norton was; she had every intention of dragging the ex-cop to the witness stand if need be.

Norton continued to gaze outside. Jay had no doubt the man's brain was speeding as fast as a bullet train, picking up things, discarding them, searching to find the perfect bone to throw. Something good enough to keep Jay and DI Sutton quiet, but not that good that it would rebound on himself.

Finally, Norton said, 'You could try and find a guy called Mikhael Ragulin.'

'He's Russian?'

The ex-cop didn't move, didn't blink. He said, 'Goodbye.'

On the way home, Jay called Tom.

'How's Warehouse Man?' she asked.

'Chaos. Every cop throughout the UK is now looking at old cases where there have been bites or weird marks on bones. So far we've five.'

'Should keep you out of mischief for a while.'

'Not half.'

Quickly, Jay filled Tom in on her visit to Philip Norton and the titbit he'd offered.

'Mikhael Ragulin,' he repeated.

'Sounds Russian.' Jay then described the tattoo of the antelope-style creature Grace had recognized on the Internet.

'I'll do a search. See if anyone like that is in the system.'

'If you find him, will you let me know?' she asked.

'Sure. You on your way back to London?'

'Yes.'

'I'll ring you when I'm up, hopefully Friday.'

'Great.'

When Jay got home she had two messages from Max Blake: one on her landline, one on her mobile. After pouring herself a glass of wine, she called him.

'You free tomorrow morning?' he said.

'Not really. I've got—'

'Good. I'll pick you up at eight. There's someone I want you to meet.' Before she could say another word, he added, 'Found the panic alarms yet?'

She looked around. 'Er . . .'

'By the front door. Big, red button. Push that and the cops will be on your doorstep in seconds. At your office as well.'

'Max, you are—'

'Gotta go, hon. In the middle of something.' He rang off.

Hon? Had she heard correctly? She stared at the phone. Unless she was hallucinating, he'd called her hon, as in short for honey. She downed half the glass of wine, unsure whether to do a tap dance or tear out her hair.

'Hey, what's up?'

Jay turned to see Denise, rubbing her short-cropped and freshly washed hair with a towel. She'd obviously just finished a shift; she always scrubbed herself head to toe after dealing with the general public. 'Why the panic alarms?'

Jay sipped her wine while she told her housemate about the break-in at TRACE's office and everything in-between.

'You think Koslov's men are following you?'

Jay nodded.

'If you need personal protection . . .' Denise made an elegant gesture to encompass her body. 'You just have to ask.'

'It hasn't come to that.' Jay smiled. 'But, if it does, you guys will be top of my list.'

'After Max Blake, no doubt.' Denise's eyebrows lifted. 'What's the story with Mr Gorgeous? You tempted?'

'No.' Jay turned away to hide the warmth rising on her cheeks. 'He's a colleague, that's all.'

'If I was into blokes, I'd jump his bones in two seconds.'

Not wanting the conversation to continue, Jay took her wine outside and sat watching the last of the light bleed out of the sky.

True to his word, Blake collected Jay at eight a.m. prompt. Today he was wearing another suit with a fine pinstripe and a silk tie. She tried not to look at his body as he walked ahead to unlock his car, but found it almost impossible. Previously, she'd only ever seen him in jeans and casual shirts, and she found having his powerful physique accentuated by the cut of his suit disturbing.

'No Discovery today?' she asked as he beeped open a sleek BMW M5.

'I needed something faster.'

Jay climbed in and buckled up. 'Chasing bad guys?'

'Never stops.' He turned the ignition. The car started with the muted burble of restrained power.

'Where are we going?'

'The office.'

Since Jay wasn't sure which office he had in mind – Blake had several, including one at Heathrow – she leaned back and enjoyed the ride, which, it turned out, was extremely short. Thames House North was barely two miles door to door from her place, which took about four minutes with a V-10 engine and a get-out-of-jail-free card in your pocket. She spent the time telling him about the Parnells and Duncan's trust fund.

'Elizabeth, along with my mother, the family . . . They don't know what to make of it,' she said. 'They're all over the place. Angry, upset . . . Cora sounded as though she'd happily kill her stepfather.'

'People don't like being deceived.'

She rolled her head to look at the side of his face. 'Have you found anything on Trent Newton?'

'Let's talk inside.'

He drove into an underground car park, lots of security and ID flashing. Jay was given a badge with her photograph displayed and the words TRACE – VISITOR stamped in red.

'I've never been here before,' she said, curiosity rising as he walked her through a barrage of security searches and checks. He didn't respond. They took a lift before walking along a corridor with glass walls on either side. She didn't think she'd seen so many computers. People were speaking into phones and tapping on keyboards, huddled together in corners, analysts and officers evaluating intelligence for border violations and terrorist threats. The air was overly chilled and she could smell synthetic air freshener and something sweet, like baking shortbread. It reminded her of her mother.

As Blake slowed to open a door on their right, she glanced in the office next door. Her heart skipped a beat. Looking straight back was one of the men who'd followed her earlier in the week. The young man in the brown shirt. He smiled.

Sixteen

'Max . . .'

Blake glanced between Jay and the man who'd tailed her. 'Yeah. That's Yevgeniy Belashev. His colleague flew back to Moscow this morning.'

She swallowed. 'What's he doing here?'

'He's with the FSB.' Max turned and opened the door. 'Sergey will explain, won't you?'

A medium-built man with a pelt of smooth, brown hair rose to shake her hand. He had no spare flesh and his face and body looked hard, as though carved from stone. He gestured her towards a chair. She sat and folded her hands in her lap, nerves hopping. The FSB had been following her? Why?

Sergey settled next to her. Blake took the seat opposite and steepled his fingers. He said, 'Sergey is also with the FSB. He's investigating the murder of his colleague, Eduard Vorontsove, and the disappearance of Eduard's daughter, Anna.'

A buzzing sounded in her mind, and she had to concentrate on keeping her expression neutral and not panicky. The FSB were after her. They didn't know Anna was dead yet, but they must have an inkling. They were hunting Anna's killer . . . and, without knowing it, they were hunting her. Fear shivered over her skin. When Sergey started to speak, she licked her lips. Her mouth had gone dry.

'Eduard was investigating Russian oligarchs,' he said. His eyes held hers, cool as pebbles beneath an icy stream.

She cleared her throat. 'The FSB are investigating Nikolai Koslov?'

Instead of answering her question, Sergey said, 'You know how the oligarchs made their money? Became billionaires almost overnight?' He didn't wait for her response, but continued, 'When President Yeltsin hit a financial wall in the mid nineties, he turned to the oligarchs to give him cash in return for shares in huge state companies. The scheme was named "loans for shares", and, in theory, when Yeltsin repaid the cash, the shares would be returned to the state. But this was a deal made under the table. The money would not be paid back, and the tycoons would keep the shares – worth far more than the price they paid for them.

'During this time there was much fraud,' Sergey went on. 'There were fake auctions of enormous companies – oil, gas, aluminium, copper – and premeditated agreements, bribes . . . All of the oligarchs were ruthless. They deliberately ripped off the state and its people without a second thought. The Kremlin wants the men who broke the law brought to justice.'

Jay thought over what she'd learned through the Internet about Koslov, from his market stalls buying people's vouchers for handfuls of kopeks to snapping up a variety of companies at bargain-basement prices. She hadn't seen anything that might have been illegal. 'You think Koslov was involved in a fraud?'

'Eduard mentioned he'd found something suspicious with the acquisition of the giant mining group Pervaya Minaya Kompanya – PMK – but before Eduard could make a report he was murdered.'

Again, she glanced at Blake, who nodded. 'Suspicious,' he said.

Not half, she thought.

'We also know that Eduard wanted to talk with an ex-policeman who used to work in Sinsk,' Sergey continued. 'Arkady Kashitsyn. He was jailed thirteen years ago, for serious assault. We discovered that although Eduard had arranged to visit him in jail, he never got there.' He turned his cool gaze on to Jay. 'I gather you met his daughter, Anna, in Moscow.'

Jay swallowed at the change of subject, and, although she tried not to, looked away.

'Tell him, Jay,' Max said. His tone was gentle. 'He needs to know.'

Still, she hesitated.

'Jay . . .'

When she spoke, it was to Blake. Somehow, it made it easier repeating what she'd said before to him, rather than to the man from the FSB. It didn't take long the second time round to cover her waking in her Moscow hotel room, meeting Vladimir and returning home to discover Duncan changed his ID in 1995. When she finished, Sergey cracked his knuckles. He was staring at her. He said, 'You don't remember talking to my colleagues in Moscow?'

She stared back. 'I'm sorry?'

'They met you with Anna at a bar on Friday evening. The Viktoria.'

At the word *bar* something in Jay's mind unlocked. Anna stood in her memory as though it was yesterday. Not the Anna she saw bleeding, dying, but the vivacious, tactile woman she'd first met. She could remember them striding down the street, Anna telling her about her alcoholic husband who she adored, but whom she eventually threw out. She went on to say that, although she'd had two lovers this year, she hadn't fallen in love since she'd met her husband.

I like sex, very much. But the heart? That is a different matter altogether.

Jay could remember the bar too. Urban chic with acres of chrome and steel and big, squashy chairs in primary colours. It was packed with men and women in smart suits and dresses, all smoking and talking fast and loud. Anna had ordered a bottle of Pertsovka – pepper vodka – which they'd taken to the far end of the room.

'Jay?'

She returned to the grey office and Blake, the FSB officer.

'Sorry. I can remember the bar but not your men.'

Blake told Sergey about the tiny bruises on the inside of her arms, where Tom believed she'd been injected. 'I think they used an amnesia drug.'

'A *what*?' Jay stared at him, her flesh crawling.

'It makes sense.' Sergey gave a curt nod. 'Certain drugs can block, dilute and even delete memories. Originally, the research was aimed at treating PTSD, the legacy of pain and misery left on the mind by horrific and often traumatic experiences, but there's always someone who'll twist things.'

'They erased my memory?'

'It's possible.'

'Will I regain it?'

Sergey raised his shoulders looking apologetic. 'It depends what they used, exactly, but yes, sometimes subjects can get total recall.'

'Only sometimes?'

Again, he shrugged.

Blake began tapping his fingers on his knee as he spoke. 'I'm wondering if Koslov knew that Jay talked to the FSB. It would give him the motivation to grab her and do some questioning of his own. Find out exactly how much Anna and Jay knew about Eduard's death. Give him the edge against you. Make some contingency plans.'

Sergey pinched the bridge of his nose between his fingers. He closed his eyes briefly. 'You're suggesting one of my men is on Koslov's payroll.'

'I'm just offering a variety of scenarios.'

'*Govno*,' the Russian cursed.

Jay leaned forward. Her breathing was tight. 'You think it was Koslov who messed with my mind?'

'It's possible,' Sergey replied.

'What has my uncle Duncan got to do with Koslov?'

Blake spoke up. 'Aside from a keen interest in horse racing, all we've discovered is that Trent Newton worked in the City and was one of Koslov's closest friends. They hung out a lot, went gambling and shooting. Everything looks above board.'

Jay told Sergey about the Parnells – Justin's mugging and his father's suicide – and that Tom was double-checking both cases.

'DI Sutton?' Sergey wrote down Tom's details. 'I'll talk with him, thank you.'

Next, she filled them in on Duncan's mother, Kristina, but she didn't tell them where Duncan's mother was. Sergey's comment that one of his men might be working for Koslov made her hold her tongue. There followed a lengthy silence. Everyone was deep in their own thoughts. Finally, Blake got to his feet. He looked at Jay, then at Sergey. 'Any more questions?'

Sergey shook his head, and although Jay was sure several would come into her mind the minute she left the building, she said, 'No.'

Blake called Jay a taxi and escorted her outside. He said, 'What's next?'

'I'm going to make an appointment with my sister-in-law. See if she can help me. I remembered the bar just now; she might help me recover my memory faster.'

He raised his eyebrows.

'She's a shrink.'

He took a step forward and brushed a lock of hair from her face. 'You need me, I'll be there.'

She smiled. 'I know.'

Seventeen

Sandra's front door was opened by Zamira, the babysitter. Jay said hi, but hi was never enough for the Macedonian girl, who gave her a hug.

'You look great,' Jay told Zamira.

'New jeans,' the girl said, beaming. She ushered Jay inside. Sandra was waiting in the hall. Zamira waggled her fingers at Jay. She said, 'See you, Jay.'

Sandra's office, or therapy room as she called it, was on the second floor of her house. It was light and airy and overlooked the Thames, which was busy with summer pleasure craft and the odd rowing boat.

'I've never been in here before,' Jay said, looking around at the desk and computer in the corner, the colourful rug that she knew Angus had bought on a business trip to China last year, the two upright chairs and a couch. She eyed the couch warily. 'Do I have to lie down for this?'

Sandra smiled. 'Of course not. You can sit anywhere you like, but some clients prefer the couch. They say it helps them relax.'

Jay chose an upright chair. 'OK. So how does it work?'

'We talk. I want you to feel comfortable with me, Jay, before we do the EMDR. This might mean we don't do it today, but tomorrow or the next day. Is that OK?'

'You're the doctor.' She gave a smile, but it was tense.

Sandra sat opposite her and folded her hands. Her expression was kind. 'I can see you're worried. If I can allay any fears, I will. You just have to ask.'

Jay looked through the windows. A small motor cruiser drifted past, a man at the helm, a woman at his side. Both were wearing identical red baseball caps.

'Have you ever had a client who's confessed to doing something wrong? Like really, really wrong?'

Sandra put her head on one side. 'Can you give me an example?'

'Say they hurt someone. Knifed them, maybe. Attacked them.'

'Yes, I have.'

'Or even murdered someone?'

'What's on your mind, Jay?' she asked gently.

'It's just that I think . . . I might have hurt someone.' A knot grew in her throat. 'A friend. But I can't remember.'

'Oh, Jay.' Compassion rose in Sandra's eyes. 'I'm sorry.'

'Do you have to tell the police?'

'No, I don't. I do, however, have to inform them if I believe a crime is about to be committed.'

Jay bit her lower lip. 'So you're bound by patient confidentiality.'

'Yes. But don't forget I'm also bound by my friendship to you. You are my number-one priority, whatever we discover together.'

It was the right thing to say because Jay felt the knot in her throat began to dissolve. 'Thank you.'

'My pleasure.' She smiled. 'So. Tell me what's happening.'

For a moment Jay didn't know where to start, but once she began talking she found it difficult to stop. Whenever she paused for breath, Sandra would ask a question like 'how are you feeling right now?' or 'show me where that feeling is?' and 'what colour is it?' and Jay would point at her heart or stomach and describe its colour before continuing. Somehow she wasn't surprised that black and red dominated her experience in Moscow, the colours she associated with depression, fear and anger.

After pausing to pour them both some water, Sandra said, 'Do you think you're ready to try it now?'

Jay pushed aside a little flare of alarm. 'Sure.'

'OK. I'll have to sit closer to you.' Sandra moved her chair across so that she was facing Jay, almost side by side but not quite. 'Can you follow my finger?' She moved her hand across Jay's vision. 'How does that feel? Comfortable?'

'Fine.'

'OK.' Sandra dropped her hand. 'What I want you to do is watch my finger as I move it back and forth, just as we did then. As you do this, we'll be stimulating the brain's information processing system. This should access the traumatic memory network and bring your memory back. Are you comfortable?'

'Yes.'

'Right. I want you to talk about what you can remember after you said goodbye to your boss, Nick, at Heathrow. OK?'

'OK.'

'We'll do it in several stages. Occasionally, I'll stop and we'll discuss what you've experienced before we continue. Allow us to process what's going on and keep moving forward. Are you ready?'

Jay gulped. 'Yes.'

'Watch my finger. And don't forget, we can stop at any time.'

Feeling a bit ridiculous but determined to give it a try, Jay let her eyes slide from side to side.

'Where's Nick?' Sandra asked.

'He's behind me.' She was surprised how clearly she felt his presence. 'He's in the driver's seat of his car, closing the door, and I'm turning to go through the electric doors of the departures lobby.'

'What can you smell? What can you hear?'

To her shock, Jay could see the queues of people waiting to check in as if they were right before her. Intellectually, she knew she wasn't at Heathrow, but it felt as though she was. She could hear the buzz of conversation, the rattle of suitcase wheels on linoleum and a tannoy announcement asking a Mrs Weale to go to the information desk where her husband was waiting. The odours of takeaways – pizza, cheese, coffee – permeated the air.

'That's amazing,' she said. 'It's like I'm there.'

Sandra led Jay through her arrival into Moscow, checking into the Hotel National – over a mile from the Hotel Oktyabrskaya II where she'd woken five days later – before she headed for the *Moscow News* offices and then to the bar with Anna.

She couldn't remember asking Anna where Duncan was, but, in a rush, she heard Anna's voice saying:

He's travelling overland to Sinsk, in Eastern Siberia. He won't have got there yet. It takes ages by train.

'Oh my God,' Jay said.

Sandra immediately stopped moving her hand. 'What is it?'

'We went to Sinsk.' Her eyes were wide as she gazed at her sister-in-law. 'Anna and I flew to Siberia . . .'

Jay talked Sandra though each recollection – fragmented, incomplete, but enough to make some sort of sense – and as she did, she gazed through the window at the sunlight glancing off the windows of houses opposite, hordes of people eating ice creams, walking dogs, pushing prams. A normal English summer's day, which felt a million miles from what had gone on in Russia.

After a while, a wave of nausea flowed through her as another memory broke through. She and Anna coming out of a canteen. They'd been telling each other stories from their lives, anecdotes and jokes. It was past one a.m. and they were laughing, clutching each other in vodka-fuelled hilarity, and at the same time there was a rushing movement and two men came at them.

Jay licked her lips. 'They kidnapped me.'

'Ah.' Sandra poured them both some water. 'No wonder you can't bear having anyone too close to you. You must be terrified it's going to happen again. This explains why you've been showing involuntary withdrawal since you returned from Moscow.'

Jay digested this while she sipped her water. Her body could remember her abduction – it had been in fight-or-flight mode ever since – but her mind was blank.

After a while, Sandra said, 'How are you feeling?'

'Angry.' As Jay said the word a hard ball of rage lodged beneath her diaphragm.

'What colour is it?'

'Red. It's like a hard, red ball.'

'I'd like you to look at this red ball and understand where it comes from. You were powerless to stop those men. You were vulnerable and defenceless, helpless, and they were large and powerful. I want you to watch the red ball dissolve.'

Yesterday, if she'd been told she would be dissolving an imaginary red ball with Sandra, Jay would have asked for a straitjacket. But there the ball was in her mind's eye, melting and dissipating into nothing. The sense of release was incredible.

'Wow,' she said. 'That's amazing. It worked.'

'Good.' Sandra smiled. 'Are you ready to continue?'

'Yes.' She trusted Sandra now. 'Let's do it.'

Jay's answer machine was blinking when she got home. It was her mother, wanting to know how she was.

'I'm fine,' Jay told her.

'You always say that. Even when you broke your wrist falling off that enormous horse of Duncan's you said you were fine.'

'I was!' Jay protested. 'Or at least I thought so.'

'You were in a plaster cast for weeks.'

'Mum, I swear it barely hurt.'

It was, if she could remember correctly, only later in the afternoon that her wrist had swollen like a balloon – and, despite the fact Jay hadn't been a child but a twenty-year-old fully fledged officer cadet, her mother constantly berated herself ever since for not taking Jay straight to the hospital after the fall.

Tucking the phone between her shoulder and chin, Jay filled the kettle and put on some toast.

'Any news on Duncan?' her mother asked.

Jay prevaricated. She didn't want to tell her mother about her memories of Russia yet. Sandra had told her there wouldn't be an instant recovery, but that it would be gradual, like convalescing after an illness. Also, she wanted to have more information before she faced the family, as well as to feel stronger. Right now, she felt about as strong as a newly hatched chick, which, although Sandra had said it was entirely normal, Jay found disconcerting.

'I saw Sandra earlier,' Jay said. 'She's been a real help.'

'Oh, Jessica.' Her mother sounded relieved. 'I'm so glad.'

'I'll tell you about it when I next come up. It's no wonder I was a bit weird last week; I was holding some seriously horrible stuff inside.'

'What, like the Balkans?' Her mother's voice was anxious.

Jay decided to be truthful and said, 'Yes. But it's OK, Mum, Sandra's going to work with me over the next couple of weeks until I no longer need the straitjacket.'

'I wish you wouldn't be so flippant.'

'I find it helps me cope.'

There was a small silence. 'Can I do anything to help?'

'Sandra said I need lots of rest. Not to push things too hard for a bit, get lots of early nights, that sort of thing.'

'It sounds very sensible.'

They talked inconsequentials for a while – Tigger the schnauzer's chasing of next door's cat, who her mother had seen in the village lately – and then they sent love and hung up. After she'd drunk a mug of tea and eaten her toast, Jay rang Tom. She wanted to talk over what she'd discovered with Sandra. Sandra had said that, now her brain and emotions could process what had happened to her in Russia, she should find things falling into place.

'It's me,' she said when he answered the phone.

'Hi, me. You at home?' he asked.

'Yes. Where are you?'

'Scotland Yard, just finishing up. You want to meet me over here? There's a new bar around the corner we could try out.'

She checked her watch. 'How about in half an hour? Six o'clock?'

She heard him talking to someone, and then he said, 'Six it is. By the main entrance.'

She arrived early on purpose, so she could duck around the corner and visit the Lebanese deli near Victoria Station. She'd discovered baklava and Turkish coffee on her tour in the Balkans and had become addicted to both. She sipped her coffee and devoured a pistachio pastry almost in one gulp. Having seen Sandra, her appetite had returned threefold. However, although she felt an enormous release, she still didn't know why she might have killed Anna. She thought back to the last few minutes of her therapy session.

'The only suggestion I can think of,' Sandra had said, 'is to return to the scene of the trauma, which is entirely impractical, given that it's in Siberia and obviously an extremely dangerous place to visit.' Sandra had narrowed her eyes in thought. 'It's a shame really, because sometimes the sight and smell of the actual place where the trauma occurred can act as a trigger. Brings the memories back, like with EMDR.'

Jay downed the remainder of her coffee, suffused with a sense of frustration. Since she had no plans to visit Russia again, she might have to face the fact that she'd have to live with the memory of Anna's death all her life, never knowing what had happened. And what about the FSB? What if they discovered she'd killed her? What if they found the right evidence, convicted her and threw her into jail? It didn't bear thinking about.

She still found it hard to believe that Duncan hadn't just been Koslov's friend, but his financial adviser. What had Anna said?

It was Duncan's brains that showed Koslov how to profit from the state.

Which meant Duncan had been tight with Koslov from the start. Had Duncan done anything illegal? Loads of accountants, tax advisers and bank managers advised clients without crossing the boundary to criminality. Certainly, the Duncan she knew was one of these, but the more she learned, the more she became unsure. When Anna met Duncan, he had told her he wanted vengeance . . . But for what?

Suddenly, her appetite deserted her, and she pushed away the remainder of her baklava and headed outside. She'd barely taken three paces when she spotted Tom climbing out of a taxi across the street. His shirtsleeves were rolled up to the elbow and his hair was awry. She was about to wave and shout, but she swallowed the words when he ducked back inside to embrace someone. A woman.

She was petite, tiny, and wore a daffodil-coloured skirt and a pair of killer high heels the same colour. She was clinging to him like a limpet.

Jay felt as though someone had crept up and punched her in the kidneys. She couldn't stop watching them. They were holding hands and talking, obviously reluctant to part. The woman raised her face for a final kiss and Tom obliged before closing the door and gesturing for the driver to continue. As the taxi drove away, he stood on the pavement watching it go. Only then did he turn and head for Scotland Yard.

Mouth dry, Jay counted to sixty before she followed him. He didn't enter the building but stood outside the front door and waited for her. When he spotted her, he waved. She didn't wave back. She could feel her heart beating, smell the metallic air of city fumes, but her emotions were encased in ice. She didn't think she'd ever felt so calm.

'Hi.' She stood a couple of paces back.

'Hi.'

'Nice day at the office?' She gestured at the offices behind him.

He looked away. 'Oh, the usual. You know how it is.'

'You've been here all day?'

'On and off.'

Two officers came through the door and skirted them, heads down and talking, but Jay paid no attention.

'And you've just come out?'

He gave a nod.

'You haven't just been dropped off by taxi around the corner by a small blonde woman, who just about stuck her tongue down your throat when you said goodbye?'

'Woah.' He held up his hands. 'Cool it, Jay.'

'Who is she, Tom?'

'It's not what you think . . .'

'*Who is she?*'

'Heather Lore. And she's not a girlfriend. Well, she was once, but not now, she's——'

'She's an ex-girlfriend?'

'Yes.'

Several more people exited the building. Jay stepped aside, keeping her distance from Tom when he did the same.

'I thought I knew all your ex-girlfriends.'

'It was a long time ago. I was twenty-one, OK?'

'How long have you been back in touch with her for?'

His eyes lifted to the sky.

'*How long?*'

'A couple of months.'

Jay ran her tongue over her lips. He'd been meeting up with his ex-girl-friend – if she even *was* an ex any more – for that long?

'I didn't tell you because . . . it's complicated.'

'What's complicated? Are you *sleeping* with her Tom?' Her voice had risen, attracting a few stares, but she didn't care.

A muscle in his jaw began to flex. 'So what if I am?'

'You shouldn't be coming on to me if you are!'

'OK, OK.' He backed up a couple of steps. 'I'm not sleeping with her, OK? However . . . the thing is . . .' He took a breath and exhaled. 'I have a daughter. Heather's child, she's mine. I didn't know, OK? Sofie got sick earlier in the year, she's got a heart valve disease, and the doctors wanted to know the father's medical history, so Heather got in touch.'

Jay felt her jaw drop. 'You have a daughter?'

'Yes. She's twelve. She's in and out of hospital, having tests done. I've been visiting her.'

'And you never thought to tell me?'

'It's not like we're an item,' he said. 'I mean, we were. But we're not right now, are we?'

Jay could feel the heat of the sun on her face and shoulders but inside she felt chilled. 'The way you've been carrying on, I thought we might be.'

He chewed his lip briefly. 'I can see how you thought that.'

'Is Heather married?'

'No.'

'Boyfriend? Partner?'

'Not since she split up with Brian three years ago. Look, Sofie's a really nice kid. Sweet. You'll love her. Having her around is a real bonus.'

'For you, maybe. I'm not interested in playing stepmother.'

'It's not like that.' He looked startled.

'What about when little Sofie has a birthday? And what about Christmas? Won't she want Daddy to drop by?'

'So?' He was frowning. 'Come on, Jay, don't jump off the deep end. Let's get that drink. Talk it through.'

'No.' She swallowed. 'Not now. I need time to think.'

She walked away without looking back.

When she got home, it was to find Angela in the shower and Denise cooking a curry.

'All right, babe?' Denise asked. 'You look a bit frazzled.'

Jay wasn't frazzled as much as emotionally wrecked. She felt as though she was teetering on the edge of a cliff, close to breaking down. She wasn't sure what to do. She'd never been this close to losing it.

'I just need a beer.'

'Help yourself.'

Jay popped a bottle of Becks and drank straight from the neck. 'Still hot,' she remarked.

'Summer of the century. God bless global warming.'

'Just wait until we start fighting over water.'

'That's way off. At least twenty years. We'll be tending our goats and herb gardens in Cyprus by then.'

'Lucky you,' Jay sighed.

Denise sent her a sharp look. 'Everything OK?'

'Sure,' she lied.

'Just checking, because gorgeously gorgeous rang earlier. Said your mobile was turned off. Sounded quite pissed off, actually.'

She'd forgotten she had switched off her phone at Sandra's. Now, she switched it back on. Five messages. All from Blake, all asking her to bloody well ring him. Except he hadn't sworn, but he might as well have from the tone of his voice. Walking into the back garden, she dialled his number.

'It's me.'

'You OK?'

'Fine. Sorry I switched off the mobile. I was in therapy, remember?'

'How'd it go? Memory back?'

'Almost. I've lots to tell you.'

'Me too. One of our guys found your uncle.'

For a second, she'd thought she'd misheard him. 'What?'

'He's in Russia. A town called Sinsk.'

Emotion wrapped its tentacles round her windpipe. An uncontrollable tremor shook her shoulders. 'I don't believe it . . . He's OK?'

'As far as we could tell.'

'Max, that's fantastic!'

'Unfortunately, our guy lost him. Hasn't seen your uncle since. Duncan's seriously spooked. You fancy a trip to Siberia? Talk him in?'

Her stomach gave a lurch, but whether it was fright or excitement was hard to tell.

Her uncle was OK. He's alive!

'Sorry?' She tried to concentrate on what Blake was saying.

'We need him, Jay. Badly. We know why Koslov is after him. And why he changed his ID.'

'Me too,' she said. 'Duncan was Koslov's financial adviser from the start. He knows where the bodies are buried.'

'Exactly.'

'But why has he gone to Siberia? Into the lion's den? I don't get it.'

'We don't either. But we need him. You up for it? I'll come with you. Protect your back.'

She thought of the exquisitely petite woman with the killer heels who had borne Tom's daughter. *Sofie's a great kid. You'll love her . . . Having her around is a real bonus.*

Then Sandra's voice. *Sometimes the sight and smell of the actual place where the trauma occurred can act as a trigger. Brings the memories back.*

Jay was meant to be resting after a traumatic therapy session, restoring her mental strength, and for a moment she hesitated, listening to the voices in her head, but the one that was screaming the loudest was Anna's.

'Can I ring you back in five minutes? I just want to check something.'

'I'll stand by.'

Jay rang Elizabeth and talked her through what she knew. Her aunt listened quietly, only asking the odd question occasionally, making Jay wonder how much she'd already guessed about her husband's past.

Jay finished saying, 'Blake wants me to go to Siberia . . .'

'Please go, Jay. Duncan needs you more than you realize . . . I'd go myself, but for the children . . .'

Jay's heart was still beating a brisk tattoo of joy under her breastbone. *Duncan's alive!*

'He's gone to Siberia to do the right thing,' Elizabeth went on. 'I'm sure of it. What was the word that Russian woman used? Vengeance. Don't you see, Jay? *Duncan needs your help.*'

Next, Jay rang Sandra.

'What was your first feeling when Max mentioned the trip?' Sandra asked.

'Scared.'

'And?'

'Hopeful. Worried. Nervous,' she said.

'The fact you haven't rejected it out of hand is important,' her sister-in-law said. 'Not only does it show how resilient you are, but also that you're not crippled by your memories. Perhaps giving you something worthwhile to do – especially looking for Duncan – might help you recover faster.'

Jay closed her eyes briefly. 'I'm worried I might crack.'

'In that case, stay at home until you feel stronger.'

But Jay didn't want to stay at home and deal with Tom and Heather and young Sofie. If Sandra thought she'd be OK taking the trip, even recover faster, then she'd be OK.

Finally, Jay rang Blake.

He said, 'You coming?'

'I'm packing my bag right now.'

Eighteen

Blake drove his BMW hard and fast along the M2. The sun was setting in a crystal clear sky showing half a dozen persistent contrails, a sign of continued good weather. Traffic was sparse. Friday's rush hour was long past. They were headed to an ex-RAF airbase at Manston where a special foreign ministry aircraft was waiting to fly them to the Bodø NATO base in Norway. After refuelling, they'd fly over the top of the world to Irkutsk, Eastern Siberia, and from there they'd hop up to Sinsk.

Part of her felt small and scared at what she was doing, but the other – the soldier and traveller – was coolly checking through what she'd packed to make sure she had everything needed, from her Swiss Army knife to a hip-flask of whisky. Both she considered essential items no matter where in the world she went.

Tom rang as Blake was driving them past Dartford. She'd already spoken to her mother and her housemates, and she'd just hung up from talking to Nick when he called.

He said, 'Jay.'

'Yes?'

'You mad at me?'

'Yes.'

Silence, then, 'Where are you?'

'In the car.'

'Where are you headed?'

'It's classified.'

'Are you with Blake?'

'Yes.'

Silence. Then, 'Any clue as to your destination?'

'Try Siberia.'

'Are you serious?'

'One hundred per cent.'

Another silence. She heard him sigh. 'OK, so talk me through the plan.'

Since he was part of the team trying to find her uncle, she couldn't very well refuse. She had to put her personal feelings aside for the wider picture. She said, 'The FSB found Duncan in a place called Sinsk, but then he vanished. Apparently, he's seriously spooked. Blake wants me to talk him in.' She brought Tom up to date.

'How long will you be gone?'

'How long's a piece of string?'

'You are *so* mad at me.'

'Yup. So why don't you go and play happy families while I try and find my uncle? I'm sure Heather would love to have you on tap.'

'It's not like that. She only got in touch because Sofie went to hospital. Heather doesn't need me. She's a barrister; she does very well on her own, including raising Sofie.'

'Bully for her,' said Jay, and hung up. She didn't want to hear any more about how successful Heather was, and she didn't answer when he rang back but let her message service pick up. He said, 'Jay . . . Shit.' Then hung up.

At that moment, Blake glanced across. 'Problems?'

'Oh, yes.'

'Does that mean I can ask you out?'

She rolled her eyes. 'No, Max. It does not.'

He shrugged. 'Can't blame a man for asking.'

She rested her head against the window and watched the last of London slide past. After a while, she said, 'I've never flown in a private jet before.'

'First time for everything.' He crowded an Audi out of the fast lane and redlined the revs until he reached 140mph. 'How was the therapy?'

She decided to be honest. 'Awful, since you ask. Not the therapy itself, I mean, but the memories.'

'You up to talking about it yet?'

'I'm not sure.'

'No rush,' he added. 'I know what it's like.'

It was the realization he'd probably experienced something similar that prompted her to make a start. 'Tom was right. They did drug me.'

'Hmm.' He made a non-committal sound.

'They took me to Sinsk. I awoke in a type of cell. Brick walls. No windows. Single bare bulb. There was a chair in the middle of the room and a bucket in the corner. . . . There were two men. They wanted to know where Duncan was. I tried not to let them know how scared I was, but in the end . . .'

Jay swallowed, forced herself to continue. 'They injected me with a muscle relaxant or something similar, because I lost control of my limbs. I couldn't think properly. I couldn't speak. Everything became a blur. I was strapped into a wheelchair and wheeled down a corridor. I remember more bare bulbs hanging from the ceiling, one every ten yards or so. We turned right, into a whitewashed room that was empty aside from a man in a white coat. He was holding a kidney-shaped bowl. They called him the Doctor.'

'Sounds bad.' His voice was soft.

'His name was Vasily. He had a face like a hatchet. Vasily told me I would feel the worst pain imaginable, but that when I told him the truth he'd administer an antidote.

'I wanted to speak straight away, tried desperately, but I couldn't, and when he injected me I thought I would die from the pain. It was like having my veins filled with petrol and set on fire. My blood boiled. My skin, every cell melted. I'd never known such pain, but I couldn't scream. They'd paralysed me . . .

'I kept passing out. Each time I came round I was so thirsty . . . desperately hot, almost dying of dehydration. He'd dribble iced water into my mouth. It was the most exquisite bliss. And then came the most dreadful pain . . .'

She closed her eyes as she continued, only half aware that Blake was slowing the car. Reliving the experience had brought back the sheer terror of being strapped to the wheelchair, powerless, and goose bumps rose over her skin as she spoke, her words becoming jerky, but she knew she had to tell him. Blake had to know what they were up against out there, as well as the fact she was vulnerable and uncertain about how she'd cope.

'I told him everything. I would have given him my bank account numbers, my mother's address if he wanted. He dehumanized me. Crushed my spirit into oblivion. And then I was taken to a concrete cell where Anna lay, bleeding, and I had a gun in my hand, a Sig, and I shot her. She's dead, Max. I killed Anna. I still don't know why . . .'

Blake had exited the motorway, and now he stopped the car, snapped free her seat belt. Leaning across, he folded her against his chest, and she was sobbing, her fists clutching his shirt like a child's. She cried for a long time, soaking his shirt, but he didn't seem to notice. He stroked her head gently, rhythmically, like he might a cat, until eventually her sobs lessened. Finally, she pulled back. He reached across and popped open the glove box and passed her a small pack of tissues. She blew her nose and began a mopping exercise. Normally, she never cried, but now the floodgates had opened it was hard to stop.

'Sorry,' she mumbled. 'I'm not normally an emotional wreck.'

He put a finger beneath her chin and turned her head towards him. 'I wouldn't have you any other way.'

'Even when my face has swollen to twice its normal size?'

'Even then,' he said solemnly.

She blew her nose again, trying to restore some equilibrium.

Blake said, 'How do you feel?'

Instead of trotting out her usual 'fine' she said, 'Knackered. Fragile.

Scared. What if they catch me again? I don't think I could stand being tortured again. It would break me. I might go mad.'

'I won't let that happen.'

She looked at the calm determination in his eyes. 'Max, you're not Superman.'

'That's what you think.' He gave a glimmer of a smile. 'You up for doing this, or do you want to stay behind?'

The soldier in her wanted to be strong, go to Siberia and face her fears, find Duncan and uncover the truth about Anna, but the woman in her wanted nothing more than to go home, jump into bed and pull the duvet over her head.

'I don't know.'

Blake nodded. He didn't look fazed. 'You want to think it over?'

'We don't have time.'

'Let's sleep on it,' he suggested. He glanced at his watch. 'I know a place near Ash. You get a good night's sleep, wake up, then tell me whether I go alone or you come too.'

'But Duncan won't trust anyone else. He doesn't know you—'

He held up a hand. 'No more talk. You're on overload right now. Let it settle. It'll become clear in the morning.' Using his Bluetooth, he made a call. 'Listen up, Pearce. Mission's been put back. Reschedule Manston for six a.m. tomorrow . . . Great . . . Yeah.'

He started the car and rejoined the motorway. After they passed Canterbury he took the A28 towards Margate, but soon afterwards ducked right on to a country lane. They passed a farm before crossing a river, and by the time he drew up outside a small brick cottage it was almost dark. Ten p.m. Jay climbed out of the car. The air had cooled and was intense with the scents of flowers and hay. She could hear water flowing nearby – the river they'd crossed earlier, she assumed.

Blake walked to the front porch, plucked a key from beneath a flower pot and opened the front door.

'Great security,' she remarked.

He shrugged. 'Nobody comes out here, and, if they did, there's not much to steal.'

Bringing in their bags, Blake began snapping on lights. The cottage was decorated in simple tones, faded pinks and beiges, the furniture neutral. Three bedrooms, one bathroom and a downstairs loo. Kitchen cum dining room, and a cosy living room with wooden beams and an open fire already laid with logs and newspaper. It wasn't flash, but it was comfortable enough to stay a while.

'Is this a safe house?'

'Got it in one.'

She followed Blake into the kitchen, where he opened the fridge and then the freezer.

'Hungry?' he asked.

She shook her head.

'You're eating anyway,' he told her. 'You'll sleep better for it.'

Curiosity nipped at her, making her open a couple of cupboards. She found basic supplies: tins of soup, beans, rice, spices. She paused when she came to the honey. Four jars: one from France, one from Somerset, and two Manuka and jellybush from Australia. One was nearly empty.

'I take it you come here regularly,' Jay said.

'Five, six times a year, sometimes more. You like a beer?'

'I'd love one.'

'Take a pew.'

She sipped beer while she watched him cobble a meal together. At one point he disappeared outside and came back with an onion, which he diced and fried. Handfuls of frozen peas and beans followed, Thai green curry paste from a tube, lots of stirring, then a can of coconut milk and some chopped, freeze-dried chicken. They didn't talk much while it simmered. Jay was too tired, and for once she was glad Blake wasn't the talkative type.

He piled rice high on her plate before spooning over the chicken and sauce. She tested it warily, felt her eyes widen. 'Max, you're a hero.' She couldn't believe it. From nothing but a handful of items, the man had made a delicious curry.

'Good job I get to keep a few staples in the cupboard or I'd for ever be hungry.' He took a long sip of beer. 'What else came up in your therapy session?'

'Just stuff I learned from Anna. How Duncan was seduced by Koslov. Koslov was trading minerals at that point. He was doing nicely, a cut above most Russians at the time, but he wasn't wealthy. Not until Duncan came along.'

'Same as we learned.'

'Anna was convinced Koslov had something to do with her father's murder. She was looking for something, anything that might trip Koslov up, when she was alerted to Duncan. What piqued her curiosity was when he vanished in the nineties. One day he was Koslov's best friend, the next he was gone. It took perseverance, sheer bloody-mindedness to find him again. She used the Internet, following Koslov, seeing which races he was attending, when she came across a picture of Duncan. It was chance, a fluke. He was at the Bath races earlier this month.'

It had been his fiftieth birthday present from Elizabeth, Jay recalled, a luxury break at Bath's fabulous Royal Crescent Hotel with a racing day thrown in. He'd been thrilled.

'He was photographed in *Horse & Hound*. Duncan and Elizabeth and a couple of friends with their glasses raised. They'd backed a winner, apparently. When Anna realized he'd changed his name, she knew she couldn't ring him or drop him a line. She'd have to see him face to face.' Jay sighed. 'Poor Anna. She said Duncan just about had a heart attack when she told him her father had been murdered and that she suspected Nikolai Koslov. She blamed herself for Duncan vanishing again.'

'How come?'

'Koslov knew she was on Duncan's trail, trying to find her father's killer. He must have had Anna followed to England.' She looked at the floor as she spoke. 'Anna led him to Duncan.'

Anna had, apparently, seen Duncan on Saturday and the next day, Koslov had dropped into Norridge Farm for drinks, scaring Duncan into running away again.

They ate the rest of their curry in silence. When Blake took her empty plate to the sink, he said, 'Anything on Arkady Kashitsyn? The ex-cop in a Siberian prison? Eduard was on his way to see Arkady when he was murdered. I'm thinking Arkady might hold the key to all this.'

'The only thing Anna said that I can remember was that Arkady, like Koslov, was a friend of Duncan's from years ago, and that Duncan had no idea he'd been jailed. Apparently, Duncan was absolutely horrified.' Something else, something important, slid like a fish at the back of her mind but she couldn't hook it. 'That's it. Sorry.'

Blake rinsed the plates. He said, 'Sergey believes that Duncan's following the same clues Anna's father did.'

Jay blinked. 'Eduard was going to visit Arkady in jail –'

'And never got there. That's why we've got to get to Duncan first.'

She slid off the stool to help him clear up but he waved her off, pointing upstairs. 'Bed,' he told her. 'Take the one on the left. I'll be in the one on the right. I'll wake you at five.'

Like the rest of the cottage, the bedroom was unfussy and plain, with a standard double bed and chest of drawers. No mirrors or pictures on the walls, but the view of the river was pretty, lit by a sliver of moon. Stripping to her knickers, she climbed into bed, turned out the light. She was asleep in seconds.

Dawn was creeping past the curtains when Jay awoke. Blake was squatting in front of her fully dressed, mug of tea in hand. His hair was slicked back, seal damp from a recent shower. He smelled of soap.

'Hmm,' she said. 'You sweetheart.' She put a hand out for the tea, blinking sleep from her eyes, half yawning.

'Christ,' he murmured.

Jay's eyes snapped open to see Blake was staring at her. Belatedly she realized the sheet had slipped. She yanked it up to her throat.

Slowly, he put down the mug. His eyes were locked on hers, dark liquid, almost black. He reached for the sheet.

Jay wriggled backwards. 'Max,' she began. 'I don't think this is such a good idea . . .'

In one sinuous move Blake was on the bed. A hand, warm as bread, slid to caress the nape of her neck.

'I think it is,' he murmured.

His lips brushed the side of her mouth and fire scorched across her skin, lighting more flames deep inside.

'Oh, God,' she said.

He kissed her. His lips were soft and gentle, nothing like she'd imagined, and she raised a hand tentatively to touch his cheek, smooth, freshly shaven. When their tongues touched, she groaned. It was the groan that made her break the kiss. She groaned like that with Tom. *Tom.*

'Max, no.' The words were gasped.

He reared above her. 'Not a word I want to hear.' His breathing was ragged.

'Sorry. I can't.' Her heart was beating fast. Thump-thump-thump. She was sure he could hear it.

'You want me,' he said.

'Yes,' she admitted. There seemed little point in denying the fact considering she was panting like a bitch in heat. Tom was right. She did pant . . .

'And I want you. So why not?'

'Tom.'

'I thought there were problems.'

'There are. But I don't want to burn any bridges. If Tom knows that you and I . . .' She took a breath. 'It'll be *over* over. I'm not sure if I want that right now.'

His eyes narrowed briefly. 'Hmm,' he said.

Jay tightened her grip on the sheet. If he made a total assault she'd never be able to resist him. She'd always known the chemistry between them was strong, that the slightest spark would ignite a wildfire, and if she was honest she'd always been slightly scared of the fact. Blake could engulf her, devour her with a single bite, no problem.

She held her breath as he leaned in to her and kissed her nose. 'Ah, well,' he said. 'I'd better make breakfast.' He rolled off the bed and padded outside. 'See you downstairs.'

Jay stared at the space where he'd been. Her lips still tingled from his kiss and her body was aching. She felt as though he'd placed a handful of hot coals in her heart, her belly. If they'd had sex, she reckoned they'd never have made it to Russia. Not until next week.

Wobbly kneed, Jay headed for the bathroom and a cold shower.

Nineteen

It was hot in Siberia, hotter than Jay could have imagined, and her clothes were wet and sticking to her skin, her hair leaking sweat. Since the airport at Sinsk didn't work at weekends, and he didn't want to waste hours sitting on a train, Blake had chartered a helicopter from Irkutsk at huge expense. What the British tax payer would think, heaven only knew, but she doubted they'd find out. It wasn't as though MI5's expenses were published in intricate detail through the national newspapers.

She nearly hadn't come. Not just because she felt tired, but because she wasn't sure if she could trust herself with Blake. There was no way she'd be able to keep her hands to herself a second time, and she didn't dare risk Tom for a night of hot sex with Blake until she'd worked out how she felt about Sofie and Heather. She'd stuffed up big time last year over Tom, and she didn't want to do the same thing again.

She'd been running the tap to wash up that morning – Blake had cooked bacon and baked beans on toast for breakfast – when he came and stood beside her. He was looking outside.

'You OK about us?' he said.

'There is no "us".' She said it quietly.

'Never say never.' He turned to face her. His expression was neutral, his eyes cool. 'You staying, or you coming with me to find your uncle?'

'You touch me, and I'll deck you.'

'It's a deal.'

And with that, he'd turned away and taken their bags outside to the car.

Jay kept looking around the town as they drove through, waiting to recognize something, but everything was alien, unrecognizable. She was surprised at the depth of her disappointment, because it was only now she was here, travelling through the place of her brutal memories, that she realized how badly she wanted an answer as to why she'd shot Anna.

'We're going to meet Sasha Korkach,' Zaro said. Zaro was Blake's man on the ground, flown in from Irkutsk last week, and currently their designated driver. 'Sasha apparently saw Duncan on Tuesday. I put a couple of men to watch Duncan earlier in the week but they messed up. He spotted them on his tail and vanished. Incompetent idiots.'

Sasha was, apparently, a policewoman who had been around since the eighties. She'd seen the area climb from the pit of poverty to what it was today. Although people weren't rolling in money, at least most had a roof over their head and were no longer starving. Rumour had it that Sasha had been involved in kickbacks from Koslov when the oligarch had bought his first mines.

Jay leaned forward so she was level with the front seats. 'You think she's got some dirt on Koslov?'

'I'm betting on it,' Blake replied. When he didn't turn to meet her eye or say any more, she leaned back. Her head felt woolly from all the travelling, and her muscles were stiff and achy. She couldn't wait to have a shower and wash away her sense of exhaustion.

Instead of heading straight for their hotel as Jay had hoped, Zaro whizzed them through town for their meeting with Sasha. They overtook dozens of trucks belching noxious fumes and clouds of oily smoke, some moving so slowly that Jay thought they were stationary until they drew alongside. Faceless grey blocks of concrete with rows of tiny windows lined the roads, utilitarian buildings cheap to erect and sturdy enough to withstand the bitter winters. Zaro pointed out a huge hospital and a large supermarket, both built with Koslov's money. They passed an oversized statue of the man himself in the middle of a roundabout. He was wearing a miner's helmet and a beatific smile. No matter how Koslov had amassed his wealth, he appeared to have earned enough appreciation to last him a lifetime.

After a while, concrete blocks gave way to wooden houses. Some were painted blue, others red or green. Horses pulled carts of potatoes and more potatoes were for sale in buckets lining the roads. Stray dogs darted between the traffic. The countryside was dull and flat. A massive, hazy-white sky pressed down.

Jay leaned back, and the second she let her mind wander it latched on to Tom and the daughter he'd sprung out of the blue. And what about his ex-girlfriend, Heather? She'd witnessed Tom kissing the woman, holding hands with her. Not that she had seen exactly where he'd kissed Heather, on the cheek or the lips, but did it matter? The fact they were so intimate said it all. Heather was everything Jay wasn't: petite, blonde and pretty. Where Jay wore boots and jeans, Heather wore tiny short skirts and sexy high heels. And Heather was single. She was also a civilian. A feeling of dismay settled in Jay's stomach. Was Tom tempted by Heather?

She suddenly realized she might have made a mistake coming out here. What if Heather used the situation to get her hooks into Tom? Jay suddenly felt like screaming. She never seemed to get things right. One day, it would be nice if things weren't so complicated . . .

Gradually, the multicoloured houses disappeared, along with the road. They began jolting down a pitted track. In the distance she could see a train pulling a line of freight cars. She wondered if it was the Trans-Siberian Railway and realized it couldn't be; they were way north. She looked ahead to see the track stretching across a baking wilderness of tundra – low, sage-coloured bushes and stunted trees.

'You've been out here before?' Jay asked Zaro.

He shook his head. 'The instructions are easy. Drive until the track runs out, and she will be there.'

'How long is the track?'

'She said it would take an hour.'

An hour passed and the track worsened. Ruts two-feet deep were edged with hard-baked soil, which clawed the bodywork like metal fingernails. The potholes became huge, the size of washing machines. After another fifteen minutes, Blake said, 'We'll give it another ten and then we're turning around. Don't want to run out of fuel.'

Jay studied the map Blake passed her. It was empty of any villages, or rivers and forests. Nothing but thousands upon thousands of acres of tundra. The track wasn't marked, nor the last village they'd seen. She wouldn't want to get lost out here.

'There.' Zaro sounded relieved. 'You see it?'

On the horizon was some form of habitation. Initially, she thought it might be a village, but when they arrived she saw it was an old army camp. The perimeter wire had long come down, the posts rotted away. Rows of single storey, wooden buildings were slumped, decaying, their corrugated-iron roofing rusting on the ground. Weeds grew everywhere.

Zaro pulled up and, as he reached to switch off the ignition, Blake said, 'Don't. Keep it running. And let's stay in the car.'

The minutes ticked away. Jay wiped sweat from her face, longing for air conditioning, a glass of iced water. She'd turned soft since she left the army. She didn't have a soldier's patience for enduring discomfort any more.

'Here they come.' Blake was staring dead ahead. 'They're armed.'

Alarm speared her when she saw three uniformed police officers approaching. Two guys, one woman. Their faces were like tombs, hard and cold. Their guns were already drawn.

'Oh, Lord,' said Zaro. The words came out on a half gasp, alerting both Jay and Blake that his adrenalin was already in full flow and that he probably hadn't seen much action, if any at all.

'I thought we were supposed to be meeting just the one cop,' said Jay.

'We were.' Zaro almost whimpered the words. 'Oh, sweet mother of God . . .'

'Pick reverse,' Blake told Zaro. 'The first sign of trouble, get us out of here.'

Jay's senses were on high alert, processing everything at what felt like twice the normal speed. Zaro put the jeep into reverse. Jay could see his hands were trembling and hoped he would react fast when Blake gave the order. At least he hadn't bolted yet, which was promising.

The cops were now ten yards away. Their faces were red and shiny, and she could see dark, sweat-soaked patches on their shirts. They'd obviously been in the sun for a while. They looked as though they were roasting.

Blake stuck his head out of the window and held up a hand. 'Wait there.' His voice was commanding.

They stopped, their weapons pointed at the car.

'Sasha,' Blake called. 'I can't have your colleagues come any closer. I'm sure you understand.'

'Of course.' Sasha dipped her head. In her forties, she was short and round as a football. The pips on her epaulettes meant she was the British equivalent of a sergeant, her companions both constables. She lowered her weapon. 'You and I, we talk?'

'And my colleague, Jay. She's Duncan's niece. The one Zaro told you about.'

'I see. If you and Jay would like to step out of the car, arms raised, I will check you for weapons, and then we can have a friendly chat.'

Before they climbed out of the car, Blake gave his pistol to Zaro. 'Keep the engine running, and keep a three-sixty alert.'

Jay climbed out of the car, allowing Sasha to frisk her before the police-woman turned her attention to Blake. When Sasha found a hunting knife tucked in an ankle holster, she chuckled. 'Nice weapon,' she said. To Jay's surprise, Sasha let Blake keep it.

They walked a little way from the car, out of earshot of the two constables. Aside from the jeep's engine it was silent, deserted. No birdsong, no insects buzzing. The sun beat down like a hammer on the crown of Jay's head. She didn't think she'd ever felt so removed from the real world and was glad Blake was taking every precaution.

'Thanks for meeting us,' Blake said.

'I'm sorry I had to bring them.' Sasha jerked her chin at her men. 'But after Eduard Vorontsove was killed, I decided on some insurance.'

'Who killed him, do you know?' Jay asked.

Sasha shrugged. 'It could be anyone in town wanting to protect their job.'

'What do you mean, anyone?' She didn't get it. She thought Koslov had murdered Anna's father.

'Eduard was employed by the Kremlin to investigate Nikolai Koslov over some business dealings he conducted in the mid nineties. If Eduard found something to put Koslov away, the town would be at risk of sliding back into poverty.'

'But the mines would keep operating, surely?'

'Yes, but by whom? Nobody else would care as much for the local people as Koslov.'

'Why?'

Sasha glanced at her constables, then away. 'He's bought their silence.'

'But not yours.'

Another shrug. 'I kept quiet for a long time. It was only when Eduard turned up that I saw there may be a way of settling old scores. When he was killed I thought I was back to square one, but then your uncle arrived.'

'Where is Duncan?'

'I don't know precisely, but he might have gone to see an old friend, Arkady Kashitsyn. Arkady's in Camp 102. It's near a town called Zigansk, north of the Arctic Circle. Koslov put him there on a false charge.'

'Why?'

'Because he wouldn't be bribed.'

Jay let the silence hang for a moment before saying, 'Sasha, tell us about your old scores.'

'It's simple.' Sasha looked past them and into the distance. 'Koslov destroyed the lives of two people I love. I want him to pay.'

Despite the heat, the hairs on the back of Jay's neck rose. 'When was this?'

'Nineteen ninety-five.' She wiped her forehead before continuing. 'Yeltsin authorized a company called Silnaya Kompanya – SilKom – to be auctioned here. Koslov made sure there were no other bidders by closing the airport and using armed police to block the roads. Weeks later came the first mega deal. The giant mining group Pervaya Minaya Kompanya – PMK – came up for sale, and Koslov went for it. Koslov also owned the company that ran the auction. He bought PMK for roughly a third of what it was worth at one hundred and twenty million dollars. Its assets had been valued at three hundred and fifty million. However, the highest bid had come from Mirovoi Kapital – MirKap – owned by Pavel Gubin, who offered three hundred million. When Koslov won, MirKap took legal action against him. This was abandoned after MirKap inexplicably withdrew its complaint.'

Her face suddenly twisted but whether in anger or pain, Jay couldn't be sure.

When Sasha spoke, her voice was hoarse. 'Arkady was my friend. He was like a brother to me. Arkady fell in love with my best friend, Alexa . . . Alexa's brother is Pavel Gubin.'

Sasha glanced over her shoulder, checking on her constables. She gave them a nod, both nodded back.

'Pavel is in a camp, like Arkady.' She reached into her breast pocket, withdrew a piece of paper and gave it to Jay. 'Alexa can tell you the story. This is her address. I suggest you visit her. Duncan may make contact with her after he's seen Arkady.'

'Duncan knows everything you've told us?' Blake pocketed the address.

'Oh, yes. It was his idea to block the roads.'

Twenty

Alexa lived with her aunt in Sinsk, in one of the modern blocks over-looking the hospital. Climbing out of the car, Jay looked around at the scorched, dry-looking trees and people in shirtsleeves walking on pavements, chatting, smoking. Again, she recognized nothing. A small doubt rose. Had the EMDR with Sandra really worked? Or had her imagination gone berserk, making everything up? But then she remembered the bruises on her body, from where she'd been manhandled into cars and aircraft, into a wheelchair. She checked for the tiny bruises on her inner arms, where needles had been inserted, but they had long gone. She had to hope she stumbled on something soon or she'd never find any answers about Anna.

Blake told Zaro to wait outside and the young man looked relieved. He'd obviously had enough excitement for the day.

'Entrance F,' Jay told Blake. 'Ninth floor. Apartment fourteen.'

The elevator groaned like an old woman as it rose, shuddering and clanking. Jay decided to walk down the stairs when the time came to leave. Blake let Jay press the apartment bell and be studied from the peephole by a brown eye. She could hear music from within the apartment, brisk jazz, and smelt something sharp and acetone, like nail polish remover.

'I'm a friend of Sasha's,' Jay called out. 'She asked us to drop by.'

'You're Jay?'

'Yes. And this is Max Blake.' Jay pulled him into view.

'OK. Please, Sasha rang us earlier. Alexa and I have been expecting you.' The door was unlocked to reveal a plump woman in a green and pink dress. She was beaming. 'We never get English visitors. It is such a pleasure. Please come inside. I am Irena.'

Inside, the apartment was small and neat. There was only one bedroom, which Irena told them she shared with Alexa, a small bathroom, a galley style kitchen and a living-cum-dining room with a small sofa and two armchairs surrounding a knee-high table. Vases of plastic flowers and white table cloths adorned every surface.

A woman sat with her back to them as they entered. She was small and slender and had a palomino plait that hung between her shoulder blades. She switched off the radio saying, 'Is that Jay and her friend?' Her words were slightly muffled, making Jay wonder if she had a speech defect.

'Yes, Alexa. They're here.'

'It's nice to have visitors. I get so bored.' The woman got to her feet and, using the back of a chair, turned around. Jay felt more than saw Max stiffen at her side. Her face looked as though she'd stepped too close to a fire and her skin had melted. Her eyelids appeared to have been sealed shut with wax and her mouth was distorted into a permanent grimace, one side of it dragged upwards, towards her cheek.

Jay immediately moved forward. 'Hi, Alexa,' she said. 'I'm Jay.' She took the woman's hand, which was smooth and scar free. In fact, the further Jay looked, it seemed as though it was only Alexa's face which had been scarred.

'Hi Jay.' Alexa's grip was firm.

Jay didn't beat about the bush. As she had with Justin, she came out with it straight. 'Your poor face,' she said. 'What on earth happened?'

Alexa turned her head to where Irena stood. 'Isn't that refreshing? Someone who isn't scared of asking. I can't remember the last time that happened. Please, would you like tea or coffee? Then we can sit down and I can tell you about it. Sasha said it would be OK.'

'Tea would be great,' said Jay.

'Same for me,' said Blake.

Jay blinked. She'd never seen Blake drink tea, he always had coffee.

As if he'd heard her thoughts, he said, 'It's Russian tea, not PG Tips.'

They settled with Alexa in the living room while Irena brought chocolates and fruit, and cups of tea so strong and black it resembled engine oil. A small bowl of home-made raspberry jam was offered around. Blake spooned some into his tea and stirred, took a sip.

'Delicious,' he said.

'The jam is a cure all,' Alexa told them brightly. 'It's been known to fix anything from flu to impotence.'

Blake choked on his tea. 'Really?' he said. His gaze wandered over to Jay, her shirt collar opened to her breastbone, then to her lips. 'I must get some,' he murmured. Then he winked.

They chatted for a while, talking about their journey, about Duncan and his disappearance from England, and it was Alexa who finally broached the subject of her scars. Like Sasha, she told the story of Koslov fixing the auction so her brother's company, MirKap, couldn't contend.

'Koslov bribed the police to block the roads, can you believe it? Arkady went insane.'

Blake said, 'Sasha said it was Duncan's idea.'

'It was, but he didn't actually think Koslov would do it. He said it as a joke.'

It transpired that when Koslov had bribed the police to put up the road blocks he'd told them that it was the start of a special relationship, that when he owned the giant mining company he'd look after them and their families, build schools and hospitals and houses, and every cop in town jumped on board. Except for Sasha and Arkady. Aside from these two, Koslov owned Sinsk, and Sinsk was happy to be owned.

Later, when Pavel went to court to take legal action against Koslov for the fraud, Koslov threatened his family, saying he'd hurt Pavel's sisters. He had three, including Alexa.

'My brother didn't believe him,' said Alexa. 'He thought Koslov was bluffing, so he pressed on with his complaint. When Koslov was served his court papers, he came to the house with his thugs. He threw acid in my face. He told Pavel if he didn't withdraw his complaint he'd throw my younger sisters in an acid bath.' She closed her eyes briefly. 'Pavel withdrew his complaint immediately. He had no choice. There were only two police officers who would help him. One was his sister's best friend, the other his future brother-in-law.'

Jay said, 'Sasha told us you were engaged to Arkady.'

'Yes. Then this happened –' Alexa gestured at her face – 'and Koslov bribed the police to frame Arkady for it. Koslov knew Arkady would kill him for what he'd done to me, so he put him away. My poor love . . .' Her voice broke, but she cleared her throat and continued. 'He was accused of doing this to me . . . throwing acid in my face. I couldn't do anything to help. I didn't know what was happening until later. I was in hospital a long time . . . I had no idea what Arkady was going through . . .'

Alexa wiped tears from her ruined eyes. Nobody spoke as she gathered herself.

'Arkady's serving a twenty-two year sentence in Camp 102. They won't allow him any visitors. They don't give a reason. I ask every month, but they refuse to allow me to see him. I write but I never hear back. I don't know if my letters ever arrive . . .'

Alexa took a breath. She said, 'Pavel was framed for fraud by Koslov soon after Arkady was arrested. He has three more years before he is freed, but I don't think he'll make it. He's got TB. I think he will die before the year is out.'

The long silence was punctuated by a clock chiming. Irena poured more tea from the samovar, and this time Jay tried it with jam. Blake was right, it was delicious, but she couldn't enjoy it against the back story of violence and corruption, people's lives destroyed in the name of ambition and greed.

'Your uncle Duncan didn't witness any of this,' Alexa said. 'He was in England at the time. When Arkady rang him, begging for his help, he refused to believe what had happened. He said he'd talk to Koslov and get the truth from him. Poor Arkady was devastated. When he was arrested, he was convinced Duncan was going to arrive at any minute and rescue him, but it never happened.'

Poor Arkady, indeed, thought Jay. How awful, and what about Pavel? He'd retracted his complaint to protect his sisters, and even then he'd ended up in jail.

Blake spoke up. He said, 'Did Arkady ever mention Koslov dealing in uranium?'

Alexa blinked. 'Oh, yes. I'd forgotten about that with everything else going on. He'd only just started that investigation. The Kremlin put him on to it. They'd heard rumours that Koslov's scientists had found some canisters of uranium in one of PMK's depots. It had been sitting there for years, apparently. Nobody knew what they were until Nikolai sent his men in to do a stock check before buying the company. Arkady told me he'd started digging on the quiet.'

'Did he tell you if he discovered anything?'

She shook her head. 'No. He'd barely begun to look into it.'

Blake tapped his fingers on his knee. His gaze was distant but Jay knew he'd be processing this new information alongside everything else he knew.

'Do you know the irony of all this?' Alexa didn't wait for a response. 'This apartment is paid for by Koslov. He looks after me and Irena. We'd like to throw his money in his face, but we can't afford to. Irena works in the super-market and doesn't earn much. Nobody will employ me as they can't bear to look at me. We'd be on the streets if it wasn't for him.' Her voice turned low. 'I hate him, but I'm grateful too, which makes me hate him even more.'

'I'd hate him too,' Jay agreed.

'He arranged for Sasha to get a promotion. If she hadn't taken it, she'd look like me. She made the right choice, but it eats away at us. We're owned by him.'

They sat in silence for a while, listening to the faint sound of traffic below.

Eventually, Jay turned to Alexa. 'If you see or hear from Duncan, could you tell him we're staying at the Koslov in town?'

A glimmer of humour showed in the woman's eyes. 'Two hotels in town and you choose that one?'

'The other's a rat-infested dump,' Blake said, shifting slightly. 'I hate rats.'

Jay tumbled into her room at six p.m. She hadn't stopped to bathe or rest all day and exhaustion tugged at her eyes. She'd accompanied Blake for the remainder of the afternoon, spent gathering intelligence from the FSB in

Sinsk and the surrounding area. Nobody had sighted Duncan since Tuesday, and nobody had any idea where he might be.

Since her mobile phone didn't work out here – apparently there was a mast, but the service was unpredictable – she called Tom from her hotel room before she went and foraged for supper. England was seven hours behind, which made it eleven a.m. in Bristol.

'Sutton,' he answered.

'Hi,' she said. 'It's me.'

'How's the vodka?'

'Sixty per cent firewater. How's Warehouse Man?'

'All chewed up. Pete's studying the variety of bite marks on the bones. He's guessing a pack of eight dogs or so.'

'Not a nice image,' she said, glad that Tom wasn't harking back to their last abrupt phone call. 'Any luck with Duncan's phone records? Who he rang from his mother's after he'd vanished?'

'He rang British Airways to book his flight to Kiev, then he called a taxi to take him to Heathrow.'

'That's it?'

'Yup.'

Jay remembered Anna saying Duncan had travelled overland in an attempt to avoid detection. Kiev to Siberia by bus and rail would have taken six days or more. He would have arrived in Sinsk earlier this week, maybe even on the Tuesday he was first spotted by Zaro's men.

'Talk about a circuitous route,' she mused. 'Any luck with Mikhael Ragulin?'

'Not yet.'

Jay turned her head when she heard a knock on the door followed by Blake's voice, asking if she'd like to join him for dinner. 'Yes!' she yelled, then she said to Tom, 'I've got to go and eat. I haven't had anything all day.'

'Say hi to Blake for me.' His voice was brittle.

'Hi to Heather.'

Silence.

'Sorry,' said Jay at the same time Tom said, 'God, I wish . . .'

Another silence.

'Jay?'

'Tom?'

'Let's talk when you get back, OK?'

'OK.' She mentally blew him a kiss as she hung up.

After a quick shower she joined Blake downstairs. The dining room was oddly deserted. Not a single person, aside from a lugubrious waiter who looked as though he'd rather be elsewhere. The room was formal, the tables covered with white cloths and pink plastic flower arrangements. Blake ordered vodka and gherkins, and, in the echoing silence, they mulled over their day.

'I'm worried about security,' Blake said.

'In what way?'

'Sinsk is Koslov's town. He gets to hear everything that goes on. Let's just be careful who we talk to about what we've found.'

'Including Zaro?'

'And Sergey.' He rolled over his wrist to check his watch. 'He meant to join us for drinks, but he's obviously running late.'

Jay was startled. 'The FSB guy I met in London? He's here?'

'Yup. He doesn't trust anyone else.'

'Do you trust him?'

Blake gave her a pitying look. 'Hon, I don't trust anyone.'

They talked over a meal of mutton stew and pickled vegetables until, in a rush, Sergey turned up looking the worse for wear, having driven from Irkutsk. His slick, brown pelt of hair was ruffled, and his clothes were rumpled and dusty. He looked far more approachable than the hard, controlled man she'd seen in MI5's offices.

Pouring himself a vodka, Sergey downed it in one then poured another. 'Shit of a journey,' he said. 'I hate coming out here. Arsehole of the world.'

'When were you last here?' Jay asked.

'When Eduard Vorontsove was murdered.' He slugged back his second glass of vodka. 'I swore wild horses wouldn't drag me back, but here I am.'

'Here you are,' she echoed.

'What news of your uncle?' Sergey asked Jay.

'Nothing. He hasn't been seen since Tuesday.'

'The policewoman couldn't help? Sasha? Or her friend, Alexa?'

Jay flicked a glance at Blake, who had folded his arms and was giving a good impression of a rock. 'Not really,' she prevaricated.

'Please don't worry, Jay,' Sergey said. 'I know what you've been doing because that's my job. Isn't it, Max? Knowledge is our business. Knowledge is power.'

Blake uncrossed his arms and leaned forward. He said, 'Sasha told us nothing you don't already know. How her colleague Arkady Kashitsyn became obsessed with Nikolai Koslov in the mid nineties, convinced he'd committed a major fraud, ripping off the State, the people . . . And that he was set up by Koslov for assaulting his fiancé, Alexa, to silence him.'

'I know the story,' said Sergey. He was shaking his head. 'Disgusting. I want to talk to this Arkady, see if he'll testify against Koslov. Do you mind?' He gestured at the dish of mutton. 'I'm very hungry.'

'Help yourself,' Jay told him.

Sergey continued to talk between mouthfuls. 'The most important intelligence I have received is regarding Camp Fourteen. Apparently your uncle visited Pavel Gubin there two days ago. We think he might be heading north to visit with Arkady Kashitsyn, but the camp commander says he hasn't heard anything, so we're not sure.'

Jay digested this information. 'Anna said that, when she saw him last month, Duncan had no idea that Arkady and Pavel were in jail. I think he's trying to gather evidence of their innocence – either to free them or get Koslov put away.'

'Who do you have up there you can trust?' Blake asked Sergey. 'To let us know should he turn up?'

'Nobody.'

'Then we use nobody, OK?'

'OK,' Sergey agreed.

Blake gave an approving nod. 'What if I go to Camp 102 and do a recce? See if Duncan's due . . . I'd like to talk with Arkady as well. Maybe Jay could visit Pavel Gubin and see what he and Duncan talked about, and where he might have gone next.'

Sergey frowned, thinking. Then he said, 'Between Pavel and Alexa Gubin we might get the bastard. If they both testify that it was Koslov's men who threw acid in her face, we could have him behind bars by Monday afternoon.' He tossed back another shot of vodka, nodding to himself with a satisfied expression.

Jay headed for the hotel lift doubting it would be as simple as that, and in the morning she was proved right.

At five thirty a.m. Pavel Gubin's body was found by one of the camp guards. His throat had been cut.

Twenty-One

'We've got to get to Arkady before someone else does,' Blake said. They were in a canteen down the street – Blake was paranoid about people listening to their conversation in the hotel – and the air was already thick with cigarette smoke. He was sipping coffee, unshaven but alert, unlike Jay, who was still blinking sleep from her eyes despite the late hour of nine a.m.

'How do we know Arkady's still alive?' Jay asked.

'Because I spoke with the camp commander half an hour ago.'

Her eyes felt gritty and sore. Jet-lagged and overtired, she'd slept badly, troubled by dreams of Vasily her torturer and Alexa's ruined face.

Blake unfolded a map between them. 'Zigansk,' he said and pointed. She leaned across the table to see the nearest town to Camp 102 was on the west side of the Lena River and, as Sasha had said, just north of the Arctic Circle. Zigansk was plumb in the middle of one of the harshest regions on earth, where the area was frozen solid for seven months of winter. They had sent Arkady to the end of the world.

She said, 'Koslov is doing his best to prevent Duncan gathering a case against him.'

Blake gave a nod. 'Yup.'

'Do you think Arkady Kashitsyn's safe?'

'I think we should go and find out.'

Jay looked at Blake's hands, the starbursts of scars on his knuckles like a prize fighter might have. She wondered if they'd feel ridged, like her own, and she had to swallow the urge to stroke them and find out. 'I thought Sergey didn't want us going to any camps.'

'He doesn't.'

'Why?'

'It's out of his jurisdiction and therefore less containable.'

She studied the way his mouth was narrowed. He knew more than he was telling. 'Max,' she said. 'I'll ask the question again. Why?'

He studied her, considering. Then he said, 'I'm worried he's going to get to Arkady first. Maybe silence him permanently.'

She stared. 'You think he's on Nikolai's payroll?'

'Someone on his team is. Otherwise Pavel would still be alive.'

Jay pushed a lock of hair off her forehead before turning her attention to the map. 'Zigansk is a long way.'

'Three and a half days. But we'll take a helicopter. Prevailing intelligence tells us Duncan is headed to Arkady. He won't know of Pavel's death . . . He's on his way up there, I'm sure of it.'

Jay mulled over everything she knew. Her instincts were telling her not to leave Sinsk in case Duncan turned up. His allies were here: Sasha and Alexa. She was convinced that if he popped up anywhere it would be in town.

'Why don't you go up to Zigansk and I stay here?'

'I need you, Jay, to talk Duncan in. I won't stand a chance without you.'

Jay looked outside at a Lada sedan disgorging two burly men in overalls. She didn't say anything as Blake cracked his knuckles and continued, saying, 'He'll be much easier to find in a small place like Zigansk. Strangers are a rarity. He'll also be much more vulnerable.'

She finally looked at him straight. 'You want Duncan badly, don't you?'

Blake glanced aside. 'I need as much intelligence on Koslov as I can get, and since he and Arkady appear to be a mine of information . . .'

'Isn't it thirteen years out of date?'

He looked at her like he might a particularly dense student. 'The people they knew back then may well now be at the top of the pole. This is bigger than you and Duncan, Jay. It's about international security. I have the backing of not just the British government but . . . I can't say any more. Let your imagination fill in the blanks.'

Her mind skittered but she remained silent.

Blake was still watching her. He said, 'Will you help us?'

So, it wasn't just Blake any more but 'us'. She wondered how much Blake had manipulated her into coming and recognized that, although he was attracted to her, his prime objective was to fulfil his mission: find Duncan so her uncle could help MI5 shut Koslov and his uranium dealings with Iran down.

She let a silence gather.

He said, 'I'll ask Sasha and Alexa to contact us should Duncan turn up, OK?'

Jay sighed at the realization he wasn't giving her much choice. 'Is it OK if I duck into town and get some supplies, just in case?'

His eyes gleamed. 'Only if they involve satin underwear.'

Jay walked into town. She was heading to the supermarket for chocolate bars, packets of nuts and seeds, anything high energy to keep them going should the chopper dump them in the middle of nowhere; Russia's aviation fleet was notoriously unreliable and she had no intention of being without some basic provisions.

She dawdled past the lofty statue of the saviour of Sinsk, surreptitiously sticking two fingers up at it. *Bastard*, she thought, *for trying to destroy so many lives in the name of your seemingly never-ending avarice.*

'Caught you.'

Blake stood behind her, grinning. She put her hand on her chest. 'Jesus, Max. You just about gave me a heart attack.'

'You going to the supermarket?'

'Yup.'

'I might join you. See if they've some local honey.'

'You think they have bees out here?' she wondered. 'I haven't seen any flowers.'

'Where there's any plant life, there's honey,' Blake said. 'Look at the Scots and all that heather. The Kiwis and their jelly bushes.'

'You're saying we might find some pine honey? That the bees have been feeding on *taiga*?'

They entered the supermarket, and, while Blake headed left for groceries, Jay turned right to see what fresh produce – if any – was available. She'd checked out the deli – lots of cold mutton and lamb – and was scanning the piles of potatoes and apples, a few wrinkled pears, when a man walked around the end of the aisle. He was holding hands with a little girl of around four years old. A wire shopping basket was hooked over his other arm.

Jay felt as though she'd been dropped down a mine shaft. Her stomach swooped, her head went light. For a moment she thought she might faint.

'What's wrong?' Blake appeared at her side. He was holding her elbow. Distantly, she noticed he had a jar of honey in his other hand.

'It's him,' she said. Her voice was barely audible. From head to toe, she started to shake.

'Who?'

She couldn't take her eyes off the man. The way he was chatting to the child, smiling. She'd never seen him smile. He looked so *normal*.

'Jay?' Blake prompted.

'It's Vasily.' She could barely get the words out. 'The man who tortured me.'

'The guy with the kid?'

'Yes.'

'You're sure?'

'I swear my life on it.'

Blake manoeuvred her out of the fresh produce department and into the next aisle. Putting his jar of honey on one of the shelves, he said, 'Wait here.'

The second he disappeared her legs softened and she sank to the floor.

She stared at a shelf of bags of flour and sugar, unable to process any thought except the memory of hour-upon-hour of pain and terror. She was shivering and felt sick.

The next thing she knew, Blake was hauling her upright. 'You've got to dig deep, hon,' he said. 'Keep strong for me. Think you can do that?'

'Yes,' she said.

She realized the little girl was standing beside them. 'You look after each other, OK?' He spoke in Russian. 'I'll be back before you know it.'

And he was gone.

Jay looked at the girl who looked back. Her mouth was trembling and tears were beginning to form.

'Hello sweetheart,' Jay said, also in Russian. Her voice was croaky so she swallowed several times to clear it. 'My name's Jay. What's yours?'

For a moment she wondered if the girl would answer, but then she said, 'Rosa.'

'Hello, Rosa.' Jay tried a smile – and, although it felt stiff and wooden and filled with fear, Rosa gave a tentative smile back.

'I was shopping for ice cream,' Jay said. 'Do you know where it might be? I'd love some help finding it. Maybe we could buy a couple of cones and taste them. What do you think?'

'You talk funny,' said Rosa.

'That's because I'm from out of town. What's your favourite ice cream? Mine's strawberry.'

'Chocolate.'

'Let's go find some, shall we?'

Once they'd bought their ice cream, Jay led Rosa outside. Although eating was the last thing on her mind, Jay forced herself to take a bite from each ice cream. 'Hmm,' she said. 'I think I like the strawberry one best.' She kept looking around, watching for Blake and Vasily, her nerves jumping, electrified every time the supermarket door opened, but it didn't take long before her body's defence system eased off and she began to calm. Adrenalin can only keep pumping for so long.

'Where's Daddy?' Rosa asked after a while.

'Was that the man with you in the supermarket?'

Rosa nodded.

'My friend's talking to him at the moment. He'll be back soon, don't you worry. They had an important business meeting. I'm here to look after you while they talk. Shall we go for a walk?'

Rosa's face crumpled.

'Bad idea, sorry.' Jay thought fast. 'How about we find your daddy's shopping basket and finish your shopping?'

Rosa instantly brightened.

Back in fresh produce, Jay spotted Vasily's wire shopping basket lying between a crate of dirt-crusted beetroot and another of carrots. She picked it up to see it contained bleach, two packets of rice, half a kilo of dried beef and another of fish, and a jar of gherkins.

'Mama wanted some sugar,' said Rosa.

'I know exactly where the sugar is.' Jay led the girl to the next aisle. 'Which kind of sugar?'

'Normal,' said Rosa.

Jay chucked a kilo of white sugar into the basket. 'Anything else?'

'Lemonade.'

They went around the supermarket in a haphazard way, Jay trying to keep Rosa happy while Blake was doing God-knew-what with the girl's father. After another half an hour had passed, the wire basket was full and Jay was wondering what to do next when Blake appeared. His eyes were flat and cold and when he took Rosa's hand in his, Jay said, 'Where are you taking her?'

'Don't you trust me?'

There was an infinitesimal pause where Jay was sure Blake could read her innermost thoughts, her doubts, her fears.

'Of course I do,' she said, but she wasn't sure if it was the truth or not.

'I'll see you at the hotel.' He looked down at Rosa. 'I'm going to take you to your Daddy now. OK?'

Rosa nodded.

Jay watched Blake walk to the rear of the supermarket, Rosa trotting at his side as trustingly as a Labrador puppy, and then he opened a door marked *Personnel Only* and disappeared.

Jay waited in the hotel bar, tormented with images of Vasily and little Rosa. She'd fantasized about meeting Vasily, stabbing him in the eye, shooting him at point blank range, extracting her revenge for the unspeakable horrors he'd inflicted, but she'd never thought of him as a family man with a daughter called Rosa.

She supposed most torturers had families. After all, even the most vicious had a father and a mother. It wasn't as though they'd decided to become torturers when they were at school, but something they probably fell into later in life. How did it happen? How did Vasily the family man live with his dual existence? Much as a soldier would, she guessed. By compartmentalizing. When he was in his white lab coat, flicking his finger against the ampoule, his face expressionless, his emotions had to be repressed. It was his job. And when he headed home at the end of his day he was bound to be looking forward to kissing his daughter goodnight before eating supper and putting his feet up.

Jay started when she felt a hand on her shoulder.

'Come with me.'

It was Blake. His stubble was dark, his eyes in shadow.

'Where?'

'Just come. You need to be there.'

'Is Rosa OK?'

'Rosa's fine. She's at home with her mother.'

She followed him outside. It was still warm and people were on the streets, drinking and talking.

'What about Vasily?'

'He wants to show you something.'

Blake bundled her inside an ancient Honda Civic that had two empty bottles of cheap red champagne in the passenger footwell and a women's bra dangling from the headrest.

Jay removed the bra, chucking it on to the rear seat. 'Whose car?' she asked.

'Don't ask.'

He drove to a building on the east side of town, not far from the air strip. Two-storey concrete, it was unremarkable and could have housed anything from accountants' offices to a brothel. No lights were on inside. It hunched beneath a cloudy sky as grim and gloomy as any gulag.

'Where are we?'

'Koslov's unofficial HQ.'

Blake hustled her to the rear of the building. Withdrawing a bunch of keys, he opened a door, snapped on a light. Jay saw the brick walls, the bare bulbs lined along the ceiling and stopped dead.

'I'm not going in there.'

'It's OK,' he told her. 'It's safe, I promise.'

'No way.'

Every nerve, every cell in her body was shrieking with alarm.

'Jay, you've got to do this.'

A scream began to build in her body as an image of Anna seared her vision. Anna cowering naked on a tiled floor with bruises all over her body.

Blake's voice was soft. 'Vasily has your answers. He's promised to tell you what happened.'

'No.'

'Here. Let me hold your hand.'

'No.'

He ignored her. She felt his fingers brush her wrist, and although her mind wanted to push him aside, reject him and run away as hard and fast as her legs could carry her, Jay's heart let him take her hand and hold it tight.

He began walking down the corridor. She walked half a pace behind him, aware she was using him as a human shield. She felt like Rosa might have done earlier in the day: uncertain, nervous, scared of what might happen.

When they came to some stairs she said, 'I can't go down.'

'You don't have to. We're staying on the same level.'

The corridor was carpeted, which somehow increased her dread. Blake pushed the door open at the end of the corridor and kept walking. He stopped at the end of the next corridor, in front of a whitewashed door and turned and looked at her.

'You ready for this?'

'No.'

'Good,' he said, and pushed open the door.

The second she stepped inside the tiled room she felt time slip, become nebulous, transparent. Oh, God. She knew this room. She knew every tile, every brick, every detail. Her throat closed as her mind's eye saw Anna, covered in bruises and bleeding from her mouth.

'How did I get the gun?' Jay asked Blake. Her voice rasped like rusty iron.

'He gave it to you,' a man said. It wasn't Blake, but Vasily. She could never forget his voice. It dogged her dreams, her nightmares. He was behind her but she didn't turn around. She didn't want to see him. Witness what Blake had done to him.

Vasily said, 'You took the gun.'

Jay saw herself standing over Anna with the Sig Sauer 9mm pistol. She heard it fire, saw Anna falling backwards, her legs kicking, blood pouring.

'Tell her,' Blake said.

'You were all over the place,' Vasily said. She heard him swallow and could hear that he had no saliva. His voice was dry, filled with fear. Like hers had been. 'You could barely hold the pistol . . .'

Jay could remember how heavy it had felt. Like a lump of lead. The effort to keep it above her knees had taken an enormous effort.

'Look behind you,' Blake said.

Jay didn't want to. She didn't know what she might see.

'Look,' he insisted. 'It's OK, I promise. You must look.'

Finally, Jay looked around. Instead of a wall behind her, she saw a gallery. A shooting gallery. There was a gun rack filled with rifles, another holding two shotguns. She saw a pile of paper targets, bullseyes and silhouettes, some ear muffs. Vasily lay in the corner. He was handcuffed to a metal ring in the wall. His face was sheet-white.

'Tell her,' commanded Blake.

'When Anna Vorontsove was shot,' Vasily said, 'it wasn't by you. Your gun was filled with blanks. It was one of Koslov's men who shot her, from the gallery. It wasn't you, I promise. He just wanted to mess with your mind.'

Jay stared at him, her mind unable to process what he was saying.

'You only took Koslov's gun because you wanted to shoot him. Shoot me.' Vasily's mouth twisted. 'But you were incapable because of the drugs. You could barely hold the thing.'

Jay turned away, her mind filled with Anna's groans, the stench of her bowels as she died, the way her arms spread wide, one leg twisted beneath her, tears streaking her face. The way she looked at Jay, holding her eyes, forgiving her.

Something deep inside her snapped and rage reared, burning, gathering heat until it was white hot.

Jay strode to Vasily and, drawing back her foot, lashed out as hard as she could. 'You had me believe I killed my friend! You fucking bastard!'

She lashed out again, relishing his groan as her boot connected with a rib, and she was about to kick him again – aiming at the side of his head for some serious damage – when she felt two steel armbands around her ribs and she was hauled aside.

'Get a grip.'

'He tortured me!' She was gasping, engorged with fury. 'Ruined my memories. Christ, Max! I nearly went crazy!'

'And Rosa's waiting for him at home.'

At the mention of Rosa she fell still. She looked at Vasily, the monster of her nightmares, and she saw he was around the same age as her, barely thirty. She'd made him older, bigger, more powerful, but she'd been kidding herself.

'OK,' she told Blake. 'I'm OK. You can put me down now. I'm in control. I swear.'

When he loosened his grip she went and stood over Vasily. 'Look at me,' she commanded.

He tried to meet her eyes but he was so scared, his eyes kept slipping aside. She remembered doing the same.

'Where's Anna's body?'

'We incinerated it. The hospital has an incinerator. For medical waste.'

She stared down at his bowed head, the balding patch on his crown.

'Get another job,' she told him.

He gave a jerky nod. Gulped.

'Preferably one that'll make your daughter proud.'

Twenty-Two

When Blake parked her outside her hotel room she didn't know whether she wanted to cry, pass out or get drunk. Or all three.

'You OK?' he asked. His shirt collar was askew, and he had a smear of what might have been blood on his cheekbone.

'Not really.'

There was a small silence.

'You want me to come inside?'

'Yes,' she said. Then, 'No.'

'OK,' he said. 'How about we settle you in and then see how you feel?'

Taking her hotel key – on a brass orb the size of her knuckle – he opened her door and walked inside, turning on the bedside lights, the one in the bathroom, pulling closed the curtains. With the TV on low, the bedspread drawn back, the room looked as normal as a hotel room could but she still felt confused – deeply vulnerable and scared and angry.

Blake stood in the centre of the room, not too close to the bed, but not too close to the door either. He'd picked the most neutral spot he could have, she realized.

'You want me to stay the night?' His tone was careful. 'If I touch you, you deck me, am I right? So I'll take the chair in the corner. Or the floor. But if you want me to stay, I will.'

She nibbled her lower lip, unsure, her emotions wild, her mind flashing over Vasily and Rosa, the ampoules of yellow liquid and the blissful, heavenly dribbles of water Rosa's father had squeezed into her mouth.

'OK.' Her voice was small.

'OK,' he repeated. 'You want to use the bathroom?'

'OK.'

She went inside and ran the shower. As she pushed her hand under the tap she saw herself kicking Vasily, lashing out at him, wanting to hurt him as much as he'd hurt her. Hate filled her, white hot, racing from the soles of her feet into her heart and then Rosa was there, standing at her side and looking up, clutching her chocolate ice cream and smiling shyly.

'Rosa,' she said. She wanted to say something to the little girl but she didn't know how to form the words. The heat of hate abruptly turned ice cold. She was so cold, bone cold, that she was shaking, so she turned the tap to hot and kneeled beneath the spray. She didn't realize she was still dressed.

She closed her eyes, wishing the water would wash away her feelings, the emotions clawing at her mind and heart, wishing it would heat her from inside to out, but it wasn't hot enough so she rose to turn up the temperature but someone said, 'Don't,' so she sank back down and buried her head in her hands, letting the water pound her head and neck, hoping it would rinse her spirit clean . . .

She was only half aware that someone was peeling her sodden clothes from her body. The shower was still running and, as she raised her second foot to shake free her soaked combats, she took comfort from the hot beat of water, the steam rising.

She said, 'Am I clean yet?'

'Yes, you're clean.'

She felt someone wrap her in a towel, pat her dry and, taking her hand, lead her out of the bathroom. She didn't see the bed, or the lights turned down low. She simply tumbled into a vortex that felt like cool milk against her naked skin and that was all.

Jay awoke, her mind clear, her senses sharp, but she didn't move. It wasn't dark but it wasn't light either, and she guessed the sun was starting to rise by the warm tinge to the edges of the room. She began assimilating her surroundings, checking through what she remembered, testing what was real and what was imagined.

Someone on Sergey's team, if not Sergey himself, was working for Koslov. Koslov had a tiled killing room cum shooting gallery. She hadn't murdered Anna, but Koslov had orchestrated it so she thought she had. Vasily and Rosa, torturer and his sweet, lovely daughter. Max Blake. Who was lying on top of the bedcovers with his arm looped over her hip and breathing gently, rhythmically against her ear, fast asleep.

She glanced at the bedside table but the digital alarm clock wasn't working. They were in Russia where things weren't always dependable, how could she forget? Carefully, not wanting to disturb Blake, she reached out for her army wristwatch resting on the table. The luminous dial was faint, but she could just make out the time. Five ten a.m.

'Mmm,' Blake murmured. His grip tightened as she tried to slip out of bed.

'Max,' she whispered. 'Let me go.'

'No.'

'I need the bathroom.'

He raised his arm so she could wriggle free. 'Coming back?' he mumbled.

'Sure,' she lied.

Wide awake, Jay brushed her teeth and got dressed in the bathroom. Her combats and T-shirt were hanging neatly over the shower rail, still damp, so she dragged on jeans and a stretchy vest before going to grab her wristwatch from the bedside table. Blake was lying with his arms behind his head, watching her. He wore no shirt, just his jeans, and she tried not to look at his torso, finely muscled, or the dusting of fine, dark hairs across his chest.

'I need breakfast,' she told him. 'I'm going to see what's open. Maybe there's a worker's cafe near the railway station.'

'Give me a minute and I'll join you.'

'I'll wait outside.'

Blake emerged looking bright-eyed and rested.

'Thank you –' she gestured vaguely at the hotel room – 'for last night.'

'You needed company.' He sounded matter of fact.

'And, er . . . thank you for not . . .' she trailed off, embarrassed. The man had undressed her, for goodness sake, before patting her dry and tucking her – naked – into bed.

'For not taking advantage of you in your vulnerable state?' His eyes began to sparkle.

'Yes.'

'Hon, when we get it together, I want you with me one hundred per cent, all faculties intact, OK?'

Jay thought it wisest not to answer him.

After breakfast, Jay returned to her hotel room and called Tom.

'What's new?' she said.

'You get my message?'

'The service has been down since I got here. Anything important?'

'I had a hot dream about you last night.'

She didn't know how to answer that, with Blake looming so large in her life, so she said, 'How's Sofie?'

'Fine, thanks. How's Blake?'

'He's fine too.'

'I'm going to try and look on the bright side of all this,' he said. 'At least I know the man's capable of protecting you.'

She decided it was time to change the subject. 'How's Warehouse Man?'

'We've tied his death to five other cases from London to Manchester.'

She was disbelieving. 'Serial killer dogs?'

'It's going to make a great Lassie movie.' She heard the dry humour in his voice, but it didn't bother her. Sometimes it was the only way to cope with horrific events; the Marines and SAS were renowned for their morbid jokes.

He said, 'How's it going your end?'

'Mixed.'

She was glad he didn't ask any more questions she'd have to avoid answering. She didn't trust the hotel room phone not to be tapped.

'Watch your back,' he added. 'Because I quite like you. Sometimes.'

'I quite like you too. Sometimes.'

Jay woke up, disorientated, to hear someone knocking on the door. It was four p.m. She couldn't believe she'd slept away the day. After speaking to Tom she'd lain on the bed thinking she'd have a brief rest before tracking down Sergey for an update, and she'd gone out like a light.

Scrambling up, she called, 'Who is it?'

'Me.'

She opened the door to see Blake. His eyes went to her hair. 'Nice nap?'

'Yes, thanks.'

'Fancy a drink? The bar does coffee as well as beer.'

'Sure. I'll see you down there.'

After dashing her face with cold water and dragging a brush through her hair, she joined Blake in the hotel bar – a tiled, echoing space reminiscent of a public toilet.

Blake was on vodka. She decided to join him.

He said, 'Chopper's ready to go six a.m. tomorrow, OK?'

'OK.'

She looked away, and she was wondering if she'd ever get over her fear of flying when a man she'd never met before shambled across the room and sat down next to her. He was unkempt and unshaven and reeked of old sweat, unwashed clothes and alcohol. She almost gagged as his odour filled her lungs, but as she made to move seats he said, 'Don't. I have a message.' He spoke in an undertone.

Jay sank back. 'Who from?'

'Sasha. She says she has a friend she wants you two to meet.' He rattled off directions. 'You must come alone. No police, no FSB. She has something important for you. She said to give you a password so you know she is genuine. A horse's name. Chomp.' A look of concern crossed his face. 'Is that right? Chomp?'

Jay stared, almost unable to believe her ears. 'Yes, that's right.'

'OK.' The man looked relieved. 'I go now.' Grabbing their bottle of vodka, he stumbled back outside.

'Wow,' she said. Her voice was hoarse. 'If he's undercover, he's pretty good.'

'I'll say,' Blake agreed. 'What's Chomp?'

'You have ears like a bat,' she told him.

'So they say.'

'Chomp is a grey Shetland pony of Duncan's. His real name is Maestro, but he's nicknamed Chomp because he bites.'

There was a small pause as he digested this. He said, 'So, Sasha knows where Duncan is.'

'Sounds like it.'

Jay thought it interesting that neither of them were galloping on to the street to Duncan's rescue.

'What was the address?' Blake asked. 'I only heard the first part, something about Shanghai.'

'Shanghai Town. It's named after the Chinese population that used to live here years ago. At least that's what he said. Do you think it's a trap?'

'We'll take precautions.' He got to his feet. 'Ready to go?'

'You bet.'

Jay followed Blake outside. They walked past the hospital and sports ground, along the main street, pretending to look at the shops. Beyond the railway station she could see a random conglomeration of shacks and huts that she guessed was Shanghai Town, but before they got any closer Blake suggested they do some dry-cleaning to make sure they weren't being followed. After Jay had swept through the supermarket and around a small clothing store, she paused on the pavement before readying herself to stalk through the hotel opposite – the rat infested dump Blake refused to contemplate. Pedestrians were backed up on each side of the road, waiting to cross, and Jay looked right, waiting for the traffic to clear. She saw a couple of army jeeps escorting a gleaming black Mercedes and, as it swept passed, she glanced in the back.

It was only a glimpse of him, but she couldn't mistake the mop of shaggy fair hair, the boyish face and casual air, the thick cigar clamped between his lips.

For a second horror flooded her in case Koslov might see her, but the Mercedes was already past, vanishing around the corner behind a branch of Gosbank.

A robust woman with a handbag the size of a car bumped into her from behind, cursing, and she realized everyone was crossing the road. She hurried to keep up. *Concentrate*, she told herself. *You're dry-cleaning. You can tell Blake you saw Koslov in a minute.* After she'd swept through the Hotel Sokol, and a grotty guest house that smelled of urine, Blake declared them clean.

'I saw Koslov,' she told him when they proceeded east, as Sasha had instructed. The thought of going to Zigansk suddenly appeared extremely attractive.

'In the escorted Merc?'

'Yes.'

'The sooner we get your uncle,' he said, 'the sooner we can get out of here.'

After crossing the railway line, they entered the shanty town, a jumble of homes made of old boards and packing crates. There were no house numbers, no way of knowing which alley was which in the seemingly endless rabbit warren. After a while, Blake stopped at one of the shacks and asked for Sasha. One of the men inside directed them to another jumble nearby, and eventually they found the policewoman. Off duty and out of uniform, she was sitting on a stool drinking tea with a friend in a tumbledown hut that consisted of a single room containing two beds and a chair. An upturned crate served as a table.

Sasha's eyes lit up when she saw them. 'You made it!' Then her expression sobered. 'Were you followed?'

'Yes,' Blake replied.

Jay blinked. She hadn't seen anybody.

'But we shook him off at the Hotel Sokol,' Blake added. 'We're alone.'

'That's good.' She turned to her friend, a plump woman wearing a dress the colour of faded marigolds. 'Rozalina, quick, go and fetch him. Tell him his niece is here.'

Part of Jay was reserving judgement, unable to believe it was going to be so simple, but then Duncan stepped inside. For a second, she didn't recognize him. Not only was he filthy and sporting a thick beard, but he'd also lost a lot of weight. His clothes hung off him.

Then she took in the breadth of his shoulders, the slight roll of his body as he limped into the shack, and then he looked straight at her. His eyes were the same deep brown, and gentle. He was staring at her as though he couldn't believe what he was seeing.

'Duncan,' she said. Her throat closed.

'My God,' he rasped. 'It really is you.'

He stepped forward to take her in his arms, hug her, but she drew back, looking him straight in the eyes. 'You're OK?' she said.

'A bit tired. But yes, I'm OK.'

She stared at him for a handful of seconds. Then she said, 'What the hell's going on?'

He said, 'Jay . . .'

A rush of emotion flooded every vein, every corpuscle. She felt the blood rush to her face. 'How dare you leave Elizabeth and the girls like that?'

'Jay, I'm sorry, but . . .'

She had no saliva in her mouth.

Emotion and heat.

'They've been going insane! Do you have any idea what they've gone through? Or Cora and Fitz? They've cried themselves to sleep every night since you buggered off without a word. They can't eat, can't get on with their lives.' She stepped close, her hands clenching and unclenching. Her voice dropped low. 'And what about me?'

'Jay . . .'

She felt as if the ground beneath her feet was boiling. Underneath her flowed a river of red-hot lava which was filling her up with fire.

'Thanks to you, I've been kidnapped, drugged and tortured. I've lost almost five days of my life and thought at one point I was losing my mind. I had to see a goddamn shrink because you were too fucking selfish to explain to anyone what the *fuck* was going on!'

'Jay . . .'

At that point, Jay slapped him.

Silence fell. Nobody moved.

'I hate you,' she said. Tears began to fill her eyes and she dashed them away. 'I hate you for what you've done to me. What you've put your family through . . . I hate you.'

Twenty-Three

Duncan stood there, his cheek stinging from Jay's slap. He didn't think he'd ever felt so useless or so stupid. How he thought he'd get away with travelling out here without causing a storm he couldn't think. Jay was right, he was selfish, but only because he wanted to protect them. The fact they had no idea of his past kept them safe from Nikolai.

He could barely believe Jay was here, his niece and one of the most courageous and loyal people he knew. Not that she saw herself like that, and nor did she see how very precious she was, how very lovable. She was still lecturing him, pale with anger, and Duncan felt he ought to say something in his defence, but what words could he use? He stood there clutching hope to his heart, praying she'd find it in herself to forgive him.

He'd known the family would call on Jay to find him, not so much because she worked for TRACE but because she cared. She'd do her hardest to track him down and find answers as to why he'd taken off, and look where it had brought her. Six thousand miles from home, to one of the most remote regions of the world.

'Jay . . .' he tried again.

And then silence fell, smothering him.

'What?' Jay said. Her hands were on her hips, her hair almost snapping with rage.

He glanced at her companion, a lean, unsmiling man with dark hair and cautious eyes, and Jay made a curt gesture towards him. 'Whatever you say you can say in front of Blake.'

Duncan was glad Sasha and Rozalina had withdrawn. He didn't want an audience. If Jay trusted Blake, then he would take a leap of faith and trust him too.

'Duncan?' Jay prompted.

He spread his hands. 'I'm sorry,' he said lamely.

For a moment she looked as though she was going to slap him again, but instead she moved to the other side of the shack and turned her back.

He tried again. 'I disappeared the way I did on purpose. To protect Elizabeth and the family—'

'From Koslov, I assume?' She spoke over her shoulder.

He took a breath. 'How much do you know?'

'Not enough.' Finally, she turned to face him. 'For example, why did you abandon your godson, Justin? Crispin has never forgiven you, you know. He hates Trent Newton. Loathes him.'

He felt the shock of it against his heart that she knew his real name. Did Elizabeth know?

Jay had turned around and was staring at him, drilling his soul with her syrup-coloured eyes. 'Why did you set up that trust for Justin?'

He worked his mouth, forced the word out. 'Guilt.'

Uttering that one syllable took all his strength and he slumped on to one of the wooden chairs and buried his face in his hands. The old emotional wound had been ripped open and was seeping blood. In a rush he said, 'I was a coward. I took the easy option and ran away . . .'

'The day Magnus Parnell died.'

He managed to nod.

'Tell me, Duncan. Tell me what happened, so I can understand.'

'OK.' He stared at the ground as he started to speak. Whenever he thought of his godson, he thought of the racing stables, the smell of horses and manure, straw, the steady warmth of the kitchen with the Aga burning all year, drying out horse blankets, dog towels, Barbours, wellies . . . He could almost taste the sweet heat of sloe gin sliding down his throat on a winter's evening, the sound of Magnus's laugh. Magnus had been their trainer for twelve years, a friend for ten, when, to his surprise, Magnus had asked him to be Justin's godfather. Justin was eighteen, Crispin twenty-five, and apparently neither of them had been christened, but, thanks to his new girlfriend, Justin had found religion.

Magnus was half-amused but mostly sceptical. 'At least I can trust you not to fan the flames of Christian fanaticism,' he'd told Duncan. 'You're the least churchgoing man I know.'

It wasn't the best reason to become godfather, but he'd still been immeasurably proud and had got quite choked up at the little village church witnessing the manly form of Justin bowing his head for the sprinkle of water at the font.

Those days had been heady, intoxicating, and as he gazed at the walnut-coloured, earth-packed floor, a part of him found it hard to believe they had been real: standing by his first Derby winner, slimed with horse sweat up to his armpit but ecstatic and laughing with Nikolai; sprawled in the back of a chauffeur-driven limo, watching Nikolai tuck a fifty-pound note into a call girl's G-string; flying Concorde to New York for a weekend of Christmas shopping; Nikolai splitting his sides watching his first attempt at ice skating on the outdoor rink in Vienna; sharing a private jet with Nikolai to Paris for lunch, another to Cannes, Rome, Berlin.

Duncan was no longer seeing the shack or Jay or the wary-eyed Blake.

He was seeing Nikolai, his eyes creased in laughter, his fair hair always ragged and in need of cutting, the humour in his eyes always disarming, always charming.

And then he was walking past Nikolai's secretary, with a plaster cast from her wrist to her shoulder and fear in her eyes, refusing to acknowledge his suspicions. He was stubbornly refusing to listen to Anatoloy that Nikolai had blocked the roads around Sinsk and virtually stolen the giant Russian mining group, PMK, from the Russian people, and that Arkady was going after him. He was in the darkened chasm of his worst memories where the walls were drenched with blood and violence. He'd thought he was innocent because he'd never punched anyone, never pulled a trigger, but he was wrong. He was guilty by default.

His soul shivered as the years poured away.

He wasn't Duncan back then. He was Trent Newton, and he'd just turned thirty-seven. He was bounding across the cobbled yard, snuffing the scent of hay and country air, as happy as a boy at the start of the summer holidays. TGIF, he'd been thinking. Thank God It's Friday. He deserved a break after a heavy week, but he couldn't complain, not with an Aston Martin parked in the driveway, an apartment in Canary Wharf, a four-storey home in Chelsea, another on the outskirts of Bath, an unlimited expense account, endless credit, and a weekend stretching ahead with his favourite people engrossed in his favourite pursuit: horse racing.

Nikolai's Ferrari was here, but he couldn't see him anywhere, so he headed for Magnus's kitchen. The TV was on as it always was in the corner, tuned to racing wherever in the world – tonight it was Kentucky – and the dogs were padding around, tails waving. The smell of horse and leather balm permeated the air. A bottle of champagne stood open on the table – two thirds full – and Duncan poured himself a glass, took a swig.

He'd already rehearsed what to say to Nikolai on the way down. Something along the lines of a weather forecast might amuse him. *Fair to good. A little stormy in the east, but it shouldn't affect us if we hold our nerve.* He'd learned never to give Nikolai details of the financial markets. Nikolai liked broad brush strokes, to get the mood, the atmospheric pressure of what was happening around the world. Nikolai had likened Duncan – Trent as he was then – to a barometer.

'You have an uncanny sense for when things are going to change,' he once said. 'I tap you and the needle swings just so. Always in my favour.'

He wasn't going to bring up Arkady's call until after the weekend, when Nikolai was relaxed and hopefully feeling expansive after watching his horses win. The Sinsk policeman had rung first thing, almost hysterical, imparting a wild tale about the PMK deal that Nikolai had completed last week and saying that the auction for the giant mining group had been rigged. According to Arkady, the opposing bidder – Pavel Gubin, owner of MirKap – had put in the highest offer, but it had been rejected in favour of Nikolai's, nobody knew why.

Arkady had wanted Duncan to check the legality of the deal his end, go through Nikolai's contract, the paperwork, and it was only because he liked Arkady that he'd agreed. He was sure there was some mistake, and had assured the policeman he'd call him back on Monday with an explanation, but when Arkady had launched into another wild story over PMK's shipping documents – something about a couple of canisters of weapons-grade uranium – Duncan had finally had enough and had hung up.

He poured a second glass of champagne, enjoying the hit of alcohol, the way it began to unwind the stress of the week. He kept glancing around, expecting Magnus or Nikolai to arrive at any moment, and when nobody appeared he took his glass to the yard. He looked over Zhivost, a speedy bay mare that had done them quite well this season, and then Slava, a big, black gelding with a mean eye that hadn't. Both he and Nikolai had lost more than a few thousand on him at Newmarket. 'Fame and glory, like hell,' Nikolai had remarked on the gelding's name. 'I'm tempted to send him to the knackers. Turn him into Pedigree Chum.'

Duncan was humming happily, halfway across the yard when he heard a man shouting. To his shock, he recognized Magnus's voice. Shoving his glass aside – he couldn't remember where – he ran for the loose boxes at the far end where the shouts came from.

'You fucking bastard!'

Magnus's voice cracked from the force of his shouts. Wary, unsure about interrupting a major row – perhaps Magnus was bawling out one of his stable boys? – Duncan slowed as he approached the corner of a stone building, a loose box that overlooked another, smaller yard.

'You crippled him!' Magnus yelled. 'You crippled my boy!'

'I told you I would.' Nikolai's voice was calm. 'You were scamming me, remember? Inflating your fees, expenses, vet bills, everything in-between. I asked you to stop. And I told you that if you didn't I would smash Justin's legs.'

'I stopped, I swear I stopped!'

'No, you didn't. You preferred to think I was stupid. You thought a few thousand here and there wouldn't be noticed . . . You honestly believe I'm that brain-dead that I can't see when I'm being ripped off?'

'But he'll never walk!'

'Don't blame me,' said Nikolai. 'Blame yourself. I warned you.'

Duncan crept to the edge of the stable. Peered around the corner. Magnus stood in front of Nikolai, a shotgun wavering, half pointed at Nikolai's groin. Behind Magnus, creeping up on him, as silent as a cat on soft-soled shoes, was a broad, hard-looking man. Mickey Ragulin. Duncan's breath jammed in his throat. Mickey was Koslov's bodyguard. He held a cosh in his right hand.

'I'll kill you.' Magnus's voice dropped. 'I'll fucking kill you for destroying my son's life, for being such a fucking BASTARD!' His voice rose and, as he raised the shotgun, Mickey broke into a run.

Duncan stood riveted, a silent shout lodged in his throat.

It happened fast.

Nikolai spun aside, sprinting to his left. The shotgun followed. There was a blast as it fired but Nikolai didn't pause, didn't fall. Magnus took aim again and that was when Mickey hit him full force from behind. The shotgun flew to one side and discharged fruitlessly against a wall.

Duncan could hear horses skittering around the yard, hooves clattering through straw and on to stone. One or two whinnied, but quickly fell silent.

Mickey was on top of Magnus. He had him in a headlock. Duncan could hear Mickey panting and see the strange tattoos on his neck, on the backs of his hands.

Nikolai walked across. He brought back his foot and kicked Magnus in the ribs. 'You fuck,' he said. 'You think you can kill me? You're nothing but a useless piece of shit. You couldn't shoot fish in a fucking barrel.'

He went and picked up the shotgun. Broke it and checked the barrels. Clicking his fingers at Mickey he said, 'Find me a cartridge. Search his pockets.'

Duncan felt sweat trickling down his flanks, across his shoulders. He didn't know what to do. He ought to call the police. Do something . . . He began to inch backwards when his foot caught on a stone.

Instantly Nikolai stiffened. 'What was that?'

Mickey turned his head. 'I didn't hear anything.'

'Keep quiet,' Nikolai commanded. 'Someone's there.'

Duncan held his breath, locked in a motionless tableau. He was aware of nothing but his trembling muscles, straining to remain still, and sweat pouring.

Finally, Nikolai said, 'OK, let's do him.'

Immediately Magnus started to buck, but Mickey held him fast. He had at least sixty pounds on the trainer and Magnus made little progress. Nikolai bent over and fished through Magnus's pockets, brought out a handful of cartridges, broke the shotgun and loaded it, snapped it shut.

'Open wide,' he told Magnus.

Duncan's throat bubbled into a whimper, but he swallowed it. He didn't dare make a sound for fear of giving himself away. A mantra ran through his head: *no-no-no*.

Magnus continued to struggle, making it difficult for Nikolai to shove the barrel in his mouth.

'Shit.' Nikolai stood back. 'Knock him out or something. Stun him.'

Mickey let loose a right hook that snapped Magnus's head back. The trainer's eyes rolled and his body slumped. After that, things happened fast. Mickey grabbed Magnus by the hair and held him steady while Nikolai jammed the barrel into his mouth.

'Got to keep it low, like he's done it himself.' He positioned the gun between Magnus's knees. 'Stand back.'

Mickey stood to one side, holding Magnus's head by his hair, and then Nikolai pulled the trigger. The back half of Magnus's skull vanished in a spray of blood and brain matter, and, when Mickey released his grip, Magnus's body slumped to the ground with a soft thud.

Bewitched with horror, a distant part of Duncan's mind registered that they'd orchestrated their moves so easily, with such little fuss, that they had to have done this before.

'Let's tidy up,' Nikolai said.

As Mickey and Nikolai began to cover their tracks, making sure there were no extra cartridges to give the game away, no unpredicted finger-prints on the stock of the shotgun, Duncan crept away, heading for his car. Bathed in sweat, his heart thumped so loudly he was terrified Nikolai might hear it and come after him and blow out his brains too.

He fumbled with his keys, fingers trembling as he approached the Aston and beeped it open. He was about to open the door and slide inside when he heard somebody rushing behind him and he lunged for his car but it was too late.

Mickey grabbed his collar and dragged him backwards and let loose a punch against the side of his head that poleaxed him to his knees. Head dangling, ears ringing, he tried to get up but his legs wouldn't work.

'Got a problem?' It was Nikolai, standing over him.

'No,' he gasped.

'Going to the cops?'

'Never.'

'Mickey.' Nikolai turned to his bodyguard. 'If you could give him some-thing to remind him of his promise . . .'

Mickey stepped close. He was holding a baseball bat.

'No, please.' Duncan felt his stomach turn to liquid. 'I won't tell anyone, I swear . . .'

Mickey swung the bat and, with a single blow, smashed his knee into three pieces.

'They dropped me at a surgery in London,' he told Jay. She was squatting beside him. She was holding his hand. 'A tame doctor of theirs. Mickey drove my car back to my house. The doctor strapped me up, medicated me and called me a taxi. Nikolai fully expected me to limp into work on Monday, like all his other lackeys. I spent that night swallowing painkillers and getting as much together as I could. The next morning, five a.m., I vanished.'

He scrubbed his eyes with his hand. He didn't dare look at Jay. He couldn't bear to see her contempt. She wouldn't have run away. She would have faced Nikolai head on.

'Duncan,' she said. Her tone was soft. 'Look at me.'

He shook his head.

'Please.'

He was almost sweating with the effort to meet her gaze, but instead of derision there was only forgiveness. Which was, he realized with a flash of insight, worse than her contempt because it made him feel inadequate, unworthy. He suddenly felt like crying.

Twenty-Four

Jay spent the rest of the evening with Blake and Duncan, talking. At one point Rozalina came and cooked a stew of lamb and mushrooms, which they ate with boiled potatoes and glasses of beer.

When Blake told Duncan about Pavel's murder, Duncan didn't move for a while, just stared into space. Eventually, he said, 'We're in great danger now he knows you're looking for me. He can't afford to let me live. I know too much. I came here to find enough evidence to take to the FSB so they can prosecute Nikolai for fraud and throw him in jail. I want him to suffer, like he's made others suffer . . . but he's blocking me at every turn.'

Settled next to Duncan, Jay tried to work out how they could go forward together to fight Koslov. 'I think we're better off in the UK,' she said. 'We might get him for Magnus Parnell's murder. It's better than nothing.'

'*Might* being the operative word,' said Duncan gloomily. 'It's his word against mine.'

'What about the radioactive dust?'

'Circumstantial.' He spread his hands. 'It's why I came here, Jay. I hoped it would be easier to find something that would stick to him.'

'Maybe we can help,' said Blake. 'You run me through everything you know about the PMK deal, Koslov's past trades, and we'll see what we can use.'

Duncan studied Blake carefully. 'On one condition.'

Blake shifted forward in anticipation.

'I want you to get Arkady Kashitsyn out of jail.'

You could have heard a pin drop.

Blake said, 'Say again?'

'Koslov arranged for Pavel to be killed. He'll do the same with Arkady. I'll tell you everything I know, but only when Arkady's free.'

Blake and Duncan stared at one another. Jay knew how important fresh intelligence was to Blake's operation and wondered how far he'd go to get it. After half a minute or so, Blake said, 'OK. You answer every question I ask you right now, I'll consider it. Until then, no.'

Long silence while the two men continued to appraise one another, and, finally, Duncan dropped his gaze. He said, 'OK. Fire away.'

Blake began grilling Duncan about Nikolai's past financial affairs, the

British companies he owned. Although Duncan answered each one care-fully, his memory was rusty, and Jay could tell he was quickly getting tired.

'Alexa mentioned Arkady had begun investigating a rumour that Nikolai inherited some canisters of uranium from PMK,' Blake said. 'Do you know anything about it?'

'Only what Arkady told me. It's so long ago . . .' He rubbed his fore-head.

Jay propped her shoulders against the wall while Blake explained Nikolai's possible link to nuclear trade with Iran. He finished saying, 'Politically, the allegations against this British company hold potentially huge ramifications for diplomatic relations between the West and Tehran. If we can prove Nikolai – a Russian – is behind it all, it would take the pressure off.'

'And I thought you came to rescue me out of the goodness of your own heart.' Duncan gave a twisted smile.

Blake didn't say anything. Just waited.

'All I remember is our last conversation,' Duncan said. 'Arkady going nuts about the PMK deal being fraudulent . . . And then he started raving about uranium. In all honesty, I was barely listening. I thought he'd started to lose the plot. Arkady and Nikolai had had a bust up the previous year, and I thought it was Arkady's way of coping, to try and make his old friend sound like a criminal . . .'

'Can you remember anything of what he said?'

Duncan groaned and put his head in his hands. 'He was shouting at me. Really yelling. Something about shipping documents. That they were from the UK . . . I wanted to speak to him when he'd calmed down . . .' He slumped. 'I hung up on him.'

'Anything else?' Blake said, leaning back in a relaxed pose that belied the light in his eyes. 'Take your time. Don't rush.'

'You don't ask for much. It's been over a decade . . . Would you remember every little detail of such a conversation?'

'He probably would,' said Jay dryly. 'Every MI5 officer has to be born with a computer implanted in their brain or they're not admitted.' She smiled, teasing Blake, then rose and crossed the shack to fire up the Primus stove. She needed more coffee to keep awake. It was already past midnight. Picking up the gallon plastic container of water in the corner, she topped up the saucepan and put it on to boil.

'Good heavens, you're right.' She turned at the excitement in Duncan's voice to see he was sitting up straight, his expression enlivened. 'It was when Jay said MI5 . . . There was something. I remember now. He said he was sending them to England. The shipping documents. I can't remember if he said where or not. He was almost hysterical, ranting about government and intelligence services, MI5, and I was trying to calm him down . . .'

Blake didn't move a muscle, but Jay could sense he was quivering like a leopard about to launch on its prey. 'Perhaps you might have an idea where he might have sent them?' he asked neutrally.

Duncan scrunched up his face in concentration but finally shook his head. 'Sorry.'

'He didn't have any other friends in the UK?'

'Only me.'

'Hmm.' Blake fingered his chin. 'I'd quite like a chat with your friend Arkady.'

Duncan's face lit up. 'Does this mean you'll—'

Blake held up a hand. 'We'll see.' Bringing out his mobile phone he walked outside. He was gone for a good twenty minutes before he returned. He was frowning. 'Nobody likes it, least of all me, but let's talk it through. See if it's possible.'

Jay stared at him. Was he serious? They were going to spring a prisoner out of a Siberian gulag?

'You saw Camp Fourteen, Duncan,' Blake said. 'What was its security like?'

'Average.' Duncan took an audible breath. Jay could see the excitement on his face, the way he was trying to dampen it, remain calm in order to persuade them to save his friend. Digging in his pocket, he withdrew a packet of Polo mints and offered them around.

Jay chuckled. 'Only you could produce Polos at a time like this.'

'Never travel without them.'

Jay took two, popping one in her pocket for later before sucking on the other while she made coffee.

Duncan said, 'Most inmates don't bother trying to escape because they know their chances of survival outside are minimal. Because they can't rely on the generators a hundred per cent, they don't have electric fences. Just the dogs. They're the real deterrent. They're trained to kill.'

Jay passed around mugs as Duncan described the camp's defences, the barbed wire and dry moat, and wondered if all camps were the same. Part of her couldn't believe Blake was actually contemplating springing Arkady from jail. Would it be possible? How do you find one person in five thousand or so and spirit them away? Or was Blake thinking of something larger, like using the chopper? She couldn't picture it, not without Arkady knowing their plans. That's if he was still alive.

Blake put down his coffee and began to pace. She didn't think she'd seen him so animated. He said, 'I'll fly up there tomorrow and do a recce. If it looks good, I'll go in and talk to Arkady, prep him—'

'No,' Duncan interrupted. 'I'll do it.'

'They'll be waiting for you. They won't know what to do with me. I'll pretend I'm FSB. I've got the documents.'

'I can do that as well as you,' Duncan said. 'They won't know it's me either. Nobody knows what I look like.'

'Your limp.' Blake was brutal. 'It's a dead giveaway.'

'I don't care. I'm doing the recce. Arkady trusts me. Why should he trust you, a complete stranger?'

Jay didn't say a word. She had no intention of going into Camp 102 if she could help it. The inmates probably hadn't seen a woman in decades, and she might never get out.

Blake rolled his eyes to the ceiling. He looked as though he was counting to ten. Slowly. He said, 'No.'

Duncan got to his feet. 'This is my mess.' His voice was trembling. 'I will not have you meet Arkady when I can. If something happens, it should be me who suffers. And if Arkady is already dead, and it's nothing but a trap, then so be it. I will die. But I will not have you stick your neck out for my past mistakes. Agreed?'

Jay watched as the two men faced one another. She could see it was more than a battle of wills for Blake; he was evaluating and assessing every part of the plan from a different angle and trying to see if it would work.

Finally, Blake said, 'Agreed on one condition. That Jay says she'll forgive me should you get killed.'

'Thanks a lot.' She flung up her hands. 'Why do I get the final word?'

'You don't want Blake to die, do you?' Duncan said.

'I don't want you to die either.'

Duncan didn't say any more, he just looked at her with his round brown eyes, pleading.

'Oh, all right,' she conceded. 'I'll forgive Blake, but Elizabeth will never forgive me—'

Duncan held up both hands. 'Let's not go there or we'll never get to the end of it. I'm doing the recce and that's that.'

'Right,' Blake said. 'And after the recce you return with a report. I'm thinking a snatch and grab, using the chopper.'

It sounded the best idea, considering the dogs, Jay thought. She said, 'What about the guards? Their firepower? Won't they be able to bring the chopper down?'

'Not if you give us covering fire.'

'From the helicopter? Jesus, Max, I haven't been in a war zone for years, let alone fired a gun. I might not be able to shoot a barn at fifty paces.'

'Then I'll get you a nice, big machine gun that will have them diving for cover.'

Since he appeared perfectly serious she fell quiet, but her stomach was churning. She didn't want to do this. She'd found her uncle – her mission was complete – and to launch into a potentially life threatening situation, where Duncan might get killed along with her and Blake, wasn't high on her list of things to do this weekend. However, the soldier in her, who'd been trained to protect her country and stand shoulder-to-shoulder with her fellow soldiers against any enemy, couldn't be denied. She could no more allow Duncan and Blake go into Camp 102 alone than she could blowtorch her big toe.

At that point Sasha and Rozalina joined them. 'We miss much?' the policewoman asked.

Duncan said, 'Just the plan that we're going to spring Arkady from jail this weekend.'

Blake looked as though he'd swallowed a hairball. Jay knew he hated more than two people knowing a plan of attack, and now there were five. The scheme was peppered with pitfalls and risky as hell, but as Jay accompanied Blake back to their hotel she had a spring in her step.

Deep down, she realized, she was a bit of an adrenalin junkie.

The next morning was frantic, organizing kit. Blake sourced the weapons and ammunition from a hunting store on the other side of town, which included two Heckler & Koch machine guns, three handguns, a selection of hunting knives, a box of grenades, some tripwires, plastic explosive, drums of paint and several detonators. The only weapon he took with him was a sniper rifle and a box of ammo.

Jay stocked up on medical supplies, which were woefully inadequate. No sterile gauze pads, no antibiotics or morphine, no butterfly sutures, just loads of cotton wool, antiseptic and roller bandages. Next, she put together a survival pack for each of them: sleeping bag, high-energy bars, matches, torch, flint and compass.

At midday, Blake picked up Jay and drove her out of town before handing her the sniper rifle. It had a bolt action and an infrared, telescopic sight with a dead-accurate six-hundred-metre range. 'It's been a long time,' she said, automatically checking the chamber was empty. 'I can't guarantee I'll hit much.'

His mouth curved mockingly. 'I've seen the medal.'

Sometimes, she could throttle the girl squad. It had been Denise who'd put her biathlon disc on the mantelpiece one drunken evening, insisting it should be displayed at every opportunity. The name biathlon described any sporting event made up of two disciplines, most often involving cross-country skiing, but Jay's seven-point-five-kilometre sprint had consisted of running and shooting.

'It was only a bronze,' she said.

'Enough for the job in hand.'

Which was to lie hidden outside the camp and provide covering fire when the helicopter went in. Should a guard get too close, her job was to disable them. Blake had suggested shooting a couple of guards at the main gate as a diversion, but she'd baulked. 'I won't shoot anyone that isn't directly threatening you guys, OK?'

Blake looked as though he was about to argue, then relented. 'OK.'

She spent the next ten minutes sighting the rifle, firing at a finger of a branch first four, then five and six hundred metres away while Blake acted as spotter beside her, watching through a set of binoculars. Once she was satisfied it fired accurately, they returned to town.

Come one p.m. they were ready. Jay double-checked their kit while Blake arranged their weapons' delivery at a quiet spot he'd found well out of town, an open, grassy area that was flat and free of boulders. It was Sasha who drove them there. She was barely recognizable in a dress and shawl, a scarf over her head and sunglasses. When the policewoman saw their arms dealer was already waiting, she stopped a good five hundred yards away to let them out.

'Come back safe,' Sasha told them.

Blake was already climbing out of the car, Duncan too, but Jay leaned forward and squeezed the policewoman's shoulder. 'You've been fantastic.'

Sasha smiled and gripped her hand back. 'Anything to bring that bastard down.'

Jay stood with Duncan while Blake conducted the final transactions.

'You OK?' Duncan asked her.

'Nervous.'

'Really?' He was surprised. 'You don't look it.'

'I never do. You?'

'Petrified. I'm an accountant, remember?' He gave a weak smile. 'I'm not cut out for this kind of thing. I threw up my breakfast.'

'Good,' she said, 'because you'd only have lost it on that.' She gestured at the horizon, where what looked like a heavy, metallic beetle had just cleared a string of trees.

'You've got sharp eyes,' he said. He was squinting.

Within three minutes the Russian-built Hind had landed and Jay and Duncan joined Blake to load the aircraft. Jay felt a peculiar sense of *déjà vu* as she passed one of the machine guns to Blake, the sound it made – metal clanking – as familiar to her as the sound of her mother banging shut the oven door. *Click, clunk.* It reminded her of countless ops, the initial anxiety and fear gnawing at her guts until the action started and the training kicked in . . .

The pilot and co-pilot introduced themselves – Ivan and Valentin – the same guys who'd flown them from Irkutsk four days ago. When Ivan saw the machine guns, he gave an approving nod and gave Blake the thumbs up.

'What do they know about our mission?' Jay asked Blake.

'The fact that it's dangerous, and that they're getting paid a shitload of money.' He glanced at the pilots. 'They're both ex-forces, and neither of them can wait to be part of a jailbreak. Apparently, this is the most fun thing they've done in years.'

It didn't take long before they were ready. Jay took the seat next to Duncan and strapped herself in. As the rotors lifted into a clattering roar, the machine began to tremble, everything shaking and juddering in the sudden din. The runners were just about to lift when Blake glanced across.

He yelled, 'Duncan!'

Duncan looked across, startled.

'Hold her hand, will you? She hates flying!'

Although Jay was determined not to hold hands with Duncan, when the helicopter gave a violent swoop to the left a few minutes later – she was convinced it was going to drop out of the sky – she grabbed his wrist, a yelp lodged in her throat.

'I never knew you hated flying,' Duncan said. She could hear his voice clearly through the headphones Ivan had supplied. 'How on earth did you cope in the army?' He held her hand firmly in both his.

'I just got on with it.'

'Brave girl.' Reaching into his pack, he brought out a family-sized pack of Polos and gave her a roll. 'To keep you going, eh?'

The journey was noisy and mind-numbing. The monotony of the country-side was matched only by the monotony of the flight itself. There was nothing to do, no in-flight magazine or movie, and, after the first hour, conversation ran out. There was no air conditioning, and everyone felt hot and dusty. The doors weren't snug, and there were cracks in the metal along the floor. Jay stared at nothing but endless open space, mostly marsh-lands with rough hunks of grass; steppe rolling to far-off hills in every direction. Towns were almost non-existent, and those that did exist were all on a railroad line – shanties for the railroad crews, who maintained the links between north and south, east and west.

Their journey was the equivalent of flying from the south end of England to Scotland's northernmost tip, forcing them to refuel after three hours at an oil terminal the pilots knew. As the fuel was hand-pumped into the aircraft, Jay spent an hour sprawled on her front, half studying the maps Blake had bought of the area surrounding the camp. After drinking some mineral water and eating an energy bar, she took a nap, and then it was time to be airborne.

Before they landed at Zigansk, Blake got Ivan to fly over Camp 102. It wasn't precisely where they thought it was – some maps were still out of date from the Second World War, when they'd been altered to confuse the enemy – and they had to do several sweeps before it came into view. Ivan kept the helicopter moderately high, at a cruising speed, and didn't fly directly over the camp to try and avoid alerting the guards to the fact they were being studied.

'South-west corner,' Blake called out. 'What do you think?'

It looked like a parade ground. It had a platform at one end. There was just the one watchtower. Further west, and behind another fence of barbed wire, she saw maybe two or three hundred men enclosed in a broad, sandy space. Most were sitting down with their shirts off, some were in their underwear. All had their faces upturned, watching the aircraft.

'Looks good,' Jay called back. 'If we take out the watchtower on our way in, it might help.'

'My thoughts exactly.'

'Let's hope Arkady can get there.'

Then the camp was sliding out of view. They checked out a couple of potential landing sites not far from the camp, then the perfect vantage point for Jay and her rifle. Having confirmed their choices, Ivan pushed the throttle and they swept over a dark carpet of spruce trees, unbroken until they came to Zigansk. Ivan flew the helicopter over the town – a ramshackle collection of dwellings with satellite dishes and half a dozen gawping children – heading for the gravelled airstrip on the other side. Theirs was the only aircraft. As they approached, Jay spotted a man in overalls jump into an old army jeep and tear towards a fuel tank at the southern end of the runway. As Ivan gently set the helicopter beside the tank and switched off the engine, the jeep arrived.

While they refuelled, Jay joined Blake as he talked to the man. She felt torpid after being bounced and shaken in what felt like a giant blender for six hours. As usual, she was amazed that she'd arrived in one piece. The sun pounded down out of a clear sky, making her squint. She was glad she'd brought two crates of mineral water; they were all sweating buckets.

Blake asked the man whether they could hire a car.

'Sure,' the man said. Black, thick brows. Black stubble and coarse, black hair. He smelled of stale sweat and vodka. 'Hertz is on the main street, Avis opposite.'

Blake dutifully laughed and clapped the man on the shoulder. 'You have a good sense of humour, my friend.'

'You need it up here.' He glanced at the chopper then at his jeep. 'You can rent that from me, if you like.'

'How much?'

When they'd agreed a price, Blake asked where they could stay the night. The man thought for a bit, then he said, 'My place is comfortable. Me and the wife can stay with her cousin to make room. I'll get her to leave you some food.'

They all piled into a wood-built house that, as the man had said, was comfortable. There were two double beds, which the guys shared. Jay took the sofa.

The next morning, as Blake talked to Duncan, Jay chatted with Ivan and Valentin. She'd seen the photographs stuck around the helicopter's wind-screen – wives, friends and family, children – the postcards and odd letter, and it transpired they pretty much lived in their aircraft. They went where it was required, sometimes spending weeks away from their families, some-times having to sleep on board.

'It must be hard on your families,' she said.

Both men shrugged. 'At least we can send money home,' Valentin said.

Duncan came over. Blake was driving with him to the camp. While Duncan visited Arkady, Blake was going to wait outside. He hoped his pres-ence would prevent anything happening to Duncan. Duncan's cover as an FSB officer was as good as it could get, but it didn't do any harm to have a visible backup sitting there. Meantime, Ivan, Valentin and Jay were going to fly to the RV point just east of the camp and wait for them to return.

Blake checked his watch. 'If we're not at the RV point in two hours, move the aircraft.' He gave them a map coordination. 'And if we haven't turned up at the second RV point by dawn, make your way back to Sinsk and Sasha. She'll help you with the next step.'

Blake looked at Jay. 'Kiss for luck?'

She hesitated.

He stepped forward and wrapped his arm around her waist and pulled her close. His kiss was warm and brief, and as she watched him and Duncan drive away her lips were still tingling.

Twenty-Five

With two prison guards shadowing him, one to the left and one to the right, Duncan walked to the processing centre. There, his papers were inspected. He tried to look insouciant, but when the guard passed them back, with a nod, it was an effort not to slump with relief. Thank God for Blake, he thought. The man knew his stuff. The guard jerked his head, and his shadows took him into the next room where he was searched, thoroughly and at humiliating length. He was surprised when one of the guards apologized. 'Can't not do it, sorry.'

'It's a tough job,' Duncan remarked. 'I hope they pay you well.'

'They pay shit.'

Which was why corruption was rife. After they had declared him clean of weapons, he gave them a packet of cigarettes each, as Blake had suggested. 'Here. You need them more than I do.'

The guards both grinned. 'Hey, thanks. You're a real friend.'

'You're from Sinsk?' the guard asked Duncan as he began walking him to the administration hut. He had a neat, black moustache and soulful, brown eyes. 'I've heard it's a rich town.'

'It is, in some respects.' He gestured at the man's US army camouflage fatigues. 'I hope you don't mind me asking, but how come the uniform?'

'Black market, courtesy of the Georgian army,' he explained. 'The Americans give them as part of an aid programme, and the Georgians sell them to people like me. They're good quality, very comfortable.'

They passed the parade ground. A gust of wind made a miniature dust whirlwind just ahead, and then it dropped. Aside from the faint rumble of generators, there was little sound. No birds calling, no traffic, few voices. The atmosphere felt empty, devoid of energy and life.

The visitors hut was, like all the other buildings, built out of logs. It had a wooden ceiling and floor and a wood burning stove with a chimney. Again, there were no windows. At the far end were two aluminium chairs. The guard indicated that he sit down while he took up position by the door saying, 'The prisoner will be here shortly.'

In fact it was at least half an hour before the prisoner arrived, during which Duncan sat with his eyes closed. His stomach was churning and acid clawed his throat. Part of him couldn't believe he was here, but the other part, the one that burned with rage against Nikolai, was coolly contemplating his old friend's downfall. If they could get Arkady, an ex-policeman, to testify . . .

When he heard the door shut behind him with a bang, he opened his eyes. A bowed man in a dirty, shapeless prison smock and trousers smeared with clay stood just inside the door, peering about. His hair was white and shorn close to his scalp. For a moment, Duncan thought they'd made a mistake, but then the man stepped forward.

Dear God, he thought. He looks as though he's been eaten inside from a parasite. Poor Arkady had been reduced to a skeleton covered with loose, leather-dark skin.

Duncan rose to his feet. Glanced at the guard and barked, 'Out. Now! I need a private interview.'

'But, sir—'

'Do you know who I am?'

'Yes, sir.'

'Then do as I say or I'll arrange to have you leave this camp today and return tomorrow as an inmate!'

'Sir!' The guard gave a salute and, to Arkady's obvious astonishment, left the hut.

Arkady said, 'Who the hell are you?'

'Don't you recognize me?' His voice cracked. He cleared his throat. 'I'm sorry.'

Warily, Arkady stepped across the room. Stared at Duncan.

'My God,' Arkady said. 'I can't believe it.'

'Arkady,' he said. 'I had no idea. I'm so sorry.'

'You're fat,' Arkady said. His tone was disbelieving. 'You look half my age.'

'I'm sorry.'

Duncan reached to shake Arkady's hand but Arkady jerked it aside. He said, 'Where the fuck have you been?'

'Something happened when I got to England . . .' He leaned forward, whispering urgently, *I became someone else. Duncan Bailey. Trent is dead and buried.*

Arkady appeared unmoved. He said, 'I waited for you.'

'I'm sorry.'

'Do you know what it's like in here?'

Duncan shook his head. 'Sorry,' he said again.

'Thirteen *fucking* years I've been here. They built this place seventy-eight years ago, do you realize? It's been repaired and rebuilt again and again, but it hasn't changed. The huts were designed to hold twenty men, but contain up to eighty. Half the inmates have TB, HIV . . .' He leaned close so that Duncan could smell the stench of his unwashed clothes, his sweat, the eggy odours on his breath, but Duncan didn't flinch. 'We never get enough food. We are hungry of every minute of every day . . .'

Arkady opened his mouth and pointed at his gums. He was missing at least half a dozen teeth. 'I was punished for no reason, except to prove that they're omnipotent.'

Duncan shrank inside.

'Imagine waking every morning at five a.m. to use a latrine trench that stinks so bad it makes your eyes water, using the same trench before you go to bed. I bring in moss to spread on my bed when I can. It's board. No mattress, no snug feather-filled eiderdown, just a thin blanket that's been used a thousand times before . . .'

Duncan let his old friend rant. Thanks to Blake, he knew he was Arkady's first visitor since he'd been sent here. Duncan was Arkady's first witness to his misery, his pain. So Duncan stood and listened, without interrupting.

'The young men do OK here, but once you're over forty it becomes hard, especially for the men who have lived leisured lives in cities and are unused to physical work. The mortality rate is high. Some days I wish I was old so that I could die too.'

Arkady's gaze was accusing, but Duncan held it.

'Food and cigarettes are the only commodities of value. You can forget money, it means nothing.' A glimmer of something dark rose in his eyes. 'It would be nice if Koslov could experience life here and see money for what it is. A material to burn, to keep you alive in winter.'

Duncan raised his finger to his lips at Koslov's name. At last, Arkady sank on to one of the chairs. Duncan took the other.

'So,' Arkady said. 'Life seems to have treated you well.'

Duncan had to stop himself ducking his head in shame. 'Yes.'

'When you didn't call me back, I thought it was nothing, a blip, that you'd turn up any day. But you didn't. And then I was arrested.'

'I heard you got set up. I'm sorry.'

He couldn't meet the leap of hope in Arkady's eyes. 'Have you seen Alexa?'

'Not yet.' Duncan once again leaned close and whispered, *You're in danger. Pavel has been murdered. You're next.*

Arkady stared at him, blinking. Then he nodded.

Duncan continued, *We're going to lift you out by helicopter tonight. Can you be at the parade ground at two a.m.?*

Arkady jerked with shock. He mouthed, *You're joking?*

Duncan shook his head.

Tears sprang to Arkady's eyes. Duncan gripped his arm and gave him a shake. He mouthed, *Be strong.*

In between bouts of conversation to deceive any eavesdropping guards into thinking that everything was above board, Duncan whispered the plan to Arkady. There would be a diversion at the main gate, and while all the guards were concentrated on that, the helicopter would swoop on to the parade ground where Arkady would be waiting. The heli would pick him up, and bear him away. It sounded simple and completely unreal.

Duncan mouthed, *Can you be there?*

'There is a chimney in my hut,' Arkady murmured. 'I can use that to get on to the roof . . . I will be there.' Then he said quietly, 'Why?'

Duncan looked away. Why, after all these years, had he come to rescue his friend when he could have stayed at home and out of danger? Duncan held a fist over his heart when he spoke. 'Guilt.'

Arkady grinned. The skin around his mouth puckered in a strange way, like dried parchment being stretched, and Duncan guessed he hadn't smiled properly in years.

'Good old guilt,' Arkady said, obviously amused. 'Always gets the good guys in the end.'

They were grinning at one another, not seeing the men they'd become but seeing themselves as they were thirteen years ago, fitter and stronger and filled with visions of a bright future.

When the time came for Duncan to leave, he said, 'I swear I won't let you down again.'

Twenty-Six

Jay looked out from her vantage point. She wasn't that high, but she had a good view of the camp and the main gate. When she looked through her scope, she could practically count the nose hairs of the guards in the watchtower. She hoped she wouldn't have to shoot any dogs – she liked dogs – let alone people. She knew she wouldn't hesitate if it came to defending her team, but even so. The guards were civilians, and they weren't an enemy. If one of them tried anything, she'd do what she could to wing him, maybe get him in the leg rather than the torso or the head. Which would be pretty nigh impossible with the adrenalin pouring through her, but she'd give it her best effort. She may not have regretted killing three men in the past, but instinct told her that she'd rather not have one of these guys on her conscience.

She shifted her hips slightly and breathed in the heavy scents of the forest, tendrils of pine coating her throat and tongue, thick as honey. The sun had sunk below the horizon, but the sky still held a lot of light. She wondered how Blake was getting on. He'd planned on creating a fireball in the trees opposite the main gate. Hopefully, the guards would rush to see what was happening and concentrate themselves in the one area, well away from the parade ground, leaving it clear for the heli to land.

She'd always known Blake was driven, but until this mission she hadn't seen how deeply it ran. He was obsessed with nailing Koslov, and, if she didn't know him better, she'd be tempted to think it was personal. Well, it *was* personal to him, she supposed, because Blake lived for his job. To serve and protect his country pretty much at all costs. He considered anybody that threatened national security his enemy, and Koslov was currently at the top of his hit list. In an ideal world he would have spirited Duncan and Arkady to a safe house and gleaned every speck of information from them, but here he was instead, potentially about to lose both sources in the hope of freeing one who might provide the documentation Blake needed. Talk about risky.

Jay glanced at her watch. She felt sick, her stomach looped with nerves. One fifty a.m. Ten minutes to go. She scanned the arc of forest in front of the main gate but couldn't see any evidence of Blake or his drums of paint rigged with plastic explosives, detonators timed to blow at two a.m. He'd wanted to set up tripwires across the road, attached to grenades to fuel further panic, but because darkness never fell he couldn't risk being seen.

She checked the parade ground through her scope. Studied the shadows carefully, not rushing. Her breathing was steady. There! A shadow moved. She could just make out the shape of a man's shoulder and elbow, and then he moved and was lost from sight.

It had to be Arkady. Everyone else was locked inside their cabins. The target was in position.

Quick glance at her watch.

One minute to go.

She felt everything with a cold clarity: the soft breeze across her bare hands, the rocks pressing against her thighs and ankles, the snug fit of the stock of the rifle against her shoulder. Although she could taste copper in her mouth, her emotions were encased in ice. She was one hundred per cent on the job and any feelings would be processed only when the mission was over.

In the distance, she heard the faint clatter of the helicopter's rotors. She began breathing steadily, deeply, keeping calm. The sound of the rotors increased, and she was wondering if Blake's self-timing detonators were accurate when there was a massive explosion. An almighty boom, a huge flash of light lasting two seconds or more, then an orange column of fire shot through the trees, pouring black smoke. Further along there was another blast. The ground trembled. From the camp, she heard screams and shouts. Guards were running towards the main gate.

Another explosion, and a wave of hot air washed over Jay. Then she spotted the helicopter. Flying fast and low it was skimming the tops of the trees. It was barely eight hundred yards away. She swung the scope to where she'd seen Arkady. Nothing. She scanned the parade ground. Nothing.

Back to the main gate where the guards were gathering. There was a lot of shouting, dogs barking. A couple of jeeps roared to a halt by the gate. Guards piled on board, bristling with weapons. The gate opened and the jeeps shot through.

The helicopter began to descend, hard and fast.

From Jay's right suddenly came a series of explosions that she thought would never stop, more blazing comets rocketing into the sky.

She turned her concentration to the parade ground. The helicopter descending, kicking up clouds of dust. A figure rocketed from the shadows and raced towards the aircraft: Arkady, bang on time. Jay shadowed the area. No guards. The helicopter's runners were brushing the ground, the door already open, and she was urging Arkady to bloody well *get a move on* when two guards ran on to the parade ground and let loose their dogs.

Jay swung her scope across. She had about five seconds to get them. She didn't think about her affection for dogs, how she admired them, enjoyed their company. They had become a liability, a danger that had to be eliminated. She aimed at the first animal, squeezed the trigger and aimed straight at the next, dropping it with her second shot.

She turned her attention to the guards. They both held rifles, levelled at Arkady's racing form. One of them fired and she thought she saw Arkady stumble, fall to one side, but she couldn't stop to watch. She aimed at one of the guards and squeezed off a shot. She didn't wait to see if he went down but swung the rifle smoothly to the second but he was now zigzagging so violently it was hard to keep him in sight. Steady, she told herself . . . steady. She fired the second time, convinced she'd missed.

But she didn't miss.

He fell and remained still. Face down in dirt.

She heard a series of pops. Realized more guards were pouring on to the parade ground. Four more dogs.

Quick glance to see Arkady flinging himself through the helicopter door – a glimpse of people inside, reaching for him – then back to the guards. They were firing indiscriminately at the aircraft. She could hear the bullets striking the fuselage.

Forget the dogs. Jay took a breath and aimed. She had to prevent the guards damaging the helicopter. She fired. Aimed again. Fired.

The guards scattered, shouting.

Almost simultaneously, the helicopter rose. Jay continued to fire, covering the aircraft. As soon as the chopper was clear of the wire, still rising, it dipped its nose and accelerated.

Jay reloaded fast and continued firing, keeping the guards down until the helicopter was out of range.

Then she got to her feet, slung the rifle over one shoulder, strapped on her pack with her survival kit and set off at a smart jog. She had half an hour to get to the RV point, a mile away and across the western ridge. There was ample time, but she didn't hang around. She didn't want any killer dogs set after her.

Jay arrived at the clearing early to find nobody there. No helicopter, no Blake or Duncan. For a moment she panicked, thinking she'd got the wrong place, but, after checking her compass and map, she confirmed she hadn't made a mistake. She sank on to the ground, bathed in sweat. Her legs felt abnormally weak. She hadn't yomped in years, and, although she wasn't wearing much kit, it was harder than she remembered because she wasn't as fit and had forgotten how rabbit holes and rocks took it out on your shins and ankles.

She eased the rifle on to the ground next to her and looked around. Nothing but trees. She wanted to relax. She wanted to let go completely, down some vodka and talk about it, decompress, go slightly hysterical, laugh – but she couldn't until everyone arrived safely at the RV.

The minutes ticked past.

Gradually, her tension mounted.

She listened hard. Nothing.

Had the helicopter been hit? Maybe a bullet had punctured the fuel tank? She ran through the scene again but couldn't be certain. It was more likely that the Hind had suffered a mechanical failure of some sort and crashed.

Her dread increased as the minutes passed.

She recalled what Blake had said: *If we haven't arrived by two forty-five a.m. start walking for the next RV on a northerly bearing. If we're not at RV Two by midday tomorrow, make your own way to Sinsk and Sasha, who will help get you home.*

When three a.m. came and went, Jay felt like screaming, lashing out and kicking something, but she didn't. Instead, she picked up her rifle and began to make her way north, towards Zigansk and an abandoned cottage hidden in the forest that they'd chosen as their safe house.

Come eight a.m., Jay was already dog-tired. But she carried on walking, sometimes jogging, trying to keep her speed up, trying to stay awake and watchful. She considered how unfit she'd become over the past few years, how until this mission she hadn't done anything physically exhausting, like climbing a mountain or completing a marathon. Jogging through the night was the only physical exercise she'd had recently, and she felt as wrecked as if she'd done a biathlon. Maybe the stresses of her memory loss, meeting her torturer face-to-face, had drained her of her energy, every last drop. Yet her legs kept moving. That's what army training did for you. It showed you that you always had more to give, even when you thought you hadn't.

She came across a road, flat-pack gravel and free of traffic, and checked her map. She was bang on course. It was a relief to no longer be stumbling over roots and tussocks. To help keep herself going, she sucked on a Polo mint.

At least she was alive. She could smell pine, feel the morning sun burning her cheeks and the sweat pouring down her back. It wasn't all bad, she supposed. She began to hum Monty Python's *Always look on the bright side of life*.

The yomp seemed to be taking forever, and when she spotted a tendril of smoke ahead her spirits lifted. Civilization. Maybe she'd find someone to give her a lift. Jay pondered the rifle and decided to ditch it. It would only draw more attention, and she could always collect it later if necessary.

The village was called Tevriz and was a shambolic collection of wooden cottages with vegetable plots. Chickens pecked and scratched alongside foraging pigs. An old woman stared at Jay as she passed, and then a younger woman called out and waved at her cheerfully. It didn't take long for Jay to find someone willing to act as taxi and, after striking the deal with a local farmer called Viktor Daletsky, she was on her way.

Viktor was in his thirties and ginger-haired, with luxurious growths sprouting from the collar of his shirt and the backs of his hands. He had a powerful body, short sturdy legs and long arms, reminding Jay of an ape – except for the knowing look he gave her when she asked if he could keep their taxi deal a secret should anyone come asking questions.

Viktor's car was a rusting box of a Lada Niva; a small three-door four-wheel drive that used to be red, but over the years its paintwork had faded to a pale pink. It had no suspension, spewed black smoke from its exhaust, was filled with clumps of straw and stank of sheep. Jay hoped it would make the journey. However, despite the deathly rattle beneath the bonnet, it was the perfect vehicle to use. Nobody would look at them twice in this heap.

Bringing out her Polo mints, she popped one in her mouth and offered one to Viktor, who took two. Viktor, it transpired, loved mints almost as much as Duncan did.

The road wound through a muffled forest. Occasionally, they would come across a clearing and Jay would gain a sense of proportion – see how tall the trees were and that there was also an abundance of birch and larch. Then the forest would swallow them again and the vastness of Russia would, once more, press into her consciousness. Thank heavens she wasn't walking any more. Her legs felt numb.

When they came across another clearing, Viktor asked to stop. She watched him walk behind the nearest tree to relieve himself, her ears ringing in the silence. The wind keened quietly through the trees, soft and scented with pine. Viktor had just reappeared when she heard a vehicle approaching. Her heart faltered. They hadn't seen another vehicle in hours. Why now?

She climbed out of the car, waving to Viktor. 'Whoever it is,' she called, 'if they stop and question you, tell them you're alone.'

Viktor looked alarmed. 'I thought you said you were visiting your sister in Zigansk?'

'I am. I'm just being cautious, that's all.'

'Shit. I don't want any trouble.'

'You won't find any if you say you're alone.' She quickly unzipped her bumbag and withdrew a hundred dollar bill, showed it to the man. 'OK?'

Viktor licked his lips, glancing from Jay and then behind him, where the vehicle was approaching fast.

'OK,' he said.

Jay ran to the Lada, grabbed her survival pack and raced into the forest. After a few yards she took up position behind a pine, heart thumping. Cautiously, she peered around the trunk to see Viktor standing by a birch tree, pretending to urinate. The vehicle's engine noise increased, filling the forest, and then it barrelled into the clearing. A big, black VW four-wheel drive; a Touareg. For a moment, Jay thought it was going to drive straight on, but then the driver of the Touareg jammed on the brakes. The car fish-tailed to a halt, wide tyres churning on the soft mulch.

Viktor went and stood by his tatty Lada, staring as two men in dark trousers and skinny windcheaters climbed out. One of them went to the Lada while the other stood over the farmer.

'What are you doing here?' he demanded. His voice carried in the stillness of the forest as clearly as if he had a loudspeaker.

'Took my sheep to the market in Tevriz.'

'Oh, yes?'

Viktor didn't respond, but dropped his gaze to the ground.

'What did you get for them then?'

'Not much. Enough to pay the doctor's bills for my mother. She's sick. Got the cancer.'

'Play another violin,' the man sneered. 'I bet you sold them to keep you in vodka for the next week.'

'Whatever you say.' Viktor didn't look up but his body seemed to sink.

'Yeah, whatever I say.' The man spat on the ground. 'Useless piece of shit. I bet you don't even know what day it is, let alone how to scratch your own arse.'

Silence stretched.

'You married?'

Viktor didn't speak, didn't move.

'I'm not surprised. A woman would need to have a bag over her head before she'd fuck a ginger creature like you. God, you're ugly.'

More silence.

'Have you seen any other cars on this road?' the man asked. He stepped even closer to Viktor, crowding him, but still the farmer didn't raise his head.

'Nothing.'

The man turned to his colleague, who had opened the Lada's doors and was pulling out the contents – a box of tools, some twine, rope, a sweater, a container of oil – dumping them carelessly on the ground. To Jay's horror, he found a piece of Polo wrapper. Bright green with a flash of white, it looked as distinctive as a wasp sitting on top of an ice cream cone. Completely unmissable, if you weren't blind. Transfixed, she watched the man peer at it, then chuck it aside without a second look.

'Anything there?'

His colleague glanced at Viktor and then picked up the container of oil, unscrewed the lid and poured the contents steadily on the ground. 'I hope your sump doesn't leak,' he told him before throwing the container aside.

Without another word, both men climbed back into their shiny Touareg and drove off.

Jay stared after them, sweat forming under her collar.

They were FSB. They'd been called in over the jail break. Things were getting hot. The area would soon be crawling with cops, maybe even some troops. She had to get to the RV point and fast.

'Bastards.' Viktor hawked and spat on the ground before walking to the rear of his car and collecting his discarded possessions. Jay crossed the clearing and helped him.

'I'm sorry,' she said.

'You're not visiting your sister, are you?' he said.

Jay shook her head.

'Why do they want you then?'

Jay followed her instinct and decided to be honest. 'I helped break a friend out of Camp 102. We got split up. I'm trying to get to the rendezvous.'

'You're kidding!' His eyes were practically on stalks.

'Nope.'

'Holy crap. What was your friend in for?'

'He was stitched up.' Jay gestured with her chin at the forest, which had swallowed the black Touareg. 'They framed him for something he didn't do. They destroyed his family's life.'

'Well, what a surprise.' Viktor was watching her closely.

'He's a friend of my uncle's. I came to help.' Jay glanced up at the tiny patch of sky, hemmed in by swaying pine fronds. She felt as small and insignificant as a forest beetle at that moment. 'But it's all gone pear-shaped.'

'I'll say. What's next?'

Jay looked at Viktor, the red, broken veins on his face, his weather-tanned skin and the strength in the man's shoulders, his neck and legs. She said, 'Get to the RV point I arranged with my friends last night and see who's there.'

Viktor walked to the driver's side of the car and hopped in. 'So what are you waiting for?' he called. 'Another pear to make a fucking fruit salad?'

*   *   *

They hadn't gone far when Jay suggested that when they neared the RV point she should walk the rest of the way.

'What if nobody's there?' Viktor said. 'You going to walk back to Sinsk? Let's just see what happens, eh? The shits. They think they're God's gift, above the law. If we can get one over on them, then I'm all for it.'

At that point, the Lada rumbled around the corner and Viktor stamped on the brakes. 'Fuck me,' he said.

Before them stood a roadblock. One cop car, a plain, beige Lada sedan with a rack of blue lights on its roof, and three big four-wheel drives, including the Touareg. The second the Lada popped around the corner, all hell broke loose.

Twenty-Seven

A wave of dark-clad men appeared, scattering like pebbles thrown across a beach of sand. Jay couldn't believe how many there were. One second there'd been three or four men and now there were over a dozen. She saw them fling themselves at the two Touaregs, wheels spinning, churning, both headed their way, hunting, seeking their prey.

She felt a moment's disbelief at her stupidity.

The Polo wrapper. The man had picked it up, studied it briefly and thrown it away, thinking nothing of it at the time, but later he must have mentioned it to someone. Someone who knew Duncan loved Polos. That Polos were British. Alien. She shouldn't have taken them from Duncan. How stupid could she have been?

Viktor jammed the gear stick into reverse, stuck his foot on the accelerator and rocketed the Lada backwards, off the road and into the forest. Jay tensed, waiting for them to hit a tree, but miraculously Viktor spun the wheel and the Lada followed in a tight circle, narrowly missing a birch trunk by centimetres.

'Hang on!' Viktor yelled.

The Lada hurtled forward. Trees whipped past, branches smacking and scraping the car's flanks. Jay shoved her feet in the footwell and braced herself as best as she could. She had no seat belt. No air bags. She glanced over her shoulder but couldn't see anything. The forest was too dense.

Viktor's knuckles gleamed white as he gripped the steering wheel. He was hunched forward, his broad body filling the space between his seat and the windshield.

'Tell me when you see them!' he told Jay.

She realized Viktor didn't have any wing mirrors, or a rear-view mirror, and positioned herself, half turned, to gaze through the rear window.

'Nothing!' she called.

They bounded and roared their way through the forest, dodging and ducking trees with the occasional thump from a branch hitting the windscreen or the bodywork. Jay was wondering where Viktor was taking them when one of the big VW Touaregs bounded into view behind, headlights blazing.

'They're behind!'

Viktor swung the Lada for a thickly forested incline, snaking and winding his way upwards. Every time Jay thought they wouldn't be able to squeeze between two trees, Viktor managed it. Soon the Touareg dropped back, having to take a longer route, slowed by its size.

'Where are they?' Viktor wanted to know.

'Slowing down.'

They bounced over the lip to be met with a fallen tree. Viktor slammed on the brakes but the Lada was going too fast. Jay held her breath, feet jammed into the footwell, preparing for the collision, but to her astonishment the car came to a stop just as the bonnet touched bark with a small, sharp *crunch* of metal that Jay felt in her chest.

'Nothing serious!' Viktor rammed the gear stick into reverse and executed one of the speediest turns Jay had witnessed. They were scooting to the left when the big VW soared over the incline, all four wheels in the air.

She could see the driver's face, his mouth open in shock, as he saw the fallen tree. His passenger went white. The Touareg slammed into the forest mulch and kept going, ramming the tree with an almighty thud and crash of glass. The last thing she saw were two pale mushrooms of air bags filling the broken windscreen.

Viktor continued working the steering wheel, skidding down the hillside, the car twisting and jerking, thumping over branches, breaking them, sometimes dragging one along for a while until it tore free.

'Keep a watch!' Viktor commanded.

Jay sat twisted in her seat staring through the rear window, heart in her throat, praying they'd lost their pursuers. She was knocked sideways when the car jolted to the bottom of the slope but Viktor didn't give any respite. Swinging west, he barrelled along a small, shallow stream they'd crossed earlier, stones cracking and clicking against the wheel arches as they bounded and bounced, Jay's head smacking the roof of the car every yard or so. Water sprayed the windows. Viktor switched on the wipers but only one worked. Jay was glad it was on the driver's side.

They'd just dropped over a mini waterfall, dousing the bonnet with water, when Jay spotted them. She stared in dismay at the two four-wheel drives hurtling effortlessly downstream. They were both BMWs, huge machines that appeared to be doing twice the Lada's speed.

'Here again!' Jay yelled. 'Two of them!'

'Courage! We're nearly there!'

Nearly where? Jay wondered wildly. She was riveted by the Beemers. They barely seemed to lurch or roll. It was as though they were on railway tracks, their shock absorbers like mattresses.

Abruptly, the forest vanished.

She glanced forward to see they were tearing towards a river with steep, slippery banks of sheer mud.

'Jesus,' she said. 'Won't we get stuck?'

'Have faith!'

Both BMWs erupted from the forest at the same time. Both went wide, blocking the Lada from possibly returning to the shelter of the trees. Mud and stones sprayed, engines roared.

When the Lada hit the water it gave an initial jerk, as though it was about to be swept away, and then the wheels dug in. Viktor kept the engine speed high, and despite the battering of water against the car, the shaking and juddering from the current, the car kept going. So did the BMWs behind them. With sick dread, Jay saw how much faster they were going. They would catch up in the next minute or so.

Glancing forward, she took in the muddy slide of the opposite bank. It looked as steep and slippery as a water slide.

Viktor's shoulders were hunched forward as though he was willing the Lada forward. The bank was getting closer, and then the front tyres were churning, spinning on the soft, muddy bank, and Jay held her breath as Viktor pulled the steering wheel from side to side, trying to get the tyres to bite on to a rock, a stone, anything for them to grip. Suddenly, the nearside tyres dug in and the little four-wheel drive crawled up the river bank. Viktor didn't change gear, but kept the revs steady, allowing the Lada to haul itself upwards without breaking traction. When they reached the top Viktor paused, glanced over his shoulder. Jay did the same.

The two BMWs were yards away, but they weren't going anywhere. The weight of their massive frames and engines had taken their toll and they were stuck in the middle of the river, their axles sunk in mud.

If Jay hadn't been so scared, she might have smiled at the fact that one of the cheapest, crappiest cars on this side of the planet had won.

As Viktor raced for the tree line Jay saw the men inside the BMWs struggling to open their doors against the current. One of them was buzzing down his window, gun raised, but by the time he'd wedged his torso outside, taken aim and fired, it was too late.

The forest had swallowed his prey.

'Are you sure?' Jay asked Viktor half an hour later.

'Of course I'm sure. You think I don't want to see what happens next?'

'You're a sucker for punishment.'

He turned the Lada and began driving north once more, but this time the route he took was through the forest, avoiding any roads. Viktor apparently knew the disused cottage – his cousin's wife had lived there for a while before her husband died – and reckoned it would take just over forty minutes to get there. Jay checked her watch. After the chase they'd had to stop and change a tyre, taking up valuable time. Now it was two o'clock, which would make her two hours late. Would they have waited for her? She could picture Blake's face, immovable as Duncan argued in her defence, Blake striding for the helicopter, the jeep, whatever transport he'd arranged with determination. An order was an order . . .

She closed her eyes and filled her vision with Blake's face, his dark, almost black eyes, the narrow mouth that was softer than she ever imagined, and, as she looked into his eyes, she willed him to wait for her. *I'm nearly there. Just wait a little longer. Please.*

She'd never been superstitious, but she could almost feel Blake's presence as they bounced their way past spruce and birch trees. Her mother believed in telepathy, saying she always knew when Jay or her brother Angus were going to ring, but Jay had never really thought about it before. She crossed her fingers and hoped it worked today. The thought of battling her way back to Sinsk on her own was scarier than she liked to admit.

'Here we are,' said Viktor, inching his car through the trees. She craned forward and immediately recognized the rear of the abandoned cottage due to the rusting tractor propped beside it.

'I'll get out,' she said. 'Have a look.'

'Be careful.'

He kept the engine running while she walked around the side of the cottage. She couldn't hear anything else, no voices, nor could she smell cooking. Surely, if they'd been here, they would have cooked something up? They must have gone.

She'd been running, walking on the promise of hope, and now it was about to be dashed – that they'd abandoned her – she felt her legs soften, about to collapse. She forced herself into the clearing in front of the cottage and her lungs contracted.

The chopper. It was here.

And then Blake was running toward her and she was in his arms and he was holding her so tightly it almost hurt and saying, 'Christ, Jay. Christ,' over and over, and all she could think was that he didn't swear, he never swore, and he felt so good . . .

Still holding her, he leaned back to peer into her eyes. 'You're late.'

'Well, if you'd been at the first RV, there wouldn't have been a problem. What happened?'

He glanced at the chopper. 'Sprung an oil leak. We had to put down to fix it . . .'

'It wasn't hit?'

'Nope. Just showing its age.'

Jay walked over to the helicopter and aimed a kick at its runner, let loose. 'You piece of junk,' she told it. 'What you've put me through . . .'

Ivan and Valentin came and embraced her, laughing. 'Treat her nice, Jay. She's got to get us back to Sinsk!'

'She'd better. Where's Duncan?'

Duncan appeared with a man who looked so thin that a gust of wind could blow him away.

'Arkady,' she said. He came and stood in front of her. His arm was strapped to his chest, his shoulder swaddled in bandages, and his face was drawn with pain. 'I'm sorry,' she said. She hadn't covered him as well as she thought. Despite her best efforts, he'd been shot.

'Shhh,' he said. Raising his right hand he cupped her face. His hand felt as dry and rough as greaseproof paper. Solemnly, he kissed her forehead, and then both her cheeks.

'Jay,' he said. His eyes were smiling. 'Thank you for helping set me free.'

When it came to say farewell to Viktor, she said, 'I can't thank you enough.'

They were standing by his car, and she could smell the dwindling scents of cooking meat and onions. Blake had shot half a dozen rabbits while Duncan raided the old vegetable plot. Together they'd created a makeshift barbecue. Jay had been so hungry she'd bolted her food and now had indigestion.

Viktor grinned. 'It's been a day to remember, for sure.'

Duncan came over and gave the Lada a couple of pats, like he would one of his horses. 'How old is it?' he asked.

'Too old.'

'Will it last much longer?'

Viktor shrugged. 'It'll last until it lasts.'

Duncan nodded at the typically Russian response.

'What's next?' Viktor asked.

Jay said, 'We're going home to try and nail the guy who put Arkady in jail.'

Viktor shook their hands. 'Good luck.'

'Can I send you a gift from England?' Duncan asked.

'Jay's already been very generous,' Viktor said. In fact, all she'd managed to give him was directions to the hunting rifle she'd ditched outside his village. He'd refused any offer of money, saying it had been worth every minute to get one over the FSB.

'This will be something from me,' Duncan insisted. 'To say thank you for helping my niece.'

'A bottle of whisky would be nice. Something really good. I've heard the best is Glenfiddich.'

Duncan smiled. 'A bottle of Glenfiddich it is.'

Twenty-Eight

Jay didn't think she'd seen Blake so tense. He'd returned a comatose Arkady to Shanghai Town where, fortunately, Sasha had not only a nurse to hand but also a qualified surgeon. Neither seemed concerned about the somewhat unsanitary conditions, and Jay guessed they'd worked in far worse places. As soon as Arkady was on a table – borrowed from a neighbour – they stripped off his shirt and got to work.

'I'll owe them,' said Sasha. 'But it'll be worth it.'

Jay nodded. It didn't matter where you went, China to Brazil to Canada, the world was run on favours. Jay was all for favours of this kind, but then she wasn't a cop. She hoped Sasha wouldn't be asked to do something that compromised her in the future.

While Duncan hovered outside, they worked on Arkady, hooking him up to a blood bag – Sasha having got his blood group from Alexa – and stitching him together. Jay joined Blake, who had been making calls since their return.

'I've organized a jet to pick us up,' he told her. 'They'll let me know when they arrive, probably this time tomorrow. They'll have to file a flight plan from Irkutsk, but they'll file it late so Sinsk airport won't know where they're headed until the last minute. We'll have to get in place before Koslov can pull any strings.'

It was a strange twenty-four hours waiting for the jet to arrive, and it called to mind countless ops where she'd had to kick her heels. Duncan calmed when Arkady eventually regained consciousness and spent his time providing hot soup and water, coffee, whatever Arkady wanted. The surgeon had said Arkady should be OK, if sore, and that lots of bed rest and good food would have him back on his feet in no time. Apparently, he was OK to travel as long as he didn't undertake any marathons.

That night Jay and Blake shared a mattress on Rozalina's floor, in separate sleeping bags. Arkady was on another mattress in the corner, recovering. Duncan lay at his side. It reminded Jay of Bosnia. Her platoon drawing its breath in the mountains before pressing on. She slept deeply until dawn, when she began to dream. And it wasn't the guards she'd shot that she dreamed about but the dogs. One had been quite large, long-haired like a German Shepherd, the other similar to a Labrador-cross. Both were big-shouldered and long-legged, her kind of dog, the sort that she'd say,

'Hey, you,' and they'd look up and loll their tongues and wave their tails while she rubbed their chests with her knuckles – dogs hated strangers' hands going over their heads where they couldn't see – and they made friends with one another.

She could see the first dog, clear as day, running low and fast for Arkady, a big, male dog doing his job, doing what he'd been trained to do, and then she plugged a bullet into his chest. He crashed to the ground, struggled to get up, and then lay there, twitching as the life bled out of him.

The second dog, the Labrador-cross, was inches from Arkady's legs when she fired. This time she got it wrong. She hit the animal in the stomach. It went down but then it began kicking, twisting, biting at its wound. She could hear its yelps turn to screams. She wanted to shoot it again, kill it outright to stop its pain, but she didn't have time. She had to neutralize the guards first . . .

She saw herself reload, firing again and again, the animal's screams always in her consciousness, but when she hefted the rifle on to her shoulder, and set off at a smart clip to her rendezvous, she'd forgotten about the dog. She left the scene without checking whether the animal was still alive or not, and it clawed at her heart that she'd done that. She'd shot the animal badly and left it to die in agony . . .

'Hon?' She felt Blake's arm scoop around her shoulders. 'You OK?'

She hadn't realized she was crying. 'The dog,' she said. 'It was a bad shot . . .'

He drew her close. She felt him kiss her hair. 'I know,' he said. It was a murmur. 'It's OK, I know.'

She let him rock her back to sleep.

It was late afternoon and Jay was hugging Rozalina goodbye outside the airport. As a disguise, Jay had changed into a pair of sludge-coloured, everyday worker's overalls and wore a black scarf over her head. She'd tucked in every tendril of hair, and when she'd glanced in the wing mirror she reckoned she looked like a recovering cancer patient. With a pair of enormous sunglasses obscuring her face, she doubted even Tom would recognize her.

As Blake kissed Rozalina's cheeks, Russian style, Jay slipped three fifty-dollar bills into Rozalina's handbag. Duncan tapped Jay on the shoulder and passed her a wodge of notes. Jay stuffed those inside as well. Then Blake and Duncan went to the rear of the truck and pulled out Arkady, who was lying on a stretcher, eyes bright and clear and filled with animation.

'You're on your last legs,' Blake reminded him. 'So stop looking so lively.'

'I will pretend to be a corpse,' Arkady agreed and lay back, closed his eyes. He was so gaunt, his skin stretched so tightly across his skull, that he appeared almost dead.

Between them, Blake and Duncan carried him to the wooden pole lowered across the road. Blake wore a white coat with a doctor's ID tag on a chain around his neck. Jay showed their passports to the guards. 'We've got to get him to a specialist in Irkutsk,' she told them.

'What's wrong with him?' one of them asked.

'Virus,' said Blake. 'Airborne. It's not fatal, but it makes you pretty sick. Like him.'

The guard stepped back. He glanced at his companion who was flicking through their documents.

'We've got a private plane coming in,' Blake continued. 'We want him to come in contact with as few people as possible.'

'Aren't you worried about it?'

'We've been inoculated.'

Their passports were hastily returned, and they were waved through, but, as they entered the terminal, Jay saw one of the guards was on his radio. He was looking at them as he spoke.

'We'd better hurry,' she said.

Blake kicked into action. Jay took over on stretcher duty – not particularly onerous given Arkady weighed little more than a sack of potatoes – as Blake greased palms, promised favours and wished everyone a long life if they could make sure they got to their private jet on time. Within twenty minutes they were at the opposite end of the L-shaped terminal and being processed by another set of authorities. Their passports were stamped, and then they were in a tiny, private lounge. There were two chairs, above which hung a formal photograph of Koslov, enlarged to the size of a car door. She took a perverse amount of pleasure that he had an angry red spot on his chin that glowed like a beacon.

Resting Arkady's stretcher on the floor, Jay helped him into one of the chairs. Duncan took the one next to him. Blake and Jay stood at the window – grimy and spattered with tiny black dots of oil – and watched a flurry of activity in the distance at the airport gate.

'You see what I see?' Blake said.

'Yes.'

Despite her calm tone, dread filled her. There was one army jeep bristling with soldiers and two black VW Touaregs.

'And over there?'

She switched her gaze to the end of the runway to see an HS125 land as lightly as a butterfly and taxi across.

Back at the gate, she saw the boom had been raised and that the jeep and the VWs were passing through, parking outside the terminal. The soldiers ran inside, hotly pursued by four FSB.

Jay's mouth went dry. She turned her attention to the jet. A man in an orange vest directed the aircraft to the apron outside their miniature terminal. The jet didn't switch off its engines or drop its revs. The howl remained, steady and unrelenting. Through the jet's windscreen, Jay could see the pilot and co-pilot. The co-pilot looked directly at Jay. In case they wanted an ID, she took off her scarf to let her hair tumble free. He glanced at the pilot and said something then both of them looked across and waved. It seemed incongruous, but she waved back.

Then the port side door opened and two guys in reflective jackets trundled a set of steps over.

'Please, you come with me?'

A pretty woman in a blue uniform led them outside and directed them to the aircraft. It took all of Jay's self-control not to gallop up the steps and slam the door shut behind her. She let Arkady and Duncan walk ahead of her, Blake bringing up the rear. She was all too aware that anything could happen in the next few minutes.

In the distance, she saw one of the Touaregs peel away from the terminal and make its way towards them.

Koslov had obviously received the jet's flight plan. He knew where they were, that their destination was the UK. She could almost feel his hot, hyena breath against the nape of her neck as she climbed the steps. At the top another woman, also in uniform – but this one grey with cream piping – checked their passports before directing them inside. Jay chose a seat near the front and facing the rear of the plane – the soldier's choice, the safest way to travel on an aircraft – and Blake took the seat beside her. Duncan and Arkady picked two on the starboard side, facing forward, civilian style.

She buckled up. She couldn't see the Touareg. She didn't like not knowing where it was. Sweat prickled along her flanks.

The door closed, and then they were swinging around, engines howling, and the in-flight attendant was asking what they'd like to drink when they reached cruising altitude. As the jet completed its turn it thrust forward, gaining speed towards the runway, Jay glanced over at the grimy oil-splattered window of the tiny private lounge and saw three men burst inside. All three rushed to the window and stopped, staring.

She nudged Blake with her foot and pointed.

'Cool,' he said.

The jet turned at the lip of the runway and straightened, engines at fever pitch, beginning to roll. The army jeep was flying towards them . . .

She saw two soldiers bring their rifles to their shoulders, but it was too late. The aircraft accelerated so fast it was like a pellet being released from a slingshot. They were airborne before the jeep could come within firing distance.

Jay waved. She didn't care if they saw her or not. She was laughing.

Twenty-Nine

When they landed at Manston, Arkady was whisked off by Blake's colleague, Jon Pearce, to a hospital in nearby Canterbury to be checked over, accompanied by Duncan. Arkady had slept through most of the flight, and when they arrived he looked remarkably alert.

'Sore,' he answered Jay when she asked how he felt. 'But inside –' he tapped his heart – 'I feel fantastic. Like I could climb Mount Everest.'

'Maybe you should wait to do that next week,' she told him with a smile.

Yawning, she let Blake lead her to his tatty, old, sludge-green Discovery, keys hidden beneath the car, magnetized to the chassis. 'What happened to the Beemer?' she asked.

'Needed elsewhere,' he said. 'Why, you don't like slumming it?'

She wanted to tell him she preferred the Discovery, she loved sitting high and being able to peer into people's gardens as well as ride above the spray on a motorway when it was wet, but she was too tired. She simply said, 'Slumming's fine.'

Climbing inside she buckled up. She felt she could sleep for a week uninterrupted, no problem, starting right now. The flight had been more like a roller-coaster ride than a plane trip thanks to the weather – summer thunderstorms – and she'd spent most of the twelve hours gripping her armrests and longing to be on the ground.

'Jay?' She felt Blake shake her gently awake. 'We're here, OK?'

She struggled upright, blinking sleep from her eyes. Redcliffe Road looked blissfully normal. Same cherry trees, same nose-to-tail parking. Her Golf, she saw, had a film of dust over it and bird excrement streaked the windscreen.

'Max,' she said. 'Did Arkady tell you where the shipping documents were?'

'Yup.' He was tapping the screen of his satnav, programming the next leg of his journey.

'Come on! Don't keep me in suspense!'

He paused, saying, 'He mailed them to a post office in a village near Newbury Race Course. Apparently, Duncan used to use it as a dead-letter drop for his winnings around the world, to avoid the tax man. Arkady got the idea from Duncan when he visited England in ninety-three. Arkady made a private arrangement with the postmistress when he was there. Paid her in advance. Twenty years.'

'Good foresight,' she remarked. 'Go on.'

'The post office was shut seven years ago and converted into a tea shop. The boxes were destroyed. We're trying to find out what happened to any items still inside. The Royal Mail only hold items for a couple of months but we're hoping the postmistress felt obliged to Arkady, considering their arrangement. We haven't found her yet. She retired and moved to Canada.'

Jay felt a combination of disbelief and horror. 'Didn't he keep any copies?'

'He didn't have time. He was minutes from being arrested back then, and it took immense presence of mind to address the envelope and drop it in the mail room without anybody noticing.'

She smacked both hands to her head and stared at the street. All that effort and for what? Sure, she'd got Duncan home safely, and Arkady was out of jail and free. And then there was the important fact that she'd met Vasily her torturer and discovered she hadn't killed Anna after all . . . Gradually, her equanimity returned, even more so when she reminded herself that they'd all returned in one piece.

'So, what's the plan?'

'You mentioned Tom was looking for Mikhael Ragulin. Assuming he's Mickey, the man who helped Koslov kill Magnus Parnell, and we can persuade him to testify against Koslov . . . Between him and Duncan, we'd have Koslov behind bars.'

'Duncan said he was as loyal as a bulldog,' Jay said.

'Even dogs abandon their owners when they don't feed them.'

'Would you testify against a man who wouldn't think twice about killing your wife and kids?' Jay responded, frustrated at coming up against the same wall every time. The wall of violence.

Blake finished tapping his satnav screen and turned to look at her. 'Fancy dinner tonight?' he asked.

'Sorry. Duncan asked me to see Elizabeth.'

Blake said, 'See you around, then.'

'Thanks for the lift.'

She could have thanked him for much more, for helping find Duncan and returning him to England safely, for finding the truth about Anna's murder, but she didn't need to put it into words. He already knew she was grateful and that, one day, if he called on her for a favour she wouldn't hesitate to return it. It was what good soldiers – good friends – did.

She let herself into the house, feeling the same strange sensation she always experienced returning home after being on tour: discombobulated and detached. When she was on a mission the bum-fluff of life – the gas bills, the bank statements, family commitments – disappeared, and it was only when she got back that the weight of all those things returned. It was hard to believe she'd only been away for a week. It felt much longer.

There was a Post-it note next to the kettle, where she wouldn't miss it. *Working days this week, see you anon, D&A x.*

Jay unpacked and put on her washing before opening her mail, which Denise had stacked in a neat pile on the kitchen table. Nothing of interest, aside from a postcard from her father and Nicola, sent while on a weekend break in Cannes. She stuck it on the fridge with the others. Then she rang Tom.

'Hi,' she said. 'I'm home.'

'Home, home?' he said. 'Or home as in you've just touched down in the British Isles somewhere like the Outer Hebrides?'

'Home, home.'

'You OK?'

'A bit bruised in places and generally knackered, but I'm in one piece if that's what you mean.'

'Fancy a massage?'

Her body whimpered. Tom only gave the best massages this side of Dartford. She only just managed to stop herself from caving in. 'Maybe,' she hedged.

'I could swing by in half an hour. Bring you up to date on Mikhael Ragulin.'

'You're in London?'

'Yes.' He cleared his throat. 'I'm here for the weekend, visiting Sofie.'

There was a small pause. 'How is she?'

'She's doing pretty well. They've done all the tests and things are looking good so far. Thanks. I'll tell her you asked.'

'How's Heather?'

'She's fine too. How's Blake?'

Jay noted the fact he didn't say he'd tell his ex-girlfriend that she'd asked after her. She said, 'See you in a minute.'

When she opened the door, Tom caught her wrist and pulled her to him, kissing her on the lips. He tasted of almonds and sugar and when he released her she saw why. He was holding a bag of freshly baked biscuits. 'I thought about flowers,' he said, 'but biscuits appealed more. I had to taste a couple to make sure I got the right ones.'

'Good idea,' she said and took the bag inside.

'What news on Duncan?'

'It's a long story.'

'Do I need a drink while you tell it to me?'

'Several,' she replied.

'In that case, I'll have a beer.'

Jay stuck to tea and biscuits while Tom drank his Stella straight from the can, hips propped against the kitchen counter. She tried to keep the story short, but it was difficult, considering what had happened. Tom had finished his second beer and she'd eaten half the biscuits when she came to Vasily, her torturer. She told him what had happened to Anna.

He didn't move, didn't speak, until she stopped talking. 'And they let you think you'd killed her?' he said. His voice was calm but the muscles in his jaw were jumping. In his imagination, she had no doubt he had a police-issue Glock in both hands and was firing repeatedly at both Vasily and Koslov.

'But I didn't,' she said. 'The relief . . . I can't tell you.'

Tom opened an arm and she walked into his embrace, rested her head against his shoulder. She felt him tuck some hair behind her ear and press a kiss on the top of her head. 'Do you think you'll ever stay out of trouble?'

Since it appeared to be a rhetorical question, she didn't reply. Instead, she yawned and glanced outside, spotting one of her neighbours walking an elderly spaniel. Deaf, nearly blind, Pebble was a much-loved character known by everyone in the street, and even Denise and Angela – not partic-ular dog lovers – had looked after her from time to time. Which reminded Jay. 'How's Warehouse Man?'

She took a step back so she could read his face.

He said, 'Ongoing.'

'No more chewed up bodies?'

'Not yet, thank heavens. Five's enough to be getting on with.'

Jay yawned again, tears collecting in the corners of her eyes. She'd noticed this happening before, after she'd returned from a particularly stressful mission. Her body would keep going, putting one foot forward after the other for as long as she asked it, but as soon as it finally realized it was home – heard the washing machine whirring, the cars starting up outside, the constant groan and rumble that was London – it put its legs up and demanded total R & R.

'Sorry,' she said on another yawn.

'You need to catch up on sleep.'

'Not until you've told me about Mickey Ragulin.'

'Mickey?' He blinked. 'How come you—'

'Duncan knew him. It was Mickey who helped Nikolai Koslov murder Magnus Parnell. Mickey held him while Koslov pulled the trigger.'

'If I wasn't driving in a minute, I'd have something stronger. Like a double whisky.'

'Where's Mickey now?' she asked.

'In jail for armed robbery. Ready and available for interviews whenever you are.' He surveyed her for a moment. 'What are you doing tonight?'

'Seeing the family.'

'I'm never going to get my curry, am I?'

She put a hand against his cheek. 'Never say never.'

Thirty

Jay arrived at Erlestoke Prison at one p.m. on Monday afternoon. Tom had managed to wrangle an appointment for her at two p.m., and she was too early, but better early than late. She didn't want to waste any time nailing Koslov. Beeping her car shut, she walked up the hill to the main gates, showed them her driver's licence and handed over her keys, mobile phone and wallet.

She'd spent the night with Elizabeth and the Goodwin family, filling them in as much as she could through her exhaustion. When the ceaseless flow of questions had continued the next morning, she could have kissed Tom when he rang with Mickey's appointment, giving her a legitimate excuse to leave the farm. She spent the four hour journey across the country – east to west – listening to the radio and rehearsing what she was going to say to Mickey.

Now, a prison officer showed her into the formal interview room where Mickey was waiting. As soon as she laid eyes on the man, she knew he was Justin Parnell's attacker. The man was covered in tattoos, but the clincher came when the man turned to watch the guard take position by the door: he had a mythical-looking antelope etched on to the back of his neck.

Grace's voice echoed in Jay's head: *He had loads . . . all over him. All colours. Intricate designs. Green and red, blue . . . but only one stood out . . . A funny-looking sort of reindeer.*

Mickey was in for armed robbery, a seven-year sentence, and had another six months to go. Tom reckoned that the thought of going down for the murder of Magnus Parnell – for life – might crack him. She hoped he was right. Tom had talked her through what to say and how to play it, and when she was done he would follow through. He was convinced it would work.

She took a seat opposite Mickey Ragulin and introduced herself. She played it relatively straight, telling him that she worked for TRACE and was helping her uncle come to terms with a past crime. None of which had any effect on Mickey, who sat perfectly still, arms folded, gaze flat. When the man hadn't said a word after five minutes – she may as well have been talking to a chair for all the response she was getting – she switched to Russian.

Immediately, his eyes lit up. He said, 'You know Russia?'

'I was there last week.'

'Where?'

'Siberia.'

'Shit of a place,' he said.

She said, 'You know Siberia?'

'I have family in Omsk.'

Jay let a silence settle. She could sense his curiosity and also his eagerness for recent news from his homeland. She looked around the interview room, the fresh, green paint and single Formica-topped table.

Mickey finally cracked. He said, 'How was it?'

'Hot and dusty. Not enough cold beer. Warm vodka. Good lamb stews though. Gherkins.'

His eyes gleamed. 'I miss the place. Even if it is a shithole.'

This was her opening, the fissure Tom had coached her to watch for in the rock face of the interview. She swallowed, tried not to show her sudden excitement. She studied her fingernails briefly. Let her hands rest on her thighs.

She said, 'You could be there within the year, if you played your cards right.'

The gleam faded a little and his eyes became quiet, watchful.

'But if you don't, you could remain here for a very, very long time.'

A silence stretched between them.

Jay yawned. Surprisingly, it wasn't forced. It was genuine. Her body was letting her know that she was still recovering from her Russian trip.

'OK,' Mickey said. 'So tell me what it is you're here for.'

'It's complicated,' she said.

'For who?' He was frowning. 'You or me?'

'Both of us.'

'Like how?'

Again, Jay let the silence hang, but this time he couldn't wait. He said, 'Come on. Tell me.'

In the same tone, conversational, polite, she said, 'I'm here to keep you in jail until you die for helping murder Magnus Parnell.'

He blinked twice, and she could see he was having trouble with what she'd said against what he'd been dreaming of.

'Shit,' he said.

'I told you.'

'You didn't say you were a lawyer!'

'I'm not.'

Another silence during which she saw he was trying to draw himself back in, become an emotionless rock, but it was too late.

'The police have got a witness to the murder of Magnus Parnell,' she told him. 'Someone who saw the whole thing; you holding Parnell's head while Koslov shoved a gun in his mouth and pulled the trigger. The witness left a champagne glass behind, which will tie in with their testimony nicely to put them at the scene of the crime. When he comes forward, you'll go down for murder.'

'Shit,' he said again.

'My cop friend tells me he'll do a deal. You turn witness against Koslov, then you won't go down for life.'

Silence.

When she thought enough time had passed, Jay said, 'I saw your tribal tattoos when you came in. They're Siberian, aren't they? And, funnily enough, a woman called Grace Wilson described seeing identical tattoos on a man who attacked her boyfriend and left him crippled and in a wheelchair thirteen years ago. In case you've forgotten, it was in Clifton, Bristol.'

This time, Mickey closed his eyes. He looked as though he was praying.

Jay leaned forward, willing him to listen. 'You've got six months until you get out. Do you really want me to bring Grace Wilson in and identify you in a line-up? You'll go down for at least ten years for that one, guaranteed. You should see the guy. Well spoken, educated, an active sportsman, and you ruined his life. You'll be hung out to dry. And that's before they get to hear about you helping Koslov murder Magnus Parnell.'

Mickey spoke without opening his eyes. 'If you know what's good for you, you'll keep your nose out of this business.'

'I can't. It's personal.'

He opened his eyes. They looked at her straight. He said, 'I'm sorry.'

The minutes ticked past. She'd said all she'd come to say. It was up to Mickey whether to play ball or not.

After ten minutes of stony silence, Jay finally got to her feet.

She said, 'When I'm next in Omsk, I'll drop in and see your family. Send them your love.'

He smiled sadly. 'You do that.'

Jay left the jail, her emotions confused. She'd thought she'd find Koslov's bodyguard a monosyllabic hulk, nothing but brawn, but he'd been surprisingly human and the fact he obviously missed his homeland had made her more sympathetic than she'd expected.

She called Tom as she drove home and filled him in.

'You liked him?' He sounded horrified.

'He was homesick.'

'Jay, these guys will use anything, and I mean *anything*, to get you on their side—'

'Could you send a photo of Mickey to Blake, so he can pass it to Duncan to ID him?'

'Already done.'

'And?'

'He's the same guy.'

Jay thought further. Tried to see what Koslov might be doing. Tried not to rest all her hopes on a retired Royal Mail postmistress saving Arkady's shipping documents, even though they had a rule to destroy them after five years. 'I'm running out of ideas,' she said.

'Me too.'

'Where are you?'

'Er . . . Notting Hill.'

Once again, she felt a tiny shock against her heart that he wasn't in Bristol, where she normally expected him, but in London. 'Seeing Sofie?'

'Yes.'

Her emotions suddenly went haywire. For some reason, right now her mind couldn't compute that he had a daughter, let alone a successful barrister ex-girlfriend who looked like a miniature Barbie doll. She wanted things to be the way they used to be, just him and her. Even though she knew they would never be the same again, it didn't mean she didn't long for the past, its simplicity.

She said, 'Got to go. Bye,' and hung up.

Back at home, she kicked off her shoes and went and lay on the sofa. The sky was cloudy, and she wondered if it might rain. The garden was looking parched, the grass browning at the tips, but the roses were glorious. She closed her eyes, thinking of a quick nap, and fell straight to sleep only to awake when the front doorbell rang. Scrambling upright, she saw an hour had passed. Her head was still muzzy, her muscles tired.

Padding down the corridor she opened the front door. She thought it might be Sandra or Angus popping round for a chat, or her neighbour wanting a favour – like putting their rubbish out while they were away – and when she saw who it was a wave of fear flooded her gut.

'Good morning, Jay,' he said, coolly civil.

It was Nikolai Koslov.

Thirty-One

Jay didn't say a word, nor did she move. She looked at him without challenge, trying not to show her fear. Koslov hadn't come alone. He'd brought two of his goons, bulky men with mean eyes and no necks.

Koslov said, 'Hold out your hand.' He spoke in Russian.

She took a step back, but as she made to close the door he jammed it with his foot. At the same time the goons muscled her against the wall. One of them grabbed her right hand and forced it towards Koslov.

It was at that moment that she remembered the panic alarm Blake had installed, but it was now behind Koslov, and there was no way she could reach it with his hoods crowding her.

Koslov reached into his pocket. 'Open your hand,' he told her.

When she didn't move, one of the goons prised open her fingers. Koslov dropped a piece of jewellery into her palm, along with a scrap of paper.

'If you don't leave me alone, I shall visit each and every one of your family until you do. Women and children first.'

Koslov's pale eyes looked straight at hers, almost level, fractionally shorter. She saw nothing but confidence.

God dammit, she thought. She was as helpless as any victim, dependent on Koslov not to tell his goons to beat her into a pulp.

'Agreed?' he asked.

She swallowed. Gave a nod.

'Good. Now, I want you to do something for me. If you don't do it . . . Well, I'll let your imagination do the work.' His smile was chill.

Jay managed to give a nod.

'Get your uncle to this place tomorrow, along with that piece of excrement that calls himself my countryman—'

She glanced at the scrap of paper on which was written an address in Holloway. 'Arkady's in hospital,' she lied quickly. 'Unconscious. He's close to death.'

Koslov raised his eyebrows. 'That's the first good news I've heard all week. Which hospital?'

'The Cromwell.' Instinctively, she lied again.

'Your uncle, midday tomorrow,' he said. He clicked his fingers and turned away. All three men pattered down the steps and climbed into a silver Mercedes. She watched them buckle up and drive to the Fulham Road, then turn left.

There seemed no point in activating the panic alarm now they'd gone. She looked at the amber necklace he'd given her. She put out a hand, steadying herself against the door. Her legs were horribly weak. She closed the door. Locked and bolted it. In the kitchen, she picked up the phone. Nerves made her fingers tremble as she dialled.

When her cousin answered her mobile phone, she said, 'Cora? It's me. Is everything OK?'

'Don't tell me you know about it already? Heavens, bad news travels fast.'

'What happened?'

'Two men approached me after church. Fitz was still talking to the vicar, and I was walking the girls to the car. I still can't believe it happened. I mean, in broad daylight, with so many people around!'

'Keep going . . .'

'Two men. Normal, everyday blokes, jeans, T-shirts and sneakers, one talked to Hannah and Ollie while the other demanded my necklace. I didn't understand at first, but when he said he'd hurt the children if I didn't do as he said, I took it off and gave it to him. He actually said, thank you, can you believe it? I waited until I had the kids in the car, doors locked, before I did anything . . . They'd gone round the corner by the time I started yelling, and when Fitz and half the congregation pelted around the corner after them they'd vanished.'

Jay stared at the necklace in her hand. She didn't want to panic her family, but couldn't see any way around it. She had to be honest, so they would keep on their guard. 'Cora, I have your necklace here . . .'

After she'd spoken with Cora, Fitz and Elizabeth, she said, 'I'm going to ring Tom. Then Blake. We'll form a plan. Keep all the doors locked, OK?'

'Please, God,' said her aunt fervently. 'Save us from this terrible man.'

Tom didn't answer his phone, so she left a message. Blake, however, was in the safe house with his colleague Jon Pearce, starting the first of Duncan and Arkady's lengthy debriefs.

When she'd finished talking he said, 'Mickey told Koslov about your visit?'

'I can't think it would be anyone else.'

'Loyal as a bulldog is right.' He made a humming noise that she knew meant he was thinking. Then he said, 'Sit tight. Don't rattle any cages. I'll see what I can come up with.'

Something that permanently took care of Koslov, she hoped. He'd seriously freaked her out, sending his goons to Cora, catching her on her own with little Hannah and Ollie. Every time she thought of him snatching the kids, cold horror flashed over her skin.

* * *

'I'm not hungry.' Duncan pushed away his plate.

'You've got to keep up your strength,' Arkady told Duncan. 'You'll need it tomorrow.'

It was seven p.m., just the two of them dining in the kitchen of the safe house, and scents of dried straw were drifting through the open windows. Arkady was still adjusting to the luxuries of life outside the camp: the soft-ness of the towels, the sheets, the fact he could take a shower any time he liked. Duncan had found him rolling across the lawn earlier, laughing almost uncontrollably. He'd been clutching clumps of grass in both hands and holding them to his face, hungrily breathing in the rich earth smells that were so different from the arid scents of Siberia. He said he hadn't felt so happy in years, even more so thanks to Blake, who'd promised he'd do his best to persuade the Home Office to allow Alexa and her sister to join him.

'My appetite left me the second Blake told me I'm going to be bait.' Duncan looked gloomily at his plate. 'I can't believe he's going to implant me with a tracking device. I wonder where he'll put it.'

'In your arse. Your neck, the base of your spine . . .'

'I won't be able to move two feet without MI5 knowing it –' Duncan grumbled. He was looking outside at his Range Rover, which Blake had collected from his farm earlier, along with two shotguns and his .22 rifle – 'let alone fart. The microphone's hidden inside a button on my shirt. Apparently, it can hear a pin drop at fifty paces. I'm not sure whether I find this a comfort or not.'

Arkady patted his shoulder. 'Have faith, my friend.'

Duncan closed his eyes, suddenly feeling weary. 'I wish he'd die . . . I wish he'd get killed in a car accident, a plane crash . . . I don't care how. I just want him dead.'

'Me too.'

The men looked at one another, then Duncan shook his head. 'I don't think I could do it. I've pictured it a thousand times – my putting a gun to his head, or between his shoulder blades, and pulling the trigger – but I know, when the time came, I'd bottle out. I'm not made that way. I don't have the guts.'

'It's not guts,' said Arkady. 'It's hatred.'

'Whatever it is, I don't have it.'

'Ah,' said Arkady. 'But I do.'

Thirty-Two

Nine a.m., Duncan drove into London. The address Nikolai had given Jay was in Upper Holloway, towards Tufnell Park, and, although he knew the journey shouldn't take more than an hour or so, he'd left early in case he came across any hold ups.

Rush hour had already died down, and although traffic was heavy, it moved steadily, and he crossed the city without any trouble. He rarely came to London any more, mainly because he'd been petrified of bumping into Nikolai or one of his cronies. It was only when he'd run this second time that he realized how insular he'd become, how he'd orchestrated his life so that people came to him and not he to them. No wonder Elizabeth had started to get irritated recently, saying they never went anywhere. His reluctance to leave East Anglia had just about imprisoned them.

He rubbed the nape of his neck, where Blake had implanted the tracking device above his hairline. He'd used a gun-like machine, making Duncan feel as though he was one of his Labradors being microchipped by the vet. He barely noticed the dull throb it left behind. He was too nervous. His palms were sweaty, his stomach churning. He'd thrown up three times this morning. He hadn't bothered with breakfast, just drank a glass of water, which he'd promptly thrown up five minutes later.

It was past ten a.m. when he parked in a road around the corner from the rendezvous. He'd considered stopping for a coffee but changed his mind when he realized he probably wouldn't keep it down. Besides which, he didn't want any human contact. He felt as though it might deflect him from his purpose, weaken his resolve. So he sat in his car, in a suburb he'd never visited before, and listened to the radio.

The time ticked past. He watched people come and go. Every time he thought about what he had to do, the nausea returned in a rush. Each time he licked his lips, he had no moisture. He glanced at his shotgun sitting in the footwell next to him, already loaded, safety catch on. It was a bloody stupid weapon to have brought, but having it within reach gave him courage.

He'd endlessly rehearsed what to say to Nikolai. How if he died, the letter he'd sent to his solicitor would not only be sent to each member of his family – worldwide – but also to the newspapers, including the *Moscow News*. Magnus Parnell's death would be re-investigated along with Justin's mugging. Then there was all the other muck he'd set out, carefully, meticulously, from Alexa's ruined face to the corruption throughout Sinsk. The story may only last a week, but it could do untold damage and could even result in a conviction. He just had to hope Nikolai saw the sense in letting him live, but somehow he doubted this was going to happen. The only time he wouldn't be a threat to the Russian would be when he was dead.

Finally, the clock crawled to midday. It was time.

A wave of panic washed over him, and he took a breath, trying to steady himself.

You can do this, he told himself. *You have to because you can't abandon your family by running away again.*

If he got through today, he promised himself, he would take Elizabeth to the Maldives – a place she'd always wanted to visit because of its impossibly romantic atmosphere – and ask her to marry him again. And if he didn't get through it, well, he would have tried his best. As he started the engine and headed around the corner, he wondered what epitaph would be put on his headstone.

Thirty-Three

Parked in the next street, Jay couldn't see Duncan pull his Range Rover up outside an abandoned house, but she heard all about it through the earpiece Blake had provided. Blake was in the helicopter, overseeing the operation, while four official cars – including Jay and her Golf – were in place on the ground, ready for action.

Tom wanted to be part of the operation, but his boss had other ideas, along with SOCA and MI5. Having a cop from a different force was considered more of a hindrance than a help, and he'd been told in no uncertain terms he wasn't welcome. So he'd borrowed a friend's car, a ten-year-old Saab, and was parked five cars behind Jay. To watch her back, as he put it.

When she'd told him that Koslov had turned up on her doorstep, he'd come straight round.

'This guy needs to be put away,' Tom said. He was so composed that she thought he was unmoved until she saw the tight line of his mouth and realized he was fighting to control his anger. 'You want me to stay over?'

'I've got a panic button.'

'Which wasn't of any use at the time.'

'I'll be OK. The girls are upstairs.'

Tom packed himself off, leaving her unsure whether he felt exonerated of protection duty because she had two highly trained ex-soldiers under her roof or whether he didn't like the idea of having his style cramped with her housemates around.

Now, Jay peered in her rear-view mirror and gave him a little wave. Tom raised a hand in return. Like Arkady and Jay, Tom had a set of headphones so he could hear the team's chat, Blake's running commentary, but he was under pain of death not to speak. After the briefing that morning, when Jay had asked Blake for an extra set of headphones, he'd handed over a set saying, 'Tell him if he says a single word, or gives himself away, I will personally kill him.'

Jay concentrated on what Blake was saying. Duncan had stopped his car. Apparently, three men were stepping out of a plain, blue transit van and approaching the Range Rover. Duncan didn't unlock the door for a long time – a long time in Blake's view being anything more than thirty seconds – and Jay's heart ached for her uncle, his paralysing fear of what might happen to him.

The second he unlocked it, the men yanked open the door and hauled him out, manhandling him to the rear of their van. While one man opened the door, the others forced Duncan inside. Blake said he thought he saw an arm reach from within the van to grab Duncan but added he wasn't sure . . .

'Target heading south,' Blake said. 'Now turning left on to Holloway Road. Repeat, south on Holloway Road.'

Jay started her Golf and accelerated to the end of her road to see the blue van drive past. A quick glance in her wing mirror showed Tom was behind. She waited until the MI5 cars had passed – two grey Vauxhalls and a blue Ford – and muscled her way into the traffic behind them. It had been agreed that she and Arkady would bring up the rear . . .

She was glad Arkady was quiet and didn't distract her. She needed all her concentration to forward plan her driving so that she'd never be more than three cars behind the van. Occasionally, she glanced into her mirrors and sometimes she'd see Tom's Saab, sometimes not. She decided she couldn't worry about him. She had to use every ounce of concentration to follow the blue van.

They crossed Seven Sisters Road, and at the Highbury–Islington junction the van turned left to pick up St Pauls Road. After they'd joined Balls Pond Road, the van ducked left, left again, right, into quieter streets, and Blake instructed everyone to fall back to avoid being spotted. Keeping up a commentary from the helicopter, he instructed Jay to pull over when the van vanished inside a warehouse. Jay ignored Blake. Creeping past the end of the street – a glimpse of an MOT station, a motorbike repair shop – she parked just around the corner. She wanted to be on hand if anything happened, not half a mile away. Tom pulled over well behind her.

She nibbled the inside of her lip as she listened to the chat between Blake and his team. Nobody was sure if this was the final destination. The warehouse doors were shut and they couldn't hear anything from Duncan – hadn't heard a peep from him since he'd been snatched – making Jay wonder if his microphone was working or, worse, that it had been found and destroyed.

Five minutes ticked past, then ten.

Arkady groaned. He said, 'This waiting is killing me . . .' and as he spoke Blake's voice erupted in her ears.

'The doors are opening . . . There are two vehicles exiting. Repeat, two. One white van, one blue, the same we followed earlier.' He rattled off the registration numbers.

The vans appeared behind them and turned right, straight past her Golf.

She cursed silently as she and Arkady ducked low. She'd never forgive herself if she'd blown the op.

'OK,' said Arkady. 'They're past, no problem. Let's go.'

Jay started her car and pulled out after the vans. At the end of the road, one van turned right, the other left.

'Which one's got the tracker?' she asked Blake.

'Delta four six zero,' he gave the number plate of the white van, but as she began to turn to follow it, Arkady put a hand on her arm.

He said, 'No. Follow the blue van.'

'What?'

'It's got a mark on its door, see? Like paint. It wasn't there before. I agreed with your uncle that should something like this happen he would try and mark the car he was in, somehow give us a clue . . .'

'Paint?' she repeated.

'It could be a smear of blood.'

Her stomach gave a swoop. 'You think they've found the tracker? Dug it out?'

He turned and looked her in the eyes. For the first time she saw they were deep hazel, flecked with yellow. 'What do you think?'

She watched the MI5 vehicles slot in behind the white van, heading west. The blue van was headed in the opposite direction. If Arkady was right, and she ignored him, she'd never forgive herself. If he was wrong, the white van still had three cars, eight operatives and a helicopter tracking it . . .

The blue van abruptly turned right and vanished from view.

'OK,' she said. 'Let's do it.'

She turned the wheel and rocketed down the road. They popped out at the end and, without pausing, swung right. Left was a warren of back streets that led to Shacklewell. She hoped the van hadn't taken that route, that they were headed for the arterial roads.

'See them?' she asked.

'No.'

'Keep looking.'

At the next junction Jay paused. Traffic streamed in both directions. 'Anything?'

'No.'

She had to make a decision, but what if it was the wrong one? Her heart squeezed.

'There!' Arkady was pointing south. 'A blue van, I'm sure of it, hidden behind a truck. It was turning left . . .'

Jay didn't question Arkady. She simply turned the wheel and put her foot down, burning rubber, barrelling along Kingsland High Street, swinging past slower-moving vehicles, trying to make progress through slow traffic. A pedestrian light ahead turned red but Jay didn't pause and blasted across, hand on her horn. Her senses were alive and sharp. Way in the distance she spotted a blue van. Was it the same one? She jumped a red light at the bottom, ignoring the horns that blared, and accelerated after it.

A quick glance in her rear view showed Tom was no longer behind her. Would he be able to catch up? Knowing Tom was listening in to the airwaves, she told Blake exactly where they were so he could follow.

Her heart was flipping like a stranded fish. She mustn't lose the van, in case it held Duncan. Gradually, she closed the distance between them, hoping the driver of the van wouldn't worry too much about an ordinary blue Golf two cars behind him because she didn't dare lose them at a traffic light or roundabout.

As the van swung left, easing into a roundabout, her heart hollowed when she saw the number plate.

EX32 OAM.

They'd followed the wrong van.

Thirty-Four

'Arkady,' Jay said.

Her tone made the Russian swing his head round, alarmed. 'What is it?'

Jay's hands gripped the steering wheel so hard her knuckles turned white. 'That's not the right van. We've been following the wrong one.'

There was a hideous silence. Jay began to slow the car when Arkady said, 'No, no. See the smear of paint, or blood, on its door? It's the same mark, I swear it.'

She swallowed. She hadn't seen the smear earlier. 'OK, we'll stay with it.'

As they continued to drive east, Jay tried to work out how the van's number plates had been changed. There had been no time, and she guessed a lookalike had been peeled off to reveal the plate beneath. Clever, she thought. They had obviously done this before.

The traffic spread out, and Jay dropped back. She tried to think where the men would take Duncan. Part of her couldn't believe how brazen Koslov was. She could see why the town of Sinsk was in his pocket. Behave and you were rewarded, step out of line and the consequences were brutal. Plain and simple, this was how Koslov worked, and so far it had paid dividends. After all, the Russian thug was still out there, making money and watching his horses win and lose around the world.

Jay followed the van deep into the heart of Hackney. Was Duncan all right? Was he really inside this van? She could hear Blake's commentary clear as day. The white van had passed Hampstead and appeared to be headed for the M1.

'They're turning,' Arkady told Jay.

The streets became narrow, and Jay had to drop further back to avoid being spotted, so far that she became worried they might lose the van should it make a couple of unpredictable and sudden changes of direction . . .

The houses turned into terraces with the occasional garage in-between. Weeds grew in front gardens, and the gutters were filled with beer cans and takeaway cartons. The cars on the street were mostly old models with rusting wheel arches and copious dents in their bodywork. The van turned right, then left, and Jay dropped further back.

She was just turning into the next street – a canal on one side, industrial buildings and warehouses on the other – when the van showed its brake lights. It was slowing down. Immediately, she swung to the kerb behind a five-tonne truck and switched off the engine, praying they hadn't seen her.

'They're stopping . . .' Arkady sounded breathless.

Both of them ducked as the passenger door opened. Jay peered past the steering wheel to see a man climb out of the van and open an industrial-sized metal door set in a high wall. After the van had driven inside, the door was closed. Everything was quiet.

According to Blake, the white van with the tracking device had now hit the M1 and was travelling north. Jay didn't like the fact they were now so far apart, and voiced her concern that the white van was a decoy. Blake said, 'I agree. I've already sent two cars to you. Confirm where you are?'

Jay told him – and, by doing so, informed Tom as well.

'They'll be with you in fifteen minutes,' Blake told her.

Anything could happen in fifteen minutes. She glanced across at Arkady. He said, 'Let's go take a look.'

Jay studied the wall and its razor wire curled on top, the same deter-rent that Nikolai used on the walls surrounding his Hampstead home. 'OK,' she said. Starting the car she drove past the gate. She couldn't see any CCTV cameras or any electronic surveillance. Reversing, she parked close to the wall.

A dog started barking nearby, and then another. Suddenly, the air was filled with barks, excited and angry. Jay could discern yaps from small dogs as well as the deeper boom from larger breeds. It sounded as though they'd arrived at a kennel.

Hopping on to the bonnet of her car, she scrambled on to the roof and peered cautiously over the razor wire to see a wide loading bay and a forecourt of cobblestones with a dozen trucks parked haphazardly across, along with the blue van. Her heart faltered when she took in the shiny, red Bentley Coupe parked between the blue van and the gate. Its number plate: KO5 LOV.

The dogs continued to bark. Her gaze ran over the blue van. She spotted a new mark above the rear door handle. It was a hand-print made out of blood, she was sure of it. As she turned to help Arkady on to the car roof to have a look, a man shouted. All the hairs on her body stood upright. He shouted again, and then he started screaming.

'Duncan,' she said.

'Yes,' Arkady replied.

'Get the guns.'

He dived inside the car. The dogs continued their frenzied barking.

'Max.' She spoke into her mouthpiece. 'Koslov's here, and so is Duncan.' She described the warehouse. Told him her Golf was outside.

'On my way.'

Arkady brought out the .22 rifle that Duncan used for rabbiting, and a shotgun, and rested them against the car. He passed her handfuls of shells before scrambling to join her with two car mats. Jay laid them over the razor wire. The dogs suddenly fell quiet. There was no sound from Duncan.

Jay flung her torso on to the mat. She felt Arkady help raise her legs over the wire, catching briefly, tearing through her jeans and slicing her skin. She gave a grunt of pain, pushed it aside, and wriggled across until she was on the edge of the wall, her legs dangling above cobblestones. She slid her backside forward on the mat, then her spine, and gravity did the rest. She plummeted towards the ground. The instant her feet touched the cobblestones she softened her body, buckling her knees and rolling to one side to avoid spraining an ankle, damaging a knee joint . . .

She landed well and immediately rose and jogged to the metal gates and unbolted them. With a screech of rusting hinges, she pushed one open. Jay ran to her car, where Arkady was already handing her the guns. Taking both weapons she checked they were both loaded, safeties on. Arkady grabbed the shotgun. He'd ripped his shirt and blood was pouring from his forearm. His skin had paled, reminding her that he'd only recently been discharged from hospital. She hoped that adrenalin would keep him going, and at the same time she was aware the dogs had started barking again.

She put her car keys on top of the rear, nearside tyre of her Golf. Insurance for Arkady. He nodded to show he'd seen.

Both of them jogged past Koslov's Bentley, the trucks, heading in the direction of the dogs. They trotted past a loading bay for a door further along, set in the wall next to a roller door. It was ajar. Jay took a peek but couldn't see much aside from a wall covered in cracked and peeling white paint. As she opened the door wider, she heard voices.

'You've caused me so much trouble, I wish I could do this a hundred times.'

She could feel Arkady leaning against her shoulder as he peered to have a look beside her.

Koslov and two of his goons were standing on the edge of a pit, looking down. Jay recognized Gusev, Koslov's goon from Hampstead, but not the other man. She took in the brick walls, damp with moisture, the concrete floor covered with old patches of oil and a bank of windows set high beneath a tin roof. There were three pits, where Jay guessed men used to work beneath trucks, servicing them, fixing their exhausts, but now the room was empty of tool kits and oil drums.

'For God's sake, Nikolai . . .' Duncan's voice trailed up from the pit on a half sob. 'This is barbaric. Insane . . .'

'Gusev,' Nikolai said. 'Fifty quid he kills the next one.'

'No chance,' Gusev replied, bringing out his wallet. 'Brutus is tough as nails. Double or quits.'

'Brutus is shit. He cowered in the corner with his tail between his legs after that lunatic tried to bite his ear off last week.'

'You call ripping the guy's face to pieces cowering?'

'That wasn't Brutus. That was King. We had to use four dogs to bring him down, remember?' Koslov leaned out a little and yelled, 'Stepan! Let Brutus out!'

A dog started barking dementedly, then the others joined in. Was it Brutus? Jay wondered wildly. Had the dog recognized its name? Even from her position – maybe twenty yards away – Jay could see the excitement on Koslov's face. It wasn't the money that was arousing him, she realized, but the game. Carefully, quietly, she raised the .22 to her shoulder, but her movement must have caught the corner of Gusev's eye because he turned and looked right at her.

Thirty-Five

As Jay brought the rifle to her shoulder, there was a clanking sound and at the same time the dog stopped barking. Duncan yelled, 'No!'

Gusev was already moving, grabbing Koslov and dragging him to one side, but she plugged him in the shoulder, reloaded and fired again. The .22 wasn't a heavy-calibre rifle, and she wasn't surprised Gusev didn't go down. She'd caused him some damage, but he was running for the other side of the room, Koslov hot on his heels. The second goon had brought out a pistol and was taking aim at her. She ducked back just before he fired.

Thunk. The bullet hit the wall opposite and spat a chip of paint into her face.

Duncan was shouting, the dog growling furiously, snarling . . .

'Cover me,' said Arkady, and before she could move he'd pushed past her and was running inside the room for the pit.

Boom. Arkady fired a shot as he went.

Jay stepped into the doorway and fired her .22 past him, but the goon was already running for the door. She loosed off a shot, thought she might have hit his shoulder, and then he was gone. Arkady was at the edge of the pit, shotgun against his shoulder, but he wasn't firing.

She ran for the pit.

The dog and Duncan were locked in battle. The dog was broad and solid, a mastiff cross. Duncan was naked from the waist up and pouring blood. His trousers were in shreds, great gouges taken out of his thighs. His arms were ripped and torn, his hands a mess.

Snippets of information clicked through her brain as she raised her rifle. The pit's steps had been removed. There was a dead dog lying in the corner, its neck broken. Four iron gates opened into the pit. Two gates were empty, two were jammed with dogs of all shapes and sizes, all snarling and barking, scratching to get into the pit.

The next second Arkady took the shotgun from his shoulder and dropped into the pit. Taking the gun by the barrel, he swung the stock at the dog's head.

Smack. The dog growled harder, biting, chewing Duncan's forearm, enraged.

Again, Arkady hit the dog. This time it paused for a split second before shaking its head violently, blood spraying . . .

The third time the dog went down like a stone. One second it was a growling, vicious killing machine, the next it was out cold.

Jay put down the rifle and lay flat on her belly, reached down. 'Give me your hand,' she told Duncan. He was swaying violently, wiping blood from his eyes. 'Use Arkady.'

Arkady made a stirrup with his hands, and between them they hauled Duncan out of the pit. Next, Duncan and Jay each took one of Arkady's hands and heaved him free. They paused briefly, gasping. Jay said, 'We've got to get out of here.'

Her senses leaped when the door to the forecourt swung open. Tom came pounding across.

'You OK?' he asked her.

'Yup.'

'Jesus.' He was staring at Duncan. 'What happened?'

She pointed at the pit. 'Dogs.'

'Christ.'

'Blake's guys aren't far behind,' Tom said. 'If we sit tight . . .'

From behind them came a *crack*. Tom grabbed Jay's wrist and hauled her for the door leading to the forecourt. Briefly, she tried to break free, grab the rifle, but he was much stronger, and she relented. To struggle any more would endanger them both.

Boom. She glanced behind to see Duncan hot on their heels, Arkady firing his shotgun at the rear. *Boom.*

Crack, crack.

They were through the door. Keeping low, Jay scurried across the cobbles and hid behind the first truck. Tom joined her. He brought out a Glock from his waistband.

He took in her surprise and said, 'Don't ask.'

Duncan and Arkady ran across to join them.

Tom said, 'OK to get to the street?'

They gave him the thumbs up.

'They're right behind us,' Arkady said. 'Let's hurry.'

Crack.

A bullet whacked into the truck, missing Arkady by a whisker and prompting them to move. Scuttling from truck to truck they kept as low as they could, bullets whining above them. Vulnerable without any body armour, Jay dropped to all fours for the next leg of her sprint. Her elbows were bleeding by the time they reached the shelter of Koslov's Bentley.

She glanced over her shoulder to see Duncan sheltering beside the Bentley's rear tyre. He was bent over Arkady. His fist was pressed against the man's diaphragm.

Jay felt a moment's horror. Arkady had been shot. Blood poured from his chest across the cobblestones and pooled against the rear tyre. His skin was deathly pale. Her breath closed in her throat. He looked close to death.

Tom swarmed to join Duncan and checked Arkady. Raising his head he looked at Jay, shook his head. A bullet walloped into the Bentley's boot with a metallic twang, and another smacked the rear wing, missing Tom's neck by inches.

'Tom,' she called. 'Move, will you?'

'In a second.' He turned to Duncan. 'We've got to go.'

'No. I'm not leaving him.'

'He's not going to make it.'

'It doesn't matter. I swore I wouldn't let him down again.'

Tom looked at Jay, the question in his eyes.

'Think of the girls,' she urged Duncan. 'They need you.'

He glanced up. Jay didn't think she'd ever seen such pain before. 'I'll carry him.'

'You can't,' she protested, but before she could stop him he'd risen and, in one great movement, hefted Arkady in his arms. The only cover between them and the gate was the blue van.

'Go!' Tom shouted. He was already firing hard and fast behind him. 'You too, Jay!'

Gunfire raked the forecourt as Jay sprinted for the blue van. A quick glance behind showed Duncan lumbering at half speed with Arkady's limbs flopping, his head lolling, but there was little she could do to help. Tom was loping at Duncan's side, pistol firing behind him. Breath hot in her throat, she increased her pace.

More gunshots. She didn't dare look over her shoulder, risk tripping or falling over.

Only five yards to go.

A bullet kicked up a splinter of stone in front of her but she didn't falter. Her legs and arms were pumping as she ran for her life. She could almost touch the van when a fresh barrage of gunfire echoed across the forecourt and she launched herself into the air aiming to land behind the rear tyres, hoping the unpredicted movement would save her. She came down with an almighty thump and the breath whooshed out of her lungs but she didn't stop. She rolled twice, kicking her legs until she came up against the van's front wheel, as protected as she could be against the bullets slamming into its bodywork.

Duncan was nearly there. His face was strained, beetroot red, the cords standing out in his neck with the effort.

'Come on!' she yelled, and, to her amazement, his stride lengthened.

Bullets cracked between them like whiplashes. At Duncan's side, Tom was firing his pistol unrelentingly. She couldn't believe neither of them had been hit. Please God they'd make it . . .

They were just yards away, and she rose into a crouch, readying herself. The gunfire intensified. At the last second, she rose and rushed to help Duncan, taking some of Arkady's weight across her shoulders. They collapsed in a heap behind the last van. Tom went to crouch by the nearside wheel, reloading before continuing to fire.

Jay watched Duncan brushing blood from his friend's face. Tears were pouring down his cheeks. He was saying, 'I'm sorry,' over and over again but Arkady didn't seem to hear. He was smiling.

As Jay leaned over Arkady – she was hoping she might be able to plug his chest wound, stem the bleeding – she glanced into his eyes. He was looking past her and at Duncan. He said, quite clearly, 'It's good to be free.'

She saw a flash of green in his eyes, like a spark of electricity from a thundercloud, but then something changed. The gleam of life flickered and began to fade. A chill swept over her. Her heart clenched. Everything went silent. She didn't hear the gun battle. She looked into Arkady's eyes, even though she knew he wasn't looking at her but at Duncan. She wanted him to know that she was there as well, that he had witnesses. She said *God bless you* over and over in her mind, and then the light was gone and his eyes turned glassy, lifeless. His body went slack.

Duncan rocked back on his heels and raised his face to the sky. His torso was smeared with a mixture of his blood and Arkady's. His fists were clenched. 'I hate you!' he roared.

Tom spun round. 'What the . . .'

'Arkady died,' Jay said. Her voice sounded as though it was coming from a long way away.

Tom looked at Duncan then back. 'Get him together. We've got to move in the next minute.'

He turned back to his defence position.

Jay scurried to Duncan's side. He was staring into the sky, his expression frighteningly blank. She rose to take his head between her hands. He didn't seem to feel her touch, so she wound her fingers in his hair and shook him, hard, until finally his eyes met hers.

'You want me to die out here as well?' she demanded.

He blinked.

'If we don't move, I'll die. I don't want to die. Will you help me?'

'Jay,' he said. He sounded as though he wasn't sure he was seeing her.

'Do you want me to die as well?' she repeated.

'No.'

'Then help me.'

'What do you want me to do?'

She dropped her hands, relieved his protective instinct had kicked in.

Jay pointed at the gate. 'I want you to run through it and on to the street, as fast as you can.'

She felt Tom tap her shoulder. 'You go first,' he told her. 'Give him something to follow. I'll cover you.'

'Tom . . .' Although it was good advice, she didn't want to leave him.

'Go!'

Ducking her head, she kissed him on the mouth. 'Catch up soon,' she told him, and ran.

She heard Tom firing his pistol continuously. *Bang-bang-bang.* There was a brief pause as he reloaded, and then another barrage. She made it through the gate unscathed, Duncan hot on her heels.

She paused on the street and risked a peek behind to see Tom pelting towards her. He moved fast, much faster than she and Duncan had and was with them in seconds. He planted a kiss on her lips. 'Soon enough?'

She grinned, adrenalin pouring and making her feel light headed.

He grinned back.

Jay became aware of the sound of rotors, a helicopter approaching. Two grey Vauxhalls screeched around the corner, blue lights flashing in their grilles. Jay and Tom raced to open the gates to allow them access, but the vehicle that shot through two seconds later didn't belong to MI5 or SOCA or the Metropolitan police.

It was Jay's Golf.

Thirty-Six

Duncan's hands were slippery with blood on the steering wheel, and more blood dripped on to the leather seat, the carpet. He knew he was a mess, and although he could feel the strange tugging, dullness of his wounds – the pain would come later when the adrenalin stopped flowing – he wasn't going to stop now.

Bless Jay for being predictable and leaving her keys where she always did when she stayed on the farm, in case anyone wanted to move or borrow her car.

God bless Tom for turning up when he did and for giving them covering fire and getting them out. All of them except Arkady.

As he drove into the forecourt everything appeared to be happening in slow motion, and he knew it was because his body was on extreme alert, processing every thought, every detail, at twice its normal speed.

When Arkady died, he'd been momentarily paralysed. Horrified, shocked, appalled . . . but the rush of anger that followed had shocked him even more. It had been so powerful that he'd thought it might rupture something inside, implode his soul. For a moment he'd been too frightened to embrace it and had forced it aside, damped it down, scared that it might take over. And then Jay had called on him to help her, and it had returned, bright white-red.

Anger.

Rage.

Hatred.

The fear that had nearly crippled him earlier had gone.

You can do it. For Alexa and Arkady, for Pavel, Justin and Magnus Parnell . . .

He heard the tyres rumble over the cobblestones, could feel the juddering of the car through his thighs and up his spine. One of Nikolai's goons was standing tall on the loading bay, pistol aimed at him and firing. The other goon was running for cover behind the blue van.

He wasn't looking at them though.

He was looking at Nikolai. His old boss, his friend, his enemy. Nikolai was racing for his Bentley.

Duncan slammed the heel of his palm in the centre of the steering wheel. The horn blared.

Nikolai paused. He had his back to his car. He looked across.

Duncan accelerated.

Nikolai swung a hand forward. He was holding a pistol. He backed up to steady himself against his Bentley . . .

The Golf was rocketing forward, engine howling.

Duncan's soul was splintering. He could see the girls, Charlotte and Katie, their fair-spun curly hair and blue eyes, and hear their laughter. He could see Jay and Tom, Elizabeth, Fitz and Cora. But above all he saw Arkady, the forgiveness in his eyes.

It's good to be free.

Nikolai aimed his pistol straight at Duncan, and fired.

The bullet passed straight through the windscreen and buried itself into the left side of Duncan's chest. It felt as though he'd been punched by someone's fist, and for a moment he was so shocked he was briefly paralysed, but then Nikolai fired again.

This time the bullet smacked into the left side of Duncan's skull.

He felt a searing pain, as though someone had laid a white-hot knife against his head, and then he blacked out. He didn't feel his body slump. He didn't feel his foot drop on to the accelerator, pressing it against the floor, or hear the engine respond with a shriek. He was completely unaware of the Golf leaping forward and crushing Nikolai Koslov against the boot of his Bentley Coupe, smashing his hips into shards and reducing his legs to pulp.

Thirty-Seven

'I can't believe Blake slipped you his Glock,' Jay said.

'He didn't want me killed on his watch,' Tom responded. 'Far too messy.'

They were sitting in the living room at Norridge Farm, Toast and Marmite sprawled at their feet. Evening was drawing in, and Fitz had lit a fire. During the past fortnight the heat wave had ended and the air was cool. Both of them wore jeans and fleeces and were waiting for the rest of the family to join them for the traditional drink before supper. Most of Jay's bruises had faded by now, and aside from the scabs on her shin from the razor wire she was in good shape.

Jay looked at the Labradors, comatose. 'I still have nightmares about dogs,' she admitted.

Tom didn't say anything, just drew her close and kissed her hair.

Watching the flames, Jay said, 'Any luck tying Koslov in with Warehouse Man?'

'Nothing. We have no idea if he was involved in any of the deaths caused by dogs. Luckily, we haven't found any more bodies. The count is still at five.'

'Nearly six if you think of Duncan,' she remarked. 'If it was Koslov, then he was clever enough to dump the bodies well away from his warehouse.'

They were quiet for a while. Jay's mind moved to Arkady and to the memorial service they were going to hold in the village church next Sunday. Arkady's body had been repatriated to Russia, to his family and Alexa, but Duncan wanted a ceremony of observance, and the local vicar was happy to comply.

As well as helping the authorities build a variety of cases against Koslov, the last week had been spent tying up loose ends. Jay had spoken to Vladimir last week, Anna's fellow *Moscow News* reporter, and when she'd told him about Anna's death he'd wept. He told her the FSB had already been in touch and had taken Anna's computer along with her files, but apparently they hadn't said how she'd died. He said, 'Jay, I am so sorry for you . . .' She'd had to reassure him over several phone calls that she was all right, and eventually ended up confessing that yes, she had seen a psychologist, and yes, they had been a great help. Which was true – Sandra had been a godsend, empathetic and compassionate – but Jay didn't tell Vladimir that she'd only seen her once. He seemed happier believing she was in the throes of extensive and ongoing therapy.

A log fell in the grate, sending a shower of sparks up the chimney. Jay put another couple of logs on the fire before settling back with Tom. 'So, er . . .' she cleared her throat. 'I mean, this is all very nice, Mum and Elizabeth inviting you for supper, but what about . . . um . . .'

'Sofie and Heather?'

'Yes.'

'Well, they're still around. They're not going to go away.'

She fiddled with a bobble of cotton on her cuff.

'What's wrong?' he asked.

'Well, it's not even a threesome . . . There are four of us.'

'Meaning?'

'Are we an item?' she said.

'Would you like us to be?'

'Maybe.'

He scooped her tight against him. She felt him draw breath, and at that moment her mother arrived bearing a tray with bowls of nuts, crisps and olives. Tigger the miniature schnauzer bounced beside her. Neither Labrador bothered to rise, just thumped their tails. They'd known Tigger since he was a pup.

'Darlings, help yourselves.' She put the tray down on a side table. 'I'll join you in a minute. Just want to check the pudding. Where's Fitz?'

'Upstairs with Duncan.'

'I'll take drinks up to them in a minute.'

Jay watched her bustle off, happy to be cooking for a house full of guests. The Goodwin clan was here in full force, including Duncan's mother and a ginger-haired cousin Jay had never met called Wallace, whom Duncan apparently had sponsored through university.

It was Duncan's second night home from hospital, and, although he was in bed, he'd wanted the house full for the weekend. After Nikolai had shot Duncan and Duncan had pulverized him against his Bentley, Blake's team had moved in. The gun battle was brief. Outnumbered eight to three, Gusev, Stepan and the third goon had soon surrendered.

Meantime, Blake had called an air ambulance. Duncan had lost a lot of blood from the wound in his chest, and although his hair was sodden with blood, it turned out the bullet had creased the side of his head, leaving a deep gouge and no more. Nikolai, on the other hand, was in a worse state. He was still pinned between his Bentley and Jay's Golf, his hips and legs mashed to pieces. Where Duncan was given blood and patched up, Nikolai had to have both legs amputated to save his life.

Interestingly, as soon as it became public that Nikolai was seriously injured, as well as being prosecuted for dog fighting and attempted murder, witnesses started appearing. From Sinsk to Soho they crawled from beneath their rocks, out of their dens, to come forward and tell tales of extortion and blackmail, savage beatings and hit men. It was as though once the fearsome beast had fallen, the smaller creatures swarmed to take a bite out of him. Even Mickey was prepared to turn witness now his boss was out of action.

When Nikolai eventually came out of hospital, he was going to face lengthy trials both in England and Russia. Blake had predicted he'd serve his time in England since his team had, at last, found the Royal Mail's retired postmistress. Faithful to her verbal agreement with Arkady all those years ago, she had kept his parcel of shipping documents, which apparently tied three canisters of missing British uranium to Koslov via his mining company, PMK, and his British company, Davenport Industries.

Blake had dropped round to Jay's house the previous week to talk her through it. He'd brought her a jar of Puglian orange honey from the foot of Italy. 'I was there a couple of months ago,' he said. 'I'd like to take you there one day. It's beautiful. We could take moonlit strolls on the beach. Go skinny dipping.'

Jay avoided comment by saying, 'Duncan wants Koslov to go to a Siberian camp. He reckons our jails are too soft, that he deserves some of his own medicine.'

'Doubtful. But you never know what could happen.'

He raised a hand and tucked a stray lock of hair behind her ear. They were standing so close she could smell the soap on his skin. He said, 'I go next week.'

'Go where?'

'Brazil.'

She felt the blow of it against her heart. 'Max . . .' She'd forgotten he was moving to South America. The fact he spoke Portuguese as well as Spanish. That it would be good for his career.

He said, 'Will you miss me?'

'No. Yes.' She sighed, her emotions a turmoil. 'Of course I will.'

He smiled. 'Good. Does that mean I get a kiss goodbye?'

She narrowed her eyes. 'Maybe.'

Cupping her chin in his hand, he bent his head and kissed her mouth. His lips were just as she remembered, soft, gentle, and then his tongue touched hers. She gave a groan and deepened the kiss, winding her arms around his neck and pulling him close. His hands moved to her waist, then the small of her back, pulling up her shirt, stroking her bare skin. The surge of longing for him was so strong she felt dizzy.

Then he broke the kiss.

His eyes were dark, his expression sombre. 'Don't forget me.'

'I won't.'

He didn't look back when he went, and she closed the door without watching him go.

After supper was over, the washing up done, Jay took a glass of whisky up to Duncan. He'd already said goodnight to the family and was lying in bed. For a moment, she thought he was watching TV, but then she saw he was asleep. Putting the glass on his bedside table, she was about to leave when he said, 'Jay.'

She turned and whispered, 'Sorry. I didn't mean to disturb you.'

'No, no. Sit.'

She perched on the side of his bed. 'I just wanted to say goodnight.'

'Goodnight, dearest Jay. And thank you again for bringing us all together.'

'It wasn't just me. You had a lot of help along the way. Sasha and her friend, Rozalina. The helicopter pilots. And what about Viktor? He was a bit of a star.'

A light came into Duncan's eyes. 'It's nice to know there are good people out there as well as bad, and that sometimes the good guys win.'

She couldn't have said it better herself.

Epilogue

Viktor Daletsky was mucking out the cows when they arrived. Two shiny cars: one black VW Touareg and a new-looking red Lada Niva.

He'd wondered when the FSB would discover that he had helped the English woman escape. Weeks had passed and he'd begun to hope that Jay and her friends had made it safely out of the country, but it looked like things hadn't gone to plan.

Briefly, he considered running into the woods, but he knew they'd only come back and catch him months down the line, probably in the middle of the night, and he didn't want the kids terrified out of their wits. Better to be taken now, in broad daylight. Nadia would be OK without him. He'd made sure of that. They were pretty much self-sufficient, and he'd squirrelled a fair bit of cash away from selling furs he'd shot with Jay's excellent rifle. Illegal, sure, but a man had to make a living.

He watched the driver of the Lada climb out and walk over, trying not to muddy his shiny city shoes. 'Viktor Daletsky?' the man asked.

'Yes.'

'Delivery for you.' The man tossed him the car keys.

'What?'

'It's all yours. Papers are in the glove box.'

The man turned on his heel and climbed into the Touareg's passenger seat. Bemused, Viktor watched the Touareg drive down the farm track, spattering its shiny flanks with cow muck, and disappear.

Cautiously, he approached the shiny red Lada and peered inside.

On the driver's seat lay a bottle of Glenfiddich whisky and a packet of Polo mints.

DATE DUE

APR 2 8 2010			
AUG 1 2 P.M.			
GAYLORD			PRINTED IN U.S.A.